GIFT OF PROPHECY

LINA GARDINER

Cover Design: Erin Dameron-Hill, EDH Graphics

Editor: Joyce Lamb, JoyceLambEditing

Interior Design by: Lee, Ironhorseformating

Beta Reader: Nola Richardson

Special thanks: To my brother, Manzer Young, who helped me create the Mortis!

ISBN-13: 978-0-9878573-3-0

PROLOGUE

Darla Rune woke in a sweat.

All alone.

Somehow, lying on a musty straw bed inside her dank, twenty-third-century, one-room, post-War-of-Neutrality hovel, she dreamed of fresh air and a man she didn't know. The strange part: She'd never experienced true fresh air, nor had anyone else she'd ever known.

This city—the city she'd lived in from birth—was a far cry from that place in the twenty-first century she dreamed about.

Somewhere outside her door a wild animal howled, making her flesh pebble. Hopefully her thick, mud-brick walls would hold tonight. Her place had no windows because animals from the wilds, the Nevermore, were vicious and cunning. In fact, homes on the outskirts of the city were built without windows to protect the residents.

Darla thought about the cruel dreams that haunted her nights and rammed her face into her lumpy pillow. No matter what she dreamed, she couldn't possibly know what the country had been like two hundred years ago. There were very few records. Certainly no skyscrapers.

No technology existed to prove or disprove her dream. Other than the Boneyard.

CHAPTER ONE

Creeping through the Boneyard in the pitch black, Darla Rune found a familiar narrow path zigzagging from one mountainous pile of junk to the next. She grimaced. The pungent tang of rusted metal and poached plastic hung thick in the air. So thick it always left an aftertaste.

Adjusting her shoulder bag crammed full with scrounged machine parts, she stopped at the base of the nearest heap of twisted metal and shoved the toe of her boot into an opening in the compacted debris. After testing her foothold, she slowly, carefully climbed up in search of that one piece of usable technology she needed for her current project.

The sound of deliberate movements would be absorbed by the decomposing refuse. Disintegrating metal bits and rusted bolts fell continually, creating a sound somewhat like tinkling rain on a metal roof. This Boneyard, the oldest and the closest technology dumping ground to Central City, had become her secret addiction.

Nearly there now, she found solid footing and

straightened herself until she formed a spire on top of the pile. Her breath caught at the sight of the luminescent moon rising above the city in the distance. Unusual. She'd only seen the moon twice before. And tonight its beautiful pale yellow beams illuminated the darkness, sending unwanted shafts of light across the Boneyard—just her luck.

She gritted her teeth. Normally, heavy fog and tobacco-yellow clouds blotted out the sky and gave her good cover in the dark. It was too risky up here in the moonlight, so she didn't have time to hang around. She'd look for the piece of metal she needed next time.

On the way back down, her sleeve snagged on a ragged scrap of metal. She yanked but couldn't get free. Tugging too hard could pull the whole freaking thing down on her. Benevolent hell.

"Calm down, Rune, you can get yourself out of this," she whispered to herself. Right now she needed to take it slow and easy. Sweat beaded on her forehead while she carefully moved her arm back and forth and finally worked her sleeve off the metal snag. Uvlar suits might protect her from ultraviolet light and radiation, but they didn't afford the best mobility. Snagging herself could have been deadly.

While she'd managed to free herself this time, someday she might not be so lucky.

Smart individuals stayed out of the Boneyards—period. Unfortunately, nothing scared her enough to stay away—and she'd seen some pretty horrific things happen here.

Hard to believe the world once thrived on this now useless equipment that currently made mountains out of soulless metal and plastic. These remnants of technology had existed in the past but not anymore, and never under the reign of the Benevolent government. Only someone like Darla would dare be reckless enough to go against the law. Boneyards were taboo for every man, woman and child, but what did she have to lose? She'd already been branded an outcast.

Even though last month there'd been a coup, and a new government had taken over, no one knew what that meant for the people of Central City. Their new dictator might be worse than the last. Only time would tell. As far as she knew, the Boneyards were still off limits—didn't matter, nothing could keep her out of here.

A crash to her left halted her progress. Remnants got older by the day, true, but she wasn't foolish enough to be totally careless in a Yardman's domain—especially when her life depended on it. She listened hard.

Something seemed off in the yard tonight. She felt edgy, revved up—like bad things were going to happen. She waited until her sense of danger decelerated enough to start moving again. It only took a couple of minutes to get to the path that led to the outer perimeter of the yard.

Time to get out of here.

She swung sideways and inadvertently bumped against decaying metal, causing an instantaneous profusion of images to fill her head—images of the technology, brand new and working. Drat. Not now. She had to focus. She needed every ounce of her attention on the yard.

Creak...

She shifted her head and peered over her shoulder. That had been a definite footstep.

Someone else was moving in the yard.

Her best recourse—climbing to the top of the nearest

heap to get an unrestricted view of the grounds. To her relief, she saw nothing but junk. She breathed a little easier and allowed herself a second to stare at the city in the distance.

Smoke billowed into the polluted skies of the only city she'd ever known. It appeared quite small from here. A defunct nuclear power plant hunkered in the background—a burned-out reminder of the effects that electromagnetic-pulse wars had had on the world centuries ago and the disastrous times that had followed.

She considered the noise she'd heard moments ago. If it had been a Yardman, she wouldn't have been standing here wondering about it. He'd have caught her by now. Besides, Darla had only managed to stay out of their way because the Boneyard was immense. Yardmen were spread thin enough on the grounds that she rarely encountered one. But as big and hideous as the quasi-human things were, Yardmen were renowned for their ability to slink around like feral cats. Huge and silent, they were uncanny creatures who defied logic. So what had she heard a few minutes ago? She spent nearly every day in the yard. She knew the sounds that were normal. Damn it. Time to pay attention to that inner instinct that told her something was very wrong.

Time to get out. Time to get out. Those words echoed in her brain like a clock counting down. Something followed her.

As soon as she climbed back down, careful not to snag herself this time, she jumped the last foot to the ground and streaked along the twisting paths like one of the resident rats, only this rat wanted out of the yard, not in.

One thing in her favor: She'd left her transportation just inside the perimeter. If she could reach it quickly, she'd be able to escape without being caught.

Her lungs squeezed, and her heart felt like it was beating against her rib cage, but she couldn't slow down. Loud breathing was the least of her worries right now. She made the final dash toward the bike. A quick glance showed that the fire had nearly gone out in the afterburner that fueled two tiny rockets mounted on the back. She tossed the junk scraps into the front basket and jumped onto the seat.

Icicles of dread rode her backbone. Before she kicked off, a massive shadow jumped off a pile and landed beside her.

"Oh, damn." She had given her position away to a Yardman. Idiot.

Huge hands snagged her handlebars. She swallowed and slowly raised her head.

His eyes, those soulless holes in his face, were black orbs with no whites. His mouth, larger than most humans', spread from jaw hinge to jaw hinge. Grotesque wasn't the word.

She screamed in anger and pressed the throttle for the power boosters to force the bike out of the brute's giant, filthy hands. An evil grin spread across his face, and a swollen tongue darted out and licked massive lips. She might've thrown up if she'd actually eaten today.

One foot pressed hard on the pedal, forcing the back wheel to spin in the dirt. Her bike became a mere toy in the monstrous Yardman's hands. He grunted viscerally, something that might have been a laugh.

She had nothing powerful enough to use against him. Long, dangerous-looking blades hung from a chain around his neck like a deadly necklace, reminding her of what she'd seen Yardmen do to their victims. A scream froze in her throat. Panic fluttered, nearly encompassed her—until something stronger took over. She straightened her shoulders and glared right back at the freaking deviant. "You evil bastard, don't think you're going to have your way with me. I'll dismember you first." Her chest heaved while she grabbed for the small blade in her left back pocket. She'd use it if she could get to it.

Dead eyes narrowed on her, but only because he'd started sniffing her. Maybe it had been a mistake to make shampoo scented with wild flowers. Maybe that had given her away?

His rancid breath rushed over her while one meaty, giant hand pegged with swollen fingers clawed at the front of her Uvlar outfit. He might have fingers too large to grasp her zipper, but he finally managed to get one oversized finger inside.

To Darla's ultimate relief, the zipper didn't give. He tugged hard, thrashing her back and forth while she pounded her fists against his oversized hand. Her human strength could never match his. Somewhere in the depths of his black cesspool eyes, she saw a tiny spark of something she didn't want to think about. Excitement.

Somehow, while he continued to rattle her bones without completely snapping her in two, she managed to slip the little knife out of her back pocket. He shoved her away, then pulled her forward again. Surely her suit would give under this pressure.

She nearly dropped the knife but managed to hold on to it somehow. A little dizzy now, she took a big breath and sliced it across the back of his hand. A sound emitted from the beast, not one of pain, but of pleasure. Dear God, he liked it.

A scream bubbled up inside her until a man's voice shouted behind them. "Get away from her, you giant freak of nature."

Who'd be crazy enough to alert a Yardman to his presence at a time like this? Not that she'd complain at this point.

"Get your goddamned hands off her," the man shouted again. She tried to see where he stood, but she had a mountain of stinking lard between her and the voice.

After he shook her one last time, and still couldn't get her Uvlar to rip open, the monster suddenly let go. She bent forward and sucked in some much-needed air.

Maybe the Yardman's dead, stupid eyes had portrayed something like surprise at the sound of another voice behind him—hard to tell—their mutated facial expressions were usually set permanently to stunned. His black eyeballs didn't reflect light, and she had no idea what he was thinking—Yardmen were unpredictable. He glanced around then just as quickly returned his attention to her. One massive fist rose over her head, and her skin turned icy. He was going to finish her off before going after the other person.

Her stomach roiled, and for one insane moment she wondered if she'd have time to scream before he squashed her into one of the many grease spots in the dirt.

She held her breath and closed her eyes because she couldn't bear to see that massive fist, the implement of her death, coming at her.

A crack sounded and then a loud whump. A draft of stagnant air and dust whooshed past her. Seconds ticked by and he hadn't crushed her.

By the time she finally dared a look, the Yardman lay flat on the ground with his obscene mouth open and his eyes wide enough that she saw the barest rim of white on the edges of his black irises.

Dressed in Shadow Gear—military-issue Uvlars—a dark figure loomed behind the prostrate Yardman. Blood dripped off the steel pipe he held in his hands, and she wondered if she would be next.

A squidgy feeling erupted in her stomach.

Somehow, the human soldier had clubbed the beast hard enough to take him down. Unbelievable. And since the wearers of those types of Uvlar outfits were soldiers in the deposed dictator's army of the Benevolent, he would most likely not want to save her because she didn't play by the rules. Under Vestro's Benevolent government, it had been forbidden to create anything new. Disregarding that law, she always tinkered and made things for bartering to keep food in her belly. Not to mention she'd been branded a dissident. It would be worth his while to bring her in. Dead or alive.

Her chest tightened when he took a few steps toward her—out of the frickin' frying pan and into the fire. Had she survived a Yardman, only to be killed by a soldier?

Worse, her weapon was out of reach. After she'd cut the Yardman, her knife had fallen on the ground. All she had left was a little baton jammed under her belt. She figured it was police issue, circa 2010, but it would do no good against that menacing pipe that had just taken out a Yardman.

One quick glance at her bike, and she bit her lip. How fast could she pedal without the fully fueled rockets? Relief surged when she spotted a partial fuel puck still ignited inside one of the two afterburners.

She scanned for a clear path out of the yard and slid one finger onto the forward lever so the remaining embers would drop into place and light the next fuel puck—if she got lucky.

The stranger lurched forward. "Don't do it," he said in a gravelly, urgent voice.

The bike revved. She'd leave him in her dust. "The hell with you," she said. "You can't have me either." She released the kickstand at the same time that the tiny modified rockets caught and ignited. She hung on tight, because the inertia of the blast could knock her off.

The bike lurched forward, only to be suddenly yanked to a bone-jarring halt. It flew out from under her, and she landed flat on her back. Damn it.

With the bike still revving like crazy in mid-air, she rolled out of the way, while it flipped completely around and smashed back to earth with a heartrending crunch exactly where she'd lain moments before. For the first time, she noticed the chain hooked to the rear tire.

It had been sabotaged, and she'd been too intent on staying alive to notice.

This night just kept getting worse. Without the bike, she couldn't get safely through the Nevermore, the expanse of nothing but an ancient broken highway, dead brush, tall grasses and stunted bushes between here and Central City.

Her heart sank. She stared at the tiny pucks now burning out on the ground. Just sputtering remains of her handiwork.

Cornered. She glared at the man who reached out to help her up.

"Told you not to," he said. "You okay?"

His dark mask covered all of his face except his eyes. Damn him.

She scrambled backward and jumped to her feet

without help.

"Is he dead?" She tipped her head toward the Yardman. Blood oozed out of a gaping wound at the back of his massive head.

"God, I hope so." The words came out between clenched teeth.

"Why'd you sabotage my bike? You could've got me killed." She eyed him suspiciously, trying to figure out how to protect herself from someone who could take out a Yardman. Yardmen, by all accounts, had extra-thick skulls. It took quite an impact to stop them with blunt force alone.

"I didn't hook your bike to that chain. The Yardman did. I saw him from my vantage point over there," he said.

"You gave my position away."

He shrugged and then winced. She wished she could see more than his eyes.

He scanned their surroundings. "This isn't the place or time to talk. We made quite a bit of noise taking this goon out. There might be more of them around. We should leave."

"We?" Darla put her hands on her hips. "Not damned likely. I'm going home, and if you're smart you'll go back to wherever you came from and stop following me." She narrowed her gaze on him.

"What about your bike?" he asked.

She stared down at the twisted metal that had been her safety net. The rear tire had been yanked off by the chain, and the ignition source burned out on the ground where it had fallen. "It belongs here now. I'll have to build another one."

He made a satisfied sound at her statement. As if what

she'd just said proved something. She began picking her way along the border of the compound to find the way out.

Her rescuer followed her silently.

She held her tongue until they were outside the yard. Unfortunately, wild dogs and other more dangerous beasts lurked out here. Odds of making it back were not very good on foot. Maybe having someone else with her might come in handy. He'd proved his strength back there. And if things went bad, he could serve as dinner while she got away.

"What's your name?" she asked.

"Rud."

"Strange name." She allowed him to fall in step with her, but only because she didn't have a choice.

"It's a nickname."

"What's your full name, then?"

"I only share that with friends." He sounded tense, like he was talking through teeth glued together.

"You have friends? Goodie for you." As if sarcasm shielded her against his strength.

He didn't respond.

"Why were you following me back there?"

"What makes you think I was?" he asked, jerking his head toward the ditch where twin glowing eyes followed them.

A rivulet of perspiration formed between her breasts. Would the creature attack?

The man named Rud simply stared it down. The animal stayed in the ditch. Of course, the big metal pipe he held probably didn't hurt.

"You come in handy in a dangerous spot," she said finally, even though the last thing she'd do was trust him.

At least he'd scared the beast back there.

"Thanks."

"Not a compliment. Just a statement."

"Fine," he said, and picked up his pace a little. She'd have to walk faster if she needed him to be eaten first.

She eyed the Uvlar Shadow Gear he wore. "Do you work for the Benevolent?"

"No." His voice held an edge that he didn't bother to hide. In fact, his tone sounded downright disgusted.

She hadn't survived this long by being stupid. He could very well be a soldier, pretending not to be.

She'd put up with him until she got back home. If she got back.

An hour later, and with chills still running up and down her spine from the rustling noises coming from the Nevermore, they managed to safely reach the outskirts of the city. A miracle in itself. She breathed a silent thank you to the night and cast a sideways glance at Rud before taking a left where normally she'd take a right. No way would she lead him to her place.

This area projected an almost serene scene, if you didn't dig too deeply into the lives of the people living here. And, in the dark, the neighborhood seemed peaceful enough. Proving that nothing was as simple as it seemed. Not even in the city.

He inhaled. "What is that scent? I don't recognize it."

It gave her a sense of satisfaction to smell the odor of burning sweetgrasses in her part of the city. Wood was difficult to come by, and she'd just recently perfected weaving the grasses into bricks. Thin plumes of smoke snaked out of some of the tiny chimneys in the houses near her place. "We have to burn whatever we can in order to cook our meals and stay warm at night," she said.

No way would she let him know she'd invented the process, especially since he sounded so interested in the fact that she'd created the tiny jets on her bike.

She took another side street away from her place.

"Aren't you going home?" he asked.

"Yes, I live down this way," she lied. Just how long had this guy been following her?

"Nice try. You live in the little one-room place down the side street over there." He pointed in the opposite direction.

Dread pooled in her chest. "How long?" she asked, glaring at him.

"How long what?" He walked toward her place. She had no choice but to follow.

Most of her neighbors were asleep. A fine mist circulated through the narrow streets. The unnatural quiet at this time of the night always made her anxious. Like something nasty was creeping up on her. Because it most likely was.

She spent too much time in the Boneyard.

Regardless, she had every reason to be anxious tonight. Besides nearly being a victim of the worst type of killer, a Yardman, she had a stranger dogging her home, and there wasn't a damned thing she could do about it. "I asked how long have you been following me."

"A few days."

"Benevolent hell." No sense hiding disgust at her stupidity. She prided herself on her gut instinct, but she had to admit being much better at reading dead technology than anything alive. Still, she should have picked up on the fact that someone had been watching her for that long. "What do you want with me?

She lived in the poorest section of the city. And the roughest. Murderers and thieves were commonplace here. Most Benevolent troops avoided this area unless they were on duty and doing their routine checks in groups of half a dozen. They didn't spend any spare time in the taverns here, and that's the way people liked it.

So why here, why now?

"Where'd you get the suit?" she asked in an attempt to get him to admit he was a soldier.

His eyebrows rose, and his blue eyes stared into hers. "Borrowed it from a Benevolent soldier while he slept."

"You stole it?"

His head tipped in a curt nod.

"Theft from a Benevolent is a pretty serious crime. A heavy prison sentence."

"They'll have to catch me first," he said. A rumble of anger edged his words.

People didn't joke about things like that. Not sane people. "Have you spent too much time outside without your Uvlar suit on?" She put her hands on her hips and frowned at him. UV rays and low-level radiation had a sorry side effect on some people. If only she could see his facial expression. Eyes alone weren't enough.

"I'm not one of the Benevolent. But I do want to talk to you. Can you give me shelter long enough to rest up a bit after what happened in the yard?"

"Not very likely." She crossed her arms clumsily over her chest, barely able to bend her arms in the old Uvlar suit that had seen better days. "If you want to talk to me—talk."

She glanced up and down the street. The fringe guards had a shift change at around one in the morning, a good time to get home before she ran into any of them.

"Probably not the best move to stay in the street. Someone is coming," he said.

She heard the distant footsteps, too. Damn it. Maybe the guards were early tonight.

He sighed. "I did save you back there in the Boneyard. You must know I'm not a threat to you."

She made a disgusted noise at the back of her throat. "I know nothing of the sort. Your agenda could be to get inside my place to find out what I know."

One eyebrow rose again. "What do you know?"

She growled under her breath. "Not a thing that would interest you or anyone else."

She'd noticed his eyes back in the Boneyard. Intelligent. Maybe too intelligent.

Curiosity spiked against her better judgment. "You from around here?" she asked.

"Nope."

Thick ground smog skirted the hollows of the pebble-strewn road that had once been a street. Definite footsteps echoed nearby, sounding like they came from every direction at once. And getting closer.

Whether she trusted him or not, he'd saved her tonight. And if she didn't get inside, they'd both be sorry. She made for her place. She had no choice.

She opened the locking mechanism on her door and jumped inside, expecting him to enter while she lit the candle next to the door.

He waited outside. For her to invite him in? Shit. "Hurry up and get inside," she growled.

"Thanks."

The second he stepped inside, she slammed the door shut and rammed a long piece of steel into a hole drilled into the door casing.

Not a minute later, footsteps stalled outside her door before continuing along.

"Close call," he said, glancing around her room.

Her ten-foot-by-ten-foot room had a scruffy curtain in one corner that hid a rudimentary toilet, her tiny bed in the other corner. On the opposite wall, she had a little table, a stool, a small cupboard and sink and a tiny potbelly stove. Nothing like the homes near Government House, where he probably lived.

"I noticed some of your neighbors have oil lamps outside? Isn't that a waste of fuel when people are sleeping?"

"Somehow I know you're not joking," she said, lighting two more beeswax candles. "People who can afford oil use it for extra protection at night. And not just from thugs, but from wild animals that are sometimes brave enough to slink into town in the wee hours."

* * * * *

Rud grimaced. "Why don't you move into the more civilized part of the city, where people aren't quite so lawless and animals so dangerous." He knew he'd made a mistake the minute he said that.

"I hope you're not serious, Mister I-Stole-Benevolent-Shadow-Gear," she said. "Though calling it 'civilized' is definitely Benevolent propaganda." She gave him a shove. "Take a seat."

Rud nearly doubled over. Pain ripped through his shoulder. He'd definitely injured himself when he'd swung that pipe to take out the Yardman.

Thankfully, she'd turned her back on him after the shove. Showing weakness would be downright stupid at this point. She could probably kick his ass, anyway. A few more steadying breaths, and he managed to hide the pain.

"Hungry?" she asked.

He hadn't eaten all day, and famished wasn't the word. But every time he moved his shoulder, the pain caused his stomach to protest. It had to be dislocated. He reached up with his good arm to yank his face shield and B-clava off. A fine sheen of perspiration covered his upper lip and forehead, and for a second black spots erupted before his eyes. Damn, his shoulder might be an unacceptable liability. He had to find someone to put it back in place as soon as he got home. He could try to do it himself, but he'd probably just make it worse.

"Hold on," she said. "I'd like to know a little more about you before I feed you. For example, your full name—first and last."

Crap. The pain in his shoulder made it hard to think straight. He'd saved her from a Yardman and dislocated his shoulder in the process. Surely that counted for something. "Like I said before, name's Rud."

"Rud? What kind of name is that? And you still haven't given me your last name."

Hell, he might as well tell her. Keeping his lineage secret would do no good now. "Rud James. Rud is short for Rudyard."

"Holy crap. It's not your first name that concerns me. It's your last." She shivered as if suddenly chilled.

"Oberon James, the dictator who took over the government, is my older brother." He gritted his teeth.

She paled. "You're kidding me."

"Not something a guy would joke about."

She stared at him with a cold expression on her face.

Would she turn him over to the locals? They'd love to

get their hands on a member of his family.

CHAPTER TWO

Oberon James stared at himself in an ornate gilt mirror on the twelve-foot-high wall of his new office. He leaned closer. Had his expression hardened along with his responsibilities? Was this face that of a dictator?

It hadn't been his choice to take Central City by force rather than democracy, but he accepted the repercussions of his actions.

Deeply disturbed by the suffering of his people, he stared out the third-story window overlooking City Square. Taking Government House by force had gone more smoothly than he'd hoped. But he wouldn't call his coup a victory until he knew citizens accepted him.

When his office door swung open without warning, Oberon yanked his pistol from the holster under his arm. He took quick aim and sought out the center mass of his target. His finger moved to the trigger, touched it, nearly put pressure on it, before he saw who'd entered his office without knocking.

"Damn it, man. I could have shot you. It was not a

suggestion when I told you to knock first. It was an order, especially in the middle of the night. It's a damned important order."

Felix Wicks, Oberon's aide, strode to the desk. By the casual expression on his aide's face, he had no idea how close he'd just come to a near-death experience. Oberon wanted to knock some sense into the man, but that wasn't his style. Those kinds of things were Vestro's forte.

"Sure, sure. I'll try to remember that," Felix said vaguely.

"You must remember to knock. We aren't out of the woods yet. We have to be extraordinarily careful, Felix."

Nonplussed, Felix set down a stack of papers and adjusted a miniature bronze statue on the corner of the oversized desk that had once belonged to Callium Vestro, the despot who'd called himself governor until they'd driven him out.

Oberon heaved a sigh and crossed the shining hardwood floor to look at the stack of paperwork. On the top of the stack lay the Daily Post News, printed by an underground newspaper. Quite extraordinary that the impoverished people of the city made paper and print news. Glimpsing at the headline, he sighed. His popularity proved to be no better than Vestro's had been before him. But that didn't make sense.

"You'd think they'd give me a chance before they condemned me," he grated. "How can I help people if they think I'm no better than the monster I deposed?"

Felix's eyes strayed to the newspaper while Oberon read the headline out loud. "Governor James: Worse than Vestro? Ask the starving citizens." Damn it. He'd been assured taking over the government would be the right thing, but taking over hadn't warmed the hearts of the people, or their stomachs. But having a democratic election would never have been allowed under Vestro's regime.

"Obviously, it's the only way to make some ground toward a better society," Felix reminded.

"I know. But I'm not Vestro. How do I prove that to my people?"

"You have to be tough, Oberon, or you'll lose control. We live in a dangerous time. Men who show weaknesses don't live long. Leaders must be strong, and sometimes they have to be brutal if they want the majority to follow them."

He'd heard Felix sing that tune before. The term "harping on deaf ears" came to mind. "I will never resort to torture and murder to keep my place as governor."

Felix made a familiar face. His nose wrinkled, and his front teeth stuck out in the manner that made him look like a rodent. "You'll do what you have to do, sir, or you'll fail. And you'll take us all down with you."

Oberon hated to be continuously reminded by his aide that his status made him solely responsible for the lives of his soldiers and followers, probably because he hated to be reminded of the truth.

And even though Vestro had carried out horrible atrocities against his people for many years and even though he'd been detested, people still, more often than not, believed his propaganda. Extremely aggravating.

Felix must've registered the storm swirling inside Oberon. "Besides, who would dare come here to attack you? You have loyal forces surrounding the building," Felix said.

"If you recall, so did Vestro. And that didn't stop us from gaining entry and taking power, now did it?"

Oberon pushed two fingers into his temple in an effort to pin down the location of the throbbing pain. Too bad the heinous dictator had gotten away. Oberon's coup would have been much more successful if he had had that bastard to serve up on a platter.

Felix huffed. "I think even his soldiers were glad to see him go."

"And—that, my dear Felix, is why you're not my minister of Defense." Oberon returned to his desk again and sorted through papers. Intelligence reports were still coming in from the fringes. Unfortunately, it appeared the death toll ranked higher on the boundaries of the city. And there'd been civilian casualties. Damn it. He'd hoped that wouldn't happen. Worse, he'd received word only this morning that his brother had gone missing. In fact, he hadn't been seen for two weeks. That made Oberon edgy.

"I'd have no desire to be your minister of Defense, Mister James. I'm much better as your executive assistant." Felix said almost petulantly.

Good thing the man's organizing skills were above reproach. He knew how to run an office, and he knew about affairs of state. Those abilities were invaluable to a hardnosed military man like Oberon.

Feeling the full weight of his office pressing in on him, Oberon sank into the luxurious leather executive chair and snapped the papers toward him. His gut burned twenty-four/seven these days, and his patience ran thin. Being a soldier, not a politician, the thought of being trapped in this office, no matter how lavish, made his skin crawl. "How many prisoners are in the cells downstairs?"

Felix let out a long sigh. "Too many. I'm afraid before the week is up we won't have enough food to feed them all, either."

"Holy hell. Where are the food stores Vestro had?" Could it get much worse? Only the bravest of men worked outside the city in the gardens. Years of exposure to fallout and God only knew what else had created some pretty damned feral and scary animals that were hungry for red meat and actually seemed to have a taste for men. Therefore, out of necessity, soldiers protected the farmers and the gardens. They had weapons, big guns that weren't taken out by the EMP storms, but the weapons were old and had problems. It only took a few people being eaten by beasts to scare away the farmers, and they needed the best green thumbs they could find.

Felix wouldn't make eye contact. "I thought I told you...his men moved most of the food before we completed our takeover."

"No. You didn't mention that. What are we going to do?" Oberon gripped the edge of the massive wooden desk worth a bloody fortune—a treasure from before the war. The strange part: Not much had survived the destruction of the War of Neutrality, after which people had gone crazy and turned on each other. The survivors of the war had burned everything for heat—books, furniture, paintings. It didn't matter their intrinsic value. And rightly so.

"Felix, how is it that Vestro managed to keep a virtual museum of pieces inside Government House? A building that somehow, quite nicely, survived the last two hundred years?" Oberon blew out a hard breath. He knew how his family had done it. Surely Vestro wasn't privy to the same insights?

"I would have no idea, sir. But..." He scanned the room, pausing at several priceless antiques. "Evidently, he had powerful friends with deep pockets."

"And if that's true, how did we walk in and take over so easily?" Oberon had always felt squirmy about the ease with which they'd stormed the place and taken over. "And where has Vestro disappeared to? Why didn't we capture the ex-dictator himself?"

"Those questions are above my pay grade," Felix muttered, irritation evident in his voice. In fact, Felix always knew more than he'd tell. He just didn't realize Oberon knew about his insights.

"Vestro may have disappeared, but I have the feeling we haven't seen the last of him." Oberon's shoulders tightened. He rubbed the back of his neck and wished he could've had a normal life. As normal as life could be in such hard times.

Felix's thin shoulders shifted in a casual way. "You could be right, sir. If you look at the second report on your desk, you'll see another farming area in the Nevermore has been attacked. There were several casualties, and the crops were lost."

Oberon cursed. "We can't afford to lose much more food. After harvest this fall we won't have enough left for the coming year if they keep raiding like this." He paced back and forth. "We need more soldiers on all Nevermore farms. Double the guard, right away."

"Now?"

"As soon as you answer my next question." Oberon's eyebrows met over the bridge of his nose. Hell and damnation, the man drove his irritation to full blown in seconds. "Has intelligence found the whereabouts of my brother yet?" His gut writhed at the idea of his younger brother in the hands of his enemies, especially because they seemed to be gaining in strength since last week's takeover.

In his youth, his brother Rud had taken too many chances. Probably no different than he had been at the same age, and he had been Rud's role model since the death of their parents when Rud was only twelve and Oberon eighteen. Their parents had been farming when they were lost in the Nevermore. Their bodies were never found. Oberon had done his best to raise his brother without them.

"Last I heard, he'd been seen on the fringes of the city. He's most likely safe as long as nobody finds out he's your brother. Problem is, most fringe people still harbor loyalty to Vestro. We certainly don't want to tip people off that he's in their area. It would compromise his safety."

"Fuck!" Oberon wanted to throw something. He stared at the solid oak gavel rimmed with brass on the corner of his desk and imagined tossing it across the room at a Ming vase. Benevolent hell, he needed to get out of this office. He'd been proud to be a field soldier protecting farmers. Diplomat had been a dirty word.

Diplomat. Hell. He'd become a dictator.

"Is there a reason you need him immediately, sir?" Felix stooped and picked up two pieces of balled-up paper and placed them in the waste basket beside the desk without blinking—and without immediately carrying out his orders, Oberon noticed.

"Yes, there's a very good reason. I suppose you think I should tell you what that reason is?"

"Of course not, sir. I wouldn't dream of delving into your personal matters." Felix turned and began straightening priceless books on the floor-to-ceiling shelves. Might even have been the last vast collection in

North America. Even the James family had been unable to snag that many books.

Oberon's fists clenched on his desk. "I have to risk people finding out he's my brother. I have to find him. I haven't got a goddamned choice," he gritted. "Send word to all units that my brother is to be found and returned to me."

Felix's eyebrows twitched. No secret that the man snooped into everything. "Unharmed," Oberon added.

"Certainly, sir. Unharmed." He mumbled something under his breath and slammed the door on his way out. Oberon wanted to slam a few doors, too, but he had bigger issues than a complaining administrator. With thousands of people to feed, and a battle to complete, Oberon didn't have time to mollycoddle Felix. Besides, Vestro might not have been in Government House any longer, but he remained more powerful than he should have been, given his cruelty against his own people. They still had a tendency to believe his propaganda. That gave Vestro strength.

That's where Oberon had to focus his attention. The people of the city were the real power, only they didn't realize it. As long as there were Vestro sympathizers, the average citizen remained at risk. He needed to prove himself to them, but it'd be a lot easier if his brother wasn't roaming the city, at risk of being taken at any moment.

If anyone should harm Rudyard, it'd be him. The kid should never have gone off alone while Oberon had been overthrowing the government.

* * * * *

Darla looked Rud up and down, a frown burrowing

into her forehead. "You might as well have a seat, at least until I find out why the Hades you were following me. You're not welcome in this part of town, you know," Darla said. "As it stands, people here still think Vestro was despicable, but he gave them a little food, at least. It's been even scarcer since your brother took over."

"I'm not my brother, but he's not the monster some people think he is." Rud pursed his lips and stared at the tiny stool, the only logical spot for him to sit. "Is that how you felt about the last governor, Darla? Did you think Vestro's method of rule was fair?"

"Like I'd share my political views with you, or anyone else," she said.

Rud appeared smug at the irritation blossoming in her voice.

"I wouldn't last too long around here that way." Her shoulders tightened up around her ears. Hell, she might not last long anyway.

"Yeah, you're right. I shouldn't have asked. How you feel about my brother is your business, and it should have nothing to do with me."

Darla couldn't believe she stood here in her one-room shanty, discussing Oberon James with his brother. A feeling of unease trickled the length of her spine. Taking sides proved dangerous these days. Under Vestro's rule, several outspoken people, her own neighbors, had disappeared, never to be seen again.

No way did she intend to be the next victim. She rubbed the scar on the underside of her forearm. She'd been fourteen when it happened. She cast a cold look at Rud. "You're just lucky I don't judge people by their relatives. And you may have saved my ass back there in the Boneyard. But only after you put me at risk. I owe you nothing."

"I guess I can't convince you it wasn't my fault the Yardman found you," Rud said, then grinned. "Besides, even if you blame me, I saved your oh-so-pretty butt."

She'd starting taking off her face shield, but froze when he said that.

Even he knew he'd gone too far. He cleared his throat. "I guess I'd better just shut up for the time being."

"Wise, especially if you're hungry." Darla took off her headgear and got a couple of plates out of the tiny cupboard she'd built herself. Her stomach growled loudly. "And this meal is a one-time deal, James. For the record, I don't want to get to know you better."

Not that she'd tell him, but in her opinion, there'd been nothing fair about their previous illustrious governor, Vestro. He'd wanted the same lifestyle for everyone, except himself. While he'd lived like a king, everyone else had been fed, housed, clothed—the barest minimum possible. People had starved under his two-decade regime, and worse, the most desperate of people had killed each other for scraps of food. They had been kept poor and in the dark, and that's the way he had controlled Central City.

While still an unknown, Oberon James had taken control by force. At least Vestro had created an illusion of democracy, as thinly veiled as it had been.

Suddenly, Rud dropped onto the stool. His face had gone sickly pale and his breathing ragged. Had he hurt himself taking out the Yardman?

"You didn't explain what happened back there," she said. The fact that he'd admitted being related to the dictator in power disconcerted her enough, but why had he been following her?

"Been looking for you for a while," he said.

"Why?" She grimaced at him and leaned against the tiny wooden desk she'd bartered half a year's metal collection for.

"Maybe we should eat first, and then I'll explain," he said.

"If this is information for your brother, you'd better leave right now. I don't want trouble. I'm just trying to survive."

"No, I don't want information for my brother. I don't speak for him."

"No one needs to speak for him. He simply marches in and takes over. No conversations needed."

Rud grinned despite his pallor. "I think your opinion is showing."

She cursed. "So tell me what's going on. Why would you be looking for me?" She jammed her hands onto her hips.

He inhaled and ran a shaky hand over his eyes. He looked ragged.

Her stomach grumbled again, and she remembered the hunk of salt meat and pickled beets she had in her larder. She'd even managed to steal a small loaf of flax bread from one of the Benevolent's carts before his soldiers had been run out of town. Ironic to consider feeding the brother of the man who had kept food off their tables.

"You still hungry?" she asked.

His eyes lit, and he licked his lips. "Starved. Have you food?"

"Not a lot but enough that I can share." She pulled back a threadbare rug to expose a wooden trapdoor. He started to get up to help her, but he still seemed unfit. "Stay where you are. I'll get it."

She yanked a waxy cloth bag of meat out of the two-foot hole in the earth and then pulled up a jar of beets.

"Why do you keep going to the Boneyard?" he asked.

She pursed her lips. Even if she'd known the answer to that question, he'd be the last person she'd tell.

"How did you jimmy-rig that bicycle to make it go faster?" he added.

Her shoulders tightened. "If you're really hungry, I'd shut up right now, because saving my ass or not, my patience and hospitality are starting to run out."

Rud held up one hand. "Sorry. Sorry. I have a tendency to be overly curious."

"You do know what they say about curiosity."

He nodded and shut up while she slid a generous slice of the meat and a few beets onto a cracked porcelain plate. Next, she dug out the chunk of flax bread, and his eyes widened. Even stale bread was a rare commodity. Hard to find and even harder to safeguard. That's why she kept it buried in the ground under a hidden door.

"I can't accept that," he said.

After shoving the plate into his hand, she dished up her own food. Most people didn't share. Couldn't share. Food was too scarce. She'd never followed that rule, though. If she had something, she shared it, and that's probably why she'd survived the last nine years. People had sometimes returned the favor when she'd been really hungry.

And sometimes people had taken advantage of her generosity. She stared at Rud. This was going to be one of those times, wasn't it?

She handed him a fork. She'd considered giving him a knife, but decided to tuck it away again. She trusted him to a point, but not with a knife.

He pointed at the bread on his plate. "You sure?"

She nodded. "Eat up. Someone with a body mass like yours needs food to maintain it."

He flashed a smile that proved that the size of his ego matched his brawn. A member of the James family, all right, because even though she didn't trust this guy as far as she could spit, he had charisma. She hadn't learned a lot about their newest dictator other than that he held great appeal to some of his constituents, mostly female. Stupid women. She gritted her teeth.

Maybe after they ate, she'd find out exactly why Rud James sat on her stool right now. And exactly what he wanted from her.

* * * * *

Rud watched while she sliced food for herself. She still hadn't taken off her suit, but he'd seen her without it once or twice over the last two weeks. Her body was lithe and busty, complemented by shoulder-length red hair that had natural curl. He liked the few freckles on her pretty face. Most women were rangy and straggly. Not Darla. She had pride in herself and in her appearance. He'd seen her gather wildflowers and twigs in a field on the edges of the Nevermore. Now that took guts. She'd carefully separated petals and bark and ground the ingredients into a mixture. Whatever she'd made, he'd seen citizens bartering for it almost immediately.

Then each evening she'd make sure her old, protective gear glistened under the beeswax and elbow grease she applied before slipping off to the Boneyard.

The fact that she earned her living by making things to sell or trade garnered more attention than was healthy for her. Under the previous government, the Benevolent had not wanted people to learn. To create. They'd wanted a drudge force. They'd wanted humanity to be like cattle—tame, banal and afraid. And even though Vestro had been overthrown, he remained at large, and he still had followers. Her lifestyle still proved dangerous to her.

And since Rud had found the prophecy, that meant she'd become his charge. He could help her. He touched the ancient document inside his Uvlar jacket pocket and felt heat resonate from it.

He'd beaten Oberon to the message. He'd prove himself worthy of fulfilling one of the prophecies left for the eldest in each generation of the James family. His brother didn't have to be the only one able to evoke change. Not this time.

Still, the way he'd learned how to open the vault had been strange. Unlikely shadows had moved around the entrance, and the combination had come to him from an ethereal voice with no corporeal form.

He'd heard that Maribel had once come to one of their ancestors in person, but from the stories, she'd been less ominous than his encounter. It probably hadn't been Maribel. That alone should have sent him back to the surface.

Maybe Oberon would respect him for having the guts to try to save the prophecy, at least.

CHAPTER THREE

Rud needed Darla to trust him if he had any hope of succeeding. If he won her over before he told her the truth about the prophecy, he just might be able to pull this thing off.

He didn't ask what kind of meat she'd so generously shared with him. Animals were at a premium in the outskirts of the city. Only the Benevolent had beef and lamb. He took a bite tentatively. A little tough, but the flavor and texture weren't unpleasant. Best just to eat it and not think about it. Besides, he needed the protein.

Darla nibbled her food, most likely taking her time and enjoying every morsel. Probably trying to make it last. Since he'd started watching her, there'd been something about her. An underlying aura of melancholy that he couldn't put a finger on. Then again, given her meager surroundings, she had every right to be quiet and introspective. She had nothing to celebrate as far as he could tell.

He sank his teeth into the bread and nearly moaned

with pleasure. Where had she gotten primo food like this? He glanced at her again, stiff and formal on the edge of her cot, ready to run for the door if he made the wrong move. "Why don't you take off your Uvlar gear?"

"I will," she said. "But not now. I'm hungry, haven't eaten for a couple of days, and my body's more interested in food than creature comfort."

Creature comfort? Those words had no frame of reference in this place or this lifestyle, but she meant it. No sarcasm edged her words. Guilt twinged when he thought about how he'd grown up. Protected and well fed. Educated with real books. As far as he knew, his family had been one of the very few with that kind of affluence. He'd always wondered how they'd gotten so lucky. Seeing how Darla lived made him think of his own life. How fortunate his family had been over the years, if you could call it fortunate when someone maps out your future step by step. Other than resenting his brother for being privy to information only passed on from eldest son to eldest son, he'd led a very privileged life.

"I recently heard about someone with the last name Rune," he said, picking up the lone crumb of bread left on his plate and popping it into his mouth.

"Really?" She stopped chewing and put her bread down.

She hadn't even eaten half of it yet.

Rud's mouth watered.

"Who is the Rune you know?" she asked.

"It's not someone I know. Just someone I heard about from long ago. Her name was Maribel Rune. She lived before the War of Neutrality changed the face of North America, when Central City used to be called New York."

Her back stiffened perceptibly. "No one has records like that. And we're not supposed to repeat stories from our past. It breeds avarice and will lead us to the same fate as those poor people who suffered through horrors two hundred years ago."

For someone who obviously hated Vestro, she spouted Benevolent doctrine with ease. He adjusted his aching shoulder. "You've never heard the name, then?"

"Maybe. It sounds vaguely familiar," Darla said. "But, then, I never listened to my mother's stories of the past." She suddenly looked like she regretted inviting him inside. And even though she'd just told him a little bit about herself, there'd be no more sharing.

Words echoed in his memory. She won't be easy to fool or manipulate. Strange advice that had come from an even stranger source.

Once Rud had found the secret hiding place inside his family bunker, he'd read the Rune prophecy over and over. He now knew it by heart. His task had to be to protect her from danger. A sense of accomplishment filled him. He'd been given a chance to prove that his brother wasn't the only one who could make his family proud. He didn't want to screw anything up.

* * * * *

Darla's stomach tightened. What in Benevolent hell had ever possessed her to let this man into her place? She didn't like the fact that he wanted to know things about her. And she hated even more that she'd told him something she hadn't meant to. About her mother. Dumb, dumb thing to do. She couldn't let him see that it worried her. She frowned at him then glanced at the door.

His gaze followed hers, and his mouth pinched. He got

her silent message and ignored it.

"Been living here long?" he asked.

"Nope. I move around."

She eyed him from her perch on the edge of her mattress.

"What about you? You been around this part of the city long?" she asked.

"Just a few days," he answered.

She guessed he wouldn't honestly tell her how long he'd been tailing her. She'd have to be more careful in the future.

"Is this neighborhood rougher than yours, then?" She leaned forward, watching his facial expressions. Even a tiny microexpression could give him away.

"City sections are mostly all the same, aren't they?"

Brilliantly vague. There were rumors that no one could find out where the James family had come from. They were seen occasionally, but no one knew where they actually lived.

Darla had been too young to really be interested in her family history, and after being branded, her chances of learning it had deteriorated to zero. Too late for history, too late for experiencing her mother's love. She had to stay away if she valued her mother's life. Dissidents were outcasts, and if caught in the city, she and whoever harbored her would face being branded as dissidents, too. She missed her mother. Wondered if she still lived in the same place, if she found enough food.

Most girls her age usually died after being branded. Darla, however, had found the means to survive, and the Boneyard played a huge role in her survival. For some reason she felt more connected to that old technology than she'd ever been to anything else in her life.

Had Oberon James found out about her—a dissident living in the city? Maybe he'd heard about her inventions? Had Rud been sent to find her because people were starting to talk about her knack for making things? If so, they'd make an example of her at Government House. And it would be way worse than the last time.

"Do you work for your brother?" she asked, locking her gaze with his.

"What? No. We don't exactly see eye to eye. I'd be the last person he'd want as part of his entourage."

"Entourage?"

"He has his own group of followers, fanatics who think he's the next coming. I'd rather avoid those kinds of supporters. They remind me too much of Vestro's crazies."

Darla's eyebrows lifted. "And your brother, does he foster that kind of attention?"

Rud's expression changed, turned thoughtful. He might gripe about his brother, but under the surface, he probably cared about him—she'd do well to remember that.

"Nah, he doesn't like the attention either. But he's got to put up with it. I don't."

Since she'd seen a tattered picture of their newest dictator blowing around on the street, she compared the two brothers' features. Oberon had appeared older and harder around the eyes and mouth. She imagined a cruel streak in him, whereas Rud had no calluses, no scars and a gentle nature. Well, minus being able to take out a Yardman.

The scary part: She found Oberon's features to have more character than Rud's.

But, of course she did. She'd always been attracted to

the tough guys, the not-so-pretty, rugged types. Maybe because she wouldn't mind having the extra protection of a soldier who had her back.

But, so far, no one had ever gotten close to her. And no wonder. Even if she'd fostered the attention, courting a dissident wouldn't have been a good move for anyone. Not to mention, she didn't want to be responsible for anyone being branded and tortured on her behalf.

She finished her meal, took Rud's empty plate and piled it on top of hers then set them into the tiny sink in the corner. She'd do the dishes later. For now, she just wanted him gone.

He looked like he wanted to say something, but that moment passed. "Time for me to go," he said, wincing a little when he stood and moved toward the door.

She'd be glad to see the last of him. He made her uncomfortable. Well, most people did that, but this guy tripled the edginess she experienced around strangers. Probably because he wanted something from her, and he wouldn't tell her what that might be.

Darla went to the door and opened it for him, because he'd never have been able to figure out her locking mechanism. "If you're smart, you'll make sure no one sees you in this part of the city in that Uvlar gear."

He nodded then stepped outside, angling his head down to avoid the door casing. He glanced back at her. "Maybe we'll see each other again."

She gritted her teeth. She'd avoid him from now on, but she couldn't stay away from the Boneyard. Something always drew her to that place. The truth of her need didn't make sense. Touching inanimate objects and seeing visions of working machinery had to mean she lived in Crazy Land. Yet those visions that popped into her mind when she placed her hand on dead technology were her lifeblood. They made her feel alive.

She shut the door and heard his footsteps fade away on the silent street, then set the lock and got out of her heavy gear with a sigh. She stared at the tiny sink and wished for a full-size tub. She'd give half a year's earnings for one luxurious soak. Instead, she washed the dishes, put them away, and then washed herself.

Fatigue edged at her, only broken by images of that massive Yardman's fist over her head. She donned her threadbare nightgown, dropped onto the straw mattress and found her body-size indentation and exhaled.

The nightmare started practically before her eyes had closed.

CHAPTER FOUR

Darla woke to the sound of her door crashing in. That should have brought her instantly awake, but a weird exhaustion pinned her down. Unable to react, she watched as three silhouettes broke in and starting foraging through her things.

"What's going on?" she mumbled through lips that felt thick and numb. Her gaze skittered from one shadowy intruder to another. She'd heard of Benevolent kidnappings. People sometimes disappeared in the night, and no one ever knew what happened to them. Was she to be the next one?

The closest soldier snagged her arm with a gloved hand. He squeezed until she cried out, then yanked her to a sitting position like she was a lifeless corpse. With little muscle control, she felt her head hang back, her hair dragging across her pillow. The heaviest of the lethargy began to slowly bleed out of her. Her toes began to tingle.

The jerk, still holding her up with one arm, fondled her breast none too gently. She tried to kick him, but the covers kept her weak legs trapped.

One of them stumbled into her little table in the dark. She heard the wood snap before the table crashed to the floor. Bastard! That table had cost her the moon and the stars. Real wooden furniture wasn't easy to come by.

Suddenly, another person in Shadow Gear ran into her place and started shouting. "Get off her, you freaking perverts." Broad shoulders, backlit by the unusual moonlight, were very welcome at this point. Rud had come to save her again. But against three Benevolent soldiers he wouldn't stand a chance.

The man holding her let go, and she flopped onto her pillow like she had no bones. The three infiltrators turned toward the voice. "Who are you?" one of them said.

"I'd like to ask you the same question," Rud ground out.

"Isn't it obvious, fool? We're Oberon's troops. You'd better leave before we arrest you, too."

"I don't think so. You seem to be lacking some crucial pieces of identification," Rud ground out.

One soldier glanced at another, and their lack of response said it all. They were Vestro's men.

She'd have liked nothing better than to make a run for it, but her muscles were not cooperating. Her room had an odd odor, and she wondered if a drug had been piped in somehow. "Get out. You'll only get caught yourself," she shouted to Rud, not daring to say his name out loud and putting him at risk. If these were Vestro's men, there'd be more coming. They never worked in groups of three. They worked in packs. Dangerous, bloodthirsty packs.

"I'm not leaving you, Darla," he said, and she tried to edge up onto her elbows.

The soldier who'd fondled her slapped her hard enough that she felt her teeth move. She groaned and tasted blood, while her head jammed back into her pillow. Her legs still felt heavy, but now her muscles were regaining mobility, maybe because the door hung open, letting in outside air.

Meanwhile, Rud had been fighting them off, one by one. They waited their turns, as if this game was for fun and they had nothing to lose. While that happened, she had regained the ability to move.

She slid a hand under her pillow and pulled out the pistol she'd found in the Boneyard a year ago. Bullets had been harder to get, but she'd managed to buy some on the black market. She'd use them if she had to.

Rud had taken a couple of blows to the gut, and his arm hung limply, but he stood up to them, still in the fight. He pounded his fist into one guy's faceplate, three times so fast that the guy didn't know what hit him. He dropped like a rock.

The next one attacked quickly, and she wondered how much of this Rud could take. Fists pounded him, and he fell to the hard-packed dirt floor. This soldier kicked him hard enough that Darla heard the air whoosh out of him. He groaned in pain.

Before she could force herself off the bed to help, Rud kicked out from his position on the ground and took the legs out from under soldier number two. He flew backward, barely missing her. That left her sitting on the bed with a home-repaired pistol in her shaking hands aimed straight at the jerk who'd manhandled her.

"Don't move a frigging muscle," she said before the soldier, who'd fallen next to the bed, could get up again. She rammed the pistol into his temple with enough force to prove she meant business, and to leave a bruise, she imagined. Then she prayed her shaking hands didn't make it go off by mistake. All she saw of him were his eyes, but they appeared afraid. Good.

* * * * *

Rud, still grunting in pain, got up and finished off the other soldier. One solid punch to the back of the guy's neck, and he passed out cold, too.

He spat out some blood and gritted his teeth. It felt like his separated shoulder had been ripped right off. Waves of pain made him falter. He couldn't give in. He had to get Darla out of here.

He swung around and grinned at what he saw. There in the corner, she had a freaking big pistol jammed into the idiot's head.

He carefully positioned his limp arm over his chest. "Good thing I decided to camp out across the street under your neighbor's lean-to."

Darla kept the gun on the soldier. "What are we going to do with him? Others will be coming. We have to get out of here."

Rud reached out with his uninjured arm. His fingers clamped down on the intruder's neck, and he pinched hard, squeezing until the soldier slumped sideways.

"What did you do to him?"

"Squeezed off the blood supply to his brain. He won't be out long, though. Let's go."

She jumped up, staggered momentarily, grabbed her Uvlar gear, then righted herself and headed for the door. He bit his lip and watched her. Wanted to wrap an arm around her, but she wouldn't like that much, even if he had an arm he could spare.

"I think there are more of them coming," she said. "Listen."

Footsteps pounded toward them.

"We'd better run," he said, rushing forward, grabbing her hand and pulling her down the street away from the soldiers.

He cursed under his breath when she stumbled several times, still woozy. With a dislocated shoulder, he'd barely managed to pull her along with one hand. He didn't have a clue where to go. He didn't know this section of the city very well. He'd spent all of his time monitoring her.

Around the next corner, they ran right up to the edges of the Nevermore. Without thinking, he headed into the brush, figuring it was their only choice.

She stopped dead and pulled him back toward the road. "Too dangerous," she panted. "Animals hunt on the fringes of the city, especially at night."

Crap, he needed some of his brother's expertise right about now. What should he do?

"Go that way." Darla said.

Was it his imagination or did her eyes suddenly seem to be lit from behind?

"There's a place we can hide not far down that street," she said.

They stumbled along the rutted path as fast as possible in the dim light. One hand held hers, and the other, the one that should have been poised over his assault knife, hung limp and cold, with searing pain ripping through him.

Unexpectedly, she jerked him sideways into an alley.

"Jesus, Mary and Joseph," he said between his teeth. "Warn me next time. My shoulder's dislocated."

Beads of perspiration ran down his face, and he felt like he might be sick.

"Shhh. Be quiet," she whispered.

They hid in the dark indentation of a mud-brick house while several men in blackeners ran by.

"They won't stop until they find us," she said, looking him over with a critical eye. "Turn around and bite onto something. I can put your shoulder back in place."

"No freaking way. What makes you think you can do that?"

"My mother was…is a healer. I've seen her do it plenty of times."

"And you've done it yourself before?"

"No, but it seemed easy enough."

"Jehova. This is going to hurt."

"Um, yeah. Probably." She turned him to the side and carefully grasped his arm at the shoulder and under his elbow. "Are you ready?"

"No."

"Don't be a baby. We have to get out of here, or we're both dead."

He took a deep breath. "Okay, go ahead."

She maneuvered his arm quickly. When the white noise in his head from the unbearable pain began to wane, the throbbing in his shoulder had lessened considerably. "Holy shit, you really did it."

"Yeah, holy shit." She sounded just as surprised as he had. She quickly dressed in her Uvlar gear, pleased that he had the decency to look away. "Let's go. I've got another bike nearly ready to use at the edge of the road to the Boneyard. If we can get to it, we can head out there. Not even Benevolent soldiers will go there. Yardmen are indiscriminate. They'll kill anyone they find inside."

"Yeah, including us."

"Chance we have to take," she said, looking him over. "We'll have to use leg power to get there," she said in a gasping breath while she rubbed her hands together. "Problem is, my balance is off from being drugged. I'm not strong enough."

"I can pedal, but can we both ride on one bike?" he asked.

The pervasive low-lying fog and smoke made every sound echo in the darkness. Scrabbling along the edges of the dangerous Nevermore, she managed to find the bike she'd tucked into the brush.

"If I sit on the handlebars, you can drive," Darla whispered.

Voices were getting closer, along with the sound of boots pounding toward them on the broken pavement.

"There they are," someone shouted from a distance.

Rud mounted the bike, and she climbed onto the handlebars and gingerly balanced herself. The handlebars wobbled, but Rud managed to keep the bike balanced while he pedaled toward the Boneyard. "Sit as still as you can," he said. "Every time you jerk the handlebars, my shoulder feels like it might pop out again."

"Sorry," she said.

Now, with his arm not being wrenched, and the old road fairly flat, he managed to pick up speed. This bike was in pretty good shape, so they moved along at a nice clip.

At least a dozen pairs of boots pounded on the old road behind them—trained footsteps in unison echoing through the night. The men began shouting at the top of their lungs in a military chant. It got louder as they ran down the road.

They called out in a sort of rhythm. Taking turns shouting out, then all together, the song was loud enough to scare some of the animals. A military tactic Rud had learned during his short stint. Why hadn't he thought of it earlier?

"We're making good time on the bike," Darla said. "How's the shoulder feeling?"

"Pretty good, all things considered," he said.

Shortly after that, she pointed ahead and shouted back to him. "There's the first perimeter of the Boneyard. Holy crap, we've made it through the scrub without even spotting an animal."

He stopped pedaling. They couldn't go any farther because of the barrier of junk. She jumped off, and Rud laid the bike down on the ground, where it instantly became another piece of metal.

Wading through the rubble, Rud decided to step off the tiny path to walk beside Darla.

"Stop," she said under her breath, but urgently enough that he knew she meant business. "Don't forget the traps." She lurched sideways and yanked him away from a slight mound under the dirt.

The air left his lungs while he stared at the ground. Crap. There were traps? If so, the refuse all around this thing made them virtually invisible. Worse, he'd already entered the debris field several times when he'd followed Darla. He'd had no idea. "What kind of traps are they?"

"The kind that blow up and spray your pieces all over the place," she said, grimly regarding the line of refuse ahead of him.

"Holy flying fuck. I could have died," he said, trying not to see that graphic image in his mind.

She nodded. "Yep. You could have. Now follow me,

and don't go off the path."

She moved through the yard deliberately, as if she saw the traps. He sure couldn't. Every now and then, she leaned over and touched a piece of metal. What?

"This way." Darla straightened and stepped over an old box with an X scraped into it.

Just like every other time he'd followed her, she slipped quietly along the paths between the junk, occasionally stopping to press her hand against a piece of rusted-out metal. They took a corner, and then two more. The next time she stopped to press her hand against an ancient piece of machinery, Rud listened for the soldiers on the road behind them. They must have reached the perimeter because their voices were very clear now—and too damned close for comfort.

"Who's going into the yard?" one soldier asked.

"Not me. No way, no how. We don't have to worry about taking those two in for questioning. The Yardmen will have them for dinner."

"But we were supposed to bring the woman in alive."

"Too bad. "I'm not dying at the hands of a Yardman so Vestro can have her."

"Cowards," one soldier spat out. "You don't deserve to serve under Governor Vestro."

"Damn. Apparently one of the soldiers is willing to come inside," Rud whispered. And that soldier wanted Darla. Her eyes were closed—squeezed tight against their predicament, maybe.

He touched the back of her hand, and her eyes flashed open and looked at him in a way that drew him in. His heart expanded, and his breathing got tight. Frig, the woman's beauty stunned him. If they hadn't been in mortal danger right now, he'd have liked to taste her lips.

He took her gaze as an invitation to delve the depths of her. To make a connection in a way he shouldn't.

"Rud?"

By the time she'd spoken his name, he'd closed the gap between them. With hands gripping her upper arms, he pulled her against him. Benevolent almighty, she felt good. She fit against him perfectly. And even in this world of poverty and loss, she smelled like fresh apples. How'd she manage that? There were no factories, no shampoo or soap companies like the ones advertised in the ancient magazines. Only poverty, despair and waning populations due to disease and a ruling class who killed people at will.

He nuzzled her. One hand slid up the Uvlar covered nape of her neck before Darla smacked his face so hard, he saw stars.

"Don't," she said. "Before I make you very sorry, get your damned paws off me. I don't know why you thought you could just do that without my say so. If you want to live...follow me."

His arms dropped away from her instantly. "Sorry. Must've been the rush of the moment—you know, not knowing if we're going to live or die. Plus, I wanted to thank you for fixing my arm." He shifted his arm slowly. "Feels much better."

* * * * *

She glared at him. "I can't believe you made a move on me. How's your face feel now?" she grated.

He touched his cheek with one hand and grinned. "You pack a wallop, but I'm still alive and kicking, at least."

She made a disgusted sound then scouted the rough

route ahead of them. They needed to get away from that soldier who seemed willing to brave the Boneyard to come after them.

And Rud needed to get his priorities in order if he hoped to prove himself to her.

CHAPTER FIVE

Pebbles scuttled on the path behind them. Too close for comfort.

Without speaking, Darla indicated they should hide in an old passenger bus. His expression proved he wasn't very happy with her choice. Add that to the tons of metal compacted on top of the rusted-out bus, and sweat erupted on his upper lip. The poor-quality oxygen hung thick inside. Mold and pollen spores filled the air with every step they took.

Darla expected him to panic and run back outside for a minute, but he got himself under control and followed her deeper into the bus.

"I don't think this is the safest of places," he whispered. Another groan of metal accentuated his statement.

This might have been the second-dumbest thing she'd done tonight, after the Yardman incident. "We'll be okay," she lied. "This pile's been here a very long time. It hasn't collapsed yet."

"Is that supposed to make me feel better?"

No way would she tell him that even bigger vehicles were falling to ruin in the yard lately. Might not be as safe as she hoped, but they had no choice. If given an option between being crushed by tons of technology, taken by the soldier, or raped and murdered by a Yardman—she'd take the technology.

"I'm a little bit claustrophobic," he whispered, crouching next to her between rows of cracked and rusted seating. Stuffing and little bits of leather that had dried out and had been nibbled by rodents littered the rotting metal floor.

"Shhhhh."

Footsteps thudded down the dirt path toward them. Heavy, hollow sounds that only a Yardman made when not trying to be silent. She wondered if the soldier had been able to hide on time. There'd been no scream; that meant he'd be safe for now.

Her heart stumbled when the Yardman stopped near the bus. She thought they were toast until the idiot Benevolent who'd decided to chase them into the yard called out. "I'm coming after you, so don't bother to try to hide, Rune."

How could he be so incompetent that he didn't hear the Yardman?

She gave Rud a look of utter disbelief and regret. Rud simply pursed his lips and shook his head. If she'd read him right, he actually felt sorry for the soldier right now, too.

The Yardman uttered a guttural sound that the Benevolent soldier probably couldn't hear from his location.

Excitement? Laughter? Yardmen weren't able to

speak. But she'd heard enough of their noises to figure this guy had snickered at his good luck. He probably couldn't believe an idiot Benevolent would come into his yard and start hollering.

For such a behemoth, the Yardman changed direction and moved off much more quietly than before. The dumb soldier would soon regret stepping into the yard. He should've stayed outside.

A tear leaked out, and she bit her lip when they heard the soldier scream. She slowly raised her hands and covered her ears to block out the sounds that went on for much too long. Finally, after what seemed an eternity, Rud touched her hand. But only briefly this time. She looked at him, and he nodded. The soldier had to be dead, and the Yardman would be out of their way for a while.

"Let's get out of here," she said.

She noticed the faraway look in his gaze and decided this had to be the first time he'd experienced a yard murder. Lucky him.

"Yeah, after hearing that guy's screams, I'm sure the other soldiers are long gone, too. If I heard those kinds of screams coming out of this place, I'd never come back here," Rud said, then winced when he looked at her. She felt the blood drain out of her face.

"Let's put this place behind us," he said.

She tipped her head and listened. After nearly being caught by a Yardman earlier, she didn't want a repeat of that incident. Nor to be the next one screaming. "No more talking now," she said. "Not until we get out of the yard. The Yardman might be distracted, but he's got plenty of friends or relatives or whatever the hell they are. They don't have certain territories. Sometimes they gather in one place."

"To chat?"

She shook her head and put her index finger over her lips. "Sometimes they punish Yardmen who get a little too murderous. They have a kind of law out here, Yardman law. Even the beasts can push things only so far," she whispered.

His eyes got wide, and maybe she saw admiration in them.

By the time they got back to the old highway, a long, frayed ribbon leading them back to the city, no soldiers were on the road ahead. Either they'd run all the way back, or they'd been taken by the beasts that lurked in the scrub.

Whatever had happened, they were gone.

"Those damned soldiers took your bike," Rud said, standing over the spot they'd left it. "Hell, I don't blame them."

Darla heard that clock in her head ticking down again. She'd been too lucky lately, and tonight her luck had nearly run out. It had been a miracle they'd gotten away and through the Nevermore without running into anything scary. Odds were, they weren't going to be so lucky this time.

"We need to gather anything we can use to protect ourselves," she said. "I brought my pistol, but I only have a few bullets." Next, she rummaged in the box with the X on it and came up with her second-best deterrent, skunk scent, in an old squirt bottle.

"What if there are more than two creatures out there waiting for us this time?" he asked.

She sighed. "Especially the wolves. They run in packs."

The two of them stared at the broken tarmac in the

unusual fractured moonlight. Birds and strange animal calls suddenly grew louder and echoed from the brush like warning sounds. A breeze swished through the grasses, making the branches way too noisy for comfort.

"Damn it, I usually have weapons with me when I leave the city," he said.

"Wait. You saying you leave the city often?" she asked suspiciously.

His lips formed a solid line, and he didn't answer.

Benevolent soldiers left the city on a regular basis. So why didn't she think he was one of them? He acted like one. Maybe he'd lied about being Oberon James' brother? Other than a resemblance, what proof did she have?

"I had to do a stint in the army under Vestro. Only two months long, thank the night, and probably Oberon," he said, sounding a little bitter. "Oberon takes it upon himself to keep me safe at all times. He doesn't realize I'm all grown up and I can look after myself."

"You can certainly wield a pipe," she said and watched his face light up for the first time since she'd met him. The kid needed a little bit of confidence-building, she guessed.

She glanced down at the ground. "We should have one of the land mines to take with us. Also, grab another iron pipe. That'll be a good weapon for you."

"Land mine. As in explosive device? Set to go off when stepped upon?" He looked at her like she'd gone crazy. "How do you propose we do that?"

She grinned. "Very carefully. Besides, they're pressure mines, so we won't put any pressure on them. Just dig around them and gently lift them out of the ground."

He slowly pulled a two-foot length of pipe out of the debris field in front of him. "I don't think that's a very good idea. Don't know about you, but I'm rather fond of having hands and arms."

The hip-high grasses and reeds continued to rustle under the intermittent gusts of wind that blew tonight. A dry rattle that ended in a swish had Darla's hair standing on end. The swishing sounds worried her the most. Something nasty had been sneaking up on them.

She grabbed a sharp piece of metal and slowly began digging in the dirt, revealing the outline of a circular mine, easy pickings to her practiced eye. She'd had to use one before. The only problem, they were so old they sometimes didn't go off at all. And they were definitely unstable. Risky enough to hold, but deadly dangerous while being dug out of the ground.

Snuffling from the brush made fine hairs stand up on the back of her neck.

She stopped digging long enough to look at Rud, who held the steel rod at chest height and looked battle ready. Good thing.

"Don't move, and don't make a noise," he said, while a huge wild pig with sharp tusks ran from one ditch, across the tarmac and into the grasses on the other side.

"Why'd I have to stay still for a pig?" she asked. "I bet that pig would make good bacon." She'd actually never seen a wild boar before. It made her mouth water.

"More likely he'd make bacon out of you. They're vicious. And they're dangerous. Not wise to cross unless you're with a hunting team."

She stopped digging in the sand and stared out at the grasses waving in the night. "People are hungry in the city. Why don't we go on hunting trips more often?"

"Some do. Some even live long enough to bring fresh meat home. Our ancestors had things called zoos, where they kept all sorts of wild animals that weren't from this continent. After the war and the collapse of the civilized world, animals from zoos escaped into the wild."

She stared at him. "That explains the animals, but what about the Yardmen?"

"I don't think they're explainable." He shrugged. "They're a freak of nature, maybe? And they're freaking killers. Why do you do it, anyway? Go to the Boneyard, I mean."

She sucked in a breath. "I have to admit I didn't know about the animals from zoos." The honest truth: She had to come here. And, no matter how dangerous, she couldn't stay away, but she'd never justify that to Rud. As for the Yardmen, up until today she felt they'd had a kind of pact. If she didn't bother them, they didn't bother her. She might've been wrong about that.

* * * * *

Oberon signed paperwork until he couldn't sit still any longer. He let out a long, tired breath and glanced through the UV-tinted, bulletproof window opposite his desk. He glanced at his watch. It'd been hours since he'd sent Felix to find Rud. Someone should have found him by now. In a small city like Central, a man couldn't hide from trained trackers for very long. It should have been easy to find him. Especially since he had a tendency to go to the bars.

Wait a minute! Felix should've been back with news by now. He got up and opened the door and stepped into the hallway.

Fine hairs prickled on his arms.

A voice, a whisper, came out of nowhere.

He extricated his pistol. "Who's there?"

"Someone has broken the pact I made with your family. The vault has been opened, and the prophecy has been taken," a woman's voice said.

His jaw dropped. Somehow in his heart he knew the prophet herself, Maribel Rune, had come to him. But how could he physically hear her?

"Yes, Oberon, it's me. I've always been connected to your family. The connection is strongest with the eldest child."

Maribel herself had come to him? His family had survived the apocalypse because her messages left in sealed compartments had gotten them through the horrors and the starvation after the War of Neutrality. "Are you saying the vault has been opened?" His back tightened.

As far as he knew, only one other person should have been able to find Maribel's prophecy meant for him, because no one else could get into their underground bunker. Rudyard.

"I don't know how you've managed to come to me now, but I guarantee I will find the prophecy and fulfill it."

"It's not just the paper that the message is written on, boy. It's the Neo-Verolli Casket. Most powerful and meant for my great-great-great-granddaughter. She and she alone can use that casket. If it's lost.... You must have it in order to fulfill the prophesy. Do you understand?"

Oberon had read the prophecies from the past two hundred years. He knew the importance of his role. Hell, he'd taken over the government as a result of directions he'd received. But to never be able to bring Earth back to its lush abundance would be devastating. Their endgame. What had Rud done? "I'll make it right, ma'am."

The hollow sound in his ears stopped suddenly, and the woman disappeared. He turned and found his guard walking toward him. "Where have you been?" he demanded.

"I'm sorry, sir, in the latrine next door." He appeared terrified, and for good reason. Soldiers weren't supposed to leave their posts, especially when they were on guard duty outside the governor's door. This soldier seemed young. Too young. "Why isn't one of your superior officers here, soldier?"

"They've all been sent out to find your brother, sir."

"You look familiar. Were you a Benevolent soldier?" Oberon asked through gritted teeth. He'd have Felix's balls for this. They had others who'd defected to his army, but they were supposed to be under scrutiny until they proved they weren't spies.

"I was, sir." His voice remained subservient, but his eyes were angry. "Just like you, sir, if you'll pardon the comparison."

He had to grin at that comment. Oberon himself had been one of Vestro's top soldiers, and he'd taken over the government. The kid had guts.

"Carry on, soldier."

"Definitely, sir."

"Governor." A high-pitched voice like nails on a chalkboard called from the end of the hall. "Where are you going?"

Oberon stopped halfway down the hall and returned to talk to Felix. "Has my brother been found yet, Felix?" If Rudyard had the prophecy, he'd gone against Maribel's wishes, and he'd put himself in grave danger. The last thing they needed was for Vestro to get his hands on the one thing that kept the James family a few steps ahead of the ex-dictator.

Following the prophecy could be dangerous. If anything happened to his brother, it would finish Oberon.

"No, sire."

Felix lived in the past. Calling him sire made him sound like he was some lord from the Dark Ages. But then again, they'd left the enlightened years and returned to the Dark Ages. Oberon still hated the title, but he didn't make a big deal out of it. He had more important things on his mind.

He motioned Felix back to his office. "After we talk, get my Uvlar suit. I've got to go out."

Felix inhaled sharply. "You can't. It's too dangerous for you."

Oberon's expression hardened with intent. His eyes narrowed, and he felt Felix wither under his glare. "This isn't a request, Felix. Have it brought to me immediately. And don't tell anyone I'm leaving Government House."

Felix's fluffy head bobbed in agreement.

"Bring me one of the captain's stallions, too. I'll go in the guise of one of my soldiers."

Felix bowed stiffly. His electrified orange hair stood on end, and when he leaned over, Oberon saw clear to his scalp, which had turned beet red under his executive assistant's rising blood pressure.

"If you're found, you'll be killed instantly, sire."

"If I can't protect myself, what hope do I have to protect my people?" he grated. "And since the soldiers haven't been able to find my brother, it looks like it's up to me to do it."

"I pray you know what you're doing."

Oberon frowned at Felix. "I'd feel much better if you had more faith in me, Felix. If you don't, I'm not sure why you're here."

Felix squirmed for a moment, and his gaze shifted away.

It was Oberon's turn to frown.

CHAPTER SIX

Darla and Rud had been walking as fast as they dared, considering she currently carried a freaking old land mine. Rud had offered to carry it, but it was her dumbass idea, so she didn't figure it'd be fair to let him. Besides, he'd never believe she could touch it and know for a fact that it wouldn't go off until she tossed it at something. Crazy as it sounded, her intuition had saved her butt more than once. But the fact didn't exactly soothe her nerves while she carried a live mine down a rutted road in virtual darkness. She could still trip—her insight didn't carry over into her own actions.

When the snarling started, Darla and Rud were still too far from the city to make it to safety. Six mangy wolves, bigger than she would have thought possible, bounded out of the brush and surrounded them on the road. Glowing yellow eyes sent a cold chill up her spine, and her hands started shaking while the muscles in her arms burned from carrying the land mine for so long.

No surprise, digging up the mine now felt like the best

thing she'd ever done. She glanced up at that rare view of the moon and appreciated its silver light. Being able to see the wolves gave them the same advantage the wolves would have had in the dark.

Rud spoke quietly beside her. "Whatever you do, don't drop that mine."

"No kidding."

The beasts snapped and snarled but seemed to be taking their time before attacking. The larger alpha paced ahead of the rest. Growling amplified by five canines reverberated in the marrow of her bones. She'd never truly felt mind-numbing fear until now. She tried to swallow, but her throat had gone completely dry.

A wolf lunged at Rud, then ducked back from the swinging iron pipe. "I think it's time to throw the mine."

Unable to take her eyes off the terrifying, slavering wolves, she was inundated by the thought of being torn apart.

"Darla? What are you waiting for?"

She clamped down on her terror until it dissolved into a tiny burr at the back of her brain stem. "I'm going to lob the mine up and let it drop on the road in the middle of them. But, when I raise my arms, I'm guessing the wolves will attack, so be ready. The bad news is the blast will be closer than it should be. There'll be risk of shrapnel at this range."

"Risk of what?" he said through gritted teeth. "Sometimes you use language I've never heard before."

She sucked in a strengthening breath. No time to tell him that she learned the words every time she touched technology. "Flying bits of metal."

He made a grim sound of understanding.

Darla lobbed the mine up so it would hit the ground

hard when it fell. Hard enough to go off. "Drop," she shouted, pumping the spray bottle quickly then grabbing his hand and yanking him down to the broken tarmac with her.

Rud started gagging and coughing. "Holy shit. What is in that bottle?"

Before she could answer, the blast erupted on impact, and the percussion hit them harder than she'd hoped.

* * * * *

Oberon left the horse two blocks back and sneaked from one pool of shadow to another, making absolutely sure he hadn't been followed, until he finally entered the abandoned remnants of the old factory yard. He'd rather be riding to the Nevermore to find Rud, but first he needed the Neo-Verolli Casket that Maribel had demanded he get.

He had to remain alert since his safety net of darkness would be lost at dawn, in an hour or two. He moved lithely over the downed walls and slipped under a piece of fallen roofing that strategically appeared random but had been specifically placed to cover a private trapdoor.

Old New York City had been built over myriad snaking tunnels. Not many people knew about them anymore, because the tunnels were mostly in the Nevermore, where he believed the biggest part of the pre-war city used to be.

His family had hidden in this underground bunker within Central City for two centuries. As far as they could figure, it'd been the only accessible tunnel inside the city. And the entrance had a security pass code that kept out anyone who might find this place by accident.

He spun the numbers on the lock to the secure bunker

then turned a giant wheel to open the foot-thick steel door. He stepped inside, quickly pulling it shut behind him.

According to family records, this bunker had initially been designated for a top government executive who'd died when his plane had gone down. All planes had gone down when the new form of electromagnetic pulses started, wreaking havoc and taking out electricity instantly. The whole continent had been zapped back into the eighteenth century within a week, and society had consequently broken down. Some people said the EMPs were part of a newly developed time rift technology. Apparently, Maribel had been high up in the government and had quickly moved the James family into this secure bunker.

Oberon opened another sealed door and took a metal ladder down to a sub-level. Here, walls seemed out of place, covered with solid, polished steel. A vault at the end of the hall housed several locked drawers, each one coded shut with a manual number dial. An attempt to key in the wrong combination would lock down the whole set, never to be opened again. No one dared open a drawer without knowing the correct code. The fact that Rud had attempted such a thing worried him.

The drawer meant for him hung open. As Maribel had indicated, the small box that had housed the message, the Neo-Verolli Casket, remained in the drawer.

Rud had really taken the message.

How had things gone so wrong? What in hell had Rud been thinking?

Bad enough that Oberon had become a dictator as a result of one of the messages drawn from the vault upon his birth. His gut twisted. Holy hell, he needed to believe in her. To believe in what he'd been directed to do. Their country needed help, and if being a dictator was the only way to empower that change, he had to believe that message.

But for shit's sake, Rudyard knew he shouldn't have opened the drawer, so why would he? Oberon uttered an angry oath, and the air in the vault changed, feeling hollow, as if he'd pressed his ear to the end of a long tube or something.

A shimmering form of a woman appeared before him, and Oberon gasped. The vaporous beauty with long red hair threw her hands into the air. "I put a message of great importance inside the casket, Oberon," Maribel spoke to him again. "What your brother didn't realize: The casket itself is important. The casket and my granddaughter. Your brother is with her right now. They're in danger. Grave danger. Only you can save her and reunite her with the casket when the time is right. Keep it hidden and safe for now. That little box is powerful but not as powerful as Darla. She is as connected to that box as she is to you. She'll never attain the level of abilities meant for her without it."

"What happens in that case?" he said.

"Failure. Two hundred years of your family's blood, sweat and tears gone, your family's honor and hard work—all for nothing. Worse—civilization's last hope gone."

"How can I find them?"

"Go to the southern fields on the road coming from the Boneyard. They're in terrible danger." After she disappeared and her voice faded away, the changing pressure in his ears made them pop.

Heart pounding, he locked the bunker and made his

way to his horse, where he put the casket carefully into his backpack tucked into his saddlebag. To blend in, he wore a poorer-grade Uvlar suit, the same as any other soldier. It would have been better if he hadn't had a horse, but giving up his means of fast transportation wasn't an option, especially if his brother and the young granddaughter of their seer were in danger.

He took off through the city at speeds that were reckless, both to him and the horse. Idiotic as his brother could be, Oberon would lay down his life for him.

* * * * *

The lead wolf growled, and its nose wrinkled back to expose its yellow teeth. He dove at Darla and bit down on her leg.

"Get off me, you bastard." Darla kicked the beast's face with her free foot. The wolf had knocked her to the ground. Thankfully, her high leather boot gave her a little protection, but the pressure felt excruciating. At least those sharp teeth hadn't sliced into her flesh yet.

But, oh, cripes, it hurt like hell. Desperate, she leaned forward and smashed her fist dead center into the wolf's nose. It yelped and backed off.

"Spray the liquid again," Rud shouted in between beating off another hungry wolf with his iron pipe. Her quick survey before being attacked let her know that the blast had taken out four of the wolves, but there were still two left. And those two were hell-bent on getting dinner.

She sprayed the scent again, just as a gust of wind circled them. "Blowback's a bitch," she shouted.

Rud began coughing and gagging. "What is that horrible scent, anyway?"

"Skunk—only it gets worse when it's concentrated."

The alpha wolf yelped and backed off, shaking its massive head a couple of times.

Darla's stomach balked at the scent, too. Unfortunately, the wolves were not leaving. Rud grabbed for the scent bottle and hurled it at the alpha's head. It bounced off its nose and rolled back toward them.

Stupid move. As disgusting as the stuff had been, they might've been able to use it again. Since the wolf had let go of her leg to shake its massive head, she jumped to her feet. Unfortunately, her leg buckled, and she dropped helplessly to the ground in front of the alpha, in an even more vulnerable position. And Rud currently had his hands full.

At this point, if the wolf pounced on her, he'd go for her throat. She'd put an arm up to protect her face and neck when she heard horse hooves pounding toward them. The rider fired a crossbow, and the arrow buried itself in the wolf's neck just as it lunged for her throat. She actually had it by the scruff of its wide neck with its teeth snapping at her face when it dropped onto her, forcing the air out of her lungs.

If that arrow had missed the wolf, it would've gone into her head.

She crawled out from under the beast with the urge to tear a strip off the shooter, who had dismounted his horse. His features were obscured by his face shield. Those eyes, however, were vaguely familiar, and they were angry.

She heard Rud swing the pipe at the remaining wolf, and it yelped when it hit its mark but it didn't go down. "Help Rud," she shouted, pointing at him.

"Rud can handle himself." The stranger's deep voice penetrated her. It grated against her like fire ants under her clothing. He acted like he knew Rud. So she'd been right, Rud had to be a Benevolent soldier. She bit her lip and stared at the soldier in full military regalia before her.

With a final bash of the pipe, Rud took out the giant wolf, as predicted. "That was too close," he said, cradling his recently dislocated shoulder. He turned to the rider. "Thank you for…" He moved closer, stared into the eyes of the man whose face was hidden behind a shield. "Oberon? What are you doing out here?"

"Who else would risk his ass to save you in the Nevermore, brother? Most people would have more common sense." He sounded irate, and Rud's shoulders slumped noticeably. That made Darla angry.

"Your brother saved me from a Yardman. Took him out with one swing," she said, narrowing her gaze on the dictator. No wonder his eyes had been familiar. She hated how easily he'd just belittled his brother.

Oberon's brows formed a dark line. "You damned fool. Why would you bring her out here to be killed? Do you have any idea how important…" He let the sentence fade away and glanced at her again. "I'm sorry my brother put you in such danger, Ms. Rune."

"Nobody puts me in danger. I can do that very well all by myself." Hands on her hips now, she wanted to punch the idiot governor in the nose. And how did he know her name? She managed to get to her feet, but if she dared take another step, she risked falling on her face again. She'd have to take it easy. Her leg might be injured worse than she dared think about.

Rud coughed to cover a laugh. "I can vouch for that."

Big brother pulled off his hood and let it drop to his back momentarily. His face revealed exactly what Darla had expected from his photos, only tougher and probably more dangerous. His salt-and-pepper hair surprised her. Prematurely graying, she'd guess. He didn't look much older than early thirties.

And, damn it, she felt an unexpected attraction to this dictator, whom she should detest on sight.

She glanced from one brother to the other. Why did they both treat her like she had something they wanted?

"Used to getting into trouble or not, what in the name of Benevolent hell are you doing out here in the wilds?" Oberon asked Darla. When she ignored him, he turned his questioning gaze on Rud. "And without weapons."

"Soldiers chased us out here. They tried to kidnap Darla. Broke into her place dressed in Shadow Gear." He strode to Oberon and stared him down. Two brothers facing off. Darla managed a step back. It had been a crappy night. She just wanted to find a safe hole somewhere and get some sleep.

"My soldiers?" Oberon said. "I sent them to find you, not Ms. Rune."

Darla's back tightened.

"How'd you find us?" Rud asked, no doubt as grateful to be found as Darla had been. Being ticked at his brother's overbearing attitude could be ignored this time, given the circumstances. To accentuate that point, she spotted a wolf carcass on the road ahead. It must've been taken out by the blast and thrown...well, parts of it had been thrown quite a few feet.

The wind shifted suddenly, and Oberon's nose flared, and he stepped back "Holy hell, what is that odor?"

"My animal deterrent." Darla slanted a look at the glass bottle, miraculously unbroken on the ground. If he said one more thing she didn't like, he'd find out personally, because there was still a little liquid left inside.

Placing the back of his gloved hand over his nose and looking at the wolves' carcasses on the road, he said, "Didn't work against them, though, did it? You both could be dead right now. Ripped apart."

Neither of them replied—hard to deny the truth.

"Are you sure my soldiers chased you, Rud? Did they have the James' insignia on their chests?"

Rud's gaze flicked to Darla. They'd already figured the soldiers had been Vestro's, so why pretend otherwise? It was because Oberon had made him feel like a loser, and he'd struck back at him the only way possible.

Oberon's unmistakable expression proved he considered his brother naïve. He didn't understand life the way she did. The way his older brother apparently did. Rud had obviously been protected from the reality of normal everyday existence, and more than likely Oberon had everything to do with that.

Lucky Rud. His brother cared enough to come looking for him during such a dangerous time in his coup, and all alone.

A sliver of jealously stung her. She wondered if Rud knew how lucky he was. One thing she could respect the governor for: loving his brother, if not helping him to be streetwise.

Another animal made a sound in the distance, and Darla's skin went cold. "Time to get out of here before something worse finds us?"

Oberon's horse whinnied nervously, and its hooves scraped the ground. Its head lifted, and its eyes opened wide, nostrils flaring.

Whatever it was, the creature wasn't far off. Darla felt

it almost as definitely as the horse did.

Oberon touched the horse's neck to calm it. "Easy, boy."

"Something's definitely coming," she said matter-of-factly. Call it a feeling, call it dread—didn't matter, because they needed to get out of here, now.

But, damn it, her leg ached, and she balanced herself so she wouldn't put too much pressure on it. What had that wolf done to her? She took a couple of tentative steps.

"Why are you limping?" Rud asked, moving in to check on her.

"That wolf nipped me," she said, pushing back her shoulders and gritting her teeth against the burning pain.

Before Rud could get to her, Oberon dropped to one knee in front of her. "Let me see your leg."

"Piss off."

He raised an imperious eyebrow in her direction. "Well, if you're right and something is coming, then you'd better let me have a look at your leg, because we're not leaving here until I know how seriously injured you are."

"Do it, Darla. If you don't, he'll be insufferable," Rud said. "He served a term as a medic in Vestro's army. He thinks he's a doctor."

She reluctantly pushed her leg forward. Oberon unzipped the side of the boot and pulled the leather back. He hissed. "This is much worse than a nip, I'm afraid."

She avoided looking at the damage the wolf had done. She had plenty of intestinal fortitude, otherwise she wouldn't hang out in the Boneyard, but she hated the sight of her own blood. Just thinking there might be blood made her stomach do a little dance. When he lifted his head, his expression scared the bejeepers out of her.

"Help me get her on the horse," Oberon ordered Rud. Rud's jaws worked, but he moved in to help.

She held up her hands against the two men. "Back off. I can walk."

"You're bleeding heavily, Ms. Rune."

She hated the way he used her last name. Almost like an insult—like he resented her. And how'd he know her name? Crazy. She'd never met him before, why would he have any feelings toward her one way or another?

"If we can get you on the horse with your leg up, maybe the bleeding will lessen and we won't scent the air for every vicious creature that might be lying in wait."

To accentuate his statement, a large feline of some sort growled nearby. Then they heard more growling and scuffling sounds, and she monitored the road ahead. The wolf that had lain there just moments before had disappeared. Gone.

And then another big cat roar came from the other side of the road in the bushes beyond. They were being surrounded again, but by something even worse than last time. The horse started to fidget. Definitely afraid.

"Those predators might be distracted by the carcasses for now, but we need to get out of here," Oberon said in a low, quiet voice.

She limped toward the horse with every intention of mounting it herself, but Oberon moved too quickly for her. He helped her up, handed her the reins and touched her leg. "Can you sit so that your leg can rest across Tantalum's back?"

"I think so," she said. The impossibility of being lithe in an ancient Uvlar suit meant her leg got stuck on the pommel. She tried several times to lift it over, but her energy had flagged.

"Let me help you," he said in an irritated voice that ticked her off even more. Too bad she couldn't do anything about it. He manipulated her leg over the pommel, very gently, without saying another word. Next, he took the reins, and the two men led the horse toward the city. She'd seen Oberon give Rud a gun, and now they watched the Nevermore as intently as she did from her higher vantage point.

While they walked toward the city, they whispered back and forth. Totally pointless, because she heard every word they said.

"Rud, you and I have some serious talking to do when we get back."

"This dictator thing has gone to your head," Rud grumbled. "Besides, I have no reason to talk to you about anything."

"You know exactly what I mean. You've done something that might ruin everything our family has worked toward over the years. I can't believe you did it."

She didn't have a clue what they were talking about. After everything that had happened to her tonight, had these men colluded to put her danger? Had Rud set her up with the Yardman? Had the two of them sent the soldiers to make her feel at risk so they could rescue her? So she'd trust them?

She reached down to pat Tantalum's back. His skin rippled under her touch, and he whinnied a response. There's only one living thing she trusted out here in the wilds right now—the horse.

CHAPTER SEVEN

Oberon glared at Rud because he still had the prophecy. His prophecy—and until Oberon read it, he wouldn't know how much they could tell Darla.

Worse, never before had the wrong family member taken the prophecy. Who knew what that would mean for their future?

Grinding his teeth together, Oberon raised the gun in the direction of the big black cat about to pounce on Rud. He shot the beast between the eyes, and it dropped with a thump. Too close. His brother turned pale and flashed a reluctantly thankful glance his way.

Darla appeared to have been impressed by his quick reaction, too. She smiled at him, actually smiled. His pulse raced, and he pushed down the emotion she easily elicited inside him. He had no right to her. None at all.

They entered the city where small, thatched roofs sprouted up in groups. No doubt a few brave souls had lost their lives gathering grasses for these poorly made shelters. The scent of wood and burning grasses drifted in the air, reminding him that summer wouldn't last forever and winter meant cold and starvation if his people didn't get help.

And if they found him here, they'd probably lynch him.

He stole another glance at Darla. She was in pain. Her face had blanched even more than when he'd first found her. Her eyes constantly fought against closing. Either dead tired or in shock.

"Where are you taking her?" Rud asked under his breath.

"To Government House."

"She's not going to like that. And I'm not sure I like it, either," Rud grumbled.

"That's too bad, little brother. You know how important she is to us. And you had no right to do what you did."

"Why not? I'm just as capable as you. Besides, Maribel herself told me how to get the message."

"I very much doubt it," Oberon said between gritted teeth.

"Why?"

"Because Maribel sent me to you—to save her granddaughter. She also told me you'd taken the final prophecy."

"I don't believe it," Rud said. "You just want me to back off so you can have all the glory. Maribel led me to the prophecy."

Oberon shook his head. "I'm afraid I've protected you too much, brother. You're naïve. And I don't really care what you believe. Give me the prophecy," he said, holding out his gloved hand. "I'm the one who is supposed to carry it out."

"I am not naïve," Rud said angrily, even though some of the fire had gone out of him. Maybe he'd realized he didn't understand the underbelly of society quite as much as he thought he did.

Oberon cursed inwardly. He hadn't done his brother any favors by protecting him from the realities of their lives, but he didn't want to break him, either.

"I've got the prophecy, and I intend to carry it out," Rud said. "Why shouldn't I?"

"Because it isn't intended for you," Oberon whispered, glancing up at Darla again. How much of this could she hear? She looked to be asleep, gently bobbing back and forth as the horse strode along while they argued in whispers.

She might just have her eyes closed, but someone who lived in the toughest regions of the city by herself would never let her guard down.

"Halt, who goes there?" Five soldiers approached the city boundary from the east.

"At ease, men." Oberon pulled back his face shield temporarily to identify himself.

"Governor James? What are you doing out here without your elite guard, sir? It's not safe. Especially in this part of the city. We've had reports of Vestro's soldiers impersonating us. The streets are still too dangerous for you—especially alone."

"He's not exactly alone," Rud said in a sarcastic tone and frowned at the officer leading the small group of haggard-looking men.

The soldier ignored Rud and spoke only to Oberon. "May we accompany you back to the House, sir?"

"What are your current orders, soldier? If we're taking you from them, we can make it back unaided."

"We've just returned from a skirmish, sir. We were cut off from the battalion earlier. We caught one of them, though." The soldier pulled another similarly dressed man forward.

"Who is he?" Oberon asked.

"We can't get him to talk yet, sir." The prisoner's hands were tied behind his back. "Maybe when we get back to headquarters, sir."

"By Benevolent hell, he will talk," Oberon ground out. "Or he'll join his friends in the brig."

At that moment, Oberon caught Darla's open eyes. Wide awake all right, and her expression indicated she wanted to stab him in the heart herself. Wasn't she supposed to be on his side?

"Follow us back to Government House," Oberon said. "We can use the safety detail until we get," he glanced at Darla, "our charge safely inside."

"Yes, sir." The men immediately surrounded the governor's small group with one in the front with their prisoner, one on each side and one at the rear.

* * * * *

Before the soldiers arrived, Darla had been listening to the brothers arguing under their breath. She'd heard the name Maribel in their conversation. What did her so-called relative have to do with anything? It didn't make sense. And what was that talk about a prophecy?

They reached the outer gates more quickly than she expected. The horse fidgeted under her, probably because he felt her building tension.

A thin man with frizzy orange hair ran outside as soon as they stopped in front of the main doors. His hands flailed in the air. "Where have you been? I've been frantic. I thought you'd been taken."

"Felix, what do you mean taken?" Rud said, looking at his brother. "Taken by whom?"

Felix cast a disbelieving glance at Rud. "By our enemies, of course."

"It's like that, is it, Oberon?" Rud said.

Oberon made an exasperated sound. "Of course it is, Rud. What did you think? We've just managed to overtake the government. We can't possibly have total control already given the vastness of Vestro's army. Some of his men went AWOL at the first sign of the fall. Those were the people who didn't want to be in his army. The rest did. And there are still fringe groups, pockets of soldiers out there trying to take back the government."

At that moment, Darla comprehended the real scope of how dangerous it had been for Oberon himself to come looking for them. Even though the brothers appeared to be antagonistic to each other, the fact that Rud's brother had risked everything to save him said something about his character.

"Help the woman down," Oberon said to a soldier and walked away without a backward glance.

She hated him all over again.

"The woman has a name," she shouted after him and pushed the soldier's extended hands away to dismount by herself. Unfortunately, when her foot touched the ground, pain streaked through her leg and the soldier managed to grab her before she fell. Damn it, her leg hurt worse now than it had in the Nevermore.

Even so, Oberon could have at least asked her what she wanted to do before he walked off and left her sitting on his horse. She wanted to go home.

She turned to Rud to ask him to help her, when he

said, "I'll find you in a minute," he said, seeking her out before he took off after Oberon.

She had actually felt ill the second they passed through the gates of Government House. So many citizens had been taken here to die. To be tortured and killed. Her fate next? She was a dissident, after all.

Her leg twinged, and she hissed when a second soldier helped to pick her up and carry her toward the House. He jostled her and inadvertently touched her torn flesh. "Ouch, damn it. Watch what you're doing."

"Sorry, ma'am,"

"Take her to the medic wing. But stay with her," the man named Felix spat out then raced off behind the governor and Rud.

She gritted her teeth. Like they'd caught some common criminal. She leaned forward to see her leg through the torn boot that Oberon had left partially unzipped. Her leg looked like shredded meat, and for a moment she thought she saw bone. Her vision wavered, and stars appeared in her blackening lack of focus. Stupid. She had to look... More stars. Darkness enveloped her.

When she came to, she lay on a comfortable mattress. An extremely comfortable bed in comparison to the straw mattress in her tiny home. She scanned the small white room devoid of windows. Several oil lamps lit the room and Rud dozed in a chair beside her.

"Rud?"

His eyes opened immediately, and he bolted forward in his seat. "Darla, how do you feel?"

"What's going on? Why am I here?" She took in the white cotton gown someone had put on her, and when she pulled the covers up, she saw her leg had been bandaged from ankle to knee.

"Besides doing quite a bit of damage, that wolf gave you a bad infection. You've been out of it for three days. You could've lost your leg, but Oberon's doctors are pretty efficient. The infection is clearing up really well in such a short time."

"It'll take more than a stupid wolf to finish me," she said, irritated that she'd been at their mercy for three days and hadn't even been aware.

She lifted her head off the pillow to better view her surroundings. "When can I get out of here?"

"They say you need a full course of medicine before you can leave," he told her.

No wonder she felt like her veins were on fire. Either the medicine or the infection still flamed through her body. Goose bumps erupted over her flesh. "Can you get me another blanket? I'm really cold."

"Certainly." Rud opened the door and spoke to the sentry outside.

Why did she have a sentry outside her door? Rud ordered him to find a blanket and received a cold stare. Apparently, soldiers didn't take kindly to the dictator's brother bossing them around.

Rud heaved a disgruntled sigh and looked back at her for a moment before returning his attention to the sentry. "Okay, tell me where I can get one, then. I'll get it myself."

The sentry pointed. "Third door on your right."

She tried to sit up, but her leg pained like it had been scraped raw with sandpaper. She shivered and closed her eyes again. Sleep weighted her until she had no choice but to succumb. At the last moment before she drifted off, Oberon's imperious face popped into her mind.

* * * * *

Rud found the supply room and gathered two of the softest blankets he could find. And that wasn't saying much, since they were as rough as burlap.

When he got back, she'd fallen asleep again. Fine beads of perspiration glistened on her pale face. He sighed. He'd wanted to protect her, but he had failed her. She'd be dead right now if Oberon hadn't arrived in time to save them both.

Rud had been so sure he could carry out the prophecy and protect the girl. He'd certainly proved himself. Not.

He covered her gently and made his way out of the room. "Take good care of her," he said to the soldier, who merely glanced at him before ignoring him again.

He'd been trying to get an audience with Oberon for three days without luck. He had no idea where he'd find his illustrious brother's office, but, by hell, he'd find it.

Government House had marble floors, with pillars and artwork that made the place look like pictures he'd seen in books—places called museums. Of course, museums didn't exist anymore. He touched the creamy, bronze-veined marble and felt the chill of it. This place shouldn't exist in this world. Almost all of the structures from before had been destroyed. Other than their family's underground bunker, he couldn't imagine anything topside surviving in pristine shape like this place had.

He turned a corner.

"Where are you going?" a soldier demanded, stopping him with a raised weapon.

"I want to see Oberon." He must be going the right way, at least.

"Not possible," the soldier said without hesitation.

Acid spiraled in Rud's gut. Being a dictator probably

took up all of his time. Rud might not be the right person to carry out the prophecy, but by accessing the prophecy and saving Darla, he'd proven to his brother that he wasn't just a royal fuck-up. His brother, the almighty leader, had bossed him around when they were kids, but he'd probably never guessed Rud capable of anything like this.

He glared at the soldier. "Make it possible. I'm his brother, and we have urgent business to discuss."

The soldier hesitated. Rud put his hands on his hips and raised his eyebrows.

"Come this way," the soldier said. "We'll see what Lieutenant Vaughan says.

In a small office not far away sat a bald man with shoulders twice as broad as any man Rud had ever seen. Lieutenant Vaughan stood and approached them. His muscles bulged under his uniform, and his sharp gaze measured Rud quickly.

"This man wants to see the governor," the soldier said.

The Lieutenant eyed Rud and nodded his head. "Pleasure to meet you, sir," he said. "Follow me. Your brother actually asked me to bring you to him as soon as you'd visited with Ms. Rune today."

"Thanks." Rud glared at the soldier who'd held him at gunpoint.

If Oberon had told him about his damned coup, he would have been there for him. It pissed him off that he'd been left out of the loop. He could've helped.

Remembering that, helped him make up his mind. He'd be damned if he'd give up the prophecy. Darla was worth fighting for.

The lieutenant knocked on a door at the end of the hall.

"In," Oberon's voice shouted.

The lieutenant saluted Rud and stepped away for him to enter. At least Oberon has some staff who knew how to treat the governor's brother. He tipped his head in thanks and stepped inside the room.

Oberon stood in front of a window overlooking the city. In the only three-story building in Central City, he could see clear to the boundaries where the wilds had grown up to become the Nevermore. And, in the looming distance, mountains of gleaming piles of metal, the Boneyard. Imagine that. A telescope aimed out at the city, its column of gleaming brass and glass out of sync with their world, but it might still work. Rud itched to give it a try.

Oberon sighed. "What's going on, Rud?"

Rud ignored his question.

"Rudyard, where have you been the last two weeks?" Oberon's fists were clenched at his sides.

"None of your damned business, Bron."

Oberon's face darkened. "I've always fulfilled my duties to the family and to Maribel. I can't believe you've gone against two hundred years of our family pledge."

"Well, it's too late now, isn't it? Now that I'm the one who found Darla, I'm the one who's going to continue to protect her."

"Goddamn it, Rud. Don't you understand what I'm saying to you? You might change the path we've always led because we've followed Maribel's prophecies to the letter. If she wanted other relatives to carry out her wishes, she wouldn't have adamantly directed the eldest to get the messages."

Other relatives. Just the term "relative" made Rud broil under his skin—Oberon made him sound like some distant cousin and not his brother. Did his brother really think he was so special? "Fuck you. You don't tell me what to do. I'm a James, too, and I'm proud of my heritage. If I carry out the prophecy before you do, then all the better. "

Oberon's face remained grim. He opened his mouth to speak then closed it again. He inhaled and gazed out at the city. "Somehow, Maribel came to me in person, Rud. She wants you to give me the prophecy."

"I don't believe you." Oberon just wanted the glory for himself. How much glory did one man need?

"You don't have the whole message, Rudyard." Oberon always used Rud's full name whenever he wanted to make him feel stupid, and making him angry only made him more stubborn. "The note alone is not what will save us."

"What are you talking about? It's always just been a parchment with directions for each generation. What kind of game are you playing?"" Rud asked.

"No game. The parchment you took from the vault is meant for me, and there's more to it than the written message. The prophecy can't be completed without both halves."

"What a crock. You expect me to believe that?" Rud said through gritted teeth.

"I can throw you in jail with Vestro's men if you don't comply."

"You wouldn't."

Oberon sat at his desk and opened a drawer. He took out a pen and began writing. "It'll only take my signature on this piece of paper, Rud."

"I know you can be selfish, Bron, but this goes way past that."

"I've been given a job to do. A job with very important ramifications to the future of our people. Do you think I wanted to become a dictator? Do you honestly think I woke up one morning and thought I'd like to overrun a government? I think I'll forge an army and go to battle?" He dropped the pen as if it burned him. "Surely you know me better than that."

Rud gaped. "Holy shit. You did this part of Maribel's prophecy? Why didn't you tell me?"

Oberon's mouth tightened. "Not something I wanted to talk about. It wasn't easy for me."

Rud felt a lump in his throat, and it swelled until it hurt. He'd been so quick to condemn his brother for the takeover of the country, and all the while Bron had carried out the damned family prophecy.

CHAPTER EIGHT

Getting past the residual skunk odor on her skin, Darla snuggled into her pillow. Floating on a cloud of cotton, she sniffed the scent of clean linen and wondered how she'd managed to get her sheets to smell so good. She stretched, then yawned and opened her eyes.

"Morning," a man's voice said from the chair beside her bed.

She quickly yanked the blanket up to her chin and reached for her pistol under the pillow and found nothing. Then it all came back. She'd been snagged by the dictator. And when she focused on her visitor, she saw the dictator himself sitting beside her, tall and straight in the chair. His gray-blue eyes remained impenetrable while he stared at her.

"Why am I still here?" she demanded.

"How are you feeling this morning?" he asked.

She moved her leg. It still stung and felt raw, but the sensation of fire ants crawling through her skin had ceased. She should be able to get out of here.

"Where's Rud?" she asked.

Something like irritation flickered in Oberon's eyes at that question. "Who knows? Rud's a free spirit."

"Sounds like you're jealous of that."

Oberon's shoulders tightened. "Don't be ridiculous."

Just like he had in the Nevermore, this man said things that set her teeth on edge, and she wanted to slap that smug expression off his face.

Then she remembered Vestro's laws. As their newest dictator, Oberon could make an example of her if he wished. She could be taken to the town center and tortured, or worse.

"Where are my clothes?" she asked. She wanted out of here ASAP.

"Being cleaned," he said. "Do you realize you're being exposed to too many toxins in that old Uvlar thing?"

"And yet my suit is twice as good as most citizens'. Imagine how they must feel." Bitterness crept into her voice.

Oberon leaned forward. She swallowed but continued to assess him, right down to his bunched muscles and strong hands. Callused hands.

He rose. For a hopeful moment she believed she'd driven him off.

But he merely clasped his hands behind his back and turned away from her. "I'm glad you're here, Ms. Rune. I wanted to meet you."

"Why?" She frowned and shoved her messy hair behind her ears.

"Your reputation precedes you." He turned back and leaned against the end of her bed. Other than covering her head with the sheet—and she actually contemplated that—she had no choice but to look at him.

"I have a reputation?" Damn, she'd done it this time. Totally screwed up, in fact. She'd always tried to be invisible, but more and more people had been seeking her out for her inventions.

What did he intend to do to her? His corded neck muscles and broad shoulders belonged to a man who'd worked hard in his life. A man who'd fought hard in his life. She wished she knew more about him, in particular whether or not he was cruel, and if he'd carry on in Vestro's footsteps.

"Is your leg still paining?"

"It's fine. I'd like to leave now."

"It's too soon. You should rest. Make sure the infection is under control."

She considered his answer, almost like she had a choice. But did she really?

He appeared thoughtful. "I've been thinking about how you used skunk-scent repellent in the Nevermore. It could be a good tool for my men. How do you get the scent?"

She said nothing.

"Soldiers could use that method while they're guarding the gardens in the wilds."

"That so?"

"I'm sure you realize that putting food on people's tables is a very dangerous undertaking. We lose soldiers too often. Something as simple as your skunk scent might help. It might keep attacking predators at bay long enough to be taken down."

She stared at her leg. It hadn't worked very well on the wolves.

"What other tools have you created?"

She shrugged. "I want to leave now."

"Would you consider working for me?"

She didn't have to say the words—because "never in the reign of hell" had to be plastered on her face. That said, she knew enough to never turn down an offer she might not be allowed to refuse. She had no idea what this man could be capable of. "I'll consider it."

"Do you have a supply of the scent at the moment?"

"A little. There are disadvantages to the scent," she said. His nasal passages moved, reminding her that she still smelled like skunk. The medic had bathed her, but the odor still clung.

"Yes, it could be a hazard if the wind isn't cooperating. Still, once the soldiers are covered with the scent, I imagine there are some animals that wouldn't find them quite so interesting."

She moved her leg and winced. "Apparently it doesn't work on wolves."

His brows drew together. "Did my brother put you in that kind of danger?"

The question surprised her. "No."

"Are you sure?"

"Why would your brother put me in danger?" In her estimation, governors of Central City were always corrupt. She didn't trust anything this one said, either.

"He's been misguided lately. He thinks he's doing the right thing, but it's for the wrong reasons."

"Don't blame Rud. Those men broke into my place and drove us out into the Boneyard."

Another flicker of anger, and this one barely masked. "What about Rud? How'd he end up with you in your place?"

She sat forward, gripping the sheet to her chest. As if

she'd tell him even if she really understood. "Why am I here?"

"Why don't you want me to know?" he asked, his expression indicating an underlying suspicion.

"Because it's none of your business."

"I'm making it my business. Did he tell you anything about our family?"

"Nope." Not really.

Oberon tried very hard to appear at ease, but he was obviously roiled under the surface. Curious. "I hope that's the truth," he said.

"Look, I don't care if you believe me or not. I'll be out of your way the moment I can walk."

"You'll have to stay for a little while. Besides, we have to talk when you're feeling better."

"We're talking right now." She hated that she'd been drawn to his face over and over again. What in the name of the Benevolent had happened to her?

His mouth formed a grim line. She'd bet he wanted to curse at her. She bit back a grin. At least she got the satisfaction of irritating the bejesus out of him. He might think twice next time he held someone captive who had a backbone.

"We have some important things to discuss." His voice came out in a low, dangerous tone this time. That's the tone of a dictator, she thought.

"No. We don't. And although I appreciate the medical care, I don't feel the least bit beholden to you."

He expelled an irritated breath and paced back and forth at the end of the bed. He obviously needed to put some distance between them. She'd pushed him too far this time.

"I'm sorry you feel that way." He appeared sorry, too.

Maybe just a good actor.

She slumped back down under the covers and watched him glower at her. Was he trying to decide her punishment? Had she gone too far? "I'd like to speak to Rud."

Suddenly he smiled, putting her instantly on her guard. He had dimples. So rare these days.

"I'm afraid Rud won't be around for a while. He's otherwise engaged."

"What does that mean? Otherwise engaged."

"What it means, Ms. Rune, is you might as well focus on healing and getting back on your feet. Rudyard won't be coming to see you again."

"Never?"

"Probably not."

Even though she'd just met Rud a few days ago, she didn't believe he'd just walk away. He'd told her she was important to him. "I don't believe you," Darla said. "Where are my clothes? I want to go home."

"What about the soldiers who tried to kidnap you?" He continued pacing back and forth at the end of her bed. "Aren't you worried they might find you again?"

"Are you going to send them after me again?" Why'd she say such things to the one man who could make her very sorry for opening her mouth?

His smile remained but had lost its effervescence, and his gaze strayed pointedly to her bandaged leg. "These are dangerous days in Central City. Maybe you'd be better off at least letting your wounds heal before you think about going home."

"Yeah, not happening. I demand you give me my clothes. I'm leaving."

"They'll be returned to you when they're clean."

"I don't believe you." She yanked the blanket up and started to wrap it around herself, then slid her legs off the bed. When her foot touched the floor, her leg flared with streaking, spiking pain. Damn, it hurt. She felt the blood drain out of her face, and the room began to fog up and slip sideways.

"You've gone sickly white, Ms. Rune. You'd better lie down before you crash onto the floor and injure something else."

"I'm going to be sick," she said and flopped back onto the bed.

Instead of calling for help, he grabbed a kidney basin and held it for her while she threw up. She vomited twice before she finally sank into her pillow, every muscle in her body spent. He retrieved and handed her a cool cloth to wipe her face. She took long, slow breaths until the nausea passed. "I'm okay now. But keep the basin nearby just in case."

He took the pan into the bathroom, and she heard him rinse it out. He came back and set it on the table next to the bed. Then he ran more cold water onto a clean facecloth and returned and placed it on her forehead. How many people got this kind of attention from a dictator? He had minions to do his dirty work. And holding a basin for a woman to throw up in didn't fit the image.

"For now, try not to think about leaving. Get rest. Sleep. You need it."

"Guess I don't have much choice." She wouldn't get far if she passed out.

"That's right, Ms. Rune. You have no choice."

She really didn't like the finality of those words. And she didn't think he'd merely mimicked her last statement.

He turned and left, shutting the door quietly with only the smallest snick. Until another grating sound in the keyhole.

* * * * *

Callium Vestro slammed his fist onto the rickety desk. He missed his Victorian, heavily scrolled beauty of a desk. He missed his books, and he missed his artwork. "How many of my soldiers are imprisoned at Government House?"

"Three-quarters," said the shadowy vision wavering in the corner.

Vestro pulled a syringe out of the desk, filled with glorious, reassuring, clear drug, an appeasement to his tormented soul. Whenever he took it, though, he couldn't make the connection with Rhino, who'd been giving him insider information on how to control everything. And control it he had, until Oberon James seized power and forced him into exile.

Well, it wouldn't last long. He'd reformed his army. He had strengths James could never dream about or protect himself from. Vestro grinned. James would be sorry for his foolishness.

"What advice do you give me today?" Vestro asked, still pissed off that Rhino hadn't forewarned him about the coup. He'd have been ready if he'd known. Apparently, Rhino wasn't as all-knowing as he professed.

"I am working on our situation. For now stay low, and don't get caught. And stay away from that fucking mind-bender you're injecting yourself with. You're in enough trouble. If you hadn't been high for a week straight, I'd have been able to tell you what was coming." Rhino's dark features nearly formed a clear face. Sometimes he could project a fairly good image. Other times it didn't come through as well. Something about time rifts causing disturbances in the energy fields.

Rhino's gaze pierced Vestro, impaling him in his seat. Those eyes always scared him. They were the eyes of a killer. Of a man with no conscience. Vestro made a face. Rhino enjoyed torture as much as he did, maybe more.

Vestro rolled the syringe between his fingers, the urge to ignore Rhino and fall into mindless oblivion building to a temptation that was hard to resist.

"Put that fucking thing down and pay attention to me, Callium."

He slapped the syringe onto the desk but kept it close. Every now and then he glanced at it for reassurance that it remained within reach.

"What do you want? I'm tired, and I need some rest."

"Is that what you're calling a drug haze these days? Rest." The shifting image made a disgusted noise.

"It helps me clear my mind."

"It bends your thoughts, puts you in a continuous dream world of nightmares."

Callium grinned. "The nightmares are the best. And I get visions. Visions of the past. How are things in your world, Rhino? The perfect world you destroyed in order to leave us with the fucking scraps."

"You've been comfortable for too many years, Vestro. You've forgotten how you got where you are. And who helped you. And you've enjoyed the power without realizing that you eventually would have to repay me." Rhino's vision shifted again and nearly faded out before he came back again. "I'll soon have the answer to time travel. I'll be able to come there in body, not just in projection. That time is coming, and I want you to have a clear head when I arrive."

Vestro frowned at Rhino.

"What'll I be then? Your first minister?" His patience dimmed. "I'm the real governor here. People do what I say. They won't follow you."

Bone-chilling laughter crawled up Vestro's spine. Only Rhino could scare him like that. Almost as much as the nightmares. That nightmare would be much more real if Rhino ever managed to transport himself in body. It didn't seem likely. After all, he'd been trying for decades, and so far, he could only project himself as a watery shadow.

Rhino whipped his head sideways. "What do you want?" he grated. Callium sat straighter and leaned forward, listening for another voice. This had never happened before. Rhino was talking to someone else in the room with him.

"I told you not to interrupt me," he said to someone behind him. Rhino cast an irritated look back at Vestro before he disappeared.

What the hell.

Ah well, didn't matter. Vestro, flesh and blood—right here, right now. Rhino, for all intents and purposes, a shadow of the past who would probably never make the transition to the future. Otherwise, he'd be here right now.

Besides, Vestro had no intention of giving up his rightful place in this country even if Rhino ever made it here in the flesh. In the meantime, Rhino supplied him with the kind of information he needed to stay one step ahead of Oberon James.

If he'd had time, he would've eked more information out of Rhino. Vestro grinned. Funny how one little interruption in Rhino's life could be so damning and so elucidating. Rhino had a problem, Vestro had read that much in his expression when he'd been interrupted. So—someone else knew about his plans. He grinned and tapped his fingertips together, then greedily reached out and snagged the needle.

The mere act of touching the glass syringe began the experience. His synapses fired and welcomed the oncoming buzz. Joy, fear, terror and then oblivion.

CHAPTER NINE

Rud strode down the broken pavement with his hands jammed in his pockets and his shoulders slumped. "I can't believe that goddamned brother of mine threw me out of his house. And without Darla," he said out loud.

Oberon had been royally pissed when Rud decided not to give him the prophecy. Rud couldn't believe his brother actually had a soldier frisk him before kicking him onto the street. Oberon might have Darla, but without the prophecy he wouldn't know what to do with her. And if he hadn't been such an overbearing jerk, Rud might have even given it to him. Might have... but... probably not.

Still fuming inside, he strode toward the center of the city. A dark sky hung low with bilious clouds. Yesterday's heat had given in to a cool, moist breeze. Unusual at this time of year. It cut through his shirt and made him shiver.

Streets in this part of the city were whisper-quiet at night. People were still afraid, even though the curfew had been lifted, thanks to Oberon. For the first time in decades, people didn't have to hide in their homes at night, but they still did. Change would take time and trust.

He stopped and checked up and down the street and spotted an open door with a light burning inside. Hold on. He strode toward an honest-to-God establishment still open at this time of night. He heard voices and stepped into Bender's bar. At least Bender had been enterprising enough to try to make a living after curfew time.

"Rud James, you dirty dog." Rud heard the familiar voice before he saw the face.

"You didn't tell me your brother was going to run roughshod over the country and take control."

Rud turned in the direction of the voice. "Brody. Good to see someone else dares to be out tonight."

Brody Larson, a large man with shaggy brown hair halfway down his back, squinted at him from a table in the corner. Rud deliberately ignored the topic of his brother. Especially now that he'd pissed him off, totally.

Making his way to the bar, he put down a silver coin. The bartender snapped it up and shoved it into his pocket, then poured a large glass of ale for Rud.

Stomping across the ancient wooden floors, Brody dropped onto the bar stool beside him. "Good to have somebody else to talk to." Pickled, if his watery eyes and sloppy grin were any indication. At least he'd dared to come out when no one else would.

Rud eyed the empty mugs at the table where Brody had been sitting. Normally, people couldn't afford to sit and drink. Money didn't exist for most. "Work must've been good for you lately."

Brody snorted, and his lips curled back for another

drink from the mug he'd carried with him. He wiped his mouth with his sleeve afterward. "Been working the farms out in the wilds." He shivered. "Good-paying job, if you live to collect."

"Shit, man. No wonder you're celebrating. When'd you get back?"

"Yesterday." Brody's gaze turned on Rud. His muddy-blond hair in thick curls partially blocked his meaty, dirty face. Desolation and despair showed in the depths of his eyes. "We lost three men this week. Eaten by the beasts. There's one mother beast out there that is too damned cunning, and it's hungry for human flesh. It hunts us and picks us off one by one in the western territory. It's getting so bad out there, there's some talk of avoiding that territory all together."

"What animal is it?"

"Don't know. Anyone who has ever seen it dies. There's tales of the noise it makes when it kills. But word is you never hear it coming until it's too late."

"Benevolent hell."

Brody nodded, and his jaws bunched. He pushed his mug forward for another refill.

The bartender came back quickly and offered a toothy grin and made Brody's coin disappear, too. Tending bar probably hadn't earned this much real money on mead in a month. Only soldiers and politicians had real money. Everyone else bartered for what they could get. Two chickens squawked in a cage outside the door to prove his point.

Rud's mouth watered at the thought of roast chicken, and he wished he could afford a decent meal, but he had only enough to have a few drinks. And right now his thirst overtook his hunger. His damn brother could have at least fed him before he tossed him out without the girl.

Rud tapped the secret pocket in his Uvlar jacket. At least he still had the prophecy. Oberon's soldier hadn't found it.

"'Nother mead, Rud?"

"Sure." The two men picked up their mugs and downed them in unison, then pushed them forward for refills. "I'll pay for my friend's mug, too," he said to the bartender and pulled out the last of his cash and slapped it on the bar.

"Thanks, Rud. No one's ever bought me a beer before."

"Yeah, it's awful that it's so expensive. This should be something every hardworking citizen can afford."

"You got that right."

"How long were you in the wilds?"

Brody swished the ale around his mouth, obviously savoring the flavor. He swallowed noisily. "A month."

Rud took a gulp of his brew. "Crap. That's one long stint."

"Yeah. When I left I worked for Vestro, and the second I got back and heard news of the takeover, I immediately signed up for Oberon. He's a good man, your brother. He'll never be like Vestro."

Double crap. Rud had been working up to asking a huge favor, but if Brody already liked his brother, his request might not be quite so easy. "Will you continue working in the fields?"

Brody nodded. "It's a dangerous job, but it has its upside." He put one hand on the side of his mouth. "Don't tell your brother this, okay?"

Rud nodded. Yeah. Maybe he'd have an in, after all.

"We get all the meat we can eat, and lots of

vegetables, too. Food doesn't all make it onto the carts. A guy needs to have his belly full to fight bears, tigers, grolars and shit-only-knows-what that mysterious monster is."

"I don't blame you one bit," Rud said. "Hey, are you still doing contract jobs on the side?"

Brody set his drink down. "Yeah. Always. Got four kids."

Rud's gut twinged. He had to prove he was every bit as good as Oberon. Besides, he'd been given the codes to get the prophecy. It must be the right thing to do.

"Brody, I'd like to hire you for a job," Rud said.

"I'll reserve the right to refuse until I hear what it is," Brody said.

Rud glanced over his shoulder. He didn't want the bartender to overhear their conversation. He pushed away from the bar. "Let's sit over there," he said, indicating the table Brody had been sitting at earlier.

"I'm thinking you're about to propose something that'll earn me some major dinero." Brody rubbed his thumb and two fingers together, making a grating sound with his sandpaper skin.

"Yeah, you'll earn dinero, all right. Plenty, if you succeed," Rud said once they sat at the table. "Thing is, I want you to help me break into Government House. It'll have to be done like a black op."

"A what?"

Rud cringed. He loved the books from the twenty-first century. Unfortunately, not many others got a chance to read books. A terrible loss to society. Maybe under Oberon they could institute printing machines for more than weekly news. But only after they improved each and every citizen's quality of life. That thought alone made him feel worthy of Maribel's task.

"It's an undercover job. We'll dress in Uvlar Shadow Gear and go in silent. Get my property and break back out without anyone being wise to us." He planted his hands on the table. "You in?"

Brody's bushy reddish-blond eyebrows went up, and he rubbed his large nose. Thinking. "What's the target?"

"Need to know. You don't need to know, yet."

Brody frowned. "Man, if you think I'm breaking into Government House with no idea what we're going after, you're crazy."

"Yeah, you're right." Rud dug deep to come up with a plausible story. "It's my girlfriend. Oberon's got her inside, and he won't let her go."

"Why would your brother keep your girlfriend away from you?"

"He's...jealous. He wants her for himself."

"Shit, man. That sucks."

"I know. I only want to break her out. She's in the medical ward. Luckily, it's not as heavily guarded there." He squinted at Brody. "You still up on your abilities?" Brody had always been the best first-floor man he knew. He could open any lock out there.

"How much?" Brody eyed him in a way that told Rud he didn't quite believe him. Apparently, if the payday was big enough, he didn't care. Rud and Oberon had both been given fairly large inheritances when they'd each turned twenty-one. He'd barely spent any of his. "Two thousand dinero?"

"Five"

"Okay, Five. That's a king's ransom."

"Yeah, and if we get caught, I'll rot in prison. And my wife will have to look after our children alone. At least she'll have the money to provide for them." He drained his beer. "Not likely your brother would throw you in prison, now is it?"

"I wouldn't be so sure of that." Rud remembered how angry Bron had been when he found out Rud had the prophecy and wouldn't give it back. They'd had their differences as kids, but they'd basically gotten along quite well.

It seemed they were going to fight over Darla.

And neither of them would back down. Hence his need to break in and get her back.

* * * * *

As far as Darla could tell, she'd been here at least a week. An army medic or doctor, not sure which, checked on her at regular intervals. Every time he left the room, she heard the snick of the lock. And every day it bothered her more that they kept her locked in like some criminal.

She'd improved a great deal since she'd arrived. She could even stand on her injured leg today without feeling like she might pass out. She kept that information to herself. She needed every advantage, because first chance she got, she'd get out of here.

While there were no windows in the outer room, the bathroom had a window large enough for her to squeeze through, but with her leg injury, she couldn't climb up to see what was on the outside—yet. She had no idea if she'd been transported to the ground level or the second or third floor.

She leaned against the steel tub that was long enough for her to completely immerse herself in. Only in her dreams. No way could she get her injury wet at this point.

And she didn't intend to be here long enough to

experience the tub.

She hadn't seen the dictator since the day she woke and found him watching her. It had taken a couple of days for her to realize they were giving her sleeping draughts in her water. She'd found out from the medic that she'd slept for nearly forty-eight hours straight. While it did help in the healing process, she hated that she'd been tricked and left vulnerable.

Wait. Had she heard someone in the outer room? She washed her hands to cover her attempt at surveillance and peeked out. Damn it, she'd been caught out of bed.

"Afternoon," the dictator himself said. "It's nice to see that you are doing much better. The doctor told me you still couldn't put pressure on your foot." He eyed her clinically and suspiciously. And he had every reason to be suspicious, because she'd get out of here the first chance she got.

"When I tried this morning, it was still very painful. The medicine helps with pain," she lied. She hadn't taken any of their medicine since she found out they were keeping her practically comatose. And a prisoner behind a locked door.

Luckily, they were using a topical salve to heal her wound, so she wouldn't have to worry about infection when she escaped. She'd actually slipped one of the jars of salve out of the cart when the medic had applied it last time, so she'd be able to continue with the antibiotic cream when she got out of here.

Exaggerating her limp, she went back to her bed. She didn't want him to get the idea she could get around easily. Especially since she'd just found the window to possible freedom.

Since his expression seemed more serious today than

the last time she'd talked to him, she hoped those broad shoulders were currently experiencing the weight of his job. The worries of their society. Would Oberon James save everyone or add to their problems?

"Now that you're feeling better, you and I need to talk," he said. "I'd prefer we don't do it here in this hospital room. It's not the right atmosphere."

Seemed like a strange thing for him to say, but she normally spent more time outside the city at the Boneyard than she did in her house. Suddenly, she needed to see the yellow clouds, feel a toxic breeze on her face. Besides, even though oil lamps created more light than her candles at home, she didn't spend this much time inside. And, being locked in a dark room lit only by oil lamps had a depressing side-effect.

Not to mention, maybe get some bearings that might aid in her escape. She'd been in so much pain when they arrived she hadn't taken note of her surroundings.

"I could use some air," she said. "Can we go outside?"

Taut hands pressed against the metal rail at the end of her bed and he seemed to be contemplating her request. She expected a resounding no.

"I don't see why not. There's a beautiful courtyard. I'm sure you'll like it. And that way we won't have to have my bodyguards follow us."

"Why bodyguards?"

"It's not safe to wander around outside just yet. Not until people get to know my plans for their future."

"But you followed Rud and me into the Nevermore? You were alone that night."

"Of course. Rud is my brother. Even though he's a pain in the ass, I'd never trust anyone else with something so important as saving his life—not if I could get there first, at least. Even if he is being a stubborn idiot right now with a head as hard as a post-apoc rhino." He shook his head. "The boy tries my patience at times," Oberon said. "As you probably noticed, we're not exactly seeing eye to eye."

"I'd hardly call him a boy, either," she said. After all, she'd seen him without his shirt. "But if I had a sibling, I'm sure I'd feel the same way about protecting him."

His grin surprised her. His dark features softened in response. "Are you sure you're up to walking to the courtyard, Ms. Rune?"

She slid her feet out from under the covers and stood again. Dressed in a fine-woven beige nightgown, she ran a hand over the soft, lovely cloth. "You might as well call me Darla. I certainly don't intend to call you governor."

"I'll get you a robe," he said drily before looking at her bare feet. "And some slippers." He turned to the door. Two hard knocks, and the guard opened the door. Oberon leaned out and mumbled some directions.

Moments later, he led her down a massive hallway.

Marble and other stonework created a sense of chill and beauty. "How did this building survive the war?" she asked.

"That's a good question. Not one that any of us have an answer for. You haven't seen everything yet. There's more. Much more."

A pain drove through Darla's shin for real, and her tread faltered.

"You sure you're ready for this?" His hand touched her shoulder, and she shrugged it away. He pulled his hand back and clenched it.

"I'm fine."

"Idiotic of me. I should've gotten you a chair to wheel

you outside." He raised one hand and snapped his imperious fingers. Two men ran to do his bidding. Darla gritted her teeth until they both heard the creaky sound of wheels coming toward them.

"I'm quite capable of going under my own steam. Please, send your…servants away."

"My soldiers," he said, but nodded, and the two obedient men disappeared again. They were never really far away.

Oberon slowly walked with her down the hallway until they reached a door in the middle of floor-to-ceiling windows. She stared through the glass to a delightful garden with green foliage beaded with bright flowers. Flowers she'd never seen in her life.

He opened the door and let her go through. The first thing that struck her had to be the fragrance of the air. She inhaled and held the fresh air in her lungs as long as she could. She didn't want to let it go in case she never breathed anything that good again. In fact, she felt a little lightheaded, suddenly.

Almost the fresh air of her dreams. Not like the stale, moldy air of Central City. But how? She looked up. A glass dome covered the garden, and it surprised her to learn they weren't really outside. Disappointment edged at her.

A trickling sound caught her attention. "Is there a stream?"

His shoulders appeared taut while he moved down a stone path ahead of her and motioned for her to take the path to the right. They walked through a luscious maze of green plants growing with the aid of hoses that dripped water onto the plants. She inhaled several times and felt almost giddy from the effect of fresh oxygen in her lungs.

Unbelievable.

They reached the center of the garden, and Darla gasped at the sight of the huge marble fountain. A beautiful carving of a naked female sitting on a shell stunned her. "Who is she?"

"Aphrodite."

"Someone you knew? Or Vestro knew?"

"No. Someone from our past. Our history."

Anger burned inside Darla instantly and threatened to overflow. "Vestro allowed this? While we were punished severely if we even mentioned something from the past? That bastard."

"I've searched every record I could find since I took over the government to find out why he wouldn't allow us to discuss the past. It seems backward. Our history is important. It's part of who we are, yet he tortured and maimed his own people if they were caught repeating anything from our past."

Oberon's gaze wandered to the statue, his expression haunted.

"A few families dared to keep our past alive," she brazenly admitted. Still against the law, as far as she knew. If Oberon wanted to charge them, he'd have to find them first, and she'd never tell who they were.

Oberon stared at Aphrodite as if she could solve all of his problems. "I'm glad to hear it. We've lost so much. Our people aren't educated. We have no one who can re-create even the simplest of conveniences from our past, and even if they did, EMP storms would simply wipe them out again. We've lost our brightest minds."

"I'm sure there are still people who can learn," she said.

"But who will teach them? We need salvation in the

worst way, and there are very few options other than starting over from scratch."

Water cascaded from the lip of the shell and into the pool below, creating a musical sound. Flowers grew here, too. Floating flowers. Something gold flitted under the water. She leaned over and stared into the clear blue water. "What are those golden creatures in the water?"

"Fish."

"Real fish? Living creatures from before Neutrality?"

He nodded. "There are more aquatic animals in another section of the house, too. An aquarium with thousands of varieties. Vestro kept them to himself."

"Why? He could've fed people with that many fish." She'd heard that fish could be quite tasty.

Oberon strode to a bench near the fountain and motioned for her to sit. She limped over and sat at the other end, leaving plenty of space between them.

"I think he was rebuilding the fish stock. Maybe with hopes of seeding the waters again?"

"But our water is so polluted. Surely the fish could be lost if he did that."

Oberon shrugged and again watched the statue of Aphrodite. "We'll never know, unless we find him and he talks."

Darla straightened and listened to the soft tinkling of the water, the sounds of foliage moving in a breeze caused by the tiny waterfall. She touched the structure and saw a vision of a windmill on the roof circulating the water. She hated that Vestro had kept so many things from them. She hated that he got to enjoy this beauty while torturing and killing his people.

"Are you going to change things?" She might as well come right out and ask it. "For example, will you invite people to this amazing courtyard?"

His expression darkened. "No."

Her stomach clenched, and she tasted bile. "I knew it—you're just as bad as he is."

"Believe me, I will share these plants when the time is right. This is a delicate ecosystem that might be ruined if too many people trample through it. It has survived two hundred years of devastation outside. It'd be a crime to give people a glimpse of heaven, only to ruin it forever."

She hated that she saw his point. "And the fish?"

"Same thing, I'm afraid. I must find out what Vestro was planning to do with them. If there is a possibility to restock the rivers and the oceans, even with a handful of fish, it'd be better than losing them forever. If the water can sustain them, eventually they'll restock themselves."

"How'd he get them? Where'd they come from?"

"I don't know," Oberon said.

Darla reached out an arm to touch a frond that looked delicate but felt like leather. Nature at its finest, she imagined. The sleeve of her robe slipped back to her elbow, exposing her forearm. Exposing her shame. The brand that had been burned into her at the age of fourteen. She'd been near the marketplace that day when citizens decided to revolt against starvation, and even though she hadn't been part of that short-lived revolution, she'd been branded with a hot poker and left to die.

She grabbed her sleeve and pulled it down her arm again, but it was too late. Oberon's gaze was glued to her sleeve. He reached out and pulled the sleeve back again. She squirmed. Tried to break his grasp.

He stared at the ugly scar. The letter "D" burned into her flesh marked her as a dissident.

His face contorted into anger, and his gaze searched

hers again. He watched her as if he'd never seen her before.

"Never been in the company of an honest-to-God dissident before?" she asked sarcastically. Big brave words, hell yeah, but inside she'd been quaking. What would the new dictator do to a dissident?

The darkness behind his features spread. He seemed so angry. And that scared her. For a moment she'd seen an inkling of humanity behind his façade, but now she saw a man who would kill if necessary.

He let out an angry breath, and she actually cringed back.

"Who did this to you?"

"Who knows? Who cares?" she lied. She'd been branded by a soldier only a few years older than herself at the time. She'd seen tears in his eyes when he'd burned her, or maybe she'd imagined that in order to keep her own version of faith in humanity.

"How long ago?" His voice sounded choked. Maybe he wasn't going to kill her, but rather the man who did this to her?

Other than his eyes, she hadn't seen the young soldier's face because he'd worn a B-clava and face shield.

"Ten years," she said, then wished she hadn't spouted the timeline quite so quickly. She'd given away the fact that being branded did matter to her. "He didn't get away without a fight, though," she said.

"What do you mean?" Oberon James' expression made her a little nervous. She slid a little farther down the bench, creating even more distance between them. She covered her arm with her hand.

"Look, I was punished years ago—and, for that

matter, I've been punished ever since. Surely you're not going to make me pay again for something I wasn't even guilty of in the first place." She shouldn't show her vulnerability to him, but the way he was looking at her made her nervous. "I was in the wrong place at the wrong time, and I paid dearly for it."

"The brand meant you got food from the bread carts only after everyone else had their quota," he said with his voice wandering off.

"Yes, and more often than not, the food didn't stretch far enough for dissidents to get any." The memory burned at the backs of her eyes. "Most branded people die from hunger. Even citizens shun us because they're afraid they'll be seen as supporters." Even though it had happened to her at such a young age, she'd fought tooth and nail to feed herself. She'd learned to forage and steal, if need be. And she'd learned to venture into the Nevermore to hunt for food.

"What about your family?" he asked.

"What family?" Surely he knew she couldn't have gone home after being branded. If she had, her mother would have been branded as a dissident, too. That had been the worst part of her sentence. She missed her mother terribly.

"What about the man who branded you? You said he didn't get away with it without a fight. What does that mean, Darla?"

"After he'd burned me..." She had to stop for a minute, because her voice would give away too much emotion, even now. She distracted herself by gazing into the water, and soothing her damaged soul for a few seconds. "I grabbed the brand from the coals and burned his shoulder. I'm not sure how much the Uvlar protected him, but it did burn through the fabric, so I can only hope he suffered as much as I did."

Muscles in his jaw moved, but his mouth stayed glued together. His expression burned so fiercely he nearly lit the foliage on fire with a mere look.

"I'll find him someday and make him pay for what he did to me," she said. "Turning that branding iron on him gave me some satisfaction, but it wasn't nearly enough. He needs to pay for what he did." When she realized she'd let down her defenses and told the dictator something so personal, she cringed. Had she signed her own death sentence? "What are you going to do with me now?"

"What are you talking about?" He sounded impatient.

She squeezed her eyes shut and imagined herself in the Boneyard. Her place of reality. Oh, how she needed that reality right now. She inhaled and tried to block the wonderful scents in this room from affecting her understanding of air. She could never have this again, so she had to negate it. When she opened her eyes, he watched her and, to her surprise, he'd slid closer. Too close.

She quickly checked his belt for a weapon. If she could grab it, maybe she could force him to let her go.

"Look, I'm truly sorry for what happened to you, Darla. I know you'll never believe it. But I need you to know that as a fact."

"I don't accept your lies," she said in a monotone. "Besides, none of what happened has anything to do with you. Please take me back to my cell."

"It's not a cell. It's a hospital room," he corrected. He stood, his back ramrod straight and his hands clenched at his sides while he waited for her to rise.

Disappointed that he carried no weapons, she bit out, "Oh, excuse me," she said. "I'm being guarded and locked in because my infection might escape?"

His mouth tightened. "I see we cannot come to terms today."

"You're right. We'll never come to terms until I'm standing outside this place as a free woman."

His mouth thinned. "You are free."

"Really?" She dragged out the word sarcastically.

"Well, technically you're free, as soon as you and I come to an agreement."

She pressed her hand over her faded scar and bit her lip. She'd seen fresh scars on his hands and arms, too. More than likely injuries received as a soldier in Vestro's army.

"I'm not feeling well," she said. "Take me back to my cell." She stood, and he grabbed her shoulders to support her, because he apparently expected her to faint again.

"Please don't," she said, actually feeling fatigue setting in.

He instantly bent over and picked her up. She struggled for a second, but he merely waited for her to stop before carrying her to the door. "Bring the chair for Ms. Rune," he said to the soldier waiting outside.

He held her until it arrived. She wanted to push away, to avoid contact, to believe he was made of marble and not taut flesh and bone. She wanted to think of him as anything but a man.

CHAPTER TEN

As agreed, Rud waited behind the pub for Brody to show up the next day. Brody was late.

"Where are you, man?" he said out loud, looking up at the quickly darkening clouds. Electricity zinged in the air—the only place left where electricity existed anymore—in the sky. A bolt of lightning hit somewhere outside the city. A storm approached from the north, a bad one if the wind and electricity in the air meant anything.

Didn't matter. Maybe in the long run, it would be the best time to carry out his plan. Oberon's soldiers would be scrambling to hold down the fort during the storm. They wouldn't expect a break-in.

Wind picked up. Leaves and debris swirled in tiny volatile tornados. The weighty black clouds grew darker, and even though it was only two in the afternoon, it had turned as dark as twilight outside.

A crack of thunder sounded at the very moment a hand touched his shoulder. "Frig." He jumped like a scared kitten. Embarrassed, he tried to cover up with a longer streak of profanity.

Brody laughed. "You're jumpy, Rud? Gotta have your wits about you to break into Government House. You got the uniforms?"

"Yeah. Lucky for me, Oberon served in Vestro's military, and he had uniforms at home. I borrowed these from his closet."

Brody grimaced at the outfit and then down at his own body. He hissed out a pained sound. "It'll fit, but I won't be overly mobile. Good thing the pants are stretchy."

The outfits were dress uniforms. Similar to Uvlars but with skin-tight breeches and button-up jackets with a crest on the pocket. "Just pin this over the one on the uniform," Rud said, pulling out two family crests.

They dressed in the alley and shoved their clothes into a bag. Rud tucked the bag behind an outbuilding.

"Will someone steal our clothes?"

"Hopefully not. Let's go."

They made their way to the center of town. No one bothered them. Citizens avoided officials of all types. Within minutes, they reached the outer perimeter of Government House and the outer fence.

The wind had blown into a major gale, and they could barely see through the grit from the streets. Black clouds, heavy with unfallen rain, scudded across the sky.

"How're we getting inside?" Rud asked Brody in between gusts.

"Front door," Brody began, walking to the main gate with Rud close behind.

"What kind of plan is that? We'll get caught."

"We're more likely to make it in the front door than any back doors."

"What about the guard? Isn't there a sign-in sheet?"

"I bought us a couple of IDs. You'll owe me extra for that, by the way. Your name is Jake Black, and I'm Vince Kole. Don't forget your name."

"Are they real names?"

"Yep."

"What if they're already inside?"

"They're not. They're at the pub swilling ale on your dime."

Rud couldn't help but gape. "Ingenious. Expensive, but ingenious." That said, he worried about Oberon. His own soldiers had been bought to stay in a pub and drink while someone broke into the House. Not good. Damn. In a way, he hated doing this to his brother. As soon as he liberated Darla, and put the next part of the plan in action, he'd come clean with Oberon and warn him about his soldiers' lack of loyalty.

"You know, this whole thing seemed like a huge adventure until right now. I don't like doing this to my brother, but I intend to carry it through," Rud said under his breath while they walked up to the main door and signed in. The guard witnessed their signatures, checked them off another sheet and waved them through.

"Reality's a bitch," Brody said once they were inside. "Which way is the hospital wing?"

"Down this hall about halfway, then take a right."

"Why are you still working the farms, Brody?" Making small talk calmed Rud's burning gut. "You should be on Oberon's security detail. A man with your abilities should be working by his side. You'd obviously be able to point out flaws in his security."

"I'm guessing you'll put in a good word for me if this plan comes off without a hitch?"

"Sure, I will. As long as Oberon speaks to me again after we pull this off."

Two soldiers marched down the hall toward them. "Head up, Jake, shoulders back. Look like you belong," Brody said.

The soldiers nodded and continued down the hall.

When they rounded the corner and made their way to the hospital wing, it surprised Rud to see no guard on the door. How'd his break-out attempt turn into such a horrible breach of security? Had Brody paid off this sentry, too?

Unaware of Rud's rising concern, Brody picked the lock in seconds and they were inside. Darla wasn't there.

"Damn it."

"Is she gone?" Brody asked.

They scanned the rumpled and unmade bed. A full glass of water waited on the bed stand. "We'll have to wait. I don't think she's been moved."

"Hold on, where will we wait?"

Rud turned in a circle, spied the bathroom door and glanced inside. "In here."

"And if she doesn't come back?" Brody asked.

"If she doesn't come back, I have no plan B. I don't know where Oberon would keep her." His gut twisted. Not completely accurate. He worried about Oberon being alone with Darla for more reasons than the obvious. He'd seen the way Oberon had watched her.

Worse, Darla lived an impoverished life. Oberon could give her the world, literally. And Oberon needed her. But so did Rud. And they both wanted her. That much was unquestionably obvious.

They'd barely stepped into the bathroom when the outside door opened and they heard her voice.

* * * * *

Darla actually welcomed the bed. She sank back into it and covered her legs. "I'm feeling better. If I want to leave tomorrow, will you let me go?"

Silence stretched out until Oberon spoke. "I'm sorry. No."

"Why not?"

"You wouldn't understand right now."

"So, what about the little walk in the gardens today? Just a trick to get me to open up and admit that I'm a lawbreaker. I am your prisoner."

He cleared his throat. "For your own safety."

"Safety from whom?" Darla managed to force a laugh. "Every person in Central City faces that kind of reality every day. We don't live in safe times, Mister James." Blaming him for all their troubles wasn't technically fair, but he wanted to be the leader, so he'd have to wear the thorns.

"Life isn't easy, but maybe that could change for you if the right person came along," he said.

"Ridiculous. I don't know what kind of game you're playing, but I want none of it."

His eyes were a turbulent gray-blue right now, and she hated the fact that she noticed.

Even from inside this room she heard the wind outside. Somehow, impending storms always sent frissons of energy through her. Pent-up energy. She wanted out. She needed to get out of here.

"I'm tired. I need to rest." Her leg ached in earnest. And she felt a little faint, so she guessed he'd believe her. She'd probably turned pale.

Muscles worked in his jaw while his piercing eyes threatened to undo her resolve. He was a good actor.

Pretending to be seriously repentant at having to lock her up again went a little too far.

"Darla, I…" He moved toward her.

"Please, just get out. Leave me alone." He wouldn't leave her like this, so she changed her tack. "I have a lot to think about, at least give me time to do that?"

He nudged the toe of his military boot against the end of the bed. "Yes. I understand that. Will you join me for breakfast in the morning? I'd like to show you what I'm trying to do for Central City."

"Maybe." She turned on her side, effectively showing her back to him. She heard him leave and quietly shut the door. She waited. Held her breath. Then the door locked. Double dirty bastard. Did he really think she could be bought with food and air?

Darla had already closed her eyes and had nearly dropped off when the bathroom door creaked opened and startled her awake. She jumped up in bed and grabbed at her chest. Holy hell, she was locked in this room with someone who had obviously been hiding in there. She nearly screamed for the sentry, before Rud stepped out. "Rud. You scared the crap out of me. Why didn't you warn me?"

"How could I do that?" he whispered. "Couldn't let Oberon know I was here. He threw me out the other day. He wants you all to himself."

"You're not kidding, are you?" Her eyes got wider when another man stepped out behind Rud. Both were dressed like Oberon's soldiers.

"This is my friend, Brody. We're here to get you out."

Her spirits lifted considerably. "Can we go out the bathroom window?" she asked, pushing back the covers and feeling suddenly less tired.

"Nah. I already checked it. It only leads to the garden in the center of the building. Don't worry, though, we have a plan." Rud grinned then glanced at the big, hairy man named Brody. "Or, I should say, Brody has a plan."

She turned her attention to the big brute and nodded to him.

"Ma'am," he said. "Let's get this show on the road. No time to waste."

"But we're locked in, and there's a guard on the door."

Rud slid next to her, held out a hand and gently helped her off the bed. With his dark hair, freshly clipped, and a shadow on his chin, he looked even more dangerous. And young. The last thing she wanted to do was get him in more trouble, but she needed to get out of here, and this would be her best chance.

Rud pulled her toward the door. "Brody is a master break-out artist."

With that, Brody pulled out a couple of pins and a file of some sort and, without making a noise, he had the door open in seconds.

Rud pushed her forward until she peered around the door and smiled at the witless guard.

The soldier stepped toward the door, looking perplexed that she'd managed to open it. "I'm sorry, ma'am, but you're not allowed to leave your room. Please step back inside."

Another nudge from behind, and she stumbled farther into the hall. "Sorry. I can't go back inside that room— please help me. I'm tired of being locked up."

He hissed out an irritated breath. "Look, don't think I'm going to lose my week's wages because I didn't obey orders." His voice got louder and instantly angry. The jerk had absolutely no sympathy for her. He reached out and grabbed her arm. She yelped with emphasis.

Before the bastard knew what had happened, Rud and Brody dragged him into the room, gagged him and tied his hands and ankles. The two men worked in unison. A silent, efficient team.

Finally, they shoved him into the bathtub. "I don't think your leader would appreciate the way you just mistreated Ms. Rune," Rud ground out. "He may be many things, but he doesn't manhandle women."

The soldier struggled and tried to cry out, but the gag effectively muffled his voice as did the bathroom door when they shut it on him.

Rud grinned at Darla. Step one had been a breeze. "Dare we hope the rest will go as smoothly?"

He sounded a little too optimistic for her liking. With his mussed hair and a grin producing dimples, she could almost like the guy. If only he wasn't using her, too.

At least she knew where she stood with him. Thanks to being an outcast most of her life, she didn't mind using him right back.

"Brody, you go first, then you, Darla. I'll take up the rear," Rud said.

They marched down the hall with her acting as their prisoner, until an officer stopped them. "What are you two doing with this woman?" he barked.

"Taking her to Ob...Mister James, sir," Rud said.

The officer frowned at the two men. "Are you new here?"

"Yes, sir, we signed up as soon as Mister James took power, sir," Brody said.

Must've been the right answer, because the officer's brow smoothed and he nodded and waited for them to salute. They did. "On your way, then."

Brody led them to an unguarded side door that would have been impossible to find without first knowing its location. Rud had to hope Brody hadn't used this door before. They left quickly.

"That was easy," Brody said, cupping his hands around his mouth so he could be heard over the roaring wind outside.

Wind whipped Darla's hair around her face so wildly she could barely see.

Storms brought out her odd abilities even more than usual, and she didn't need that distraction right now. She had to have her wits about her. Someone grabbed her arm and dragged her along. She pulled the housecoat tighter around her. She'd be a lot more comfortable in her own clothes, but they'd been taken from her. Her hard-earned Uvlar suit.

Now, it would take her months to be able to afford another one, if then. Damned dictator.

Brody motioned to an unmanned gate. Probably locked, but he didn't seem to have any problems with locks. True to form, he had the gate open in seconds, and they were off the compound.

Rud winked at her but remained silent. Her leg pained, but not as much as she'd feared it would while they made their way into the city center.

"Where are we going?" Darla shouted to be heard over the wind.

No one heard her. Unexpectedly, Rud yanked her sideways, and they stumbled through the door of a pub.

"Great," she said, realizing where they were. "Good place to be in pajamas."

"Not to worry. Take a seat. I have some clothes for you. I'll get them as soon as Brody and I change."

"Rud, you think of everything," she said sarcastically. Free of her prison, now she just wanted to disappear. And she'd do that the first chance she got.

Before they did anything else, Brody and Rud went to the bar and ordered a round of drinks. They returned to the table, and Rud leaned down to whisper to Darla, "We're going to change into our street clothes now. I'll bring your clothes when we return."

If the bartender considered their attire strange, he didn't let on. He'd obviously met Rud and Brody and probably knew they weren't Government House soldiers.

She waited until they left before she approached the barman. "Have you got a bathroom?" In her mind, the real question had to be, Have you got a back way out of here?

He pointed to a back hallway. "Through there, second door on your left."

She limped down the hall and instantly spotted what she'd been looking for. A back door. Her chance to get lost once and for all, and to do it without Rud knowing. No telling how long he'd wait in the bar for her to return. That'd give her a chance to get far away before he went looking for her.

She made for the exit, opened the back door and jumped outside into a refuse-strewn alley partially protected from the wind.

Dust swirled and blew into her eyes. She blinked and rubbed her eyes to clear her blurred vision. "Going somewhere?" Rud asked.

Damn it. He and Brody were out here in the alley in the midst of this storm, changing into their own clothing.

"Just needed some air." Lying came so easily to her these days.

"Sure you did." Rud put his hands on his hips and stared her up and down. "Well, now that you're here, here's your clothing."

He handed her a leather satchel. She dug inside to find a dress made of the finest fabric she'd ever seen. Absolutely beautiful, and appropriate for nothing in this city. She wore pants, Uvlar pants, most of the time. What would she do with a dress, besides barter it? She touched the fine silk. It would probably be worth some good bartering, though.

Her eyebrows rose. "What am I supposed to do with this?"

"Wear it. It'll look great on you."

"I don't wear dresses. I wear Uvlar. Dresses don't protect people from the elements."

Brody laughed. "I told you that, man. Women like her don't wear pansy clothes. She's the real deal."

Rud raised his hands. "Hey, it's all I could get my hands on at the time."

She sighed and reopened the satchel. "Hold on. I can barter this dress for appropriate clothes."

"Wha…"

She didn't care how much her leg hurt, she made tracks for the storefront with the two men close behind. Brody was still buttoning up his pants as they chased her half a block to the best secondhand Uvlar gear shop in the city.

Jack Wetmore, proprietor, was sipping some dark brew and playing chess with a friend in the corner when they entered. Bells jangling, the three of them were practically blown inside, leaves and debris dancing in at their heels.

"Hey, Jack. I need another Uvlar suit," Darla said.

"That's great news," he said, grinning, apparently pleased at the prospect of another sale.

"Yes. I lost my other one. But I've got something even better to barter with so maybe you can give me better-quality gear this time?"

Jack seemed dubious until she pulled the silk dress out of her satchel.

"Whoa. Clothes like this don't exist anymore. It's beautiful," he said, running his tailor's fingers lovingly over the fabric in her arms.

Darla imagined how nice it would feel on her skin. A beautiful blue slim-line silk gown, with gold and black flecks, would suit her coloring. She peered down at the dress. Its buttons were golden in color and intricately designed. A little too intricate for a button. She turned one over. 14K. Son of a... They were gold.

She shot a glance at Rud, who grinned and shrugged sheepishly. Unbelievable.

"The buttons are gold," she said, shoving the gown at Jack. He got out an eyeglass and checked the dress over closely. His fingers smoothed over the silk, and his Adam's apple bobbed several times. "This dress is worth a fortune," he breathed. "It doesn't have a single blemish. Not a single moth hole."

"Good," she said. "Get me a top-of-the-line Uvlar outfit, then."

"You sure you want to part with this, Darla?" His gaze slid down her body, apparently not in the least surprised to have a customer standing in his shop in a housecoat and slippers.

"Yes. The sooner, the better."

He gently laid the dress down on his sales counter and led her to a rack of suits. He rifled through the clothing and pulled out a pretty decent Uvlar suit. Darla couldn't believe she'd ever be able to afford one like this. She went into the change room and pulled it on. "Boots should be included for that dress, Jack," she said.

He held them over the top of the curtain. Seemed he had already picked them out. "I've thrown in a couple of other things you might need, Darla."

He'd given her fine underthings. She really liked Jack. In fact, he was probably her favorite vendor in the city.

She pulled the boots on. They fit perfectly. These duds were the best quality she'd ever worn, and she hadn't even had to beg or cajole or bargain with Jack for these near-pristine Uvlars. That dress must have really rattled him.

She exited the change room, glanced at herself in the mirror, and ran her hands down her hips. She felt more like herself now. "That's better. Thanks, Jack." She tossed him a smile, and he blew her a kiss.

Outside, the gale-force winds hadn't lessened, but she felt much safer from the elements in her suit. Donning her headgear and face shield, she set off in the opposite direction of the pub.

"Hold on," Rud shouted to be heard over the wind, taking her arm and turning her back toward the pub. "We have a round of drinks waiting for us. And you and I still need to talk."

"No, thanks," she said, pulling her arm out of his loose grasp. "I'm going home."

Brody picked up his pace, and Rud stepped up to her other side. Neither man touched her, but it didn't change the fact that she was being softly strong-armed.

"My friend here wants to talk to you. It's the least you can do, since we went to all that trouble to rescue you,"

Brody said in a friendly voice that held more than a hint of warning. Okay, so she'd have to listen. At least she'd escaped her palatial prison.

"Only if you agree I'm not your prisoner." Like she had a choice, anyway.

"I think you'll want to stick with me when you hear what I have to say," Rud said.

She considered his statement. He gave the impression of being tough, dangerous and, at the same time, pampered. She liked him even though she shouldn't. She couldn't say the same for Oberon. That overbearing bully thought he'd keep her against her will. He'd rubbed her the wrong way from the very first moment she'd met him.

After they re-entered the pub, the bartender served their drinks and didn't even blink at their change of attire. She guessed he saw all kinds of things in this business.

Captive audience or not, her mead tasted like ambrosia. Brody swallowed his in a few gulps and stood. He looked at his ancient watch, then patted his belly. "I have to leave you both. I have another appointment. I'll see you later, Rud. Don't hesitate to contact me again if you need anything else…" Then he held out a hand. Palm up. He wanted money.

Darla's eyes rounded at the sight when Rud reached into his pocket and pulled out a wad of cash and slipped it to Brody. Brody quickly closed a tight fist over it, and it disappeared into an interior pocket in his ragged, off-duty Uvlar suit. He saluted with two fingers and left.

Darla's spirits deflated. Damn it, he'd paid all that money to get her out of Government House? By her own rough standards and morals, she owed him, whether she liked it or not.

"What do you want from me, Rud? Why'd you pay so much to rescue me?" Not to mention, where'd all that money come from?

"You're more important than you realize," he said, then flushed. "That didn't come out right. Of course you're important. What I mean is, you're destined for a very important role in our future."

She laughed.

He pursed his lips. Obviously a little disappointed. "I don't mean the two of us, though I hoped we'd be friends."

She frowned and ignored the reference to the two of them. "If you don't mean the two of us, what do you mean?"

"I mean everything. Central City. North America. Hell, the planet maybe. I'm not sure."

She sobered. "What are you talking about? Have you been outside without your Uvlar gear for too long?"

"Let's not forget who just saved you again," he said in a petulant way.

"Let's not forget who got me captured," she reminded.

"I might have inadvertently tipped the soldiers off to your position, but they were looking for you, not me. They would have found you on their own eventually," he said.

She digested that. He might have a point.

"Don't forget I helped you get away from Oberon, too."

"Thank you for that." Now go away. She glanced at the door. She needed the Boneyard.

"There's something different about you, isn't there?" he asked. "Inside, I mean. You're not like everyone else."

"I'm not sure what you mean." But she was sure. Who

else touched dead technology and had it speak to them? Who else felt more alive in the Boneyard than anywhere else? Rud had been right about one thing. Freak of nature, or maybe just a freak, she'd admitted long ago she didn't fit in normal society. But what did he know about it?

He cleared his throat and took a quick drink. "I'm sure you heard the rumors about my family having a hand up through the two decades after the War of Neutrality?"

She inhaled. "So?"

"It's true. We did."

Darla gaped at him. She hadn't expected him to say that. "You did?"

Instantly, Rud's eyes gleamed with excitement. Like he got to be the first person to give a baby a tasty treat. "We did," he said. "And your ancestor helped us. Your great-great-great-grandmother, Maribel Rune."

Darla gave him an incredulous look. "How's that possible?" No one had been exempt from the nuclear fallout. No one had been exempt from the poisoned food sources and water. Everyone had suffered. So how, in the name of Hades, had they managed so well?

"Maribel Rune," he said quickly, excitement evident in his voice now. "Protected us from the fallout. We lived underground in fallout bunkers until it was safe to return to the surface. She gave us food, and resources. And she gave us the will to continue by promising us that we were meant for greater things. That we could survive the suffering and the horrors the world would experience because we would be the ones who helped save the planet, when the time was right."

She bought into his story until the last sentence. How could Maribel possibly have known the James family could help save the planet unless she proved to be some

133

kind of psychic? Her mouth dropped open. Wait a minute—psychic? Like maybe she-could-listen-to-dead-technology psychic. Holy crap. Could it be possible?

He watched her closely. "I'm guessing by the expression on your face you're beginning to believe me. And I have to wonder why you would believe it without proof. Unless you know what I'm saying has credibility."

She nodded. "I think I do."

"Did anyone tell you about Maribel before?"

She shook her head. "No."

"But you instantly believe a person can predict something that far into the future? Why is that, Darla?"

She wondered about that.

"You can do it, too, can't you?"

"No, of course I can't." She saw the past. Did he know why she touched the objects in the Boneyard? How long had he been following her?

He scowled at her. "That faraway look you get on your face when you touch that junk. You're seeing something, aren't you?"

She ignored his question. "What exactly does the prophecy say?"

Rud's brow furrowed. "I don't think I'm supposed to tell you."

She fisted her hands on the table. "If you want me to stay here for even one more second, fill me in on some of the details. Otherwise, I'm gone." He remained silent, so she started to push away from the table.

His shoulders slumped suddenly, and he raised his hands in the air. "Okay. Okay. The prophecy is all about you. It says to protect you. To keep you safe at all costs, because you're the only one who can fix things around here."

"Is that exactly how it's worded?"

"No. I'm paraphrasing."

"Paraphrasing? You use big words in an uneducated world," Darla said, unable to stop herself.

"Yet you understand that big word. How is that?" Rud asked.

She sighed and considered his question. "I guess my mother taught me. We had lessons while I was young."

"Did she have books?"

"I don't think so," she said. "Did you learn from books?"

"I did."

She made an impressed face. "Good for you. Tell me, why would this woman, supposedly my relative, let my family suffer through the last two centuries, while keeping your family comfortable?"

He watched her over the rim of his mug. "Maybe we'll find out if we complete the prophecy?"

"Smooth," she said sarcastically and for the moment was afraid to ask what he thought that might actually entail.

He laughed. She followed his gaze. Then she noticed the bartender watched them a little too intently. How much had he just heard?

The room suddenly felt claustrophobic. Quite a trick for a room of this size. The thing of it was, she didn't like people around her all the time. Being a loner, she desperately needed a fix at the Boneyard—soon.

"What did the prophecy say that you're not telling me?" she whispered this time.

He shifted in his chair. "You've got to find something important. And you're going to have to risk all to get it."

Her stomach clenched. She didn't like the sound of

that. "That's pretty vague and pretty terrifying. Did the psychic say anything else?"

He hesitated long enough that she knew he held something back. "That's pretty much it. Does it make any sense to you?"

"No." While she considered the fact that he'd sniffed too much city air, she needed the Boneyard. She couldn't deny the pull of ancient technologies. "May I look at this…message?"

"I guess," he said, reluctantly pulling the parchment out for her. She eyed the sheet, lined with fibers that must have kept it from deteriorating over the years.

She carefully unwrapped the paper. It felt funny in her hands. Made the tips of her fingers tingle. A buzzing began at the back of her head when she opened the last fold. The words on the paper danced before her blurred vision. Unable to read them, she felt them draw her in. She melded with the message, and her soul opened and welcomed it. The message spoke to her in the same way as the rotted stuff in the Boneyard.

Without ever reading a word, the message filled her mind. Suddenly, she understood the scope of her task. Not at all what she'd expected, but something much, much worse.

CHAPTER ELEVEN

With an unexplained lightness in his step, Oberon made his way down the hall to Darla's room. He kept thinking about her soft-looking skin with that rosy glow so unusual in today's society. Most people were sallow and pale. He wondered if she realized how little she smiled, at least like she had in the gardens. Hell, he hadn't realized how much she affected him until that moment. He'd been stunned. Even thinking about her smile made his knees a tad less steady.

He damn sure figured his attraction to her wasn't in Maribel's plans for their future. If they were supposed to fall for each other, he had no doubt Maribel would have mapped it out for them long ago. And did Maribel know what he'd done to Darla all those years ago?

His inner silent alarm went off when the guard wasn't at Darla's door. He tried the knob. Locked. He rattled the doorknob and heard a muffled voice inside. Planting his shoulder against the door, he shoved. It creaked but didn't give.

He backed up and rammed it.

This time it flew open—the hinges ripped out of the door casing and shards splintered onto the floor.

His mouth went dry when he saw the empty bed. His hands touched the indentation in the sheets. Cold. Not slept in for quite some time.

Another muffled cry came from the bathroom. He ran to it and ripped the door open.

The sight of the guard tied up in the tub made his gut wrench. "Where is Ms. Rune?" He untied the gag and pulled it out of the man's mouth.

"Sorry, sir. She helped them trick me."

"Helped who?"

The guard swallowed. "Your brother, sir, and another man. A big guy. A career soldier, if my guess is right."

"My brother kidnapped Ms. Rune?" His jaw tightened, and he wanted to hit something—hard.

"No. She wasn't being kidnapped, sir." He held his hands out for Oberon to untie. "She helped them get the jump on me."

"Damn it," Oberon said.

The guard rubbed his wrists before bending down to untie his own feet.

"Report to your commanding officer the minute you're able," Oberon said and charged back to his office. Once inside, he grabbed his Uvlar gear out of the closet and started yanking it on.

Felix, as per usual, opened the door and entered without knocking.

"Governor, what are you doing? You're not going out again. You can't. You have a responsibility..." He stopped midsentence when Oberon flashed him a get-the-hell-out-of-my-way look.

Felix adjusted two books on the ornate teak shelving, but his hands shook just a little. For once, the man knew when he shouldn't push.

"How did Rud and another man get inside Government House, of all places, without being noticed?" Oberon finally said through clenched teeth.

Felix frowned. "That is alarming. I can get our head of security to find out." He tapped the tips of his fingers together nervously.

"I don't have time to wait for him," Oberon said, sealing the last two neck closures of his uniform with practiced ease. He pulled on his hood and face shield, then turned calculating eyes on Felix.

"Where are you going, sire?" Felix asked.

"To find her. Them." He glanced toward the window that overlooked the streets. In the distance he spotted the edges of the Nevermore. He had the feeling he needed to go there. An instinct perhaps? Or maybe Maribel was inside his head now, sending him in the right direction. Whatever, he knew what he had to do. But first he had to find out where in the Nevermore they might be headed.

"But you can't just leave. You're the head of the country. If anything happens to you, we'll be in a bad spot."

"Grant Ford is my second-in-command. He's more than capable of handling things in my absence."

"Hardly," Felix drawled.

Oberon laughed. "Good to know one person believes in me."

He strode out the door and down the hall, ignoring the calls of Felix in the background. Hell and damnation, how could he leave his office right now? But if he didn't find Darla, and solve the prophecy, there might not be a country left to protect. According to the culminating prophecies over the years, Darla was the endgame. The end solution, and their salvation.

* * * * *

Darla handed the message back to Rud without reading anything. "I know what I have to do."

"But you didn't read it. You opened it and stared off into space."

"And I received a message from Maribel—somehow."

His expression morphed from surprise to growing excitement, and he scanned over his shoulder to make sure the bartender wasn't listening.

"What is it you have to do?" Rud whispered in a conspiratorial tone.

"I'm sorry. I can't tell you that."

He sat straight again. "But I'm supposed to protect you. How can I do that if I don't know?" Rud said on a frown.

"You're not the one who's supposed to protect me. Your brother is." The words came out flat, and she tasted bile. Yeah, well, the prophecy didn't say she had to like Oberon, or vice versa.

Rud shoved the note quickly into his pocket. "Oberon is otherwise occupied right now. You'll have to make do with me." He took a long drink of his ale and slammed the empty mug down.

She watched him closely, could feel the anger emanating off him. Jealousy had always been a palpable thing for her. He loved his brother, but he resented him, too. That much was evident.

"But how can you touch the paper and know so much?"

Darla sighed. "Honestly, I don't understand any of it, but I am surprised by your lack of belief. According to you, your family has followed my ancestor's messages for centuries, and when I get a message, you don't believe it?"

Rud shifted uncomfortably. "You don't seem all that sure of it yourself."

"Doesn't matter," she said, standing and adjusting the strap on one of her boots. "We have to go."

"Where?"

"Into the Nevermore," she said. Funny how she could suddenly understand what she had to do, but once the knowledge formed inside her head, she knew. Why hadn't her grandmother come to her before? Did she need the piece of paper to access the information? It made sense; she had to touch technology to see how it worked.

"I'm beginning to understand why you need protection," Rud said. "You might have a tendency to be reckless."

"Something we have in common, I gather," she said, then laughed. "Still think you're the man for the job and not Oberon?"

"Of course I am."

She waved a hand toward the door. "Let's go then." A quick glance around the bar told her the bartender had disappeared. "Where'd the barman go?"

Rud jerked a glance over his shoulder. "Damn good question. Let's move before we have to find out the hard way. I never did trust that man."

"Now you tell me," she said. "Had it occurred to you that this might not have been the best place for our discussion, then?"

Though sheepish, he didn't respond. She sighed as

they stepped outside. The storm hadn't let up much. The wind still whipped around them. Grit and leaves swirled in the air, and lightning struck a building to their left. Sparks flew in a spray of yellow, blue and white, but no apparent damage ensued. Black clouds still hung overhead, swirling and dark with a life of their own. Almost close enough to touch.

Electricity in the air raised the fine hairs at the exposed nape of her neck. She reached back and rubbed her skin, as if she could brush off the sensations flowing through her. She pushed her Uvlar collar back into place.

She couldn't believe how important her task would be. Or how dangerous. She'd learned all these things from merely touching the prophecy.

Vestro might be deposed, but he was still dangerous to every man, woman and child in Central City. His perverted vision for humanity would eradicate everything normal about their lives. And if her vision had been accurate, he still had more powerful weapons than Oberon realized.

She jumped when Rud grabbed her arm to get her attention. Otherwise, she'd never have heard him over the wind. "We can't go to the Nevermore in this storm," he shouted to be heard. "We need to find shelter."

"No. We go. It has to be now. The weather will give us cover to get to Vestro before he suspects what we're up to."

"Vestro?" Rud sounded confused. "This is about Vestro? But Oberon is the leader now."

"Vestro isn't ready to go down without a fight. And this time if we fail, what's left of mankind will lose."

"How?"

"I'm not exactly sure yet. That information seems

sketchy. One thing I do know is that we need weapons," she said. "We can't go out there unarmed."

Wind blew hair into her face. She yanked some of it out of her mouth, pulled her face shield into place and tucked her hair back into her hood. It seemed Rud accepted her statement, because they began trudging through the gusts toward the ancient rail line that led to the Nevermore.

Suddenly, Rud stopped, and she almost ran into him.

"What's that?" he asked, pointing at something dark on the sidewalk ahead of them. It took a moment to realize they were looking at the open edges of an Uvlar jacket flapping in the wind.

"Uh oh, I think it's your friend Brody," Darla shouted and ran to him, where she dropped to her knees. He'd gone ghastly white and had a painful-looking lump over one eye. "Rud, check his pulse. Is he breathing?"

Rud pulled off a glove and pressed two fingers to his carotid artery. "He's alive. But who.... The bartender. He saw me give Brody the money. I bet it was him."

Brody moaned and moved a little. "Shit, my head hurts." He raised a hand and came away with blood on his fingers. "My money. Is it gone?"

"Most likely," Rud said.

Brody shoved his hand into an inside pocket without lifting his head. The air turned blue for about ten seconds. "It's gone. All of it."

Brody's shaggy blond hair hung limply, tipped in mud, and his forehead was already bluish green.

"I think we should get him to a doctor," Darla said.

Brody rubbed a hand across his forehead. "No. I have no money to pay. My family can't afford a doctor on a soldier's wages. I have a sick child..." He moaned again and pushed himself up on one elbow. "I'll kill the bastard who did this to my family."

Darla felt his pain. She had no children, but she'd seen the waifs on the streets. She'd seen babies die in their mother's arms.

"We'll figure something out," Rud said, looking up at the sky. "At least the storm's letting up."

And, true to his comment, the wind had died down considerably.

"Maybe we could hire Brody to help us," Rud mused.

Not so sure it was a good idea, she mulled his suggestion over. Finally, she realized they had little choice. "Is he up to it?" she asked before checking his swollen face again.

"I'm up to it if it means I can make up for the money I lost." He staggered to his feet, wavered then steadied himself without help.

"He's tough. And he knows the wilds better than we do." Rud gave Darla a quizzical look. "On the other hand, maybe not any more than you do?"

Her eyebrows knitted together. "I only know the Boneyard. I don't wander very far into the Nevermore. I'm not crazy."

"Boneyard? You spend time there?" Brody asked. "Frig. I wouldn't even go there." He stared at her with something akin to respect. Or maybe he suddenly believed her to be crazy, and maybe this task would prove her insanity.

"We have a problem. We need weapons," Rud said.

"I know where we can get as many as we want, and I have a key," Brody said then spat a mouthful of blood onto the sidewalk.

Darla watched the clouds swirling overhead and

wondered how much more blood she'd see before her journey ended.

"You mean you have the key to the armory?" Rud asked.

"Yeah, I do," he said.

"But aren't you putting your military career at risk?" Darla asked.

"I need the money now. I'll take my chances."

Trusting a man that desperate for money worried her, but they did need weapons before they went deeper into the Nevermore. By all accounts, animals were even more vicious out there.

* * * * *

Oberon stepped outside the gates and wrapped the horse's leather reins around his hand. Tantalum wasn't up to this trip, so he rode his own horse, Satan. The stallion whinnied and rolled his eyes as if he had a sense of what they were about to do.

"Easy, boy, you and I are going to have to do this together," he soothed. He had a vague idea where to look for his brother and the woman.

He didn't normally do risky things on something as flimsy as a feeling. Well, not on his own feelings, anyway.

His mount snorted and bucked suddenly, hooves pawing and pounding into the ground while a gust whirled down the street and a cold pocket of air warped over them in a wave. His shoulders tightened. That breeze had been unnatural, and it reinforced his need to find Darla as quickly as possible.

He urged Satan forward, and they rode through the dirt streets and ancient houses that had become the buttresses for Central City. He gritted his teeth. People needed a governor who could help them. They deserved it. Homes were in even poorer repair in this part of the city. He hadn't been here for a long time, and that had been his mistake. As governor, he had to know what his people were dealing with.

When he passed a few people on the streets, they stared at him with suspicion on their faces. They were dressed in ragged Uvlar suits, so their faces weren't visible, but he could practically see their bones jutting through the uniforms. They were starving, and he was their only hope.

Not quite true. Darla Rune could help them if he could make her understand the gravity of the prophecy. If he could make her see past his position, which she obviously detested.

Glad his hood kept him from being recognized, he continued on. He passed a couple of Vestro's followers. They wore his crest on their suits, unafraid of being caught by Oberon's men. He didn't want to consider why they'd follow a man who'd starve and torture them at a mere whim. He knew as a member of Vestro's army that there were no limits to the dictator's depravity and cruelty.

When Oberon reached his first destination, he took a deep breath through his face filter and tasted mud. Even the filters were failing them these days. Number 429 Streams Street appeared to be a mud-brick house with a straw roof. A shingle hung on the rickety door. The woman inside, by all accounts, made her living as a fortune-teller.

He dismounted and tied Satan to a wooden stock that might once have been the corner post for a fence. Satan's eyes rolled, and he whinnied again. Oberon rubbed his nose and gave him a pat. "Don't be a scaredy-cat, boy. I'll be back before you know it."

Satan stamped his hooves and shook his head as if he understood.

A quick rap on the door, and he listened. Even though he heard someone moving about inside, no one came. He knocked again, more forcefully. He didn't intend to waste much more time. He'd break the door down if he had to.

The door opened a crack, and a woman in her fifties peered at him.

"Is your last name Rune?" he asked. Like most women in society, she might look older than her years.

"My name is Marilee Rune. What do you want?"

The scent of dinner on the stove made his stomach grumble. It smelled like a stew. That's when he remembered he'd dressed as a soldier and she might be afraid he'd come to arrest her. Taking off his hood and mask would do little to allay her fears. Hopefully, she'd listen to him before she panicked.

"I'm here to ask if you know where I might find your daughter," he said, slowly undoing his collar snap. "Please don't worry. She's not in trouble. And neither are you."

Even though Marilee Rune's expression turned to stone, she still blocked the doorway. She had long, wavy, reddish-gray hair and the same green eyes as her daughter. Dressed in a worn but clean and tidy dress, she swayed for a moment and pressed two fingers to the bridge of her nose. "I sense you're telling me the truth. Come in."

Okay, that surprised him. What would she do if she realized he was the governor?

It was almost uncomfortably hot inside her little hut, and steam escaped the pot bubbling over the fireplace. Vegetables had been hard to get under Vestro's rule, but he smelled turnip. A skinned rabbit sat on a plate on the table.

He removed his face shield and hood. He hadn't been in power long enough to chance food distribution and sales yet. He sniffed. Somehow, this woman had found meat and possibly vegetables.

Two old leather couches faced each other in front of a fire, a small metal table in between. She motioned for him to sit at a larger oval table with tiny iron chairs on each side.

He felt like a giant sitting down for tea on a chair made for children, but he sat, his legs nearly shoved up under his chin.

She sat opposite him, faded irises searching his face. "Do you know my daughter? Why are you looking for her?" She sounded slightly wistful, but he understood why.

"She's with my brother at the moment. I need to find them, and I hoped you might have an idea where they might be?"

She reached out and took his hand in hers, turned it palm up, searched the lines carefully. "What is your name?" she asked.

"Bron." He gave her his nickname. If she didn't recognize him, it'd be better.

"You've got strength, Bron," she said, then pulled her hand back.

"Go on," Oberon replied.

She shifted her gaze away from him. "You realize this is how I earn my wages."

How stupid of him. Of course. He pulled out his wallet and laid several bills on the table. Obviously, she hadn't seen money in a long time. She picked up a five-dollar bill and turned it over and over in her hands. There were no banks to back up the money's worth, but people still valued it, and it could still be used to buy goods.

Oberon hoped to reinstate a financial institution so that people might once again earn a living and have wages to buy their needed supplies.

She took his hand again. "I see that you will achieve your goals in life." She paused and frowned. "No. That might not be true. Something very important is unsure. There is more than one path you could follow. If you take the wrong path, you won't succeed."

Wasn't that life in general? Fifty-fifty chance? He sighed. Somehow he'd hoped she'd be as capable as Maribel. Apparently not. "I'm not here to have my fortune told," he admitted. "I want to find your daughter. Do you know where she's likely to be on a stormy day like this?"

Marilee Rune pursed her lips. "I have no idea. I've heard rumors about her being seen in the Boneyard." She broke off and flashed a worried look at him. Maybe she did know who he was, after all.

"I don't care about the Boneyard. Would she be there today?"

"I don't think she is." She reached out and touched a polished black stone on her table. Striations of crystal worked through it like veins, and for just a second, he imagined he saw the veins pulse. He blinked hard. "She is with your brother and another man. I can see a path with scrub and small trees on both sides of them. The path is gravel, and it extends out into the…" she gasped. "The

Nevermore. Oh, my dear child, what are you thinking?" Marilee said to herself more than to Oberon.

"Do you mean to tell me you can see exactly where she is right now?"

"Yes, one of my gifts is remote viewing. It's the only way I've managed to stay sane without my daughter."

A strange thing for her to say, but Oberon shrugged his shoulders and bit his lip. "Which direction are they heading?" Why wouldn't he believe this woman, the descendent of Maribel, the woman his family had followed for centuries?

"West."

His heart clenched, and he sensed Marilee Rune's message had been right. West. The worst possible area in the wilds. He'd lost too many men out there under the maniacal leadership of Vestro. At Maribel's direction he'd become one of Vestro's officers before the coup, Oberon had never believed in Vestro's policies, but installing himself as one of Vestro's right-hand men had been the best thing he'd done to get a better idea of how Vestro thought. And, he knew there was some sort of secret outpost out there. He'd never seen it himself. Vestro had spent a lot of his time there before the coup, and he'd probably be holed up there afterward.

But why would Darla go there?

CHAPTER TWELVE

"You grab the sniper rifles," Brody said, wrenching open another door. "I'll get machine guns."

Darla watched the men working. She didn't know much about guns. They didn't work for her like dead technology, because these things actually still functioned. If she touched them, she wouldn't gain quite as much knowledge. Besides, her little pistol held enough firepower for her. Unfortunately, her pistol wouldn't do her much good where they were going.

When she'd held the prophecy awhile ago, the message from her grandmother had been strong and urgent. Vestro had to be stopped before he could release weapons upon mankind more devastating than those used during the War of Neutrality.

Another vision, like undulating water, filled her thoughts. She saw beasts with little conscience, controlled by Vestro. Not Yardmen. Much worse than Yardmen. Her gut tightened, and she felt a little queasy.

She faltered, closed her eyes, and when she opened

them again, her leg pained.

"You're not saying much," Rud said when he stopped next to her with stolen weapons under each arm. "And you suddenly look worried. Is there something you're not telling me?"

She took in the firepower the two men were toting and ignored his question. "That stuff looks heavy. How far do you think you can carry it without leaving some of it behind?" She hoped they were strong enough to carry it all the way to wherever they needed to go, but doubted it.

"I'll carry the ammunition," she said. After Brody packed a rucksack full, she yanked it over her shoulder. Heavy, but she could pull her weight.

"Let's get going. It'll be dark before we get to our destination if we don't leave now," Darla said.

"What exactly is our destination?" Brody asked, deep lines burrowing into his brow. "So far we're following you blind. Where are you taking us?"

"There's an old military compound out there that Vestro's using." Funny, Darla thought. She'd been keeping her psychic side buried for most of her life. She hadn't allowed it to surface other than to feel the machinery in the Boneyard, and now it broiled to the surface whether she wanted it to or not. Truth be told, she felt overwhelmed.

"Holy Benevolent hell." Rud stepped in front of her and looped a weapon over his shoulder. She felt a moment of disquiet. She thought about Oberon. His muscles were real. He'd created them doing hard work. When they'd sat in the garden, she'd sensed his deeper angst. His mental war wounds came from soldiering and surviving in the wilds through sheer will and brute strength. Rud, on the other hand, though young and strong and eager, might not have the experience they needed to carry this thing off.

She glanced at the man who'd signed up with Rud. Brody probably had experience, but she didn't trust him the way Rud did.

They were still in the metal building near the route to the farming grounds in the Nevermore. Brody said he had keys because of his job with the military, but he'd lied, and it didn't take a psychic to figure that out.

Only a mercenary had the kinds of skills that Brody exhibited. That's why he'd helped Rud get into Government House after all. But who else did he work for? Something squirmy slithered in her stomach, but she chose to ignore it—for now. What choice did she have?

How could she have ignored her deeper intuitive abilities her whole life? Or maybe she'd been using them without realizing it. While she'd never considered her abilities in the Boneyard as anything other than weird, maybe she'd been warming up for whatever had been written in the prophecy.

Rud touched her shoulder. "You okay, Darla? If the backpack's too heavy, I can carry it," he said.

Yeah, he would carry it, too. In his youthful exuberance, he'd burn up all his energy and have nothing left when he really needed it. Images flashed through her mind, and she squashed them. Images and sounds of what they were going to face in the Nevermore. She heard screams and saw flashes of claws and blood before she managed to block out the visions again.

She wanted to shut it off. But sooner or later she'd have to face the truth, and the horrors of the future.

Brody opened the armory door a crack. He peered left, then right and waved them outside into the daylight.

Darla squinted against the light. The clouds seemed to have dissipated more than normal after the storm. Most days, the sun beat down through a haze of contamination. Where was the haze today?

The brightness felt too sharp, and it seemed to underpin the job ahead of them.

Hours later, they were still trudging along an ancient, overgrown railway line that arrowed deep into the Nevermore. Her leg still hurt, but it was holding up much better than she'd hoped.

A voice kept whispering in her mind. A woman's voice. Like smoke on the air. She couldn't grasp it, but she caught the occasional hurry and be brave.

"Easy for you to say, old lady. You're safe in the twenty-first century," she said under her breath.

"What'd you say?" Rud strode up next to her. For the most part, he'd been staying behind her, with Brody taking the lead.

"Nothing. Just talking to myself."

He grinned. "You bored or something?"

"Something," she said. "Can we stop for a rest soon? We've been walking for hours, and I don't know about you, but I'm starving." And they hadn't brought any food that she knew of.

"We'd like to stop as soon as it's safe," Rud repeated a little louder so Brody could hear.

Irritation sparked in his expression when he glanced back over his shoulder, but he said, "Right-o. Should be a spot where we can stop safely in about five minutes."

She knew from traveling through the Nevermore to the Boneyard that some of the more seminocturnal animals would be out soon. That idea sent chills up her back.

Brody halted and held up a hand. "We'll have to go

into heavier brush for a while. There's a garden about a mile ahead. Soldiers will arrest us if they catch us out here."

It'd be worse than that—not a thought, but knowledge that lived inside her. The onslaught of images and feelings built. More intense than last time.

Two long breaths. Slowly. Very slowly, the nausea abated. She scanned the medium-size, stunted trees and thick shrubs where, no doubt, creatures slithered, slunk and crouched while waiting for people to be stupid enough to venture deeper into the foliage. Behind thick clouds, the sun edged lower in the sky now, making shadows long in the scrub. And even longer in her imagination.

They stepped off the path and followed closely behind Brody, who had a blade in one hand and a gun in the other. Rud slipped in behind her again, and she heard the slide and click of metal and knew he'd drawn and cocked his weapons as well.

She'd tucked her pistol into the waistband of her new Uvlar suit where she could grab it at a moment's notice. The suit fit her like a glove, and if she wasn't about to die by having it torn to shreds, it was too good to lose.

They hadn't made it two feet off the path when a branch snapped in front of them. The bitter scent of crushed leaves assaulted her nostrils. Something snorted and grunted, snuffled in the dirt nearby. A wild pig nosing for food perhaps.

They stood still. Everyone knew enough to do that.

Minutes later, the tusked pig raised its head above the brush. Its beady little eyes missed them, and it turned and ran off.

Now, wandering in the Nevermore, she realized she'd

somehow agreed to risk her neck for a weird voice in her head that told her to go after the deluded ex-dictator. Had she gone insane? Maybe she took chances in the Boneyard, but this was moronic.

"Don't talk until we're past the farm land," Rud whispered to her.

Brody snorted. "The soldiers hear noises in the brush all the time. They won't come looking unless they see us. There are too many deadly things out here."

"Gee, why doesn't that make me feel better?" she said.

"Me either," Rud said.

"I'd actually like to see the farm." Darla stretched her neck to steal a peek.

"Not on my shift, babe," Brody cut in. "I have to work with these men. They don't take kindly to soldiers who supplement."

She could understand that, because she didn't trust Brody, either. She figured he supplemented whenever the mood suited him. Case in point, Brody seemed to know this route a little too well. The tiny trail they were currently following outside the farmlands might be an animal trail, or it might be a Brody trail. He knew his way better than he should.

That left the question—just how well did Rud know Brody?

She managed to see a tiny bit of the farm in a small opening through the brush. Compared to the rest of their world, it appeared lush and green and amazing. Crouching low on their way by so as not to be spotted, she saw people working the land with horses. They were plowing in between the rows and fertilizing by hand. She'd love to be able to walk into the center of the vivid green field and soak in the energy from the vivacious plants. Maybe taste real carrots, or tomatoes, or whatever they grew there.

Looking back at the scrub, she noted that everything appeared dull in comparison to the green of the garden. The rest of the Nevermore consisted of browns and grays, with dirty burgundy stalks bearing stunted, odd-shaped leaves. The Nevermore reminded her of Yardmen. Genetic deviants.

"Move along. We've been here too long," Brody said under his breath.

With reluctance, she did what he said and caught Rud's expression of sympathy.

"How much farther do you think we have to go?" Rud asked.

"I'm not sure. I'm not even sure what I'm seeing in my head is real. Maybe I'm just crazy. Have you even considered that?" she whispered.

Brody had moved several paces ahead of them, taking the lead again. Had Rud even noticed he seemed to know where he was going without asking her for directions?

"No. I haven't. I trust you, Darla."

It'd be better if he questioned her motives once in a while. He was too quick to do whatever she said. It didn't make sense, prophecy or not. He should have opinions, worries.

"Better pick up the pace, Brody is getting ahead of us," she said.

In fact, Brody had already started moving to the east before she could tell him which way to go. She slanted a look at Rud, and he finally frowned, too. "We'd better be on our toes and stick together," he whispered to her.

"I agree. We might be walking into a trap."

"Maybe, but I don't see how he would've gotten a

chance to send word about us."

"I think I do," she said. "Remember the missing bartender? I have the feeling I know where he scuttled off to. And by all accounts, Brody shouldn't have had the means to spend time in the bar drinking, so why was he there? Especially not if he really has a family to look after."

"You think his family has been fabricated?" Rud said under his breath and between gritted teeth.

"How long have you known—" She cut off her question when Brody stopped and turned to watch them. His hands were on his hips, his expression distrustful.

"What are you two whispering about back there?"

Rud grinned at Brody. "Just trying to convince Darla to go out with me when we get home," he said quickly.

"Fat chance of that." Brody frowned at both of them. He didn't believe what he'd been told.

"It's okay," he said. "We're far enough from the farms not to be heard now." Brody waited for them. He must've realized he'd been taking the lead without any direction and they might be getting curious.

And he'd be right. They were on to him. His bruises and swelling weren't faked, but it would be easy to get someone to pound him and leave him on the sidewalk to be found by them. To feel sorry for him.

* * * * *

Rud wanted nothing more than to punch Brody in the face and close his other eye. A double-dealing traitor. He should've been more curious about how easily Brody had gotten them inside Oberon's compound and back out again. Mercenary or not, it shouldn't have been that easy.

"We'd better get a move on," Brody said, looking at

his watch. "We don't want to be here when the sun sets."

"Sounds like you have some experience in this part of the Nevermore," Darla responded.

Rud's muscles tightened. Don't give us away yet, he willed. Neither of them was strong enough to fight Brody off.

"Yeah, I came out this way on a rescue mission once. We got as far as the next clearing before three of the men were taken by the beasts. Those of us who escaped swore never to return. The only reason I'm here right now is for the money. For my family."

Greed filled his eyes. Rud suddenly wished he hadn't trusted Brody quite so much. He thought he knew the guy...but now...he wasn't so sure.

"Will we be able to make it to Vestro's stronghold before dark?" Brody asked Darla. Clearly, he already knew the answer to that.

"No, I don't think so," Darla said, squeezing her eyes closed. "I see a clearing among some maples. They're actually growing without being stunted."

"Which way?" Brody asked, but he'd already turned in the right direction.

"You're on the right track," Darla said. "Just keep heading away from the setting sun. We're going east now."

It amazed Rud that they'd been able to spend this much time in the Nevermore without being attacked. Hold that thought. He saw something moving in the scrub, a distance out, but slowly moving toward them.

"Beast approaching from our left," he warned. The slanted eyes of a cat of some sort stared at him. It mimicked a house cat, but times that by twenty. Muscles worked on the animal's body, and its eyes watched them with ferocious singularity.

"Weapons ready," Brody shouted. "These cats don't hunt alone."

They heard a growl from the other side of the trail to verify his statement. They were being tracked by two of them.

Brody fired the first shot and hit one enormous cat. One slash of those claws or even a single bite between its massive, crushing jaws would easily finish a human.

Rud shot and wounded the next one. "Get your pistol ready, Darla, in case you need it."

"The soldiers. Will they hear us?" Darla asked. The shot had sounded like a cannon going off.

"I don't think so," Brody said. "We should be far enough away by now. And, as I said, they don't go into the Nevermore without good reason. Hearing a gunshot won't necessarily bring them this way."

The wounded cat yowled like a banshee. Rud took aim again and finished it. Its glassy eyes and bloody teeth were grim reminders of the dangers ahead.

Soon after that, the sounds of bones cracking and flesh tearing and being chewed sent chills up his spine. Something had taken the cat? Had it been following them all along?

"Benevolent hell," Rud said.

"Don't stop moving. We've got to get to the clearing." Brody sounded more afraid than Rud had ever seen him.

If Brody was a traitor, Rud would throw him to the cats himself, but not yet. They still needed him to keep them alive.

They rushed along the trail carved out by animals, fully aware that this path had been most traveled by beasts in the Nevermore. They didn't dare to move through the scrub right now. Besides the man-eaters, there were other things that lurked in the brush. Snakes. As venomous and deadly as the two monster cats they'd just killed.

When they made the clearing that Darla had foreseen, they were all out of breath.

"I can't believe it's really here," Darla said, pushing one hand into her side while she tried to regulate her breathing. She dropped the heavy pack of ammunition.

"Considering that we're following you into the wilds, it's a damned good thing that you were accurate," Brody barked, his breath wheezy and hard.

Rud noticed the glance she slanted at him. He acknowledged her look with a terse shake of the head. Once they'd left the dead cats, Brody hadn't needed a single direction. Before, it might've just been a coincidence. Now, Rud could only call it a certainty. And when his life had depended on it, Brody made straight for sanctuary. The problem: It damn well wouldn't be sanctuary for him and Darla. Had he allowed Brody to lead them into a trap?

Had he taken the prophecy, and risked her life without considering the consequences? He'd stolen the prophecy because he'd wanted to prove himself.

Brush began to snap around them. Something coming. Lots of somethings. Heavy, too. Thundering toward the clearing. With all hell breaking loose, he barely had time to consider the full consequences of what he might've done by bringing Darla here.

Oberon would never get the chance to fulfill his destiny if things went fubar tonight.

CHAPTER THIRTEEN

Oberon rode into the Nevermore giving Satan his full lead. He made the farm in record time. Maybe the soldiers had seen Rud or Darla?

He heard the alarm sound before he saw anyone. "Who goes there?"

"Oberon James," he shouted.

A soldier in a heavily fortified sentry building peered out with his weapon aimed at Oberon's head. "Not fucking likely," he grated.

Another voice spoke beside him. "Shoot him, Harve."

Ironic that Oberon's first command had been to double up the sentries. Oberon waited.

"No way. Jerome, you need to calm down. The shift is getting to you." The one named Harve, the one with common sense, turned back to Oberon. "I'm sorry, sir. Would you mind proving to us that you are who you say you are?"

Oberon raised one hand to remove his face shield. He noticed that made Itchy Fingers Jerome antsy. The man needed some R&R, and he needed some medical treatment. Oberon had worked with soldiers like him. He knew the signs. Living this tough life affected some more than others.

"I'm just going to remove my face shield," he said. "Corporal Harve, please tell your sergeant to take note that I'm obviously not holding a weapon."

"Sergeant Jerome," Harve said. "Please listen to what the man is saying. No matter who he really is, he's unarmed. And we've got him covered. If he moves to get a weapon, we'll take him out."

"That makes me feel so much better," Oberon said drily before he yanked off his face shield and hood. The corporal gasped first then lowered his weapon and saluted.

"My apologies, sir."

"Has anyone come by here today?" Oberon asked.

The two men stared at each other in shock. People didn't visit the Nevermore. "No, sir." Jerome seemed to have pulled himself together. Oberon made a mental note to get these men some relaxation time and some medical treatment for stress. He'd spent a few years at this job himself.

"Nobody came through here. We would've spotted them, sir," Jerome said.

Oberon searched Jerome's face, then Harve's. Corporal Harve nodded his agreement. "Thanks." He pointed to the east. "I'm going in that direction. If I don't come back in two days, I'd appreciate a detail coming to find me."

"Sir, may we be of assistance? You shouldn't go out there alone," Jerome said.

Oberon glanced at the fields being guarded. Saw the

farmers hoeing and weeding turnips that virtually kept city folks alive. "These people need your strength and protection more than I do. I can look after myself."

The two soldiers saluted.

His horse whinnied and started stomping the ground, his rump shifting back and forth. "Easy," Oberon said, leaning down and patting the black horse's muscled neck. When Satan settled, Oberon yanked his hood back on and pointed the horse in the direction he needed to go. Satan obviously didn't like the idea, but he moved into the brush. Good horse.

Images of soldiers they'd found ripped to shreds out here during his tours of duty assaulted him, but he pushed them away. Rud might not have much experience, but surely he could figure out how to protect Darla and himself. He knew how to use a weapon and stay alive if he had to.

Darkness would settle over the Nevermore within the next hour or two. No human should be out here after dark.

Even a strong, well-experienced soldier would have a hard time surviving the wild animals on the hunt out here at night. And every soldier alive knew there were worse things than they could even imagine out here. Something hunted men. Something big and deadly. Something his soldiers had never seen and lived to talk about.

* * * * *

Darla deliberately fell a few steps behind the men. The sound of something approaching grew louder. She held her pistol tight. Standing in the middle of this field, in tall chlorotic-yellow grasses with their feet mired in squelchy muck, wasn't the best place to be right now. The trees surrounding them were the tallest she had ever seen. At least forty feet. Amazing to see. Their leaves, more green than yellow, tinkled and waved in the breeze. Or maybe they were trembling like she was?

What was coming?

Rud backed up until he reached her. He wrapped one arm around her shoulders and held a machine gun in the other. "I'm sorry, Darla, I shouldn't have brought you out here. I should have listened to Oberon. He's the warrior, not me."

"Doesn't matter. I would have come alone if you hadn't come with me," she said. She turned just in time to see the back end of Brody disappearing into the tree line.

"Should we follow him?" Rud asked.

"I don't think we'd like the people he's gone to meet."

"Probably right," she said. "Got any ideas? I have the feeling whatever is coming isn't going to be good."

Rud's bright blue eyes suddenly stunned her. If she closed her eyes right now, would those be the blue eyes of her dreams? She'd only ever met two men with blue eyes in her lifetime. Rud and Oberon. But she'd been dreaming about a blue-eyed man her whole life.

"What are we going to do? Should we run?" she asked.

"I have the feeling that's exactly what we shouldn't do. We're in the open, though. We need cover."

"Good point," she said.

"Can you climb?" he asked.

"Climb?" She'd spent half her life climbing heaps of defunct technology at the Boneyard. "Yes, I can climb. But what? Where?"

"If we can make it to the edge of this clearing, we'll climb that tree." He pointed at another tall tree—

unbelievable. "See it? The tallest one?"

"The bark on the trunk looks fairly smooth, but if you boost me up to the first branch, I think I can handle it from there," she said.

She could feel vibration in the ground under her feet. Maybe a stampede? But of what? "Let's hurry."

Not only could they hear trampling of brush and thundering coming their way, but they also heard snorting and heavy breathing. They didn't have much time.

Darla glanced at her boots, saturated in the sulfurous-smelling muck, and wondered how quick they could be. She thought about the ammunition she'd left back there in the field. It was too late to go back for it now. They made their way with a minimum of mud-sucking and dripping sounds somehow. He boosted her to the first branch of what had to be the largest tree in the Nevermore. She shimmied higher with Rud close behind her.

Now at least thirty feet off the ground, she squeezed her arms around the smooth bark of the tree and breathed in its unusual aroma and prayed for a miracle. If only more full-grown trees like this one existed. Most trees' habits were stunted, barely ten feet tall with thin branches and yellowish, wilted leaves. They mostly looked like they were going to die at any moment. So how had these trees flourished? She gazed through the thick cover of leaves down at the soil below. It appeared to be dark and rich. Maybe if she survived this day, she could package up some of that soil and take it home. See if she could grow something in it.

A roar filled the air and quaked through her bones. Their position may have been hidden by the leaves, but they could still see through the canopy. She spotted the massive creatures when they breached the tree line and rumbled into the opening. She wanted to scream but held it inside. When she met Rud's gaze, she saw he was just as shocked.

Yardmen had nothing on these creatures. Half man, half animal of some sort. She'd heard Vestro had been dabbling with animal DNA in his labs. Creating abominations.

Something like a man but two feet taller. They had cloven hooves, tails, horns. She'd once seen a picture of the devil, and these creatures were similar, only they had the wide slash mouth of a Yardman, sharp teeth and a forked tongue. Their skin appeared mottled with blues and greens, and the tails similar to the thick hide and scales of a water-dwelling creature.

Their eyes were tiny in their heads, and that might be a disadvantage. They had large, vibrating nostrils. Maybe their sense of smell made up for their possible poor eyesight.

The creatures' ears were barely there, and they had hair like wild boar tufts. Hideous didn't even come close to a description. Four of them entered the glade, dressed in some sort of military outfits that covered their torsos. Their enormous weight and their hooves made the thundering noises she and Rud had heard coming. And probably more than that with the armament they were carrying on straps on their chests and backs.

"Find the girl," the lead one said in perfect English. Darla half expected them to only be able to grunt.

"What about the man?" Creature number two sniffed the air and licked his lips. "I haven't tasted sweetmeat for at least six months."

"That's because you've scared them so badly they

won't leave the farms and venture into our killing grounds. It's your fault," another creature said.

"Shut up. We're not here for a snack. And we won't be killing the sweetmeat. We have to take them back to Father."

At the mention of "Father," they all bowed their heads in supplication, each chanting something under their breath. Four devils chanting in a glade. Creatures that might have come from hell. Darla's chest tightened, and she gripped the tree tighter.

Neither she nor Rud spoke a word. If they did, the creatures might hear them.

The devils stood back-to-back in the glade, watching all directions. One of them straightened and tipped his head toward Rud and Darla. His slash of a mouth opened slightly, his lizard tongue licking the air.

Darla's heart rate tripled, and she swallowed too hard.

"Over there." The beast pointed at the tree they were in.

"We're dead," she whispered, but Rud put one finger over her lips and shook his head vigorously and pointed toward the field. A rarely seen twelve-point buck had entered the grassy area to graze. A beautiful creature, as undamaged by the elements as the trees. The sheer beauty of the animal, its grace and fluid movement, captured Darla's breath.

"Snack time," said one creature.

"Be quick," the leader said. "We have people to hunt. They can't have gotten far."

Darla watched in dismay while the beasts surrounded the magnificent animal. Within seconds, they'd slashed open the screaming buck's throat and gutted him still kicking.

A clotted scream froze inside her. She'd seen horrors in the Boneyard but had never witnessed the death of something so beautiful. So innocent. The creatures made quick work of the animal. They strung it up into a tree and left its hollowed-out body hanging for later.

With fresh blood on them, they were even more shocking to look at.

"If you're done dicking around, they're in the tree," Brody called from somewhere in the woods behind them. "Damn deviants, I thought you were better hunters."

The main devil growled low in his throat and turned in the direction of the tree where she and Rud hid. Brody stayed out of sight. Most likely afraid of them, too.

"What'll we do?" Darla whispered.

"I don't think we stand a chance against them. At least they don't want to eat us."

"They do want to, but they have orders to keep us alive. Doesn't mean they will," she said.

"S'pose you could be right."

"Well, I'm sure as hell not going down without a fight. You?"

He shook his head. "Nope."

She watched the four monsters approach the tree. "They look like they can climb better than we can. They might have hooves, but they've got really big hands with claws that'd be great for tree climbing."

"I'm sorry I put you in this position. I should've listened to Oberon." Rud said, as if suddenly ashamed. "He said there was another part to the message, and I didn't believe him. I should have known he was telling the truth?"

She wanted to reassure Rud. But she couldn't. If she believed what she'd learned from the voice in her head, it was the Oberon's quest to keep her alive, not Rud's. And if they survived today, she'd have to be ready to give up everything to save society. She didn't know exactly what that meant, but she had the sense she'd know when the time was right.

One of the devils took a gun out of a holster on his back and aimed it at them.

"That's the biggest barrel on a gun I've ever seen," Rud whispered.

"Get out of the tree," the beast said in a guttural intonation. "Get out now or I'll blow you out, and if I do that, there won't be much left of you. If you get out voluntarily, I'll let you live."

"What about me?" Rud asked. "Sweetmeat?"

The other devil licked his very thin, wide lips and grinned.

"Neither of you are going to die today. I have orders to bring you in."

"To whom?" Darla asked. "Who do you work for?" As if she needed to know.

They all laughed. "We don't work for anyone," the leader said. "We revere. And we do what we're told. And we've been told to bring you in. End of story. Now get down or I'll bring you in with a few extra holes."

"One thing I know for sure, I damned well hope I get a chance to get my hands on Brody and that no-good bartender," Rud said on his way down the tree.

Darla followed him down. Even from here she could smell the blood on the beasts from the fresh kill. She gagged once, but held the rest in.

Dread pooled in her stomach. She heard Rud grunt when he touched bottom and one of the beasts grabbed him. She didn't dare look to see if he was still alive. After what they'd done to the buck, he might not have even had a chance to scream.

She'd barely stepped onto the ground when a hand came around the tree, grabbed her by the collar and pulled her out of the line of sight of the beasts.

"Where'd she go?" They roared and thundered their feet on the ground.

Darla snapped her head around to see who'd dragged her backward like a kitten being carried by its mother. Surely not Brody?

She turned and punched him in the gut. Air vented out of him. "Bloody hell, what are you doing?" he said in a low voice while blue-blue eyes narrowed on her. It was Oberon.

Again, the leader of the country had come to save her. He had a weapon in his hand. Large. Powerful. The name Barrett inscribed on the side. He fired twice. The powerful bullets killed two of the beasts instantly.

Smoke hung in the air from the spent cartridges.

"Stay back here. Don't move unless I say so," Oberon said in his usual curt tone. He moved behind another tree and fired again.

A flurry of gunfire broke out. She watched with terror while chunks flew out of the trees around them. One shot nearly cut the tree in two that hid Oberon. He didn't budge, other than crouching lower. His focus remained on saving his brother.

Suddenly, the gunfire ended. Smoke made her lungs ache even with her face shield in place.

Oberon stepped out from behind the mangled tree and motioned for her to follow him.

Her stomach squelched when she saw the massive bodies blown-apart in the clearing. Then, as if it couldn't get any worse, she heard animals growling from the edges of the Nevermore. The scent of blood had drawn more beasts already.

Oberon returned and held out a hand. "Get up. We have to move."

"Rud?" She didn't dare look.

"I think he's okay," Oberon said, pulling her toward the mutilated body of one of the four downed devils.

She searched for Rud. "Where is he?"

"I'm down here," an exhausted voice said. She looked down and saw blue eyes staring up at her. The rest of his face was covered in blood and the monster's arm covered his torso.

"Get me out of here. This creature is crushing me."

Oberon sighed. "Good thing it's only his arm pinning you down. If he'd really fallen on you, you'd be my younger brother pancake right now."

Rud grunted while Oberon and Darla worked together to move the massive arm off him. Like a huge sandbag, it weighed him down. Darla gasped when they finally got him free and she saw he was covered with blood. "Are you hurt?"

Rud got to his feet. "No, I think it's the beast's blood."

Growling grew louder around them. "Unfortunately, it's ringing a very loud dinner bell to the predators around us," Oberon said. "You'll have to take Satan back to Central City."

"You think I'm going to skulk back to the city alone? And leave you and Darla here? Without your horse?"

Oberon took off his face shield. His expression worried. "Little brother, I honestly do appreciate what you're trying to do for Darla. For us. For everyone. But covered in blood—out here in the Nevermore—even on my horse, you'll have to ride like the hounds of hell are after you. Because they will be." He closed his eyes for a second then squeezed Rud's shoulder. "I pray you make it, brother. Give me the prophecy, and I'll take it from here."

Rud bristled visibly, but in his state, saturated with blood, he didn't have much time to make a decision. They all turned their attention to the tree line now. The growling got louder. The creatures wanted the carrion in the field, the fallen devils, and for the time being, they were staying back because of the humans in their way. That wouldn't last long.

Rud reached into his interior pocket and, with two fingers that marked the paper with blood, pulled it out and handed it to Oberon. "I'm sorry, Darla. Oberon is right. I've failed. I tried to fulfill the prophecy, but it couldn't work because Oberon had to be the one all along who carried it out. And, just now, he's proven he's the right man for the job. Who am I to argue with proof like that?" He shuddered and his shoulders sagged. "I'll go for help, though. And I'll come back for both of you. I'm not giving up."

Oberon nodded his head. "I know you will, brother. I'm proud of you for doing this. You've certainly proved your strength today."

"I wish that were true."

Oberon whistled, and his horse cantered into the clearing. The black stallion's eyes were rolling, and his feet stamped nervously. Oberon went to him and patted his neck. The beautiful black horse whinnied and nudged Oberon's shoulder.

"Calm and easy, Satan," he said to the horse. "Take Rud home. Ride as fast as you can."

Rud watched Darla through a curtain of blood. "I'd give you a hug if I could."

Darla smiled at him. "Thank you for everything. Stay safe. Don't let the beasts get you."

He nodded and climbed up onto the spirited horse that Oberon soothed. "I'm ready, brother. Be careful."

Oberon whispered something into the horse's ear. "See you soon, Rud."

Rud pulled on the reins and dared a quick glance back at the two of them. "You, too, Oberon. Get out of this field before you're both on the menu yourselves." He saluted and galloped off.

"Let's go," Oberon said, stepping over one of the dead devils. "I know of a place where we can hole up for the night." He adjusted his heavy weaponry in leather straps on his back and grabbed her hand. They ran as fast as they could across the field.

The sun had begun to set. Brazen eyes of encroaching animals followed them from everywhere. Luckily, the heavy scent of blood and four dead beasts were more tempting right now. Oberon managed to get them both out of the clearing without a single attack—that alone a minor miracle in her book.

"Where are we going?"

"As I said, I know a spot where we can hole up until morning."

"How do you know about this place? I heard no one comes out here."

"Vestro's elite guard were the only ones allowed to travel out this far on hunting excursions."

"Hunting for what?" she asked.

"For materials that Vestro can use in his labs. I've never seen the actual building but he has a lab out here somewhere, where he creates monsters like those back in the glade. Sometimes the monsters get loose. Some of them are the most dangerous animals on the planet."

"Good thing your gun was more dangerous," she said. "Otherwise, I'd be Vestro's prisoner right about now."

"Thankfully, for both of you, Vestro wanted you alive. Otherwise, I wouldn't have made it in time."

Darla took a step forward and tripped on a root, but Oberon snagged her elbow to keep her upright.

"I'm fine," she said, snatching a nervous peek at shadows in the brush caused by the growing dusk. They left the field and walked for quite awhile. When they'd finally stopped, they seemed to be in the middle of nowhere without a landmark in sight except one slight hill in the distance. Even so, she had no doubt that Oberon could keep her alive. He'd trained to be tough. Tougher than Rud and twice as irritating.

"See that hill? There's a cave there. We'll be safe inside overnight."

Great. Stuck in a cave with him overnight. Could life get any better? Hitching her shoulders back and treading over the uneven ground, she gritted her teeth and followed in Oberon's footsteps. Hopefully, all the predators for miles around were drawn to the scent of blood in the valley and not the fresh meat walking straight through their hunting grounds.

Somehow they made it to the hill before dusk fell. "The cave's right there," Oberon said. "Let me climb in first in case something is inside."

"Good idea," she said. "Though, in retrospect, what good would it do me to be out here alone if you are eaten? I wouldn't last long."

"I think you'd do just fine," he said. "I understand

you've spent a lot of time in the Boneyard. Not many people can do that and survive."

Had she heard a modicum of respect in those words? Probably just her imagination. "Yeah, well, last time I wouldn't have survived. Rud saved me from a Yardman."

He grinned and shook his head as if surprised. "Given his lack of experience, it was quite a feat."

"You two don't like each other very much, do you?"

Oberon's blue eyes shifted to scan their surroundings before he returned his attention to her. "It might seem that way, Ms. Rune, but I'd give my life for my brother. And I'm pretty sure he'd do the same for me."

Her eyebrows rose.

"I'll do the same for you, too, if you let me. Now, keep watch while I check the cave," he said, handing her the massive gun and extracting a very sharp-looking knife from his belt. He started inside then hesitated. "You okay with this? Being out here alone?"

She gave him an incredulous and disgusted look. "I'm tougher than I look," she said and wished she believed it.

He eyed her up and down, his expression unreadable. When he crouched down and crawled inside, she shivered, watching him disappear into the small opening. With her full attention on the brush again, she pulled out her pistol and held it in her other hand.

A low growl made her jump then, embarrassed, she realized it had been her stomach.

Grass and brush shifted and moved in the breeze. Birds of prey flew in a circle in the distance. She prayed that Rud would made it back to the city.

Covered with his attacker's blood, it wouldn't be easy.

CHAPTER FOURTEEN

"You can come inside," Oberon said, his voice echoing in the cave. "It's safe in here."

Darla peered over her shoulder at the barrens behind her then leaned down to scope out the dark entrance. "Is there room for both of us in there?" The fine hairs on the back of her neck rose, and her stomach gurgled in protest.

"Plenty of room," he said. "Hurry up, will you? The longer you hang around outside, the more likely you'll be eaten."

On cue, the brush behind her rustled. Probably just the wind, but Goosebumps flashed across her skin, and she dove inside the small opening without thinking about what might be in front of her. She landed on her hands and knees and scurried the rest of the way inside before something could grab her from behind.

Most likely unaware of how much he'd scared her, Oberon had already lit torches he'd found in the cave. He'd definitely been here before.

"You can stand up now." Even he could stand to his

full height, and he stood over six feet. The cave was bigger than it seemed from the outside.

She got off her knees and stood.

When he moved past her and his body brushed against hers, she felt some kind of weird frisson between them. Even through her Uvlar gear. She didn't like that he'd affected her. She didn't want to like him.

She watched him shove a round, metal disk in front of the cavern opening. Now she understood why the size of the opening was optimal. Easy to close off from predators. Then he pushed several large boulders against the metal. "Won't be easy to get through this, and worst-case scenario, we'll hear them long before they get inside, and we can shoot them."

"Not as good as my protective hideaways in the Boneyard, but it'll do," she said.

"Do tell?" He walked toward the back of the cave and pulled out a bench-size bed with straps of leather woven to make a sleeping surface. He pushed on a strap and it broke under the weight of his hand. "We'll sleep in shifts."

"You said it'd be safe in here."

"Relatively, but not safe enough for both of us to sleep. Someone needs to watch the opening. Shoot anything that tries to come through. Remember, not all of the creatures out there are mindless animals. Some of them are part human and have been sent specifically to get us. They have an acute sense of smell, so they might be able to find us by scent alone."

Great. Darla turned her head and sniffed at her shoulder. She'd have to stop making that scented soap. It'd be the death of her yet.

Oberon pulled off his hood and face shield, then

unzipped his jacket and took it off and threw it on the dirt floor. He wore a thin sleeveless T-shirt.

"It's warm in here, and it'll get warmer with the opening blocked. You'll want to take your gear off," he said.

"What if we have to leave in a hurry?"

Oberon exhaled. "I don't think that'll happen, Darla. You can rest fairly easily for tonight. The temps rise to about ninety degrees in here though... I think it has something to do with underground thermal activity. You'll dehydrate faster in your Uvlar if you leave it on." He sat and pulled off his boots and leather pants. "Up to you, though."

He'd undressed in front of her as if she were one of his men. As if she saw men undress all the time. Some women had to do anything to survive in their world. To feed their families. She, on the other hand, used other methods.

She had no idea what normal meant when it came to anyone else, especially men. She'd grown up with a burning need to understand technology, and that had left no room for relationships when she got older. Not to mention being a dissident.

The Boneyard had been her sole obsession.

Sweat started to build inside her suit. She removed her face shield and hood and shook out her hair. Oberon seemed to watch her every move.

That made her teeth itch.

She slid down onto the ground and crossed her legs then unzipped her Uvlar just enough to cool herself a bit. She had only a bra and panties on under the suit. No way she'd strip down in front of the Overlord of North America. The man who'd kept her prisoner and who continually ogled her like some loaf of fresh flax bread.

"Where were you and Rud going when you came into the Nevermore?" Oberon asked. "Did you know you were getting close to Vestro's lab? His freak show?"

"Yes and no. I expected Vestro's sole reason for being out here was to run his equipment. His technology. Apparently, you've seen his stronghold if you know where we're going?"

He shook his head. "Never been there. No matter how hard I tried to get an invite when I was Vestro's general. But, after the takeover, I found paperwork in Government house, with schematics about what he's doing out here, and lady, it ain't pretty."

If he wanted to warn her away, he'd failed. Yes, his words scared her. Of course they did. But she needed to carry this thing out to the end. And the prophesy hinted that that might just mean her death.

"You must've known he had the equipment to keep mankind at his mercy," she said.

Oberon frowned. "What are you talking about?"

"He has EMP magnifiers. He's the reason we can't rebuild technology."

He tipped his head back and laughed, his dark hair shiny and reflecting the candlelight. "Vestro has no such thing, Ms. Rune. Is that really what you believe? What you think you're going to find?"

"It's what I know," she said, then swallowed. Unless she was crazy and having weird delusions. But, if she really had some remnant psychic abilities, could she seriously be getting information from her great-great-great-grandmother... Hell. It sounded crazy even to her.

She eyed the stone wall, the tiny fissures and bits of dirt and moss clinging to the sides, a long-legged, wobbly spider climbing up the side. As crazy as it sounded, she'd come here in search of a vision she'd seen, and she hadn't even considered that she might not make it. Well, that she might not succeed. Whether or not she survived this little quest of hers, she darned well intended to take out the EMP weapon before she died.

Her back felt sticky as the room got more uncomfortable. Oberon maintained a cool and comfortable exterior, perched on a bolder in the back corner of the cave. He'd even removed his T-shirt and socks. That made her a little uncomfortable. She had never seen that kind of rugged musculature in a man.

Because of the way he sat on the rock, Darla noticed the scar on his left shoulder for the first time. Thick scar tissue flared up his back and reminded her of the thickness of her own branding scar.

"I have something to tell you, Darla. Something the James family has never told an outsider before. We've survived the last two hundred years by following prophecies left to us by a psychic who lived before the War of Neutrality." He sighed. "At her insistence, my family moved underground into bunkers specially created for the years that would follow the devastation. While EMP weapons were used and electricity went out everywhere and homeland wars and nuclear fallout ravaged the surface of North America, we were safe in our bunker underground. My family thrived, reproduced and continued. We came to the surface only occasionally to follow prophecies. Or to find a suitable mate for the next James progeny."

"Sounds like you had it a lot better than most of us," she said, not admitting that Rud had already told her some of it.

"I'm merely telling you this because even with Maribel's prophecies, things don't always go the way we expect. Our lives are as tenuous as anyone's."

He held out his callused palms and analyzed them. "There were times when my family so badly wanted to share what we had in order to make other people's lives better. But, if we wanted to carry out the wishes of the psychic, no one else could be told. No matter what, we had to keep our underground sanctuary secret. Each generation received messages to be opened only by the eldest child. Those prophecies gave directions on how we must proceed for the next few decades."

"How could someone from two hundred years ago tell you how to live your life? How could she possibly know what life would be like in the future?" And why help the James family have a good life while her own family suffered?

"I still don't totally understand my role in your prophesy?"

"It has everything to do with you. Your name has been the topic of the prophecies since the day you were born. Apparently, you're the only one who can save us. Save everyone from the horrors of the world as it is. You, Darla Rune, are the great-great-great-granddaughter of our prophet, Maribel."

If he expected a surprised reaction, he must've been disappointed. She merely shrugged, because Rud had already told her that part, too. Not to mention, she'd received her own message when she'd held the parchment.

"But, why did my family live in poverty and despair while yours lived in luxury?"

"I don't know. It doesn't make sense to me, either."

"Yeah, well, what if the prophesy has it wrong? I'm not anything special."

The thought crossed her mind that her mother earned a fair living as a psychic. Was it in their bloodline? Maybe the reason Darla had the useless ability to reverse-engineer dead technology? "Okay, suppose what you say is true. What do you make of what the prophecy says about me?"

One hand shoved through his hair, working the muscles in his bicep. "I haven't had a chance to read it."

"Well, Mister Ruler of the Country, I hate to disappoint you, but I can't help you."

His expression remained detached, as if he really didn't care what she said. "I have to believe you must have some ability that can help us."

Darla's hands clenched at her sides. If Maribel could ensure the James family lived well, why had she been through literal hell on Earth? Her mother's life hadn't been much better. And how had Maribel been able to direct her toward Vestro in the middle of a dangerous Nevermore?

Questions. Lots of questions.

"You took the parchment from Rud. Read it."

He nodded. His ruffled dark hair made him look younger, somehow. "I'm going to once we get settled."

The heat built steadily in the cave, which was about twenty feet long and eight feet across. She unzipped her Uvlar a little more and bit her lip when she saw Oberon stifle a grin. "It's not funny. I'm not wearing underthings that give as much coverage as yours."

The smile wiped off his face instantly. His expression darkened. "That is a problem," he said.

"Yeah. I'm not used to parading around in my skivvies

in front of strange men." Certainly not in front of men she wanted to kill first chance she got.

"It's not like I haven't seen it all before," he said, as if he wasn't interested anyway. Bastard.

"I don't care what you've seen. You haven't seen me."

Oberon got up and sat on the small bolder in the middle of the cave, facing the other direction. "You're right. I'm being totally inconsiderate. Go ahead. I'll keep my back turned."

"Except for one thing," Darla said.

"What would that be?"

"The opening is in the other direction. What if something decides to break in?"

"Then it won't matter what you have on. It'll only matter that we make it out in one piece."

She wiped sweat off her brow. "You have a point." Still, she hesitated.

"Darla, you've got to get cool. We only have one bottle of water. If you continue to sweat without the ability to hydrate yourself, you'll be in a bad way. I need you to retain as much moisture as you can until morning."

Now that made sense. "Since you put it that way." She peeled off her gear.

She saw his shoulders move. Chuckling? Damn him. She could also see more fresh scars on the back of his neck. He'd been seriously injured and not that long ago if the ugly redness of the healing wounds was any indication.

"May I turn around?" he asked, his voice lowered, and this time she could tell he held back laughter.

"No."

She looked down at herself. Great day to be wearing

skimpy underthings. Jack had given them to her at the shop along with the Uvlar gear. Now she wished she'd insisted on something that covered her a lot better.

She heard parchment unfolding. Oberon read the message again. She'd like to see his expression.

Sitting on top of her leather gear, she stretched her legs out and watched Oberon's head bent over the message. It couldn't be easy to read in the faint light of the torch.

"What do you think it means?" she asked.

He sighed, and even though he stared at the wall in front of him, his shoulders knotted. "I'm not sure what Rud told you, but it seems to me this is the final message. The very last one."

"You sound saddened by that."

He swung around and eyed her—from head to toe. "I sound frigging terrified by that. This whole time your ancestor has been preparing us for a helluva fight. We've been gathering weapons. We've been building an army of people who are sympathetic to our cause. But we never knew when the final message would come."

"I'm not sure I understand the gravity," she lied. She had seen her own version of his message as a vision in her head, even though she hadn't read it. Either she stopped Vestro or all would be lost. Humanity for humanity's sake would be a memory. The deviants and creatures would take over, create a new world order, and mankind would be nothing more than sweetmeat.

She prayed the images in her head were wrong.

* * * * *

Oberon read the prophesy again. How could Darla Rune be the woman who saved them all? She'd very nearly been taken by Vestro's creatures tonight. Her obvious vulnerability had taken him by surprise. But then, nowhere on the parchment did it say she'd be a one-woman warrior—so what were her talents? How could she save them? And what did the Neo-Verolli Casket, the box that had been in the vault with the prophesy, have to do with it?

"Do you have any special fighting abilities, Darla?"

"Not really," she said after a pause. "I know how to stay out of the way, though."

His hand fisted, and the parchment twisted between his fingers. "I'm not sure how we're going to carry out this final message. It seems impossible for one woman, or one woman and one man, to carry it out."

"One woman and two men," she said. "Don't forget your brother."

Oberon hadn't forgotten his brother. Odds were, his brother had died by now. No way would he make it back to the city covered with blood. He'd been heartsick about that since he'd sent his brother on his way. Had he sent him to his death?

"Yes, my brother. He's young, and not very experienced…" But then, so was Darla. Maybe the two of them had more in common than he'd previously considered. "But Rud's heart is that of a warrior."

"Meaning mine isn't?"

"I'm sure it is," he said.

"He'll make it back," she said, as if she knew what his thoughts were. Her grandmother had been a seer, but Darla had shown no such abilities. None, in fact. Maybe Maribel had been mistaken. Maybe she hadn't realized the family's psychic abilities would wane with each generation. At least, it didn't seem like Darla had any extra abilities.

He'd seen some of Vestro's experiments. He'd found secret lab documents that not even his own council knew about. Horrific things were being done to what was left of mankind. How had Vestro gained the ability to do such unconscionable things?

He eyed his watch and shifted his position on the rock to stare at the wall again.

"You can't sit on a rock all night," Darla said.

"I can. And I will," he answered.

"Okay, never mind what I'm wearing. At this point, what does it matter? Besides, I'm really hungry, and I'm hoping since you brought water you also brought food?"

He shifted again and turned his head just enough to see her in the muted torchlight. He wasn't sure he wanted to see her. She did things to his thought processes whether she was fully clothed or half naked. He needed his wits about him, now more than ever.

"Yes, I brought some fruit, bread, cheese and dried meat." He expected the silence he got. Three of the foods he'd mentioned were nearly nonexistent commodities for most people. He'd been working on ways to get these foods back into the food chain, without causing rioting and fighting. An even and instantaneous distribution would be the only first step possible.

"I won't eat those," she said.

Now, that response he hadn't expected. "Why?"

"Why would I eat something that normal people can't have? Do you think you're better? That you deserve such food?"

* * * * *

Had she really just said that? She'd stolen bread from

the Benevolent carts on more than one occasion. Her stomach rumbled again.

"No. I don't think the distribution of food is fair. I intend to change it as soon as I can. But for now, I grabbed the fastest thing I could from the kitchen because you never know how long we might be stranded. This could be the difference between life and death for us."

She merely glared at him.

He smiled tautly. "A lot of people feel the way you do. Even though people's lives were horrible under Vestro's rule, change is scary. People just don't know who to trust, especially since my takeover wasn't democratic."

"Why did you take over by force, then? Didn't that send an equally bad message to society?"

"I didn't have a choice. Even Maribel thought so…" His words trailed off as if he sometimes disagreed with Maribel's recommendations. "As long as Vestro remained in power, there would never be a chance at democracy."

He ripped off a piece of bread and a strip of dried meat. "Eat this, and then try to get some sleep. It's going to be a long night and a longer day tomorrow."

"Oberon, for what it's worth, I think Rud is going to be okay. You're right, I'm not psychic—at least not in the powerful way that Maribel seemed to be, but I have a sense that your younger brother will make it."

He didn't meet her gaze this time. His hair was ruffled, and his bangs hung low on his forehead over one eye. A feathering of hair low on the back of his neck struck a strange chord inside her. Where had that feeling of familiarity come from? "I can tell you don't believe me. That makes sense. More sense than the fact that your family has been following words on parchments for generations."

His eyes narrowed on her, and she bit her lip.

"I know it's all confusing and unbelievable, but it's real," he said. "And you are the woman who will lead us out of the darkness."

Crap. A lot of responsibility to place at the feet of an outcast who spent too much time in the Boneyard and whose delusional daydreams about another century had led them on a quest that would probably get them both killed. She ate her food quickly. If she didn't savor it, maybe it wouldn't be quite so wrong.

"I'm tired. I need to sleep," she said, when she was done eating. She needed to allow her mind to go blank. To forget the burden of these new responsibilities.

As it got warmer in the cave, the air felt close. "Do we have enough oxygen in here?"

"Plenty. There are a few openings in the ceiling."

Her eyes widened. "Really?"

"Relax, they're not big enough for predators to get in. Just big enough to keep our air from giving out."

She settled down on top of her leather suit, pushing the clips and buttons to the side so they wouldn't stick her. Her suit might be warm, but it was preferable to sleeping on the rock and dirt.

After she closed her eyes, she heard Oberon open the prophecy again. After a long while, he sighed and folded it back up. She started to drift off.

Horns honked in the street, and Darla walked along the sidewalk to her apartment. She glanced at her watch and cursed. Shoot. She needed those papers before she could meet her client, but she'd taken too long getting home. She'd be late.

She leaned back and stared at a skyscraper sparkling

like jewels in the sunshine. A passerby gawked at her like she'd lost her mind.

She ran her hands over her outfit. Midsummer, and she wore a sunny lime sundress with lines and dots, and matching shoes and purse.

"Darling, you're going to be really late if you don't hurry," a male voice said. He came up behind her and planted his lips on the nape of her neck. She should've screamed and fought him off, but in this version of her world, she felt safe. Butterflies lifted inside her, and she turned to see vibrant blue eyes staring into hers. Laughing eyes. His fingers fiddled with her hair, and he had a wry grin on those sexy lips. "You're never going to change. Your head is always in the clouds, my sweet."

She laughed. She heard the sound of her own voice, but somehow it sounded foreign. Like she really had joy in her life. Had something to be happy about.

"I'm sorry. It's just that the buildings are so magnificent today. Look how the light is reflecting off the metal and glass. It's really something to see."

He laughed low in his throat. "Only you would appreciate something like that." He checked the gold watch on his tanned arm. He wore a short-sleeved shirt and no protection on his face or body. They both stood in the outside air, unprotected, and yet the air felt wonderful, smelled fresh.

She inhaled. "I've died and gone to heaven, haven't I?"

"Oh, sweetie, you're in some kind of altered state of reality, aren't you?" He rubbed her chin. "Earth to Darla, Earth to Darla."

"Funny," she said and smacked him gently.

"Let's get going. Your grandmother will be having a

fit that you're late again. She has some sort of congressman she wants you to meet."

A teeny kernel of worry formed in her solar plexus and began to grow. But the cacophonies of sounds made by this city were music to her ears. Horns, voices, rumbling machinery, music filtering out of restaurants and vehicles, total and continuous noise—all of it wonderful—all of it wrong.

She stepped off the curb and heard the screech of a vehicle. She heard an impact, and everything went black.

"Darla, Darla," he said, shaking her shoulder.

She moved her head back and forth, moved her fingers and legs. Were they broken? He shook her again. "Wake up. You're having a bad dream."

She shifted up onto her elbows then opened her eyes. She'd been almost afraid to see what had happened to her body when the car hit her. But when she'd opened her eyes, the reality rushed back into her dark world. She'd never seen a skyscraper. Had never ridden in a car. She'd never smelled fresh air other than that in the governor's garden. Why did she imagine these things?

Oberon pressed forward on his knees. He held out one hand and wiped at a tear on her face. "It must've been a doozy of a nightmare."

She nodded, reluctantly. Her nightmare had enhanced the muddy weight of the reality they lived in. The added weight of the dangers she faced right now.

Her nightmare faded quickly, as always, but seeing those eyes that close to her right now, his mouth so near. He felt familiar. More familiar than he had been before she'd gone to sleep.

"Have you got a gold watch?" she asked.

"What? No." He held out his right arm to prove it.

"My watch is silver. Are you okay?"

She sniffed. The dankness and stale air filled her nostrils and lungs, and she wanted to cry again. She wanted the air she'd breathed in her dream. Fresh and sweet, and rejuvenating. And the man who'd been with her…his image had faded. She couldn't remember anything but the blue eyes.

She ran a hand over her moist face. She shifted to look at Oberon. His dark brows were drawn together, and his blue eyes monitored her closely. Those eyes. Those beautiful, familiar blue eyes. "You're him," she breathed. "You're really him."

"I'm sorry?" He felt her forehead. "Did you get scratched by one of the creatures outside? You might have a fever."

"No fever," she said. Still on her elbows, she leaned toward him. His eyes widened and his crouch tightened, but he didn't back away. She pushed herself to a sitting position and grabbed the front of his T-shirt and pulled him toward her.

"This won't hurt," she said, her voice wandering off when her mouth deliberately collided with his. They fit together like a dream. The sensation of his mouth against hers made a soft buzzing sound inside her head. White noise. The perfect sound for someone whose life revolved around fake images and sounds. She needed to blot out the craziness.

He kissed her obligingly and without complaint, but with no emotion, taking one for the team. Finally, she stopped and shoved him back. The dream had gone now, and so had the need to connect with her blue-eyed man. At least, that's what she told herself.

"Sorry. I don't usually do things like that," she said.

He swallowed and smiled at her. "It's not something I'm likely to complain about. Did it help drive your bad dream away?"

She shrugged. "I don't remember the dream. It's gone." She ran a hand through her damp hair. "May I have some water?"

He handed her the bottle. "Just take a few sips. No telling how long our supply will have to last."

"What time is it?"

"About three o'clock in the morning."

"Have you slept?"

"No," he stated. "One of us needs to keep guard."

"Why don't you try to catch a couple of hours? It's not likely I'll go back to sleep now." In fact, no way in hell would she sleep again tonight.

"Good idea. We both need a few hours." He moved back to his spot on the floor. Neither of them used the makeshift bed. The aged and rotten leather wouldn't hold them anyway. "Wake me if anything happens, even the slightest scratching noise."

She watched him stretch out on his Benevolent gear. Silence filled the cave. Almost like her ears were plugged with fluid. Or underwater. She didn't like it here. Sweat dripped off her brow, and she swiped the moisture off her face. One quick glance at Oberon, and she noted his skin glistening with moisture. Funny that it got so hot in here, because it'd most likely be cool outside after dark. Even in summer the evenings were cool.

She heard a noise, and her heart started to hammer. Glancing at the piece of metal blocking the door, she didn't think the sound came from there, anyway. Something dropped from a tiny hole in the ceiling and scurried to the back of the cave.

She sighed and shook her head. "Field mouse, you're going to wish you stayed outside." Then she realized the mouse could've dropped inside to save itself from being eaten by something much bigger.

Suddenly, she respected the mouse's choice. She felt like they were in the same situation.

* * * * *

The fact that Darla had finally stripped down to her underwear affected him less than the fact that he could see her bare flesh in the low light of the cave. He stared at the horrible scar on her forearm, and his stomach contracted, threatened to expel the little bit of food he'd had.

He hadn't realized she was the girl he'd branded all those years ago, until he'd seen the scar on her arm in the gardens of Government House. He'd done that to her. To Darla Rune, their prophesied savor. Now he understood why Vestro had ordered him to brand the young girl who'd been innocent.

He'd burned her badly. But even worse, he'd single-handedly left her alone in the world to starve. Very few people survived when they didn't have access to the food carts that delivered scraps of rotting and stale food doled out by Vestro. And as a branded dissident, Darla would not have had access to the food, and she'd have been forced to move away from her family. To try to find a way to survive on her own.

And if she'd died, Vestro would have been free to rule without threat of her interference. That made him think Vestro had known about the prophesy, too. But how?

He grimaced at the thought of how Vestro had used him. But then, he remembered how she'd dared grab the brand and slam it into his back. Hell, the pain had been excruciating, but it had made him feel better somehow. He'd deserved to suffer the same pain as her.

He turned onto his side. He needed to stop thinking. To sleep. Images and responsibilities continued to swirl in his mind.

He'd only been twenty-three when he received the order from Vestro himself to brand the girl. He looked at Darla again, saw the swell of her breast, the curve of her belly, and the rise of her hip. A little on the thin side, somehow she'd survived. And she'd done it without help from anyone.

He swallowed hard and closed his gritty eyes. He could still see those large, innocent green eyes staring up at him from the alleyway that day he'd captured and branded her. She'd have been safe enough hiding in the alley if he hadn't been told where to find her.

Only fourteen. Already beautiful. Long, red hair and beautiful skin for a young woman of Central City.

She'd been so untouched, until he'd marked her with that white-hot brand in the shape of the letter D.

CHAPTER FIFTEEN

"Wake up." Darla shoved Oberon's foot with her boot three hours later. She'd dressed while he slept. It had been the tiny pinpricks of light leaking in through the holes in the cave ceiling that indicated they needed to get going. The sooner they made their next move, the better. Traveling out here would be even more dangerous if they had deviants looking for them.

While she'd been keeping watch, she'd been listening to the voice in her head. She'd seen images of where they had to go next. A stream that meandered through the wilds. An anomaly in the vast wasteland of scrub and brush. She remembered the full-grown trees in that marshy field where they'd been ambushed. The trees were like hope springing from the ashes, their green leaves not stunted but lush and reaching for the sky.

Find the stream, echoed in her mind.

"Morning to you, too," Oberon said, rubbing a hand over his eyes. "Did I get more sleep than you?"

"No. We both got a few hours. I'd say we're pretty

much equal." That said, it felt like half the sand from the floor of the cave clung to her eyeballs. Fatigue still clawed at her, but that might be partially because of the dead air inside.

He yanked his clothes on, grabbed his backpack and dug out a hunk of bread for each of them. "Wish I could offer you a cup of steaming tea to go with this," he said.

She smiled. She'd had tea once and loved it. She'd heard a small plantation grew tea somewhere out here. Only special people got tea. A reminder of why she hated the society that Oberon represented.

She had created her own herbal concoction from dried flowers and certain twigs. A nice concoction, actually. She'd even started bartering it along with her soaps lately.

"When we find the stream today, we can fill our water bottles there."

"Stream?" He frowned. "We can't drink water out here. It's contaminated."

"Well, I think this water is going to be drinkable."

He shook his head and shrugged. First time he actually didn't seem to believe in the possibility of prophecies, maybe because the prophecy came through her and not from a dried-out piece of parchment. She didn't blame him.

He handed her the water bottle, and she took enough water to wash down the lovely yet slightly stale bread.

He swallowed even less water. He really didn't believe they'd find the stream.

"Water isn't fit to drink out here unless it's been boiled, treated and filtered. As well you know."

"This water is coming from an aquifer deep underground, from a source that is no longer affected by the devastation. It's cold and pure and unpolluted." She paused. "It's a sign of change and the possibilities for the future." Whoa. Where had that come from?

He grunted and zipped up his blackener and pulled on his hood and face shield. Leaving only those blue eyes to taunt her. "It would be nice not to have to wear a face shield outside, but that's not going to happen any time soon. And, even if we find a stream, I very much doubt that the water is drinkable."

Jerk. She waited while he pushed back the steel circle that had kept them safe overnight. Guns at the ready, they both crawled out. The best version of fresh air she'd ever get, she imagined, sucking in some slightly less stale air through her face shield.

Blue sky broke through the yellow clouds in the east, only the second time she'd seen a streak of blue in the sky.

Oberon stopped and stared at the sky for a moment. "Which way do we go?" he finally asked, positioning his weapons for use.

"This way," Darla said, pointing to the west.

"Okay, stay close behind me," he said. "Without a footpath, brush is the worst to get through. Animals can get dangerously close to you, and you won't even know they're there until they attack."

She should have been afraid, but she couldn't stop thinking about Rud. "I'm sure he made it."

Oberon's eyes mirrored her unspoken fear. "He's young, but he's smart. If anyone could have made it in the state he was in, Rud could."

"Why'd you do it?"

"Do what?"

"Why'd you choose me over your brother?"

A shadow fell over his eyes. "You know why. I believe in Maribel's prophecies. So does Rud. We both want to make this hellhole of a world a better place."

"So you don't mind that he stole the papers from you?"

"That was a stupid thing for him to do, but honestly, I understand why he did it. I'd probably have done the same thing in his shoes."

A twig snapped nearby, and Darla's footsteps faltered. Had something moved in the brush beyond? She scanned her surroundings. A sea of knee-high scrub.

* * * * *

"Bring that box to me," Vestro ordered. "And make it snappy."

"Which one, sir?"

Vestro's blood pressure hiked instantly. He hated to be questioned. "The one that I always want this time of the day."

His servant, one of the few pure humans left on his staff, bowed several times then rushed to get his needle and mood enhancer. His moods were getting continually darker, so much so that he had a hard time controlling his dark side. As if his evil alter ego fought to take over.

He laughed, and his servant blinked at him nervously. Not like he ever had a good side. He'd always enjoyed doing nasty things to people.

"Out. Out of here," he said, waving the servant off. The second the door shut, he closed his eyes and injected the liquid drug into his system and felt the wave of deliciousness that followed. The wave of dark fantasy that he intended to make reality.

"You're into that drug again."

Vestro's eyes slowly focused on the apparition in the corner. "What's it to you, Rhino?"

The image wavered like a ripple on a pond. "You're supposed to be stopping the Rune woman."

"I heard from my men that she is looking for me. She's in the Nevermore, as we speak. If she's still alive, that is."

"Your men are a far cry from what you need for an army. I had you all set up as governor. You shouldn't have let that bastard James get the upper hand. You can't take over with your warped gene pool of creatures."

Vestro laughed. "That's where you're wrong."

"You knew nothing about genetics until I came along and taught you. Don't forget your knowledge comes from me. Your rise to the top only happened because I gave you the means to do so."

Vestro laughed, and his head wobbled. He held up the empty vial. "That's funny, I thought my uncle taught me the family business. Genetics. My side of the family kept labs and taught each generation how to create life and drugs down through the centuries. You can't take credit."

"Can't I?"

Vestro made a disgusted noise at the back of his throat. "You can't. And, no matter what you think you know, the tides have changed. I'm going to do what I want to from now on."

"That wasn't our deal."

"Maybe before I realized you were using me."

Rhino cursed.

Vestro's fingers floated in the air for effect. "You fooled me for quite a while, but you did help me gain knowledge and assets. For that I'm grateful. But grateful in my books means very little. I'd kill you as quick as look at you if you were here in person. You and I are done, so you can go to hell."

"You still need me, Vestro. This woman will annihilate you. She's the only one who can."

"Why would I believe this woman is dangerous? In fact," Vestro said, giving his crotch a rub, "I'm going to have fun with her if she makes it here in one piece. And she better."

"If you let the EMP machine go off-line mankind will re-create itself without you, you dumb shit. You won't be able to stop them."

Vestro blew out a languid breath. "No one can get to the EMP machine. Number one…my creatures have been well educated in what will happen to them if they let anyone near."

"Torturing your own damned deviants. That is so fucked up, Vestro."

"So much for your insights." Vestro laughed and slowly inhaled. A fresh rush of adrenaline coursed through him while the second wave of the drug reached his brain. Now the light show really began.

Tired of working in Petri dishes and with victims who'd been exposed to the atmosphere for too long, he'd revamped the program. Another nudge, and his crotch jumped to life. Yeah, he wanted her alive. He rang the bell on his desk. Holding the old school bell, he clanged it loud enough to bring the building down around him. At least, that's the way it sounded in his head.

His servant ran in, worry evident on his face.

"Send word again that Darla Rune and her companions must not be hurt. Sometimes my soldiers get over exuberant. This is extremely important." She had to die. But not yet. He wanted her first. If he took her, then killed her while in the middle of his release, he'd absorb her power.

"Yes, sir. By the way…" he swallowed hard. "The first wave of your…" the servant hesitated, and swallowed again, "Your soldiers haven't returned on schedule, sir. The second group should be returning any minute. They were sent to find out what happened to the first ones. They have been told not to harm Ms. Rune and Mister James, but I will reinforce that information immediately."

"How do you propose to do that?" Vestro felt his grasp of reality slipping. About to dive headlong into the murderous delights of his medicated delusions.

"I'm sending Brawn to give the message."

"Ah, Brawn. My most amazing creation," he said and fell head first onto his desk, a grin slicing his face.

CHAPTER SIXTEEN

"How do you explain the occasional streak of blue in the sky and the moon showing through the clouds the last two nights?" she asked Oberon while they trudged through the brush.

"Fluky."

"Really? Is that what you honestly think? It's been two hundred years since the devastation. Have you ever seen blue sky before? "

"Don't get your hopes up, Darla. You'll be disappointed." His eyelids lowered and blocked her ability to read his expression, yet somehow she felt his angst for his people.

She shrugged her shoulders back. The weight of her backpack sent stabbing pain through her shoulder blades, and they'd lost the path awhile ago. He strode through the hip-high brush, keeping a sharp eye on their surroundings. The large weapon propped on his shoulder with the butt resting in the palm of his hand must have been heavy. He wore a bigger backpack than hers, as well. No wonder his shoulders were broad and muscular. He'd earned every one of those muscles the hard way.

And if anyone could, he'd get them through the Nevermore in one piece. After all, he'd kept them alive overnight. A miracle in itself.

"I don't understand you," she said. "Especially when you see blue sky for the first time in your life. It's a sign for those who care to see it." Her face shield felt tight today. She'd like to take it off and breathe deeply, to smell the fragrant scents that she seemed to remember from her dreams. "Fresh air is like perfume," she said without thinking.

He laughed and shot her a quick look. "Did you crack your head when that beast forced you out of the tree? How can you possibly know what fresh air smells like?"

"That's just rude." She stomped past him, turning to the right and following a small path through the brush. As usual, clouds hung low in the sky—low and gray with brownish-yellow hues. Their normal world. No thin strips of blue visible anywhere now. Delusional? Maybe. "It's kind of like the air in your gardens, only better."

"Sure, it is," he said in a mocking voice.

"If we take Vestro out of the picture, maybe we'll have a chance."

"Honey, I hate to say it, but I'm afraid you're wishing on stars mankind hasn't seen in centuries."

It would have been so easy to let the derision in his voice sway her from her path. But, she'd learned to believe in herself through very hard times, and she'd learned to scrounge and fight for whatever she needed to survive. Well, now there was more than just her life at stake. Much more, and she had to believe in herself in a way she never had before. And she had to make him believe in her, too.

As much as she hated to admit it, she needed him if she were to succeed. He'd proved that yesterday.

"Stars. Most people don't even know what they are. The only reason I do is because I've seen them in an old magazine." She tipped her head. "How do you know about them?"

"My family had books. Lots of them."

She bit her lip and spat out a curse. "Of course you did. And you didn't think to share? Maybe to try to improve lives?"

"No. Vestro wouldn't have allowed books to be shared. He would have kept them for himself or burned them. And they'd have been lost forever. It's my dream to create a place where people can learn to read, and then my family will donate the books to Central City. I'd like to see your magazine, too."

Darla described the magazine, as well as the vibrant pictures of a living planet, as she followed him along the narrow path. "Colors that would stop your heart," she said finally, then realized they'd stopped walking again and his eyes were smiling at her. Her breath caught in her throat. She didn't want to think of him as a man who'd smile at her whimsy. She wanted to hate him with every breath she took. The pictures in her magazine had been faded, but the hues and the vibrancy of how the world could be were imparted in those pictures. It had given her hope for what might be.

He monitored the path ahead. "We have a long distance to go, and there's no way we'll reach those mountains today. We'll have to find sanctuary before dusk." He paused. "If we make it that far."

She gazed at the mountain in the distance, then back at

Oberon. "We have to go there. To that mountain," she said and pointed at the most distant peak.

He tore his gaze away from her and scanned the mountain top. "You're kidding, right?"

"No."

"That's not where Vestro is," he said.

No matter what he said, she strongly felt Vestro had a facility inside that mountain. "You sure?"

"I'm pretty sure. Vestro is at a power plant at the base of that mountain, though."

If his face hadn't been mostly covered, she could have seen his expression right now. The expression he'd honed as dictator du jour. Muscles would be working in his sculpted jaw while dark lashes shadowed his eyes.

A branch snapped in the surrounding brush—way too close for comfort. She jumped, felt her skin prickle, and instantly moved closer to Oberon. Then she heard the ungodly scream, like a woman being tortured.

"It's another cat," he said in a low tone.

"Not the 'here, kitty kitty' type, I'm guessing." She tried to sound light, but her teeth were beginning to chatter.

He snapped the gun from his shoulder with one arm. That explained why his arms were thick and muscled. It took strength to handle the weapons soldiers used. He held it out while releasing the safety with his thumb.

The scream happened again, and she saw brush moving to her left. Oberon had already caught the movement and fired three rounds at the animal charging them. A cat, some sort of cougar, leapt into the air just as one of the oversized bullets struck and dropped it to the ground.

She'd hadn't seen many of these creatures in the

Boneyard. But, then again, there weren't many animals there. Nothing but metal and plastic, and Yardmen, who probably ate whatever wandered into their territory.

She watched Oberon's back as he stepped forward and pushed the cat with his foot. His eyes never left the surrounding brush, and the gun remained ready to fire. Then she heard it. Mewling.

"She had kittens?" She stepped forward, but he held up a hand to stop her progress.

He shook his head in the negative. "She's a he."

"Oh." She took another look at the cat and realized he was right.

Oberon covered his mouth with a finger. "Shhhh."

She had no idea what would mimic the sound of a cougar's babies. Something smarter than a baser animal. That idea alone scared the holy living Benevolent out of her.

Oberon made a similar mewling sound. Silence, then a response. He bit back an expletive. "It's watching us. Waiting for us to make a wrong move."

"What is it?"

"An abomination of nature," he said in a serious voice. "Part human, part animal. Smart, vicious, cunning and hungry. Always hungry."

"Why do they exist?" she asked, more to herself than to him.

"That's something I hope to find out as governor. To eradicate the inhuman creatures who prey on people."

She liked the sound of that.

"Get behind me." He made the luring sound again, and his body braced to use the weapon. His shoulders bunched.

She hated everything this man stood for. That made it

hard for her to follow his orders, even when they made sense, but she'd try to do what he told her to out here.

Glad he had the strength to stand against a horrendous creature in order to protect her, she wondered again, why? Why was she important to him? To a grandmother two centuries before? She reached for her own weapon and prepared to use it.

He glanced back at her then down at the pistol in her hand. "Please point that away from my back," he said in a low voice and through his teeth.

"Oh. Sorry." Okay, so she didn't really know how to use weapons. She pointed the gun at the brush. Wind riffled through the scrub, masking the actual advance of the creature, until it died down again. She swallowed hard.

Oberon stood ready, until ten feet in front of them, the thing rose out of the brush and stood up on two legs.

She gasped at the sight. Nothing at all like she'd expected. So different from the Yardmen and the beasts in the clearing. It had a human shape, arms, legs, but the similarity ended there. It had a snout and slanted eyes more intelligent than an animal's. The teeth were jagged, and it drooled continually. It had hands, but the fingers were stubby, only one knuckle on each finger, and dangerous looking heavy, pointed nails. Skin sagged, hung over the eyes and drooped off its bones like it had melted. And it appealed to them like a small child, afraid and alone.

She gasped. The creature's expression surprised her. Like a child, somehow aware and terrified. She stepped forward. "Don't hurt it. It's afraid," she said.

A firm hand clamped on her shoulder, halting her forward momentum. "Don't be fooled. It'll attack you without a second thought if you get close enough. It's hunting you, and you're falling into its trap."

She hesitated, the sight of those heart-wrenching, sad eyes and big tears affected her. Only Oberon's warning created awareness of those claws flexing in the stubby fingers. "In Benevolent's name, Oberon. How can this be?"

"I'm being very serious, here. Get behind me, Darla. And, please, move slowly."

She stepped back and slid in behind her guardian just as the creature dove for them, baring two rows of jagged, slicing teeth, gnashing and drooling.

Oberon fired and dropped the creature.

They stood for a moment, staring down at the lifeless beast. The combination of child and monster blended into a package meant to fool and kill. A blending that would've gotten Darla killed if she'd been out here alone. She shivered, and her skin iced over inside her oven-hot suit.

Oberon didn't shove this body with his boot. He lowered his head, and for a moment Darla thought he'd said a silent prayer. Part human? She saw the man with fresh eyes.

"Let's get moving. There's too much blood here."

She nodded. She'd gotten herself through some terrifying times during her banishment, but out here without Oberon, she'd have been dead by now. The creatures yesterday would have surely captured her, and even if she'd gotten away from them, she'd have certainly died in the Nevermore last night without his expertise.

She stared back at the body on the ground. Even this little, innocuous-looking creature would have been the end of her. She'd thought she learned to be tough. She'd believed she understood the underbelly of this world. Apparently not.

A tear escaped and dropped off her face shield. Emotion, not only for the creature, but for humanity. What it had become. Is that why she had the dreams? To know the difference?

They trudged on for more than an hour without running into any more beasts. Mountains loomed in the distance, but vast miles of brown scrub lay ahead of them. Every now and then, they'd find rubble where a building once existed. Another type of boneyard, only along with the remnants of buildings were the bones of ancestors lost long ago. Bleached white and crumbling away, they'd soon disappear.

She didn't have a watch, but her internal clock worked fairly well. With a hand over her eyes, she scanned their surroundings for signs of the stream. No telling if it really existed. Suddenly, finding the stream meant everything to her. If she believed she could do something to help mankind, then this stream represented the ability to prove it to herself. But tracking a stream from a voice in her head? Yeah. Pretty crazy when she considered it again. She might have found the field yesterday, but a stream with clear water?

Yet, Oberon James, Leader of the New World, believed in the prophecy enough to follow her through the most dangerous place in the world. To protect her. Who was crazier? Her? Or him?

"Have you been out here before?" he asked so suddenly she jumped. They'd been silent for the last hour.

"I've never been past the Boneyard."

"I can't believe you spent time in the Boneyard and survived," he said, stopping and adjusting the heavy rifle, then rubbing the back of his neck. No wonder he found it hard to believe—she obviously couldn't look after herself out here.

Offering a fake carefree shrug, she wouldn't explain to him or anyone her need to touch the defunct technology. Bad enough that Rud had figured some of it out. But he didn't know the whole truth. That was something she'd never told a soul. She could reverse-engineer any dead machinery she touched. Not very useful in a world with continual EMP storms deadening everything she re-created.

"Being branded at the age of fourteen left me little recourse," she said bitterly. "I had to find ways to survive. I learned that I had an ability to create goods that I could barter for food and shelter. Very few people dared venture to the Boneyard, so I had the advantage."

His brows drew together. Anger sparked behind his eyes every time she mentioned being branded a dissident. She did it purposely, to throw it in the face of the governor. Would he make her pay for her smart mouth? Probably. Or maybe because he'd vowed to protect her, and since she could get away with it, she tormented him out of spite.

A rock outcropping caught her eye just as something slithered past her boot, but it kept going. There were boulders strewn around like some giant had played a child's game of marbles with them. She climbed a rubble pile to reach the biggest rock. "Boost me up, will you?'

He didn't say a word before he knelt down and cupped his hands to give her a boost. With his help, she scrambled to the top.

"What do you see?" he asked when she finally stood.

She pulled off her hood and face gear. The air smelled different here. She couldn't put her finger on why. "I can see for miles and miles."

"And?" She heard the disdain in his voice. Probably because her face gear was off again.

"It's all dead and brown-looking." Her voice cracked. She rarely cried, but she'd never been so disheartened. Shouldn't they have found the stream by now? If it existed.

"You should put your gear back on," he said softly. "We don't know how toxic it might be out here, and we have nothing to measure it, nor do we have medicine to counteract its effects."

Ignoring him, she turned slowly with a hand over her eyes. Yellow-brown clouds proliferated near the mountains like giant globs of goo.

"The stream has got to be here." Something inside wouldn't let her believe otherwise.

It surprised her when Oberon climbed up onto the rock and stood beside her.

"Keep looking then," he said and scanned the surroundings.

The sense of futility that had filled her moments ago dissipated. His simple act of helping her look made her regain some hope. Shortly after that, he tapped her hand. "You should put your gear back on."

"Okay." She hated wearing it. And even though it had been part of her existence from the first time she'd stepped outdoors, dreaming about life centuries past, dreams in which she could breathe fresh air, made her ache for the freedom of being outside without protection.

Just about to give up searching, a crack in the clouds

sent down a shaft of light, hitting the ground miles ahead of them. Under its golden glow, colors burst to life before them. Greens and golds and... "Look. Over there," Oberon shouted. Oberon, who sounded excited. "See the blue? I think it's your stream."

Darla started to quake inside. It really did exist. And if the turquoise clarity of the water meant what she thought it did, the water had to be untainted. It had to be.

Oberon got down first, then reached up for her. Hesitating, she climbed down as far as she could on her own before she had to accept his offer. Finally, short of jumping and breaking a leg, she let him help her the rest of the way.

* * * * *

"Okay, we've found the stream. Now, get your gear on," he said more sternly this time. His muscles tightened in his jaw. He'd used his governor's tone without thinking, probably the last thing he should do with her.

She glared at him, but she reluctantly cooperated.

She couldn't stand him. Hell, he didn't blame her. And it would have been even worse if she'd known the whole truth. That he'd been that soldier who'd branded her and walked away, knowing she'd have little chance of survival. He would always wear the shame of that moment as a scar, deeper than any physical scars on his body.

When they reached their destination, the excitement in her beautiful eyes nearly sidelined him. The stream existed. He rubbed his forehead and considered the fact that there were most likely thousands of streams out here. Didn't mean they were safe. He'd seen a few of them in his role as Vestro's general, but they weren't blue or clear like this. He could even see the bottom. He expelled a tired breath and hoped to hell this meant Darla Rune had what it took to carry out the prophecy.

"It's lovely," Darla said, climbing down an embankment for a closer look.

He followed her. Noted the animal tracks near the water. Something had been drinking here. He considered the danger and decided the beasts probably waited until dusk before coming to their water source.

Even so, he adjusted his rifle and took a watchful stance.

"There's nothing here but us," she said, taking off a glove and dangling her fingers in the water.

"Don't."

"It's clear. Can't you see that?"

"Not all toxins can be seen."

"I know that." She flipped some water playfully at him. Then, again, whipped off her face shield and hood. She inhaled deeply. He nearly panicked. What had she been thinking? Too much unfiltered air filled her lungs. How could he protect her if she continued to be so reckless?

"Take a sniff," she said. "The air smells sweet and clean. It can't be foul here."

Because he felt parboiled inside his suit, the temptation to throw caution to the wind and cool down in that clear water struck him. Hold on. Someone had to keep their senses. Someone had to be well when she came down with the shakes and vomiting. He pulled out his flask and swallowed a few drops of water. They didn't have much left.

"Drink?"

"No, thanks."

He frowned. "You need to have a little taste.

Dehydration out here can be deadly all by itself."

"Don't worry. I'll drink some in a bit."

He shrugged. Her hair hung in auburn curls around her shoulders, making her look younger and somehow unspoiled by their circumstances. She pushed her hair up off the nape of her neck, and tiny moist curls and perspiration sparkled on her smooth nape in the unusual sunlight.

He had to get a grip. Stay focused on his duty. They needed a safe place to hole up for the night. "I'll be right back," he said. "Unless you'd like to come with me?" He didn't like the idea of leaving her alone, but he most likely couldn't drag her away, even if he wanted to.

"I'll be fine. Don't worry about me." She crouched down again and dipped her fingers playfully in the clear water. He wondered if it could possibly be as cool as it appeared.

"If you keep doing that, you'll be sick by sundown," he said. Sure as the Benevolent she'd be in trouble. She didn't seem to want to listen. She'd already taken too many chances today. First, by taking off her face shield, and now exposing her flesh to toxins. He'd done very little to stop her. Great protector he was.

"Darla?"

"Um hmm?" She glanced up at him over her shoulder but didn't leave her position near the burbling stream.

"Get your pistol out and watch for predators while I'm gone." Her expression changed. She believed he was patronizing her. He sighed. "I won't be long."

"Take your time. I've got my pistol right here." She pulled it out of her jacket and laid it on a rock nearby, then sat down on the ground next to it. Not a position he liked her to be in. If something pounced, she'd never make it up on time. He opened his mouth to tell her that when her eyes narrowed on him, daring him to lecture her again.

He closed his lips. She'd survived terrible hardship for years on her own, thanks to him. Surely she could get through a few more minutes while he scoped out their surroundings.

He hadn't gotten far when he heard splashing then heard her squeal. With his heart pumping overtime, adrenaline rushed through his veins. He sprinted back to her, afraid of what he'd find when he got there. He should have taken her with him.

He stopped instantly and grabbed his chest over his heart. "What in holy hell do you think you're doing?"

She smiled up the side of the bank at him. Her Uvlar suit lay in a heap on the ground, and she paddled in the stream in her minuscule bra and panties, nearly completely immersed in the water. His legs felt instantly weak. What had she done? With the level of exposure she'd received, she'd most likely die, and he wouldn't be able to help her.

CHAPTER SEVENTEEN

"Benevolent hell, woman. Get out of there immediately."

Darla spun playfully in water up to her chest and grinned at him. The sun had come out all over again. Her smile was more beautiful than the sun itself, if that were possible.

"Wait. You don't understand—"

He cut her off. "Damn it, Darla. You don't understand." He could see every inch of her under the water. Every inch of exposed flesh absorbing God only knew what kinds of toxins.

"It's safe," she said, cupping her hands in the water and drinking from them.

His gut twisted, and he dove toward her. "Have you got a death wish?" He dropped his gear and waded in far enough to grab her hand and physically pull her out.

Of course, she resisted. He'd expected that. The last thing he needed right now was to have his hands on her smooth, bare flesh while she fought him.

Slippery, too. He grabbed her around the waist and lifted her out of the water and dropped her onto the bank, his jaw aching from the tension.

The irony of his situation: He'd agonized over his long-held memory of the fourteen-year-old he'd branded. He'd hoped and prayed she'd survived. And now, when he had a second chance by keeping her safe in the Nevermore, she did everything in her power to die. Not to mention distracting him beyond reason at the same time. Any normal man would have gone loco at the sight of this luscious peach in a place where women were normally tough and stringy. A temptation to any saint. And he was no saint.

"Get your gear on now."

"I'm soaking wet," she said.

"Your point?"

"It won't be easy to get dressed this way. Why don't I just air dry for a couple of minutes first?"

"Why not swallow another gallon of poisoned water while you're at it? Exposure will make you sick enough. I have no idea what that water is going to do to you." He swallowed hard. "Worst-case scenario—you might not make it."

He wished he didn't have to look at her again. The cold water had left her with a rosy flush. With eyes averted, he fought against his own hormones not to stare. And he wanted to stare. If she died, it'd be his damned fault. He hadn't protected her the way he should have. The way the prophecy told him to.

"I'm fine. I feel fine."

"Great. If you're still able to stand tomorrow, I'll congratulate you." He checked the sky. "That is, if we're able to find a place to hole up for the night and we don't get eaten first." It didn't give him a thrill to terrify her, but she didn't seem to get it. They were in the most dangerous place they could be, and she'd just made it ten times worse. She needed to be at least a little bit afraid of what she'd just done to herself.

* * * * *

Oberon's perturbed voice broke through Darla's euphoria. She heard the fear in his voice, loud and clear. She suddenly realized he had a deeply entrenched family obligation to her, and he was trying his darnedest to fulfill that obligation. And he must take it pretty seriously if he'd leave his comfy office to come out here in the Nevermore and put his life on the line to do it.

Alone with her. No soldiers to back him up.

She felt suddenly ashamed of her actions. But her skin still tingled and felt fresh from the water, which had tasted so sweet. Could she have been so wrong?

Newly aware of Oberon's obligations and his obvious discomfort at her near nakedness, she flushed. To try to make amends, she yanked the suit on over her damp body in jerky motions, suddenly aware of how she must look, standing here next to naked.

He must think she'd lost her mind. And no wonder, after her prudishness in the cave. Somehow, at the first sign of a clear stream, it had all gone out the window.

"I really think I'll be okay, Oberon." She used his name in a familiar way for the first time.

One eyebrow rose suspiciously.

"I was reckless, and I'm sorry. I won't do it again until it's necessary."

"Won't do what again until it's necessary? Jump in a stream in your underwear?"

"I won't do anything reckless again until it's necessary." And somehow she knew at some point, her journey would involve being reckless. She just hoped she had the strength when the time came.

"You're a confusing woman. I'd prefer it if you said you wouldn't do anything reckless again, period." He stared into her eyes, the only part of her that he could see now. His expression conveying deep concern for her craziness, but relief that she had covered herself. "Yeah. That's me, confusing."

"Why did you take that chance in the stream?"

She averted her gaze.

"If you'd stop trying to sabotage me, I'm trying to keep you safe," he said, speaking through teeth clenched tightly together. Then he cursed under his breath and scoped out their surroundings. "That is, if I can keep you alive tonight after your antics in the stream."

* * * * *

Vestro woke with a start. His back ached. Slowly lifting his head off the desk to stop the room from spinning, he smacked his dry mouth. It felt like cotton balls had been shoved in there during the night.

How many nights had he spent sleeping on his desk like this? Too many. He'd have to start taking his...medicine... in bed. That way, he'd be more comfortable when he came to.

He lifted an arm to run shaky fingers through his sparse hair. One whiff of perspiration, and his stomach protested. He couldn't abide being unclean. He took at least three showers a day.

He staggered to the shower stall and turned on the water. His servant already had the stove burning, filled with grass bricks made by some enterprising person in Central City. He gritted his teeth. He'd have that enterprising person shot. After stealing his techniques, mind you. He didn't want anyone to become enterprising under his regime. First thing you know, the people would want democracy if they grew too independent.

He felt the hot water with his fingers then stepped inside. He needed this as much as his morning coffee ritual. The greenhouses in his buildings were able to produce some of the most exotic delicacies. Products that used to be commonplace in the world had become all but extinct. Well, he had coffee and a few other things that were now nonexistent for the riffraff. Most citizens didn't even know about coffee. Or spices. He had a particular penchant for cinnamon. He even allowed his soldiers a portion of cinnamon when they did something well.

He smiled. Hot water sluiced over his naked body. Over his arms, his legs. When had he gotten so thin? His ribs were even showing. Maybe Rhino had been right. He needed to slow down on the "medicine."

A sharp rap on the bathroom door made him drop his bar of old-world milled soap that miraculously still smelled fragrant.

"What do you want?"

"There's an important matter you might want to deal with when you've finished your shower." The voice scratched like nails on a piece of tin. Sniveling and nasal. Vestro grimaced. Just a hair's breadth away from freaking out at the idiot for interrupting him, he got out and dried off, pissed off that he hadn't gotten to enjoy his shower. His stomach gurgled. When had he eaten last?

He stepped into his office to find Brawn sitting on the settee in the corner, making it look like a doll chair. A

Yardman with a twist. Only, Brawn had more intelligence. He had the body and the wide mouth, the soulless eyes, but he had brains. At least enough for him to reason—and to do what he'd been told.

Brawn watched Vestro carefully. He always did that. Vestro wondered what he was thinking. Always thinking. That scared Vestro just a bit. Except for Blip, his miniature creation, he might've gone too far this time. He'd pretty much failed with the rest of the Yardmen. That's why they were cast out into the Yards. They weren't allowed to leave the premises or they'd suffer their most-feared death—becoming fish food for his sharks.

"What do you want, Brawn? Did you get them?"

Brawn shook his oversized head, his mouth a grim slash. "No. But I found another one for you." Brawn never called Vestro sire or master like the rest of them. He never gave a name to Vestro at all, and Vestro didn't like that. It meant a loss of control.

"What other one?" Vestro frowned and leaned against his desk, suddenly tired. He pressed the intercom. "Breakfast, Blip. Now."

Blip had been standing so quietly bedside Brawn, Vestro hadn't noticed him until he tore out of the room like the hounds of hell were after him. Vestro demanded instant gratification, always. But not from Brawn. Brawn wouldn't react the way the others did.

Brawn might have to become fish food, sooner rather than later.

"I have the brother." Brawn's voice came out low and very quiet but clear enough.

"Brother? What brother?"

"Governor's brother."

"He's not the damned governor, I am!" Vestro's blood pressure nearly sidelined him. Where'd his effing breakfast go? Then he realized he'd better calm down or Brawn wouldn't give him the information he wanted.

"You've got Rudyard? Rudyard James?"

Brawn nodded, but his mouth had clamped shut. Leaving a long cut that needed stitching.

"Is he alive?"

Brawn nodded, his black eyes emotionless. "Got injured by the Beastie Boys, though."

Vestro leaned forward with his hands clamped over his guts. They were cramping, and he wanted to puke. The fact that Brawn had pet names for his creations worried him more than the other issues. It showed Brawn's intelligence might be growing.

"The Beastie Boys are dead now. The governor killed them all."

"I'm the damned—" Vestro stopped in the middle of his tirade. "Oberon killed my devils? How's that possible? They might be as dumb as pucks, but they are as big as you, and they're strong, emotionless killers. They do what they're told without question."

Brawn shrugged his massive shoulders. "Don't know how. Just found their carcasses. Then I tracked the brother on a horse, reeking of blood. I found him easily."

Blip re-entered the room with a plate of steaming eggs and some real bread. Not the fake kind they baked in the city with seeds from the Nevermore. It smelled fresh out of the oven. Vestro sniffed it first then grabbed a hunk off the plate before Blip could even set it down. He crammed it into his mouth and let out a sound of fulfillment. Goddamn, he was starving!

"Coffee? Where is it?" he said with his mouth full.

Seconds later, his tiny failed version of a Yardman staggered back into the office under the tray of coffee. He'd be considered an elf, if one believed or even remembered Irish folklore. That's the only reason Vestro kept him. He fancied reading the tales of pixies and elves. It amused him that he'd created one of his own. And Blip made a very good servant.

Blip poured the steaming cup and held it up to his master.

Vestro took it, ignoring the tiny beast, and swallowed a long, delicious sip. His stomach broiled for a second. Not sure if the brew would stay down, he paused before his next drink. Everything settled, and he finished the mug, then forked down the fluffy eggs and ate the bread as fast as he felt his stomach could take it.

"Where is Rudyard now?" he asked when he'd finally sated his ravenous hunger. He hated the fact that Brawn had stared at him throughout the whole meal. He should've created monsters with more expression. It was a definite downfall not to be able to read his beasts.

"In the Barn."

"With the wolves and the big cats?"

"He's in his own cage. They can't get him." Sometimes Brawn talked like he had a mouth full of marbles. Probably due to his overlarge tongue. Other times, he spoke very clearly.

Vestro patted his stomach. It had finally settled, and he felt like he might live another day. "You failed me, Brawn."

Brawn nodded in agreement, but he didn't cower like the rest of them would have. He didn't seem in the least worried about his failure. Why?

Vestro didn't want to push his luck with his prize

creation. He still needed to find Oberon. "I'll let it slide. This time. At least you brought one of them." He tapped his fingers on his chin, felt a crumb of bread and brushed it off onto the floor. Blip quickly fumbled for it and stuck it in his pocket.

"I'll decide what I'm going to do with him later. I need privacy right now. All of you leave." He hated the wobble in his voice when he should have sounded authoritative and commanding.

When the door shut behind Brawn with a bang, Vestro jumped. Not deliberate, he thought. The beast couldn't help it. Or could he?

* * * * *

Darla stopped for a breather, or maybe she should call it a rebreather? She smirked at her own joke. She hated face shields, so it wasn't really a joking matter. It'd been liberating to breathe without it, to feel the breeze on her body.

"Tired?" Oberon noticed her lagging behind immediately.

"I can keep up. Just needed to take a breath."

They'd been climbing straight up for the last few hours, and they hadn't even reached the mountains yet. She took stock of their surroundings. "There's more debris in the Nevermore than I expected," she said. From this vantage point, she could see for miles.

"Some areas have more debris than others. And every now and then there's a building. Intact. Like nothing happened to the rest of the world. The place with the most debris must have been where the cities used to be. I think they were the hardest hit," she said, breathing heavily. She exhaled again, and her face shield whistled at her next inhale, a warning device created for wearers not to breathe in toxins faster than the filter could handle.

"Slow your breathing," he said calmly.

She rolled her eyes and bit her tongue. As if she hadn't already known that. Hyperventilation in a Uvlar suit could be deadly. Her stomach growled, and she planted her hands on top of it. She didn't think he'd heard it because he'd already started scouting their way forward. How he continued to carry that heavy weapon on his shoulder baffled her. It weighed a ton. But Oberon James never dropped his guard. Never.

Most of the ground cover consisted of weed-like shrubs, stone and gravel. Not very comfortable to sit on, but she'd really like to rest for a minute.

Oberon stopped on the rise ahead. He never went so far that he couldn't see her, or reach her, if she were attacked.

The heck with it, she didn't want to keep up. She wanted a break. Her legs let go, and she dropped to the ground. Just ten minutes. Sweat pooled everywhere inside her damned suit. A wave of dizziness set her off-kilter for a moment. She planted her hands on the ground to slow her rotation. It didn't help.

"Are you sick?" Panic leaked from his attempted calm while he rushed back to her.

Had she made a mistake by swimming in and drinking from the clear stream? She didn't think so. "I'm hot. I'm hungry and a little dizzy, that's all."

"Dizzy!" He dug into his backpack and yanked out a water bottle. Shoved it at her.

This time she took it without complaint. She needed fluids, and she needed some food. If only she had her trapper gear with her. She could catch some fresh meat.

He'd probably think that would be wrong, too. Animals in the Nevermore were supposed to be contaminated, but she'd been eating wild meat since she'd been branded. That's how she'd survived. By her wits. So far, she hadn't grown a slash of a mouth like the Yardmen. Poor things. In some ways, she pitied them.

She shook the bottle, nearly empty.

"Drink," he said.

"But it's almost gone. Have you had any water today?" She'd taken her fill in the stream but still needed fluid. He must be parched. She had also filled a bottle from the stream, but there was no way he'd agree to her drinking any of that.

"Not yet. I'll use a water collector tonight to get us more," he said.

"How much water can you possibly get from condensation?" she asked. In fact, she'd seen soldiers showing citizens how to collect water if they were desperate. It might save a mouse. She glanced at the mountain tops in front of them. Dark clouds were building there, black on the bottom and full of precious liquid. "It should rain soon. I pray it does. Otherwise, you're the one who's going to collapse."

"I've been through worse," he said, then dropped beside her. He dug around in his backpack and tore off one of several rations of salt meat. "At least we'll have a little extra protein for a day or two." He ripped it in two and handed her half.

"You should have filled your water bottle at the stream," she said.

He gawked at her like the word lunatic had been tattooed on her forehead. "Not likely. Look at you. You're already dizzy."

"From lack of food most likely. It's hot outside today, and we're in heavy Uvlars. It's a wonder we aren't both dead of heat exhaustion."

"Yeah, well, sorry, but we're out here alone. There's not much we can do."

"Why did you come after Rud and me alone?" she asked, avoiding direct eye contact this time because his gaze seemed able to pierce her self-imposed armor. "I mean, you could've brought soldiers with you. Probably should have."

"So far I've managed to keep you alive, haven't I?"

His sharp response proved she'd insulted him. Good one, Rune. Insult the only person who might keep you alive tonight.

"Yes. And, all things considered, I'm grateful."

His eyes condemned her for lying to him. He sat beside her for several minutes without speaking. She wished she could close her eyes and take a quick nap. The heat and lack of food had drained her energy. She watched the brush waving gently in the breeze, the yellow clouds clumping in the sky overhead... Her eyes drifted closed.

"We should continue on, if you're up to it?"

She jerked awake. Holy crap, she'd gone to sleep. She'd never done that before in her life. Especially not in the Nevermore. "I'm fine now," she said, pushing herself to her feet.

This time, he stayed so close he was practically touching her. Too close. Probably expected her to collapse from the toxic water and air she'd exposed herself to. In all honesty, that bit of food had helped. Still hot, she'd have loved nothing better than to strip off her Uvlar and cool her body down again, but he'd have a fit if she did that.

What was with her, anyway? She'd never felt she could take off her protective gear before. Why did she feel differently now?

The lumpy yellow-gray sky threatened to burst overhead. She felt something coming. Something dangerous. And more than a simple storm.

CHAPTER EIGHTEEN

Rudyard jerked awake with such force the muscles in his neck knotted viciously. The stench of animal feces had probably been what forced him awake. Not to mention the animals in surrounding cages were more restless and noisy than they'd been before he passed out.

He glanced down at his blood-covered body. A couple of the gashes he'd earned during his escape attempt could probably use stitches.

He crawled to his knees and peered through the wire mesh. He'd been put dead center in the room, where every caged animal in the place watched him. Might as well ring the dinner gong.

A Yardman had captured him. This Yardman had seemed more aware than the others. He'd always heard they were dumb and brutal in general. This Yardman, who'd snagged him from his ride home, hadn't appeared the least bit slow-witted.

Something shuffled nearby, and he searched for the source of the sound. Hopefully, it wasn't an animal on the loose drawn to the scent of blood. Being locked inside a cage might not be so bad right now.

When he saw the source of the scuffling, he yanked his fingers back from the wire. A creature, no taller than a dog, stood there looking at him. A miniature Yardman?

"Benevolent hell," he said to himself, not expecting an answer.

"Cursing won't help you now."

He gawked at the little beast. "You speak?"

It nodded.

"How?"

The little creature shrugged. "Same way you do, I'm guessing." He sounded insulted. His tiny frame perfectly proportioned, and Rud marveled at his stature. Where had this little creature come from? Nuclear fallout could be blamed for some of the deviations in their society, but surely not this, a complete, tiny version of a Yardman.

"Sorry. I didn't mean to insult you," he said.

The little Yardman's lack of expression changed to definable surprise at Rud's comment. "Aren't you the governor's brother?" he asked. His tiny voice sounded like a rusty door.

"Some of us have all the luck," he replied dryly.

The little Yardman laughed. "You come from a privileged family."

The little guy used big words, too. Rud frowned at him. "What do you want?"

"My name's Blip."

"Of course it is," Rud said instantly. "Only we don't have any radar anymore, do we?"

Blip sighed. "I forgot your family had books to read. Most people don't get the connection."

"You seem to know a lot about me, Blip."

"I should."

"Why's that?"

"You're my brother."

Rud's mouth dropped open, and he practically had to use his hand to close it again. "I'm your what?"

"You heard me."

"If this is some kind of spy tactic to get me to talk, I'm afraid your attempt has failed." He wanted to laugh, but didn't want to insult the little guy. He didn't want him to leave yet, in case he could get some helpful information from him.

"Care to tell me how that happened? My father's been dead since I was twelve. You don't look old enough to have been sired by him."

Blip made an irritated sound. "I wasn't sired. I was grown in a dish."

Rud had read a few tattered science magazines, and one of his ancestors had been a geneticist. His family had little else to do in the bunker but retell stories of their past. That meant he vaguely understood how a person could be grown in a dish. But he believed that technology had been lost a hundred years ago. "That doesn't negate the fact that my father has been long dead and couldn't have possibly been used to create you."

Blip put his hands over his chest. He wore a tiny Uvlar suit, so perfectly created and sewn, amazing to see. Almost as amazing as Blip himself.

"Okay, it doesn't matter that you don't believe we're related. Let's forget that issue for now," Blip said. "If you want to get out of here, you're going to have to be a little more trusting. I'm not letting you out of that cage until you and I have an understanding."

Rud straightened. He had to fool this tiny deviant into

thinking he could trust him. But how? No way would Blip believe a complete turnaround right now.

"Your eyes tell me you want to fool me. Don't bother. I'm not as dull-witted as most of my gargantuan cousins," he said.

"Yardmen?"

Blip nodded.

"You're saying they're my brothers, too." The little guy must've been overexposed.

"We all have crosses to bear," Blip said in perfect English.

"You can let me out," Rud began. "I promise you can… You wouldn't leave your brother in a cage?"

Blip held up a tiny hand. "Do not insult my intelligence, Rudyard James. I'll know when you and I have come to terms with the truth. For now, take this," he said, handing over a bottle of water and some dried meat wrapped inside a woven bag. "Hide the bottle and the bag under the straw when you're done, if you know what's good for you."

Blip turned away.

"Wait. Aren't you going to let me out?"

"Not until I know I can trust you. I'm sorry." His little slash of a mouth turned down. "Don't make a fuss or you won't be alive long enough for trust to grow."

"I trust you," he said.

Blip turned back, his small black eyes burning with anger. "Don't patronize me, brother. I want to respect you. Please don't let me down."

With that, the small creature left. Rud heaved a sigh and pushed his hand against his throbbing head. He needed water. Maybe that would help the shrieking pain behind his eyes. He drank deeply. The water went down cold and clear and tasted like none he'd ever had before. If this was a drug or poison, then let him be poisoned. He drank more, and when half was gone, he decided he'd better hide the rest. He might need more before his stay in this animal cage ended.

He pushed his face against the wire, trying to see where Blip had gone. Animals roared around him, grunted and screamed and howled. He felt like doing the same. He clamped his eyes shut. Oberon, I hope you made it safely, brother. I hope you never end up here.

He slumped against the cage and tried to sleep, to block out the smells and the sounds in this horrible place. When something touched him, he jumped. A little hand shoved a bottle of salve at him that looked almost too big for Blip to carry. "Put this on your wounds. If you don't, you'll get infection." He shook his wee head and clicked his tongue. "It's hard to believe a man can be this cruel, isn't it?"

"What man?" Rud asked.

"You must know who's holding you prisoner." Blip eyed him suspiciously.

"Not for sure. Though I have the suspicion it's probably Vestro."

"In the flesh," Blip said. He tipped his head as if he'd heard a sound through the din of the animals. "I must go."

This time, Rud watched him scurry down the aisle between all the animals. A creature as small as he was must be very brave to come in here where everything wanted to eat him. Step one to trusting him might have just happened.

Then the doors at the far end of the building opened, and the creature who'd captured him stepped in. Next to him, stood Callium Vestro, deposed dictator and his brother's sworn enemy.

Vestro had a vile expression on his face while he stomped down the dusty, sawdust-covered floor toward him.

* * * * *

"I think we should find shelter right away." Darla managed to tear her gaze away from the building clouds.

Oberon stiffened, and he flashed a wry look at her over his shoulder. "And exactly what do you think we're doing right now? What we've been doing most of the day?" His voice held a note of incredulous irritability.

She smiled at him weakly. "Sorry. That's not what I meant. I have a bad feeling. We need to find shelter soon. I can't explain it, but I'm usually right about these things."

He halted and adjusted the weapon on his shoulder. "A throwback from Maribel's ability?"

She shrugged, the movement reminding her that every muscle in her body had been overworked. "Maybe."

He breathed heavily and squinted to scan their surroundings. "The mountains are still too far away. We won't make them before dark."

"Never mind dark, we need shelter and soon. This isn't about nighttime," she said.

"If you were anyone else but Maribel's offspring, I'd ignore your comments. But, in this case, I see a building over that way. I think we'd better go check it out."

Her gaze followed his. "I don't see anything."

He leaned down to scan from her angle. "It's there. See the broken remnants of the roof just below that rise?"

"But it's not a whole building."

"It's the only thing I can see in any direction that might suffice as shelter."

"Let's make for it, then, and fast." She started running, leaving him in her wake.

He caught up and touched her shoulder. "Until you carry the weapons, I'd suggest you let me take the lead."

"You're right. I got carried away with the feelings creeping into me. It's bad, Oberon. Whatever's coming is very bad."

"Let's get a move on, then."

They charged through the brush at the fastest pace they could, while still watching for beasts.

By the time they made the building, Darla desperately wanted out of her gear.

The building was mostly intact. It might even have a basement. Please let there be a basement.

A noise began in the distance, a loud roar like the one she'd heard only once before. Her hands shook, just a little. Oberon halted.

"Hurry," she said. "It's coming faster than you can possibly believe."

"What is it?"

"A crippler. I've seen one before. "

They rushed inside the building. Only partial walls remained. "I'm not so sure this is the safest place to be right now. If this thing comes down on us…"

Cripplers were hurricanes with an extra mean twist. They carried debris from the remnants of their fallen society. So much debris lay scattered everywhere that the winds picked up the garbage as it moved across the landscape and became a moving weapon. And, somehow, it was doubly fueled by the EMP ions in the atmosphere. If elements were just right when they formed over the ocean, they hit hot, dry land then built into a monster storm over the mountains. And whammo. These storms sliced and diced everything in their way.

Sometimes, this type of information in her head made her feel like she'd gone crazy. Right now she believed it, especially with the sounds coming from the distance like a moaning wail of a dying world.

"Holy Mother," he said, looking around them, trying to find the safest place to hide. "This looks like it used to be a sewage plant. That might save us."

"I don't understand."

"You will. Let's get downstairs and fast." Already, they heard metal hitting the sides of the building, yet the storm's center raged quite a distance away.

Darla waited for him to indicate the most likely route to the basement. But with the fallen interior walls and broken glass, it'd be difficult to find a basement entrance, if it existed. Or it might be covered by debris. "Where do we go?"

Sweat beaded on his forehead, and his skin had turned a little gray.

"Hey, are you okay?" she asked.

"I'm fine," he said and intermittently began digging through rubble. After a few minutes, he stopped digging. Breathing hard, he searched urgently for a way downstairs, but so far, no luck. "Odds are the stairwell is on the perimeter," he said more to himself than to her.

She crawled over rubble to keep up with him. They made it to the nearest corner still standing. The wind outside had risen to a shrieking tempest now, like something mechanical coming for them. Irony at its finest in a world without mechanics, she thought.

Debris pierced the brick wall near her with such force

it ricocheted then slammed through the wall above her head. She dropped to the ground and wondered how many layers that projectile would get through before it stopped.

Oberon madly dug into the rubble at their feet. She tried to help while he lifted huge chunks of material and a steel bar that seemed impossible for two people, but they did it. Material like that would garner a fine penny back in the city. Not many dared venture out here for building material, but even after two hundred years, some of the finest pieces were still intact. Good old stainless steel.

"Thank the Benevolent," he said, pointing at worn cement steps going down through a hole in the floor that had once been a stairwell. "Get down there, Darla. I'll be right behind you."

Ear-splitting noise erupted as a wall at the other end of the building sheared off and was sucked heavenward into the debris-rife vortex. She stopped on the second step from the top and stared back at the chaos until Oberon grabbed her arm and practically thrust her down the stairs before flying bits of metal started pinging around them.

Even though fallen chunks of concrete partially blocked the stairs, they managed to climb over and make it to the bottom before the world above them exploded under the howling force of the crippler.

At the bottom of the stairs, Oberon managed to shove the stairwell door shut. Good thing, too, because negative air pressure had been creating a suction effect down here. Dust and debris had started to move toward the door. They would have been sucked up into that killer spiral if he hadn't been able to block off the pressure.

They found the basement full of ancient holding tanks. While rust had eaten away at the outer surface of some tanks, most were intact. Other than that, this place might be secure, except for the risk of being buried alive by the storm overhead.

All of a sudden, things got a lot worse upstairs. It sounded like everything was being shredded above them.

"Phew. Lucky we got down here when we did," Oberon shouted, just seconds before the door began to rattle.

"Can it be sucked off its hinges?" Darla sprinted toward the other side of the room with Oberon on her heels.

"Sure can. And I'd say it's going to be. We need to get deeper below ground if we can."

She scanned the wall behind the last of the giant vats in the room. "Look, there's a door. I just hope it leads to a stairwell that takes us down, not up."

Oberon rammed against the door, but it didn't budge. "This thing's blocked."

They heard an earsplitting sound of rending metal, and then the door was sucked out and up into the spiral. Terrible pressure built. Darla pressed her hands against her ears, even though they were underneath her Uvlar hood.

She scanned the room again and spotted another small door on the wall a few feet away. Meanwhile, the metal vat closest to the stairwell door began to shriek, no doubt because it was being torn out of the concrete floor. They'd be next if they didn't get out of here, fast.

"This way."

He turned in the direction of her pointing finger. "Let's pray that door's not blocked," he shouted, barely audible above the din. Grabbing her hand, they ran toward the four-foot door. He yanked it open, and they crawled inside, slamming it shut just as vat number one careened through the ceiling and into the vortex.

They were in a small room with a ladder down into a dark hole. The steel ladder riveted to the wall seemed sturdy enough, and somehow, emergency lights lit this area. Didn't seem possible, and where did the power come from? Even with the emergency lighting, they couldn't see the bottom. It might be blocked, too. This could end up being their tomb.

"Two hundred years of rust. Do you suppose the ladder will fall off the wall when we both get on it?" Darla asked.

"It's a chance we have to take. I don't think the main part of the building will be around much longer." He had to shout even louder, because the noise outside had risen to a deafening level.

"You go first."

"No. You go first. You're lighter than me. I'll wait here until you get to the bottom," Oberon said.

Something rammed into the wall behind them and shook the reinforced concrete around them. Maybe these walls wouldn't be there much longer, either.

Darla climbed down the long ladder first. Halfway down, she said, "Oberon, you'd better start down now. This ladder seems sturdy enough."

Shrieking metal and pings of rivets and bolts hitting the walls outside the door intensified. "I want you to be safe first," he called down to her.

On the other hand, he also wanted to be around to help her accomplish her quest. "Oh, hell, I'm coming, too. Here's hoping the ladder holds."

* * * * *

Climbing down, Oberon had exerted himself to the point of near exhaustion. He needed water. Worse, his knees felt limp, and he hoped he had the wherewithal to make it without his muscles giving out.

"I'm at the bottom," Darla shouted. She sounded a million miles away. He paused, wrapped his arm around a rung and pulled his face shield and hood off and let it flop onto his back. He inhaled slowly, felt moisture bead on his face and saw brilliant sparks of light in front of his eyes. Uh oh. Could he make it?

"I can see you," she said. "You're not far from the bottom now."

Just stepping down the rungs sucked every bit of energy out of him. If her coaxing voice indicated her relative position, she couldn't be far away. He'd try to make it. Problem being, he'd lost eighty percent of his strength in the last few steps.

He had to hang on. He glanced down. Sweat ran into his eyes and made them burn. Darla's outline appeared in the dim lighting inside the tunnel. The urge to puke and pass out at the same time overwhelmed him, and he clung to another rung, breathing raggedly.

"You okay up there?" she asked.

Only a few more steps. So tired—if he could just rest. He took a shaky step and missed. Then, unable to stop himself, he stepped off into midair and dropped the rest of the way to the bottom.

Her body registered beneath him. She'd tried to halt his fall, and he was mortified that she might have been injured. His last thought, as everything faded to gray, was that he didn't know if he'd hurt her.

He felt her body squirm out from beneath him. He weighed a hundred and ninety pounds of solid bone and muscle, and he couldn't move.

Her hands grabbed his face. "Oberon. Don't you dare pass out. You've got heat prostration. If you pass out, you might never wake up again. Do you hear me?"

He moaned, all he could do to reply.

Suddenly, cool water slid over his lips, and his mouth opened to let more in. He drank it down and gasped for more.

He couldn't help her when she opened his Uvlar suit and pulled his arms out. Arms that felt boneless. At least the air felt cooler in here, though dank. Heaven, compared to baking inside his suit. Then she put something wet on the back of his neck.

"That'll cool your core down so your organs don't fail," she said. He registered the worry in her voice. Didn't blame her. She'd be all alone if he died.

At least the urge to puke had passed, and lying here, with the cool moisture on his neck and liquid in his belly, made a bit of a difference. He still felt like he could die at any moment, but hopefully the worst had passed.

He groaned while she yanked his Uvlar suit and T-shirt off all the way. The cool air hitting his overheated, dry torso helped even more.

She tipped his head and poured sweet, sweet water into his mouth. He'd never tasted water so good.

"Feel like crap," he managed to get out.

She touched his forehead. "I bet you do. Hang in there, because I'm not going to let you die today."

He tried to laugh but couldn't quite manage it. He needed to gather some strength and move. Sounds of the storm groaned through the building above. Metal twisted somewhere, and he searched for the strength to get up. They needed to move to a safer location.

"More water," he said, finally regaining some inner strength. "Not too much, though. You need some, too."

"Don't worry. We have lots of water," she said. Oh, no. He remembered her water container had been full, all right. Full of that damned toxic water from the stream.

He shut his eyes tight and held back a string of curses that might tarnish her pretty little ears. "Contamination."

"Yes, pick your poison. Contaminated water or dying from dehydration," she said. "Seems to me, water, contaminated or not, is your only option."

She tipped it to his lips, and he acquiesced. He drank enough to satiate his body's need, while making sure there'd be enough left for her.

"Have more," she said.

He wiped his hand across his mouth. "That's enough for now. Thanks." Some energy returned, enough for him to sit up. Then he actually let her help him stand. Hard on the ego.

"We can't stay here. Not safe." His breathing felt labored. His vision blurred in and out while he scoped out one of several halls leading off the stairwell.

"It looks like maintenance tunnels."

"Good," he said. "Could go for miles. If it hasn't caved in from old age." He felt her unexpected shiver under his shoulder where she was still propping him up. If they couldn't get out another way, they were trapped.

* * * * *

"We've both been drinking toxic water. Who knows what'll happen to us next?" he said, obviously trying to make a backhanded joke to offset their grim situation. At this point, water would be the least of their worries.

The tunnel appeared to stretch out for quite a distance.

Hopefully, this one hadn't caved in somewhere in the darkness ahead. She considered the possibility of being buried alive.

Oberon leaned against her a little more now, and no wonder, his body needed a chance to recoup. She spotted a bench ahead, an old stainless steel platform probably used to access the pipes running the length of the tunnel. Just the right size for a six-foot-something man to lie on.

They made it, and he fairly collapsed onto it. It held his body weight.

Yanking the water container out of her pocket, she ordered him to drink again.

He shoved a hand in front of his face. "Not until you drink some, too. Or we'll both be like this."

To appease him, she drank. Her container held a few liters, so they'd be okay for a bit, depending on how long they'd be stuck underground.

"Got anything left to eat?" she asked, sliding down the wall to a crouch beside him and taking another sip of water before handing it back to him. She shouldn't have mentioned food, because now he wouldn't stay down.

He sat up and grabbed his backpack, digging through it, then handing her another strip of salt meat. He took one for himself and sagged against the cement wall. He leaned over and looked at the floor, then on the other side of the bench. "Where's my gun?" he asked.

She'd been happily chewing on her stringy meat until she heard the concern in his voice. "I think it fell when you pancaked onto me back there at the bottom of the ladder," she said.

"Sorry about that, Darla."

"I'm fine. And, if it makes you feel any better, I'm going to go back and get the gun after I've got you situated."

He bristled at that. Probably always had to be the tough guy. "It's not safe down here without protection. Benevolent only knows what we might come across."

She sat a little straighter. "Oh, sorry, I didn't think of that. I figured we'd be down here alone."

He shook his head. "If we can find our way down, so can other things."

She noticed he didn't say other people. "Great."

He started to get up, but she held up a hand to stop him. "Stay there. Rest. I don't want your kidneys shutting down. Drink some more fluids. I'll go get the gun."

"No way, Darla. It's not safe. I'm not letting you go off alone. No telling what you might run into. We go together."

She ran her hands up and down her Uvlar-clad arms. Technically, no one could call her a scaredy-cat, but the idea of being stuck down here with unknown predators sent shivers up her spine.

He pushed himself forward. "You're not going alone."

"We could wait until you're rested," she said.

"And risk the gun disappearing?"

"Since you put it that way, I guess we go together."

He shoved himself to his feet but blanched like he might be physically ill again.

"You okay?"

"Never better," he said caustically.

They trudged slowly back toward the ladder well. How'd it get this far away? She kept an eye on Oberon's sickly color. How could she have been so stupid as to leave the weapon behind?

They turned the corner. "The gun should be right there." Her throat thickened when she realized it had disappeared.

"Damnation," he said. "We're too late."

* * * * *

The main doors to the barn opened, and Rudyard Solomon James watched an abomination against humanity coming toward him with that bastard ex-dictator trailing behind. Vestro stopped in front of the cage, and the beast stepped in behind him. Some sort of gargantuan, inhuman soldier.

"Well, well. Rudyard James, in the flesh," Vestro said thickly.

Rud stared at him. He'd swear the guy appeared drunk or something.

Vestro heaved a dramatic sigh and bent over to look at him. "You quite comfortable in your accommodations?"

Rud didn't respond.

"Prod," Vestro shouted, and accepted a metal pole from the beast. He shoved it in the cage, through the feeding hole.

Rud expected a bruise but not the shock he got. What kind of weapon of torture had they used? Every cell in his leg burned.

"Barely fazed me," Rud spat out, gasping for breath. If he could get his hands on that damned dictator, he'd crack his skull on the cage and show him a thing or two. He might get fed to the lions across the way, but it'd give him satisfaction for a short time.

Vestro handed the prod back to his oversized bodyguard. "Nice to know you can speak. I thought you were mute for a second." Evil oozed out of him. No wonder Oberon had wanted to oust him. Someone had had to.

"What do you want?"

"What do I want?" Vestro mimicked before chortling out a laugh. "What do I want?" He tapped his fingernails on his nose. Then he turned seriously angry. Hate filled his narrowed eyes. "I want... no, I demand respect."

Rud ruminated on that statement longer than Vestro liked, if his expression proved accurate.

"I want to know where your brother is. I'm sure you already know and are just playing dumb. Or maybe you got the short end of the intelligence stick in the family."

Rud gritted his teeth. "Actually, I don't know. We split up after your...whatever they were attacked us." It didn't escape Rud's attention that the abomination behind Vestro stiffened angrily. For a beast, he remained very calm and cool, and maybe reluctantly obedient. Not at all like the Yardman he saw in the Boneyard with Darla.

He hoped Oberon had gotten Darla away safely. But even if he had, they were still in serious danger in the Nevermore. Maybe they'd already been captured. They might even be in this barn somewhere, for all he knew.

"Look at me when you're in my presence, swine." Vestro walked around the cage, and Rud followed his progress. The maniac wore a purple silk robe of some sort and silk shoes. The more Rud watched the dictator's face, the more he realized Vestro was on a magic carpet ride of his own making. He was high. Not ale, either. A different high than Rud had ever seen.

The creature cleared his throat, and Vestro slanted an angry glance at him.

Rud's attention was glued to the man-like beast, who had horrifyingly sharp bones jutting through his flesh. Intelligence glittered in those marble-black eyes, and he'd swear the big beast didn't like Vestro, either.

Nearer Rud's cage now, he kept looking at him but didn't speak.

"What do you plan on doing with me?" Rud asked after an ear-shattering roar from one of the big cats. He practically had to shout to be heard over the din.

"I'm going to use you for bait. I want your brother. And he'll do whatever he has to do to free you."

So Vestro hadn't captured Oberon and Darla. Rud grinned. But that happiness was short lived. Unfortunately, he had become Vestro's bargaining chip.

His heart sank. He hadn't helped his brother or the prophecy. He'd screwed everything up. Single-handedly.

CHAPTER NINETEEN

Darla stared at the spot on the disintegrating concrete floor where the gun should have been. Besides the drag marks in the dust, there were no footprints to identify what or who might have taken it. But why would it have been dragged and not carried?

She swallowed hard and bit her lip. Her fault. She'd left the weapon behind only because she'd been more concerned about getting Oberon to a place where he could rest, and she couldn't carry everything.

She should have tried harder.

The drag marks led them down a different corridor to a dead end, and then through a small enough hole in the wall that they couldn't follow.

Except for his labored breathing, Oberon's silence proved more than she could stand.

He turned back toward the hall they'd just come from without saying a single word.

"Wait. Where are you going?"

"Back to the bench." His voice held no anger. No tone

at all. That made her insides wobble.

"But the weapon."

"Gone," he said. "We won't get it back now."

"But we have to try," she said, catching up to him and looking at his face. Her gaze found no readable expression.

"No sense, Darla. It's gone. We could break through that wall down there, and if the tunnel's big enough for a human body on the other side, we could still follow it for miles and find nothing. It's a waste of time."

One last look at the hole in the wall and shivers rode her backbone. She had a bad feeling about that area, and she always trusted her intuition. Apparently, Oberon had intuition, too.

When they made it back to the bench, Oberon sat heavily. His breathing sounded even more labored than before.

Thankfully, his Uvlar suit remained on the bench. But who could've taken the weapon? Especially since it weighed at least ten pounds. And since it had been stolen and yanked through the wall, the thief had to have been small. And strong?

"It's my fault," she blurted out.

Oberon had been leaning forward with his fingers threaded through his hair. "No. It's mine. I should have made sure I drank enough water, even if it meant drinking from the stream. I should have listened to you. After all, my family has been following your grandmother's prophecies for generations. I had no reason to distrust you."

Well, that shocked her. She hadn't expected him to say that. "But I should have…"

He shook his head slowly back and forth. "You're not

a pack mule, Darla. Even you couldn't have carried everything, especially since I was leaning on you, too. I'm amazed you were able to get this far."

She appreciated that, but no way did she intend to say so. She adjusted her tight-lipped expression to even tighter-lipped, and slid down the wall into a seated crouch beside him again. "What will we do without a weapon?"

"We'll get by. We still have your pistol."

"And about a dozen bullets," she said. Thanks to leaving the ammo behind in the field.

Unable to stop herself, she yawned.

"You need to rest."

"We both do."

"We'll take turns," he said. "Not safe..." His eyes were closing. No doubt, as badly as he wanted to be the big tough guy on guard, his body vetoed that.

She stood and leaned against an old pipe opposite the bench so she wouldn't fall asleep. She heard shuffling. Someone or something else moved around down here. She searched their surroundings and found a two-foot length of steel pipe. She knew how to wield a staff, so this would do nicely.

Considering the crippler up top was probably still ripping and shredding everything in its way, the quiet down here felt unnerving. The only noise came from the occasional dripping sounds and rustling behind the walls. Nevermore rats were ugly. They were bigger than house cats, vicious, but they were basically afraid of people. Unless the person was dead, or nearly dead. She shuddered. Either way, she'd keep them away tonight.

She paced for a bit then crouched next to Oberon before she expended too much energy. She needed to stay awake.

At some point, she must have dropped off. At the sound of rustling, her eyes snapped open. Benevolent hell. She whipped her head around. Where had the noise come from? She checked left and right then stood to check on Oberon and nearly tripped over his gun. The weapon that had disappeared lay on the floor at her feet.

Hair rose on the back of her neck. "Who's there?"

She heard the rustling again. "Don't hurt me if I show myself," someone said.

"Why would I do that? Did you return the gun?" she asked.

"I did. I want to help you accomplish your goals."

Darla had a tight-fisted grip on the pipe. "Come out and show yourself," she said, searching the shadows on the other side of the tunnel, where there were several pipes stacked on top of each other.

More rustling, but no sign of the man behind the voice.

"The weapon is still loaded. I didn't harm it. Just kept it safe for you."

She picked it up, checked the magazine and barrel. It looked to be operational, but she wasn't a weapons expert. At least not military-issue weapons. It could've been tampered with so it wouldn't fire, for all she knew.

She glanced at Oberon, wondering if he'd heard the voice. "Where are you?" she demanded, searching the lines of pipes running along the tunnel in front of her. Was there room for someone to hide behind them?

"I'm right in front of you," the voice said. She inhaled sharply at the sight of a miniature Yardman stepping out from behind the pipes. Perfectly proportioned and only three feet high, his little black eyes stared at her while his tiny slash of a mouth pressed together in a serious way.

Not something she'd ever seen in a Yardman. Fear? Intelligence? "What are you?" she asked finally, slowly reaching down and pulling the weapon closer to her.

He held up small hands. "Please, don't shoot me." The Yardman's bushy eyebrows lifted.

"What are you doing here, and what is your name?"

"Name's Blip, ma'am. I want to help you."

"I don't understand," she said.

"If you're going to win the battle ahead of you, you're going to need someone on the inside, and I'm the only person who can do that for you."

"On the inside of what?"

"Vestro's stronghold, of course," the little Yardman said. His voice sounded so different from what she'd ever expected from a Yardman. As far as she'd known, they couldn't speak in anything other than grunts. She rubbed her eyes. He seemed real enough.

"Vestro knows you're coming. He's amassed an army to stop you. You won't be able to defeat him without help." The little man coughed. "And he has a bargaining chip. He's got Rudyard. He's got something planned for the courtyard. I'm not sure what yet, but I have a feeling Rud will be involved."

Benevolent hell. Darla pursed her mouth, frowned and reconsidered this little Yardman's statement. "How is that possible? Aren't most of his soldiers being held captive in Central City?"

Blip nodded his round head, his black eyes watching her closely. "Only the humans." He switched his gaze to Oberon, who was breathing deeply behind her. "You and Mister James have been foretold to do this together, but Vestro can still stop you. He knows the prophecy, and he swears that your future is not certain. He says anyone can change it, if they're smart enough. He plans to stop you."

She had no idea how something like this perfect little Yardman could exist. "Blip, I don't understand why you'd help us if you work for Vestro. You must know I can't accept anything you say as the truth."

His mouth turned into a line on this round face. He had no lips, so when he closed his mouth, it became something akin to a scar. "I do. I know I'll have to earn your trust."

"Why do you want to?" she asked, gripping the gun tighter in her hand.

He looked down at his body, swept his small Yardman fingers down the front of himself. "Vestro created me in a lab. Just as he created all the Yardmen. I'm sure you heard that Yardmen have been around for over a hundred years, but it's not true. He's the monster who created us by playing with genetics. He's creating a workforce that will bow down to him. He doesn't care about our lives. He just wants followers. Slaves. Nothing else matters to him but his own desires, and what's worse, the Yardmen follow him. But they only do it because they're afraid of him. If they don't do what he says, he tortures them and feeds them to big sea animals called sharks. The poor, ignorant brutes don't understand anything but pain and suffering, and fear."

She felt the agony in his words, could sense it. He told the truth.

"That's horrible."

Blip closed his eyes and lowered his head. "There's more."

Darla pressed a hand over her chest. "More can't be good..."

"He's got your mother, too."

Her legs nearly buckled and her world began to crumble from the inside out. Her mother. No! After Darla had been branded an outcast, she couldn't risk her mother's life and safety by being seen with her. She'd never gone back, in order to keep her mother safe.

"What's he done to her?"

The little head shook from side to side. "Nothing yet. But he's got a plan and it won't be good, I can promise you that."

Darla stared into space. "Vestro's going to be sorry for this," she said.

Blip shook his head with an expression of severity. "And he deserves everything he gets." He looked around, suddenly nervous. "I must go. I'll find you again tomorrow night, and I'll bring my big brother with me."

Darla inhaled. A full-size Yardman.

Blip waved his hands in front of him. "He's not like the others. He's intelligent. And he's the only one the other Yardmen will listen to."

"Why? Why do I care about that?"

"Because you need an army, too," Blip said.

"Aren't they Vestro's army?"

"Oh no, miss. He has something worse. Much, much worse."

She imagined she'd already experienced the worst of his creations, but maybe not. A sound brought Darla's attention around, and she double-checked the tunnel. She saw nothing, but when she returned her gaze to Blip, he'd disappeared.

* * * * *

Oberon remained still while the little Yardman talked, watching him through nearly closed eyelids. Once, he caught Blip looking right at him, as if he knew Oberon was listening.

After Blip left, Oberon reached out and touched Darla's shoulder. She jumped and jerked around to look at him. "Did you hear?"

He nodded, lifting his head off the bunched-up Uvlar suit. He sat up, realizing his T-shirt was wet and balled up under his neck. That meant she'd seen his scar twice now. Had she realized she'd done it to him, after he'd perpetrated the most heinous crime upon her? Upon her creamy flesh that had turned so horribly red.

To this day, he still had nightmares about it.

He'd never forgive himself.

He edged away from her, probably because of the way she stared at him. Like she'd never seen a man before. He, of all people, didn't deserve that look.

"I heard," he said, yanking his T-shirt over his head quickly. Her gaze followed his movements, making him aware of his scarred, hard-muscled flesh. Unlike her, he'd been through a few battles. But, then, that was because he had. "Vestro has Rud and your mother."

"If only we knew exactly what we were supposed to do. I'd feel a lot better," Oberon said.

"You'd feel better? How would you like it if some ancient prophecy said you were supposed to do something and you don't know anything about it?" Darla asked.

"Aren't you getting small messages here and there?"

"I guess so. It just seems so weird to me. I'm not used to it. But I don't have the big picture."

"We have to believe you will have it when you need it," he said with frown lines deepening in his forehead. He grabbed his weapon and hoisted it mechanically onto his shoulder.

"What about that little creature who brought back your weapon? Do we really trust him? Is it booby-trapped?" Her stomach wobbled, and she felt sick.

Oberon looked the weapon over, pulling off all the movable parts and checking it thoroughly. "I've never said this out loud before, but I've always known Vestro could come back and take the city, if he really wanted it. We wouldn't stand a chance against a platoon of Yardmen, let alone whatever else he's growing out there."

He leaned forward. His boots were military issue, and hers were black market. Funny part, hers were better than his. People of Central City were starving and had no economy, but somewhere an underground market of food and goods had begun to flourish. He wanted to bring that to the surface and introduce it to all of his people. He needed to jump-start growth. But first, he had to protect the citizens from the Nevermore, and from a war with a psychotic dictator hell-bent on maintaining the damaged version of civilization as they knew it.

Oberon got close to Darla, too close, and stared her straight in the eye. "Vestro's afraid of you, Darla. Only you." He inhaled and took a step back, adjusting the weight on his shoulder. "And deep down, you know it."

Her hands clasped and unclasped, and she closed her eyes and squeezed them tight, fighting the urge to do Oberon bodily harm for daring to speak a truth she hadn't wanted to hear.

"I'm sorry. I know you've been through hell, Darla. But there's worse to come, and you need to face it. Right now."

She slowly exhaled then opened her eyes. "You realize

I hate everything you stand for."

"I know," he said solemnly. "And so you should."

What did that mean? She exhaled again. "What about Blip? Do you think he really wants to help us? Or is Vestro setting us up?"

* * * * *

Oberon's gut burned like acid. He was Darla's worst nightmare and had been since she'd turned fourteen. Her gorgeous bright eyes were like pools of liquid emeralds. She'd unbuttoned her Uvlar suit far enough that he saw a bit of her lacy underthing and a voluptuous curve of breast. Heat flashed over him, and he felt dizzy again. No time to get himself overheated. But Earth be praised, she drove his libido to overreact at the most inopportune times.

He'd been edgy since they'd started off on this journey. Edgy and tied up in knots. He wanted her. He owed her. He'd branded her, and she'd never forgive him when she found out.

His guts felt like they'd been sliced by knives. Worse, he'd ignored part of the prophecy because he couldn't do it, the part that said he had to brand her again to initiate the next level of her ability. And only he could do it. He'd planned to forget about that bit, until what Blip said reminded him about the terrible war coming. What if she needed help to escalate her abilities?

No way. He couldn't do it.

"Are you worried about Rud?" she asked, touching his arm with a cool hand. He drew back quickly, as if she'd burned his flesh. Worse, his reaction caused her to step away, an embarrassed flush in her cheeks.

He couldn't explain why he'd reacted so vehemently,

without admitting how he really felt about her. And he couldn't do that.

But if she gave him even the slightest come-hither glance, after that kiss in the cave, he'd be all over her.

Control yourself, man. You're the leader of the few people left. You have to be in control of yourself at all times.

"Get your clothes on," she said in a tight voice that made him feel terrible all over again.

Better if she believed he didn't care, than realize how deeply he did. He'd never forgotten her after he'd been ordered to brand her. He had forced her into a life of hardship and starvation, and then afterward, when he'd tried to find her and help her, he'd failed. He'd thought she'd died long ago. And then Rud had found her.

He drank her in. She'd done pretty well for herself, all things considered.

She turned away from him and waited for him to dress. For a man suffering from dehydration, and who felt like he still might die at any minute, he yanked on the Uvlar suit quicker than he thought possible.

When he did up the last of the snaps, she faced him again. "My mother is innocent. She shouldn't be involved in any of this." He heard the self-recrimination in her voice.

Oberon's guilt grew again. He'd gone to see Darla's mother before heading out into the Nevermore. Had he led the kidnappers straight to her door? Worse, he'd sent his brother off alone, and now he'd been taken prisoner.

So much for being the great and wonderful leader of the people. He couldn't even help his own brother. He'd proved himself to be a total fuck-up.

And now he still felt weak from dehydration. He

needed more water, and that stream back there...right now, he'd like to drink it dry.

CHAPTER TWENTY

They gathered their gear and stared down the tunnel in front of them. Blip obviously had a way in and out. But would they?

"What do you think?" Darla asked.

"Unfortunately, I think there's a very good chance that he's telling the truth about Rud and your mother."

She leaned against the wall. Her legs suddenly felt like they might give out because she instinctively knew the truth. Vestro had her mother. "What's our plan? What'll we do when we reach Vestro's place?"

"Before I left the farm land, I told the sentry to send soldiers if I didn't return in two days, so they'll be arriving soon, I imagine. I have trackers who are the best in the business."

"We need to get inside Vestro's building," she said, circling her temples with her index fingers. "I've felt that from the beginning. I have to go there."

Oberon suddenly appeared uncomfortable. His family had been following the prophecies of a psychic since the

War of Neutrality, yet it seemed easier for him to believe a message on paper than a flesh and blood woman.

"First we have to find a way out of here. Then we're going to have to backtrack to the collapsed building. Otherwise, I'm afraid my soldiers will think we're buried under tons of rubble. They'll try to dig us out."

"Luckily, the stream's not far from there. We can refill the canteens, too." She thought he'd go ballistic at that, but he merely nodded.

"Any ideas on which way should we go? The tunnels stretch out in every direction."

He grinned at her, then nudged his head up toward a small rectangular sign on the wall. Dirty, and barely readable, but enough to make out the word. Exit.

"Smart-ass." She moved in that direction with him on her tail. He didn't seem too concerned about her going first this time. But, then again, she could practically feel his breath on the back of her neck.

The tunnels went on for about twenty minutes before another rusted-out, barely readable exit sign showed up. But this exit had caved in and was completely sealed off. She waved an arm to indicate that they had to keep moving.

After walking another ten minutes, she glanced back at him. Had he recovered enough to climb the ladder when they found it? He hadn't even made it down the last one. She monitored his skin tone. At least it had improved.

He hadn't balked at the idea of drinking the water, so she wondered if, this time, he'd take a dip in the stream and cool off. Suddenly, she stopped so fast he ran into her.

"What's wrong?" He grasped her shoulders and shoved her aside, raising the gun to protect her from whatever had stopped her in her tracks.

She'd been thinking about him in the stream with next to nothing on. "Nothing. Sorry I stopped without warning you."

She had to get a grip. He wasn't particularly nice to her. He wasn't particularly good-looking. But his tough aura and intelligent blue eyes made her little heart go pitty-pat. Whether she liked it or not.

He cleared his throat. "Let's keep moving," he said.

They found another ladder about ten minutes down the line. This exit appeared to be debris free all the way to the top. But would it be buried under rubble above ground?

"No way to know if the door is covered over or accessible. Why don't you wait down here until I check it out?" she said.

She practically heard his teeth grit.

"I should go first," he said.

"Your call," she said, crossing her arms on her chest. "I don't think you should overexert yet, though."

He sighed. "You're right," he grunted in a barely audible voice. "You go ahead. I'll wait here."

That had to be hard for him to say. She grinned.

She stepped on the first rung and tested its moorings. It made rusty squeaking noises, but it seemed solid enough. Good thing they'd used so much heavy-duty steel two hundred years ago.

"Here goes," she said and climbed up quickly. The door at the top was a twin to the rounded steel back in the cave. She pushed it—it didn't budge. She shoved again. Her arms weren't strong enough, so she climbed two more steps and shoved her shoulder against the cover and slid it ajar. Just a little, but it opened. That gave her the opportunity to get her fingers on the rim to push it sideways. A few strained minutes later, she had it shoved far enough to poke her head out.

"Be careful. Don't stick your head out there without a weapon. There could be something waiting to attack," Oberon shouted from below.

Hair stood on the back of her neck and her arms. Benevolent hell, she should have thought of that. She knew better. She ducked back down, grabbed her weapon and poked up again, only this time with her revolver taking the lead.

"It's all clear. Can you come up?" she shouted.

He grunted something angry, but she couldn't make it out. Meanwhile, she climbed out and scoped out their surroundings. Downhill from here lay the remnants of the building they'd entered. The crippler had pretty much flattened the above-ground portion of the building. She thought about the skyscrapers in her dreams compared with these bones that were left. How could they ever come back from this?

By the time Oberon climbed the ladder and out of the hole, he appeared worse for wear. She reflected on offering a hand, but the determination sparking in his deep blue irises told her to let him do it by himself.

His breathing grew more labored than it should have been. He needed rest and more water. She squeezed her container and swallowed a lump in her throat. Not a whole lot left.

Oberon gazed down the valley at the shattered building. "We went a long distance underground, didn't we?"

"Easy to cover more territory in a tunnel, I guess. At least we backtracked and got nearer the collapsed building. We'd better get moving."

They made tracks through the brush, literally. Their survival might depend on Oberon's trackers finding them and soon.

Pausing, Darla pressed the palm of her hand over her forehead and closed her eyes. She hated backtracking now because they had been getting closer to their destination, and soon they'd be in Vestro's territory.

They stopped at the rubble that had been the building they'd entered. If they hadn't found a way into the tunnels before the storm hit, they'd have been buried under that heap of broken concrete and metal.

She snatched a quick peek at Oberon. His skin had become chalky, with no perspiration on the part of his face that she could see. The stream was half an hour at least from here. "Drink the rest of the water," she said, shoving the container at him.

"I can't. It's all we have."

She gave him a look that would have withered the stunted leaves in the Nevermore. He sighed and took it. Finally, the man used his common sense. He drank most of it, but she noticed, when he handed it back, there remained enough in the bottom for one last, long drink for her. She shrugged and shoved it back into her sack. At least he'd had enough to hopefully make it to the stream.

"Let's get to the water," she said.

He nodded. "Good place as any to wait for the soldiers. I'll scrape a quick message in the dirt for them."

By the time they bypassed the rubble and made it to the stream, she couldn't imagine how he'd been able to keep that heavy gun at the ready the whole way. He looked about to pass out again. "Get your clothes off and dip your body in that stream. You'll be surprised at how cool it is, even in this heat. It'll help you get over dehydration much quicker." The lure of the clear water burbling along tempted her, too, but she needed to stay on guard this time.

He handed her the gun. Now carting his ten-pound rifle, she found a boulder and sat on it with the gun on her lap. That'd give him peace of mind long enough to cool off.

She watched him strip off his Uvlar gear piece by piece, until once again he wore his skivvies in front of her. She tried not to stare, but man. This guy was built.

He squeezed his eyes shut and heaved a long sigh when he lowered himself into the water. "I hate to say it, but I think you're right about the cool water making me feel better." He dipped under the water and came up gasping but with a smile on his face. "This feels better than anything I've experienced in a long time."

"It's clean water. Look at me, I'm not sick," she said. "It's been hours, and I still feel great. Better than great." She needed to tear her gaze away from the man, at least long enough to keep an eye out for predators.

* * * * *

Oberon stood in the stream deep enough to cover his shoulders. The pebbles on the bottom felt strange under his bare toes and a little rough on his feet. The clear water ran past him, making his skin tingle with its brisk flow. He drew in a reinforcing breath before doing something that every fiber in his body rebelled against: He dipped his head low enough to take a long, refreshing drink. Being a soldier, he still kept a keen eye out for danger. Even though Darla watched occasionally, she didn't have the same gut instinct out here that she had in the

Boneyard. One good thing, the water hadn't made her sick yet. No denying it still could. Either way they'd die out here without hydration, so he chose the better of the two evils.

A thin slice of blue sky had opened over the mountains again today. Maybe it was a good sign?

He climbed out and had to admit he felt better.

If only her attention had stayed on the brush, and not on him. She watched him with such intensity he'd have felt that gaze on him with his eyes closed.

"Your turn to cool off. I'll take watch," he said.

"No, I'm fine for now," she said and handed him the water containers. "Fill these up before you dry off, please."

He took them and stepped back into the stream to fill the containers.

They were surrounded by small trees and brush. The ones nearest the stream had tender green shoots and leaves. It seemed that life had been trying very hard to return to this land. He never thought he'd see the day it would happen.

Looking for a place to wait for his men, he spotted a stunted, medium-sized tree not far away. It had yellowish-green leaves. Maybe not as healthy as the smaller trees growing near the water, but it had a wide trunk and grew tall enough to cast a cool shadow. They could wait under it for the soldiers.

Heat rippled in the distance, creating images that tricked the mind. One had to stay sharp in this kind of heat. He reluctantly pulled on his Uvlar gear again. "Let's go over there," he said.

She jumped off the rock she'd been perched on and lugged his weapon with her.

They'd barely made it to the tree when something snapped in the brush beyond them. Darla raised the weapon, but Oberon reached out and took the gun from her. She gladly gave it up to him and stepped behind him while he aimed.

The cracking and snapping of the dry brush continued. Whatever circled them watched and waited to attack.

"Why doesn't it come after us?"she whispered finally.

"Probably waiting for the cover of darkness," he said. "Some creatures in the Nevermore only hunt after dark."

She stared, unblinking, at the mountains in the distance, probably thinking it would be dusk too soon.

"Great," she said. "Maybe finding safe water won't matter much to us in an hour or so."

"Whatever it is, it'll have to come through me first," Oberon said through gritted teeth.

"Don't you mean, whatever they are?"

He should've known she'd be smart enough to realize a pack of animals lurked out there. Scenting them, watching them, and waiting for dark. He reminded himself of the time she spent in the Boneyard. She had to be better at looking after herself than he'd given her credit for.

Low growling began nearby, and it was getting closer. "Must be hungry," he said. "They don't usually come this close until dark."

Her head tilted toward him. "You know what they are, don't you?"

He wouldn't meet her gaze. Surely, she didn't want to know what they were, and how they ripped flesh from bone, torturing their prey and eating them alive. Even in his Uvlar, a bone-cold chill flashed over him. With only one heavy-duty weapon and her little pistol, they might not have enough weaponry to keep the wild dogs at bay. They were mean bastards, and they attacked in packs. He glanced up at the tree. If he could get her into that tree, she might be safe. It certainly didn't look sturdy enough to hold them both.

"Darla, do me a favor, will you?"

She must've been listening to the beasts, must've sensed they were getting nearer. She jumped when he spoke. "What is it?"

"Climb that tree and keep watch for the beasts. You should be able to see them coming from up there."

She narrowed her gaze on him. "You're not protecting me and fighting them alone down here."

"No. I need perspective. I'm too heavy for that sickly thing. It'd break, and we'd both lose the advantage."

She stared at him while the scents of heated brush and earth rose up and threatened to choke him. They were losing their shade. The setting sun found an unexpected break in the heavy cloud. Bright light flashed in his eyes and burned. The ground smelled fried under the smoldering light.

More movement in the brush. The beasts would crawl on their bellies until they were so close he could reach out and touch them. Only the most experienced tracker could see them. Unfortunately, he knew only too well, they were masters at camouflage in this landscape.

"Quick. Get up there, before we lose our advantage," he lied. He could tell she didn't quite believe him.

"I'll do it, but under protest," she said, stepping up onto a low-hanging branch, then climbing higher until she was most likely out of reach of snapping jaws and six-inch canines.

"I appreciate that," he said, continuing to monitor their

surroundings.

She climbed a little higher, and it impressed him that she managed the task so easily. "I'd swear you had experience climbing trees," he said. "Only I know that's not possible, since there are none higher than my hip around Central City."

She groaned. "I've had plenty of experience climbing in the Boneyards. The heaps of technology can be precarious and very high. This tree is nothing in comparison."

He intended to keep her talking until the last minute when the beasts attacked. He didn't want her to come down. "What do you see?"

"I can see the brush moving very deliberately all around us. They're there, but they're almost invisible."

"They have perfect camouflage," he said, suddenly aware that a pair of eyes watched him from the edge of the brush. Yellow orbs lined with red veins and black slits in the center.

It wouldn't be long now. The animals were too hungry to wait.

"Hold on, I see something else. A dust cloud not far out."

Oberon's chest tightened. "What is it?"

She climbed higher into the tree, and he feared the smaller branches at the top wouldn't hold her. If she fell, the beasts would have her.

"It's your soldiers. They're coming."

"Are you sure it's my soldiers and not Vestro's?"

She remained silent for what felt like forever while he stared down the voracious beast that grew brave enough to show itself.

"Yes, they're carrying your family crest on a flag. I'm

sure of it."

"We need to indicate our location and fast," he said, raising his weapon and shooting the beast between its yellow eyes, knowing he might initiate a full-on attack. The oversized dog dropped, and two more flanked him, hair standing on end on the backs of their necks.

"They heard the gun," she said. "They're coming this way."

"And so are the dogs," Oberon shouted. "Stay up there."

* * * * *

Darla saw the huge beasts moving in on Oberon. They'd rip him to pieces if she didn't help. She slid off the branch and started climbing down.

"Get back up that tree," he shouted, while taking aim and shooting two more of the slavering beasts. They were almost bigger than the wolves outside the Boneyard.

She dropped to the ground and yanked out her pistol. She shot two bullets into a beast sneaking up on her from behind. Each time they took down another animal, several of their kin arrived and began devouring their own brethren. That might give her and Oberon enough of a reprieve to make it until the soldiers arrived.

She shot two more, and each time, more beasts jumped out. They were huge, grayish-brown and mangy, smelly creatures with long teeth and terrifying yellow-red eyes. Their growling reverberated in her bones. If she believed in her mother's stories of the hounds of hell, these had to be those creatures.

"What're we going to do now?"

"Keep shooting and don't quit. We're not dying today, and not with the soldiers so close." He actually had to shout to be heard over the growling.

They both started shooting. Darla had only a eight bullets left, but an animal went down with every shot she took.

Some of the beasts fought over the dead, yanking their bodies back into the dense brush as quickly as they dropped.

Horses thundered toward the tree. Soldiers hopped down and approached, killing a few more dogs as they approached. Suddenly, the dogs turned tail and ran.

"Glad to see you in one piece, sir." a soldier approached Oberon and saluted.

"Thanks to you, Sergeant," Oberon said, returning the salute before running a gloved hand across his face and leaving streaks of dry dirt that just made him more endearing to her. "We couldn't have held out much longer."

At least twenty odd soldiers in well-worn Uvlar suits milled into the area round the tree, "Your men need better protective gear," she said under her breath when she stood beside him.

"Yeah. Vestro had the inside track on suits. We can't find out where he had them made for his men. We're not a technological society anymore, so I'm baffled by what he seemed to be able to manage."

"Maybe we'll find out in the next few days," she said.

"Maybe."

* * * * *

She rubbed one temple with grimy fingers and felt the grit on her face. She wondered if she was as dirty as Oberon. The streaks of dirt on his face reminded her of the camouflage she sometimes used in the Boneyard.

Bolstered by surviving their near-death experience, she said, "Look, I'm no Maribel, but we can get through this."

"Damn straight." She heard the smile in his voice and snapped her head around to check. His expression at this moment, so serious, so sexy, made her knees lose a little of their strength. Her heart squeezed involuntarily.

His lips were as dry and cracked as her own, but she'd give her headgear to a beggar for one kiss. It'd most likely be amazing. Or would it be like last time, when he had no reaction at all?

He kicked a stone with his boot, and it bounced on the hard-packed ground.

They'd just had a moment, and neither of them knew what to do with it.

An hour later, tents were up and several bonfires burned around the camp to keep the animals back. Some of the soldiers carried bits of old wood from the leftover relics of buildings along their way. Others collected worm-eaten, rotted bits of brush, but it burned well enough.

During the last hour, Oberon had been busy with the men. He hadn't given her any idea what decisions were being made about their imminent attack on Vestro's stronghold. That ticked her off. She'd voice her complaint when, and if, she got Oberon out of earshot of his men.

She picked a solitary place near the center bonfire and sipped the most amazing cup of coffee, given to her from one of the soldiers' ration packs. She couldn't believe they had coffee and they shared it with her.

Most of the soldiers gave her a wide berth. She got the occasional nod in passing, but none of them said much to her. She'd been an outcast since the age of fourteen, so being ignored couldn't hurt her feelings. Just made her feel at home.

She settled cross-legged on the ground and stared out over the Nevermore. A first for her. Yes, she'd spent many nights in the Boneyard and might have dared to enter the edges of the Nevermore, but she'd never spent a night out here, until the last couple of days. Soldiers, on the other hand, spent half their lives out here. Someone had to hunt, grow food, and find the means to keep the people going by scavenging the ruins for whatever might help.

She closed her eyes and listened to the sounds of a billion insects in the night. The whirrs and clicks and glugging sounds coming and going in their own tempos created a symphony that almost soothed her ragged soul. When she opened her eyes, it had gone from dusk to night in such a short time. The dark yellow clouds that had bubbled across the sky were nearly undetectable.

Since she'd had little sleep the last two nights, her eyelids grew heavy. The continual drone of the insects played a lullaby she couldn't ignore, while a light breeze caressed her cheeks. She reached up and removed her headgear and face mask. The breeze lifted her moist hair and moved it, cooling her overheated scalp and neck.

Even the occasional roar or screech of something unknown in the distance seemed less threatening with all the testosterone-pumped soldiers around her. They were tough, and they would be ready for whatever came at them if their scarred outfits, heavy-duty knives and guns were any indication.

She leaned onto her side and rested her head on her hand. From the background chatter, she picked up a word or two. It seemed the soldiers were concerned about her not wearing her hood and face shield. She wished she could convince all of them they could safely breathe the air here, but they wouldn't believe it any more than Oberon had when she'd said the water in the stream had to be safe.

She heard more buzzing then felt the tingle. She slapped her neck. "Darned bugs," she said under her breath. Yeah, annoying, but secretly she felt liberated that not being covered from head to toe allowed her to experience a bug bite somewhere other than around her eyes.

It surprised her that the dogs hadn't come back. Maybe since they were pack hunters, they knew the soldiers outmatched them. As much as she wanted to sleep, it didn't happen, so she got up and walked the perimeter of the camp to stretch her taut, sore muscles.

After a quick trip to relieve herself, well, not so quick in an Uvlar suit, she went to the area cleared for bedding down and found a soft bit of ground. She'd closed her eyes for about ten seconds before she heard shoes crunching on gravel and someone clearing his throat.

She slowly opened her eyes and squeezed her fingers tighter around the blade clutched in her hand.

"Please don't use that thing on me," Oberon said in a low voice that did strange things to her insides. Why did she react so unexpectedly around him? So…viscerally.

He'd been smart enough to stand back before she could stick him with her knife.

"Thought you'd like to hear about my captain's ideas with regard to making it to Vestro's building. We've been setting up a plan of attack."

She shifted and turned her back on him. It ticked her

off that he'd left her out of the loop. Not that she knew much about planning attacks. "Whatever."

"You're angry with me."

The dumb statement ticked her off even more. "No kidding. You and I are supposed to be a team. I'm not your underling or some woman who should be kept out of the planning."

He cleared his throat, and even though she couldn't see him, she knew her message had hit home.

"You're right. I apologize." She heard Oberon's Uvlar unsnap, and she really wanted to look. No way he'd dare remove his hood. But, given his strong feelings, it was a wonder he wasn't freaking out because she'd left hers off.

"We do need to do this together," he said, sounding a little closer. Most likely, he was crouching down beside her.

She shifted a little but didn't turn around. "Why? Because some relative of mine left notes and your family decided to follow them?"

"Hell and damnation, Darla. If you wanted to scare the stuffing out of me, you couldn't have said anything worse." An exasperated noise came out of him. "Don't you believe in Maribel?"

"How do you know if any of this is even real?" Okay, internally, she'd tried to ignore the inner voice that had kept her on the right path her whole life. The voice didn't have a name, as far as she knew, and was most likely her own conscious thoughts, not those of some relative who'd lived two hundred years ago. At least, that's what she'd always told herself.

Grass rustled near them. "She's real," a familiar little voice said from the bushes.

Darla jumped up and automatically moved closer to

Oberon. To her ultimate surprise, his headgear hung on his back.

The little Yardman stepped out of the brush but stayed in shadow so the soldiers couldn't see him. He tipped his head in Oberon's direction. "Mister James," he said. "It's my pleasure to meet you."

* * * * *

Oberon shook the small Yardman's hand. Going by Blip's expression, Oberon had surprised him. Blip's body language suggested he had been treated poorly by Vestro and he expected the same from the new dictator. That made Oberon's gut twist. He wasn't cruel like Vestro, but maintaining a tough aura was a necessity if he wanted to maintain control of the city. So far, he'd managed to do that without doing anything that went against his moral code.

"Darla told me about you, Mister Blip," he said. "I don't know why you've chosen to help us, but we do appreciate anything you can tell us."

Huh? Darla's head snapped around to ogle him like she couldn't believe her ears. His gaze slid to hers with nary a hint at what he was thinking.

Blip nodded eagerly. "It's just Blip. And, yes. I want to help."

"Wait a minute. You said Maribel was real," Darla said. "What did you mean by that?"

"Just what I said. Your great-great-great-grandmother was real. Is still real—inside you."

Darla shook her head. "Yes, well, I'm afraid I'm a wagonload short of whatever she had. I'm not a seer."

The little Yardman quietly regarded Oberon. "But Mister James possesses the key to you becoming much more able to see."

Oberon frowned at him. "What are you talking—"

Was it a coincidence that his words suddenly cut off, as if he suddenly did know what Blip was talking about? "What do you know?" she demanded.

"Nothing. I don't know what he's talking about." Oberon eyed Blip.

"He has a name," she said, surprising herself by standing up for the Yardman. Small or not, she'd seen the horrors they were capable of perpetrating. Blip took two steps closer to her.

"You know, too, miss. You hear the voices."

Her turn to frown. What? How did he know?

"Okay, Blip. Start talking. Why do you know these things?"

"The prophecies weren't just left for you, Mister James. There were some left for me, as well."

"Benevolent hell," Oberon said, raising his voice loud enough that a soldier started toward them. Oberon quickly raised a hand to let the soldier know he wasn't needed.

"Geez, if this is my relative we're all talking about, why did everybody but me know about her?" Darla asked.

"I believe I know the answer to that," Blip said. "Maribel knew what kinds of challenges you were going to have to be strong enough to face. She needed you to experience the struggle of survival in order to prepare you. In fact, every member of your family had to travel this difficult path to make sure you were in the right place at the right time in this future."

She raised her eyebrows, and Blip's mouth shifted. Without any identifiable lips, this movement looked odd, but she suspected it was a smile.

"So how did you receive the prophecies?" she asked.

"I also got messages from Maribel," he said, and his chest puffed out just a bit more.

You know it's true. You know I'm here... The words whispered through her mind. She tried to shake the strange ideas away, but the sensation remained. Darla's attention turned on Oberon again. "What do you know that you haven't told me?"

Oberon eyed the little man then shook his head. It must have been bad. He appeared almost agonized.

"There is something, isn't there?"

He nodded slowly.

"It must be done, I'm afraid," Blip said. "And it must be done soon. Vestro has been preparing his legion of unholy soldiers. Even the Yardmen give them a wide berth."

Darla's eyebrows hiked higher. "What in the Benevolent's name could scare a Yardman?"

"Vestro is a scientist. He's been manipulating humans since he was a very young man. He's gotten quite proficient. Unfortunately, not proficient enough before he created me."

Her heart went out to Blip. She could feel the Yardman's pain as palpably as if it was her own.

"He's the monster, Blip, not you."

Blip's head lowered. "You are nicer to me than anyone has ever been, and I appreciate your sincerity." His hard little black-marble eyes appealed to her. "You'll need that kind of compassion before we're done. If we are to succeed, you're going to have to lead the Yardmen into battle against the Mortis."

"Mortis?"

"Vestro's personal demons. Like Yardmen, they're deformed, but their deformities go deeper. Yardmen were a disappointment to Vestro, and if I can say it without turning into salt, he got it right this time, if right is creating monsters who live to kill."

"Why did he create them?" she asked.

"So that their bodies are both armor and weapons. Their bones are tough as steel and twice as sharp, extruding from their skin. They slice through their opponents' flesh easily. Even their skulls can have spurs that are like razor-sharp blades."

"How did he create them?"

"He takes people and injects them with serum that makes their bones grow out of control. A very painful process for them. In the end, there are no two of them alike, because their bone spurs occur in different locations. The serum also makes them feral and cunning. It must do something to their minds, as well. Even if they were mild before, they're killers after. Worse, if they want to live, they have to toe Vestro's line. They'll do anything just to get their daily fix. But I think it's more than that. They get pleasure from killing."

"What is their daily fix? The serum that makes their bones grow?" Darla asked.

Blip's round head shook. "No. The overgrowth of their bone structure is too heavy for normal musculature to sustain, and it will crush their internal organs if they don't get a pill every day that keeps their connective tissue strong enough to keep their skeleton from caving in on them. Not something I'd like to live with."

"So they're like Yardmen with built-in weapons? Is that what you're saying?" Darla asked.

"No. Yardmen aren't intelligent. They have low IQs."

"Not all Yardmen, apparently," Oberon said.

"Thank you, sir." Blip bowed forward slightly. "Mortis are intelligent. Extremely intelligent. In fact, they'd probably revolt against Vestro if their lives didn't depend on the daily pill that keeps them alive. One day without that little red pill is torture for them. Two days, death. Their connective tissues tear, and their bones crush in on them. I've seen it happen. It's horrible. That's how Vestro controls them."

"That's barbaric," Darla said.

"Have you never met Vestro?" Blip asked without a hint of sarcasm in his voice.

"No, I haven't. But I've suffered because of him." She rubbed her branding scar and noticed that Blip and Oberon exchanged meaningful glances.

Blip's round, hairless head bobbed. "I'm Vestro's servant. I wait on him day in and day out. He treats me like filth. He's very distrustful, but I'm the only person he thinks is no threat..." Blip pointed at his small chest. "I guess Maribel knew that. That's why I'm part of her plan."

"Interesting," Oberon said, digging at the zipper of his Uvlar jacket. On a hot night like this, he must have been sweltering.

"Take it off. The air is okay here," Darla said, running her fingers through her hair.

Blip nodded his agreement. "The air is no longer toxic and hasn't been for decades. Vestro keeps the fear going. He wants society to rely on him alone."

"How does he know the air is safe? There is no working instrumentation."

Blip inhaled a quick breath. "Vestro's technology is fully active underground. He has a bunker that was created for the once-upon-a-time president of the ancient United States. There is electricity. Machines that run, air conditioning."

Darla gaped at Blip and then at Oberon. "Is it possible?"

Oberon shrugged his shoulders. "Now we know where the Uvlar suits are coming from. And there were lights in that tunnel. If he has electricity, he must have a factory?"

Blip nodded. "He has an underground city. A booming city bursting at the seams with his created deviants, and the normal soldiers who stay with him because they get food and better conditions. I don't think they've ever stopped to consider where the Mortis are coming from. Their numbers are dwindling."

Blip tipped his head as if he heard something. "I have to go. I understand if you're not sure you can trust me. Maribel said the trust will come very soon. I'm not sure why, or how."

"What do you mean..." Oberon straightened when he heard a branch snap. Just one of the soldiers snapping some twigs to throw into the fire, but when he turned back, Blip had left and Darla stared off into nothingness.

Her expression had changed, she looked like she'd been caught in a trance, so he reached out a hand to shake her awake but halted midstream. What if pulling her out of this trance would harm her?

He considered what Blip had said. Apparently, Blip knew that he'd branded Darla and ruined her life. But could he trust what the dwarf Yardman told him or was it all a setup by Vestro? He glanced at Darla again. He prayed the answers would come if he carried out his end of the prophecy.

But how could he do it? How could he brand her

again, this time to initiate her next level of psychic ability? Yet, the prophecy had been clear. She had to suffer at his hands again. He had to brand her. Burn her flesh. Only then would she know. Understand the forces building inside her. And it had to be done if civilization stood a chance to survive. But he knew how horrible it had been for her the first time. He'd seen her stroke her arm where she'd been branded, over and over again.

Maribel better help him. He wasn't sure that he could do it.

CHAPTER TWENTY-ONE

The night enveloped her, and she stared into the intense blue irises of the man who made her bones weak and her pulse thunder through her veins. So close, his breath warmed her forehead before his lips brushed her brow, then her mouth.

She melted into the heat of his kisses. Inhaled his clean, fresh-air scent. Always fresh.

"You know I'll always love you, darling," he said in that deep, sandpaper voice that created a sense of well-being inside her.

"You'd better," she said with a grin. Her hands caressed his face then rested over his heart, the terrain of his chest intimately familiar to her.

The heartbeat that reverberated under her hand, steady and strong, suddenly stopped. But her hand remained pressed against his chest. She'd felt his heart beating just a second ago and now—nothing. Panic surged through her. How could he still be looking at her? How could he still be standing?

"What's wrong?" he asked, reaching out and stroking her hair. She barely felt his touch.

Before she could answer, his image wavered.

A cool wind swirled down the nearly deserted city street, playfully tickling leaves and bending the branches of trees planted equidistant along the sidewalks. The air moved steadily toward her, until the wave caught her hair and ripped it from his fingers and blew it into her eyes. She clawed the strands away.

The nighttime skyscrapers, like guardians, hovered over her.

The music that had been pounding inside a building across the street and the sound of a jet overhead seemed farther away. A car horn beeping in the distance. The yowl of a cat in an alley. Fading...

Before she could speak, he had somehow distanced himself from her. In seconds, he'd moved to the other end of the block, looking at her with a wistful expression. How'd he get so far away, so fast?

A tear trailed a hot path down her cheek when he extended his hand toward her. He mouthed something she couldn't hear, but she knew what he'd said. She'd have known it even with her eyes closed.

"I love you, too," she said, but her words faded on the now stale wind that turned to dust in her mouth.

He'd nearly disappeared now. He had been slowly fading from the first moment she laid eyes on him.

She woke in a sweat, the remnants of her vision leaving nothing but the cold reality of her life.

A wild animal's howl in the distance made her shiver. She noticed Oberon watching her. She ignored his attention, suddenly embarrassed by her reaction to the dream. Had he been the man in her vision? The man she'd kissed, the man she loved? What did it mean?

"You were in a trance." He said it like it happened every day.

She squeezed her eyes tight and inhaled. "I guess I was. For a second, I was back in the twenty-first century."

He digested her statement without comment. If he didn't believe her, he didn't say so. And she tried not to stare at him, to wonder if his lips tasted the same as they had a moment ago in her trance. Would his arms wrapped around her make her feel that same euphoria?

The sudden need to find out scared her more than facing the Mortis. But why would she see him in a setting from the past? Had it been a message to prove that they could rebuild their world? Or Maribel's way of making her care for him, so she'd work with him?

"What did you see?" he asked.

"A different world. Blue sky, scented air, city sounds, and happy people," she said, deliberately leaving out sexy boyfriend who looks exactly like you. She glanced around. "Where's Blip?"

"He left during your trip to nirvana."

She cleared her throat. He had no idea. "Do you believe what he's telling us?"

"He knows about Maribel. It seems unlikely he'd know the things he does otherwise."

In fact, the wind whispered it in her ear, and her mind fairly blossomed under the truth of it. "What aren't you telling me? You and Blip obviously know something I don't."

"The prophecy," he said, his voice suddenly hoarse. He unzipped his jacket and let it hang open.

"What about it?"

"It says I have to brand you. Brand you, in order for your psychic talents to open up to the next level."

She touched her scar. "I've already been branded."

"I know."

The way he said that, she jerked her head in his direction and stared into tumultuous irises that reminded her of a strip of sky. "Do you know who did this to me?"

He nodded, and his jaw clenched.

Maybe in response to his tension, muscles in her back tightened to the point that she felt immobilized.

"I can guarantee the soldier regretted his actions." He continued to undo his Uvlar jacket.

"How do you know that?" She frowned. Imagined what his eyes had looked like peering out from behind the face shield of a much younger man. "You." She jumped to her feet. "You're the one who did it." Her eyes widened. "That means I burned you, too, didn't I?" That deep scar she'd seen on his shoulder had been her handiwork.

His shoulders were taut, and he braced himself as if to stop her from dashing into the Nevermore. "Darla, I know you'll never believe this, but I've never forgiven myself for what happened. I was young. Stupid. I should have said no."

She remembered him from then. He'd been tall and gangly, and when she'd fought back and pressed the brand into his shoulder, he'd screamed in agony. At that point, she'd managed to get away.

"I don't blame you for hating me," he said. "I've hated myself forever." He turned his face away from her so she wouldn't see his own self-loathing. "I...I thought you must be dead. Most of the others didn't survive." He removed his jacket, right down to the white sleeveless T-shirt underneath that revealed the scar that twisted his flesh horribly.

"How many of those branded citizens survived?" she asked bitterly.

"Too few. After branding you, I would never do it again. No consolation for you, I know. Vestro threw me in jail, but eventually he decided my soldiering skills were too good to lose, and he let me get away without following those particular orders—ever again!" His eyes clouded over. "In retrospect, I think he'd just wanted to keep a close eye on me."

She swayed. His foot slid toward her on the gritty earth, and she cringed when his hands touched her shoulders.

Too tired. Weak and wretched. She suddenly felt like she didn't have the strength for any of this.

She hadn't screamed when she'd been branded. She'd held it all in. Saved it for those times when she needed the anger to keep her going. To force her to survive.

Probably because of the grime on her cheek, a tear ended up near her earlobe.

It surprised her when she saw moisture on his face, too.

She turned away from him because she didn't know how to forgive him. She wasn't used to forgiveness. "Leave me alone. I have to come to terms with what you've just told me."

"I'm sorry," he said, getting dressed again and putting his face shield back on and leaving.

She pressed her palms to her eyes. She had to think.

The whole thing played out in her mind. Over and over again.

She'd gone to a place in the encampment where she

could sleep. Now she lay on the ground, curled into a ball, remembering how she'd vowed to kill the man who'd branded her. But over the years, she'd forgotten those eyes. How could she have forgotten?

Over the years she'd relived the fact that she'd turned the brand on the soldier. And he hadn't stopped her. He'd barely pressed the brand into her flesh, but she'd done much worse to him.

Now, as part of the prophecy, she had to be branded again? Grandmother, are you listening? Why are you doing this to me?

A low wail wound its way through the leaves and brush, building in intensity until sand and gravel spiraled into mini whirlwinds around the camp, and the soldiers scattered to keep their gear from blowing away.

"What's that?" She heard one of them say.

"Just normal events in the Nevermore," Oberon said, but Darla saw him glance at her as if he knew it had come from Maribel, too.

The wind died down, and she closed her eyes. As much as she wanted to deny it, she'd seen the pain in his eyes. He wouldn't brand her again, even if it meant saving their world. She'd have to make him do it.

She felt more tears threatening and tried to convince herself she couldn't waste the fluids. Being branded again would bring back horrific memories. Up to now, she'd survived on sheer willpower, faced with terrors no young girl should have to endure, all because she'd been branded.

She'd practically starved until she found the Boneyard. That had been her salvation. She'd scavenged parts for people of the city, and she'd always managed to avoid the Yardmen, until Rud had come along.

* * * * *

Oberon paced to the tent set up by his men. They'd made up a cot for him inside, but he couldn't sleep in there in that kind of superior comfort. And there was no way Darla would accept the offer of using it, not after what he'd just told her. He'd seen devastation mirrored in her eyes. She'd suffered beyond what any human being should suffer, and all because he'd carried out Vestro's orders. Why would the prophecy demand it happen again?

Maybe Blip had been right. Darla had to be tough and strong to get through the challenges ahead.

If that were true, did it also mean he had to be strong enough, too? Strong enough to brand her again? His gut clenched again, and he suddenly wanted to punch something.

He'd fallen for her all those years ago in the city center. He'd never stopped thinking of her. Worse, Rud had found her when he'd given her up for dead.

Almost as if mirroring his inner turmoil, the Nevermore reacted. Wind rose, and noises rustled in the brush, along with a pervasive hot breeze that swirled around everyone and scuttled their belongings.

No one slept well.

Oberon had barely fallen asleep before daylight broke with its usual yellow, clotted clouds hanging low overhead. No strips of blue to unnerve them today. Had he really expected it to be different?

After he glanced across the camp to make sure of Darla's safety, he washed up then let his nose lead him to the fire, where the soldiers had coffee on. They were eating their breakfast in shifts. Mandatory practice in the Nevermore. They always had to be on guard against the predators waiting for someone to slip up.

Covered head to toe in Uvlar, as always, and removing their face shields only to take a bite of food then put them back on again, some of them cast strange looks his way, like he'd gone mad. Maybe he had, because he'd removed his jacket and headgear this morning and hadn't put them back on.

Another hot, sticky day. Humidity hung in the air, and Oberon sensed a storm brewing. He inhaled and grabbed a steel cup and filled it with steaming, thick, black brew. The first swallow burned his tongue, but it felt good on the way down.

From his position, he could see Darla curled up in her blanket. Probably awake. He wanted to take her coffee but knew instinctively that he had to wait for her to come to him. She had a decision to make.

And he didn't think he could comply with it.

* * * * *

Blip made it back to Vestro's office seconds before the dictator began bellowing for him. His chest heaved. It had been a long trip through the tunnels and back. His short legs couldn't cover large areas easily, and his motorized cart had stopped working once he got past the underground city's outer reaches. He had no idea why electricity worked only in certain areas.

Vestro had many secrets. There were areas of the city Blip couldn't get into. As hard as he tried, it'd been impossible. The guards were deadly serious about doing what they were told, and he wasn't foolish enough to mess with the Mortis.

"Blip, you little bastard, where are you?"

Blip held the heavy tray loaded with Vestro's

breakfast and shoved the door open with his hip. His mouth gaped at the site of Vestro, standing on top of his desk in his underwear and holding a crystal of some sort in front of him.

"I can't get it to work this morning," he said. "That bitch is trying to shut down my ability to see."

Blip crossed the room to a table nearly as tall as he was. It took all of his strength every day to hike the tray over his head and slide it onto the table.

He'd never before seen Vestro gazing into a crystal.

"I'm sorry, sir. Is there anything I can do to help?"

Vestro jumped down and slammed the crystal onto his desk. "It's cold in here. Throw some straw bricks into the fire."

"Perhaps you'd like your housecoat?"

Vestro seemed shocked to find himself nearly naked. "Damn it, where were you this morning? You didn't lay my clothes out."

"I'm sorry, sir. I thought I did." Blip ran into the anteroom, a huge walk-in closet, and climbed up on the shelving made for him. He gathered more clothes and brought them out. The man could've just walked in and gotten his own clothes, for heaven's sake.

Instead of accepting the fresh clothes that Blip had gathered, Vestro sidestepped him and grabbed his housecoat from the bathroom door and donned it, then shoved his feet into the slippers that had been warming near the fireplace. "Don't let it happen again."

"Never," Blip said. Down here in the sub-basement, it always felt cold.

Vestro dropped onto a wooden chair at his desk and shoved a mouthful of food into his yap, talking the whole while. Ranting, really, like the madman he was. Only this time, Blip's blood turned to ice.

"That son of a whore Rudyard—going to put him in the courtyard and inject him with rigorra serum as soon as it's ready."

Blip raised his eyebrows.

"Can't do it sooner because there's no serum ready, damn it." He shoved in another mouthful of eggs. "He'll be a Mortis by the end of the week at the very latest, mark my words," he said, then laughed maniacally, toast crumbs flying everywhere.

Blip had the sudden wish that Vestro would choke on his breakfast.

He knew people often forgot he was even there. He also listened very carefully when Vestro talked in his drugged hazes. Especially when he believed he was alone.

Blip dusted the room and waited for Vestro to finish wolfing down his food like a ravenous pig at a trough. The second he finished, Blip tore out of the room with the tray. No time to drop it off at the kitchen, he ditched it in a closet and made for the barn. He had to get Rudyard out of the cage today, trust or not. If Vestro's Lab people came up with an early batch of serum, he wouldn't wait. Rud would become a Mortis before Oberon could save him.

Chapter Twenty-Two

Rud ached to stretch his legs but could barely move inside the dog cage not meant for a human being. He applied a little more of the antiseptic cream to his wounds. Without it, he'd probably have been in deep trouble. Infection ran rampant out here in the wilds and was probably even worse inside this manure pit of animals.

His stomach grumbled loudly, and he jumped. For a minute, he'd thought one of the creatures crouched nearby. He had to get out of here. He couldn't even have picked the lock if he'd had anything to pick it with. The door of the cage had been structured with several layers of chicken wire, and he couldn't get his whole hand outside, just a couple of fingers.

Would he have been free right now if he'd made Blip think he trusted him? He'd had no reason not to trust him. He'd fed him, given him antiseptic. But that had been a couple of days ago. Where was he now? He'd promised to come back.

The animals hadn't been fed, either, and some of them were watching him just a little too closely from cages that didn't look too sturdy. With their massive claws, he imagined they could carve an opening into his cage to get the sweetmeat inside.

"Rud."

Rud's attention snapped to the floor. Speak of the little devil. "Where've you been? I'm just about starved." He stared at the Yardman. He had no food, but he held a key nearly as big as his hand. Yes. Freedom.

"I have to get you out of here before Vestro has the chance to turn you into a Mortis in the main courtyard." The little man paused. "Vestro told me what he plans to do with you during his drug induced ranting today. After you become a Mortis, he's going to force you to kill Darla's mother, Marilee."

"Mortis? What is that?" Then the rest of the sentence sank in. "Darla's mother is here? She's still alive?"

"She must be over there somewhere." He pointed with his stubby hand. "Right now I don't have time to explain what the drug will do to you, but the reclamation process is painful and it will turn you into a mutated killer. Not something I suppose you're interested in being, especially when an innocent woman could die at your hands shortly after." The little man shuffled around the cage, reached up and tried to fit the key into the lock over his head.

"Oh no. I can't reach it. Wait. I'll find something to stand on. Be right back."

"Hurry," he said, then thought about being turned into a monster and worse, being forced to kill Darla's mother. And then he thought about the Yardmen. Was that how they had come about? Society had always blamed the bad air. Maybe that wasn't true?

When he heard shuffling to his left, he expected Blip, but instead, saw was a pair of legs with bones jutting out of the shins and hip areas. Bones so sharp they had sliced right through the makeshift Uvlar suit the guy wore. He returned his gaze to the beast's face. Rud felt nauseated suddenly, and the cage spun slowly under him.

Sunken eyes and overgrown teeth and spurs on top of the semi-balding head—the last thing he'd expected to see here, alone. A Mortis.

The monster planted a stool on the floor, then he sat on it and stared at Rud. Rud's spirits sank. The little Yardman couldn't help him escape now. He'd just been put under heavy guard. And he had no doubt this killer was very capable of making sure he didn't escape. Its eyes were the worst, sunken and bloody, with no irises and tiny pupils. The guy's pain level had to be excruciating. Maybe that was why his skin appeared to be such a horrible gray color.

"What's your name?" Rud asked.

The Mortis stared at him, bared his teeth and growled low in his diaphragm. Maybe he couldn't speak?

They both heard movement at the end of the aisle. It had to be Blip, this time. If the little guy got caught, there'd be hell to pay. "Why are you here, Mortis?" Rud said in a voice loud enough to be heard over the roars inside the barn.

The Mortis scowled and glanced around suspiciously.

A few moments later, the rustling stopped. "Damn rats," Rud said.

Bleak eyes narrowed and shifted left to right. The Mortis might not speak, but he definitely understood what Rud had just said.

Blip had said he was going to be turned into

something like the abomination in front of him. Holy frickin' unbearable pain. He pressed his hands against his forehead. Now he understood why Oberon had to do this job and not him. A little too late for him, though.

He glanced at the end of the building where huge doors to the outside were usually left open, probably because of the stench. Would Blip have a chance to get him out now?

Probably not.

He cringed. Not only had he been deluded into thinking he'd be able to see the prophecy through to the end, but he'd screwed things up royally.

He closed his eyes and willed his brother to succeed. If anyone could do it, Oberon could.

After he wallowed in his own misery for about ten minutes, a surge of adrenaline worked its way through his muscles. He was a James, too. No way he'd give up. He'd find a way to get out of this mess, one way or another.

* * * * *

Finally invited into the war room, Darla listened in on the attack plans this time. Something had been left out. Some information they needed but didn't have.

"I've sent two scouts back to the city for reinforcements. Our army will arrive tomorrow, then we'll begin the final stages of our strategy," Oberon said.

According to their plans, they'd go in with guns blasting, and with no idea if that would work. They'd never seen a Mortis. What if they were bullet resistant? Blip had said they had extra-thick bones.

At the end of the session, she stepped away. She walked to the outer rim of the encampment, which had been set up beside the stream. It burbled noisily over pebbles of various sizes, and she couldn't resist taking off her boots and dipping her toes into the water. The uncomfortable air already warned of another extremely hot, humid day.

Scanning the stream bank, she saw there were no recent animal tracks. Camp activity had most likely scared most beasts away. Nevertheless, she kept her pistol nearby.

"You seem to like to have your body exposed to toxins in one way or another," a deep voice intoned behind her. She heard the humor in his words this time. He wasn't quite as mortified at her being out of her Uvlar gear anymore. Maybe he believed her after all.

She managed a smile. "I'd take all my gear off if it didn't serve as a deterrent against a wolf chewing on me." She poked at her ribs under her jacket. "It's darned hard for them to get through the Uvlar. Gives a gal a chance."

He laughed and, for one second, things felt normal between them. It made her think of the dreams she'd had of the two of them—if it was him in her dreams. Her gaze went straight to his mouth. She'd often tasted him in her dreams. Deep down she wanted to know if his kisses could be as world-bending as they were in her imagination. On the other hand, maybe he wasn't the one, considering the kiss in the cave.

She patted the sand beside her. "Sit with me for a minute."

His smile disappeared slowly, and he sat down. Dressed head to toe in Uvlar, he must have been envious of her bare toes dangling in the water.

"What's up?"

"I think your plan of attack is good," she said.

"But..."

"We're not ready for this fight," she said. "We don't know what we're going after. It's more than just Vestro, I'm sure of it." She pushed up her sleeve and pointed at her scar. "If this is the only way for us to do this thing and survive, we've got to do it. You have to brand me again."

"No." He started to get up again.

"Sit," she said in a tone that stilled him instantly. "We've come this far, Oberon. Your family has followed Maribel's prophecies for two hundred years. Does it make sense for you to question her now? Especially since this is supposed to be the most important part of the prophecy?"

"I can't do it," he said. She heard the agony in his voice.

"It's not like I'm looking forward to it, either," she answered. "But I think we have to. There's no other option."

He heaved a shattered breath. "Benevolent almighty, Darla. I've spent my whole adult life wishing I could take back that one moment. I should have saved you, not burned you. And now I'm expected to torture you again? How can I? I'd rather we go in fighting and take our chances."

"And die trying. Or worse, let down every living person in the country? There are worse things than branding me, Oberon. You must know that's true."

He shook his head, his mouth forming a stubborn line. "I don't know that."

She wouldn't beg. "I'm telling you to do it." She swallowed hard and glanced back at the fire burning in the center of the encampment. She opened her jacket, took it off and threw it on the ground. "Can I borrow your T-shirt? I'd rather not do this in front of all the men in my bra."

"This is fucking crazy. I can't do it."

"It's just a T-shirt." She tried to use humor to help calm him. "Is there a branding iron here in the camp?"

"Darla, how can you ask this of me?"

Her heart nearly fractured at the sight of his anguish. "I can ask you because Maribel knows you are the one person on this planet strong enough to carry this through."

He swallowed hard at the impact of her statement. "You're very sure?"

"Never been more sure of anything in my life. We must do this." Her eyebrows rose. "Branding iron?"

He nodded gravely. "Probably. Even though it's been outlawed by me, we'll most likely find one or two in some of the soldiers' rucksack contents. Sometimes, change is hard for people."

"Good thing. Go get one. And start heating it up. I want to get this over with. And the sooner, the better," she said, pasting on a brave smile, while her stomach swirled and she felt like she'd stepped outside herself. Maybe the pain wouldn't be so bad?

He cleared his throat, his voice suddenly raw. "Benevolent hell."

She touched his shoulder, and he jerked around to look at her. "It will be Benevolent hell if we don't at least try everything we can to save our people." A breeze blew around her, and for a moment she felt Maribel's encouragement. "Did you feel that? We're doing the right thing."

He slowly took off his jacket and T-shirt and handed it to her.

Darla tried to keep herself from freaking out the whole time Oberon explained the situation to his men, so they wouldn't try to stop the branding. Some of them cursed under their breath in disgust. Others were silent. The brandings had been done during a dark time in their society. Most soldiers had had to do them, and the shadows of their past hung heavily on them. One soldier stepped forward. In his hands, a piece of steel marked with a D.

A half-hour later, Oberon was sweating so hard his hands must have been wet, because he kept rubbing them against his hips. He stared at the poker buried under the coals.

Nearly ready, the branding iron pulsated that reddish-orange-white color that reminded her of searing pain. Maybe fear had blocked her hearing, because suddenly the Nevermore held its breath in anticipation. The winds died. The insects and birds were silent.

Not a sound, not a breath happened when Oberon retrieved the branding iron from the hot coals and blew on the end to get pieces of wood off. If she knew him, he'd do it quickly. It would only hurt for a while, right?

She inhaled and nodded to him, then held out her arm so he could brand her in the same place. No sense getting another scar when she already had one.

Several of the men stood around the fire, watching and waiting. One of them had salve and wet towels ready to swathe her burn as soon as possible. No doubt, the medic stood here on Oberon's orders.

"Just do it," she said. "It's worse to wait."

He pressed the brand against her flesh. It sizzled and

burned for a split second before he yanked it away and dropped it onto the ground.

She waited for the pain to hit. Her arm turned red where she'd been branded. The area bubbled for a second. The pain flashed through her, but then it disappeared, and when she expected blisters to start forming, it started to heal. What the…?

One of the soldiers shouted Oberon's name. She heard him moan and saw him drop to his knees while smoke billowed off his shoulder, where she'd branded him years ago. It burned too long. Much longer than a few seconds.

With everyone in shock, she got hold of her senses and shouted, "Put the wet towels on him, quick."

Even after the burn had been covered with a wet towel, it continued to smoke. "Get water from the stream," she shouted. "Hurry."

Even though the men still believed the stream to be beyond toxic, one of them ran and filled a jug, then poured the water onto their leader's shoulder. Steam rose up in a hiss, and then finally—finally, the burning stopped.

Oberon toppled over onto the hard-packed dirt. He'd passed out from the pain.

Somehow, the pain had transferred from her to him, only much worse than it would've been for her. She couldn't believe her arm. He'd barely singed her.

Before she could drop to the ground next to him, a howling sound rose up from the Nevermore. As if every animal out there suddenly felt Oberon's pain. Reverberations like the deep rumbling of the earth before it cracks wide open filled her ears, only they came from the living things, not the planet.

Suddenly, wind whipped her hair around her head, and

she felt her bare feet lift off the ground, just barely.

"My love, you've done it. You and Oberon. Joined in pain and in duty. You must stay with him, keep him alive. You need him more than you know."

Darla felt her feet touch down, and she dropped to her knees next to the man who'd taken her pain—and then she, too, fell into a black oblivion.

CHAPTER TWENTY-THREE

Darla woke slowly and found herself still lying on the ground where she had dropped. The men were leaning over their leader, concern etched in their condemning eyes.

She pushed off the ground and edged through the soldiers watching Oberon. He was still unconscious. "Not possible!" Darla stared at the debilitating and vicious red burn on Oberon's shoulder. It was bad. Very bad. But how?

A medic applied salve and began wrapping a bandage around his shoulder. When Darla dropped next to him, she asked to take over wrapping his wound.

"It won't help, ma'am," the medic said.

She sighed. "I know, but I'd feel better if I could try."

He nodded. "Go ahead."

The medic waited for her to finish then turned to her. "Ma'am, what about you? May I tend to your burn?" he asked.

She held her arm out. The scar barely seemed red now.

He looked as shocked as she probably did.

Oberon moaned. Still lying on the parched red dirt beside the fire, his head moved back and forth. "Where's Darla? Is she okay?" He winced when he tried to move his arm.

"A heck of a lot better than you are, James," she said. Her instinct was to baby him, but he'd hate that. Especially in front of his men.

She didn't like the way his men were looking at her now. Like she'd deliberately done this to him. The medic helped him sit up. Oberon's face had turned pale as smoke.

She'd felt odd since their horrendous ceremony had played out. Kind of fuzzy, like her head had filled with cotton that was slowly being torn out her left ear. Not a pleasant sensation, but his arm ended up being a lot worse.

"Get him inside the tent," she said. "He needs to lie down and rest."

"Hey, I'm the one who gives the orders around here." He forced a faint laugh. "But, this time, I am in agreement."

Inside, with his shoulder propped on pillows, he faded in and out of consciousness.

His men ranted outside. They'd clumped into groups and were doing so much talking, it made her nervous. After a couple of hours, Oberon's eyes opened again, and he found her in the chair next to him. "What's going on out there?"

"I don't think your men are fond of me right now," she said, pulling the chair a little closer.

"How do we explain what just happened? They're a little superstitious to start with."

Darla grimaced. At least the mind cotton had nearly gone, and a colorful world of images had taken its place. Images of things going on inside Vestro's stronghold, and none of them good. All of this information, thanks to her new and growing psychic abilities.

She blinked hard and pulled herself back to find Oberon watching her.

"Did it work? Do you have Maribel's abilities now?" he asked.

"I don't know about that, but I am seeing more than I've ever seen before. For example, I'm pretty sure Vestro is preparing to move against us. He knows we're coming. He has a spy inside your troops."

"Do you know who it is?" His dark eyebrows rose. His expression turned livid.

"No, I haven't quite gotten the hang of this thing yet."

He nodded, as if understanding how hard it would be to realize the full potential of her gifts. He had no idea.

He exhaled slowly. "I should have expected a spy. Most citizens haven't accepted me. They don't understand, before it gets better, it can only get worse. I don't have the resources Vestro has. Our people are hungry. And that makes some people desperate."

"Probably true." In fact, she'd been one of those people.

His rapt attention made her squirm. "How's your arm?"

"It's fine," she said, feeling guilty.

"Don't be a martyr." He grimaced but managed to slide his head across the pillow to look down at her arm. "Let me see it."

She held it up. All that was left was her old scar from years ago. Not even pink.

He lightly touched the bandage on his shoulder. "How did you do this?"

She hated the question in his voice, like he actually believed she could or would have done that to him on purpose.

"I didn't do it to you—not this time." She bit her lip. "At least I don't think I did."

"Whatever this is that happened between us—I guess it was supposed to go down like this." He settled his head back on the center of the pillow again. "I'm glad I took your pain away. I can live with this." His eyes closed, and she waited until she heard his even breathing again. He'd fallen asleep.

She leaned forward with her hands clenched in front of her. "Yeah, but can I?" Several soldiers gawked her way. "And can they?"

Oberon slept the rest of the afternoon away while the men worked around camp and eventually cooked dinner. They offered her nothing. Her stomach growled, but no way would she ask for food.

Rustling brought her attention to the ground at the base of the canvas. Small fingers lifted the edge, and Blip crawled under. He breathed heavily, and mumbled to himself under his breath.

"Blip? What's wrong?"

"Oh, Ms. Rune."

"Please, call me Darla," she said and gently helped him onto his feet.

His little forehead scrunched, full of worry wrinkles. Being bald and with such a round face, meant the slightest frown became highly exaggerated.

"I can't rescue Rud. I nearly managed it today, but Vestro put a Mortis on guard. He's going to start injecting him as soon as the serum's ready. It could be ready in the next couple of days, maybe even sooner. And then, shortly after that, he'll be turned into a Mortis. Then he's going to kill your mother."

"How'd Vestro find my mother? I stayed away for years, to keep her safe." Darla's blood lost its ability to deliver oxygen to her brain. She felt like she might pass out. "What can we do?"

"You must begin your attack as soon as possible if you hope to save them."

She jerked her head in Oberon's direction, and Blip's gaze followed hers. "Oh no. What's wrong with Mister James?"

"He's severely injured."

"That's bad. That's very bad." Blip started pacing back and forth, his arms stretched to their limits behind his back, his fingers barely able to touch.

"I'll be able to fight," Oberon said, opening his eyes. "We'll save them."

Darla saw images swirling in her mind's eye. This new, stronger psychic ability was more than a little confusing. She held up a hand for the two men to wait while she closed her eyes and pressed her fingers to the center of her forehead. She let her grandmother lead her where she needed to go. Images flooded her mind, and suddenly, she understood what she had to do.

She stood and held a hand over Oberon's injury and recited a phrase under her breath.

"What are you doing?"

"You'll be much better after the sun sets."

* * * * *

Oberon squeezed his eyes closed and swallowed down

a palpable wave of pain and wondered why her voice had sounded different. "Only an hour to sunset, thank the Benevolent," he grated.

Before she could put a cool cloth on his forehead, he lifted his head and caught the attention of one of his men walking by. "Branson."

"Sir, yes, sir."

"Did anyone feed Ms. Rune dinner?"

Branson slanted a sheepish look at her. "I'm not sure, sir."

"Bring her and my little friend dinner, please."

"What about you, sir?"

"I don't think I could stomach a thing right now," he said, wincing when he lowered his head back down.

Only, Branson didn't move. He stared at Blip. "What in Benevolent hell is that?"

Oberon said, "His name is Blip. Blip, this is Corporal Branson."

"How do you do, sir," Blip said, bending politely.

Branson offered an obligatory, very curt nod, and turned on one heel and left for the food tent.

"Sorry about that, Blip," she said.

"Not a problem, Ms. Darla. Usually it's much worse than that."

Waves of images continued to assault her. She grabbed onto the next one, and wished she hadn't. Sweat beaded on her upper lip and she momentarily considered ignoring it. What if it was wrong?

No. She knew in her heart it wasn't wrong. She had to say something.

"Blip, I have bad news for you. There's a spy in our camp. You're not going to be able to go back now because the spy may have seen you. You'd be in too much danger."

"Oh no. I'm sorry. I wanted to help Rud, not make things worse."

"We have to have faith in Maribel's plan, if we hope to succeed," Darla said. "And, Blip, you're very important to that plan. You're exactly where you're supposed to be."

"Maribel is talking to you now?" he asked.

"There's a definite voice in my head. I think I've always heard it. But it's clearer now."

"What is Maribel telling you?" Blip asked.

"That you must gather the Yardmen, and we will lead them into battle. But not before Oberon and his men get to Vestro's factory. First, we must cut off the source of the red pill that the Mortis take daily."

Blip's eyes grew huge, so big in fact that Darla could see the actual white part of his eye. "Maribel knows about the pills. That's brilliant. But it's also very dangerous. The Mortis are killers, deadly cunning, and they will fight like the devil to stay alive. Those pills are their life force."

"This war is going to happen whether we want it to, or not," Oberon said. "Will the Yardmen follow you, Blip?"

"Probably not, but they will follow Brawn, and he will listen to me. There's something else that will give us an advantage," Blip said, looking directly at Darla. "The Yardmen respect you, Ms. Rune. You've been in the Boneyard almost as long as they have. They know you were brave enough to venture inside, and you gave them a wide berth, in their eyes respecting them. You're a bit of an idol to some of them."

Her eyebrows hiked. "That's not what I expected you to say. But what about the Yardman that Rudyard killed?

Will that affect how they feel?"

"He isn't dead, just had a bad headache. But right now he's in worse trouble because the other Yardmen didn't like the fact that he could have hurt you. There'll be a tribunal, and who knows what his fate will be?"

"Oh," Darla said, not sure how she felt about that at the moment.

"For the most part, Yardmen aren't bright, but they're strong and hardy. They might be our only way to stop the Mortis." Blip's expression turned sad. "Though I'm sure some will have to lose their lives in order to do that."

Darla's heart felt heavy. "Yes, I'm sorry, Blip. It seems the only way," she said, and touched Blip's shoulder. "We'll make sure they understand what they're volunteering for. They won't have to do it if they don't want to."

He nodded.

Shadows lengthened in the tent. While Darla and Blip had been discussing Yardmen, Oberon had been so quiet she thought he'd fallen asleep again. Suddenly, he sat up and began unwrapping his shoulder.

She rushed toward him. "Hold on. What are you doing?"

"It doesn't hurt anymore."

"How's that possible?"

He glanced outside the tent. "While you two were having your discussion and waiting for dinner, the sun has set. You healed me."

"I spoke whatever words came into my head..."

"However it worked, I'm feeling like a new man..."

Now that the bandages were off, they could see that his scar had returned to its previous state. Apparently, they both remained scarred from their earlier encounter, but not from this one.Oberon jumped off the cot and made for the entrance to the tent. "Where are you going?" Darla asked.

"To find the traitor," he said on a growl and marched outside. Darla exchanged a surprised look with Blip. Oberon really had healed.

Darla sat on the ground to be closer to Blip. "How will you contact your friend, Brawn? Especially since you can't go back."

"I have routes no one knows about but me."

"What if he doesn't want to help?"

"No worries there. Like all Yardmen, Brawn hates Vestro. Besides, he and I have been trying to come up with a way to stop that monster's inhuman creations. The Yardmen will follow you, with Brawn as their captain. In fact, they'd probably follow you without Brawn, but he's most able to keep them in a cohesive unit."

Darla thought about all those years in the Yard. They'd known about her. They'd left her alone as long as she didn't mess with them. They'd shared a camaraderie with her that she hadn't known existed.

Dare she hope they'd be able to fight the Mortis and win? She'd seen their image in her mind. Terrifying. Almost unbeatable.

Her heart fluttered. Somehow, asking the Yardmen to fight the Mortis felt like tossing very big babies off a cliff. Then again, the Yardmen might not be as bright as the Mortis, but when it came to sheer brute strength, it'd be anyone's guess who'd be stronger.

"Okay, Blip. Let's set this plan into motion. And while you're doing that, Oberon and I will break into the drug factory. We'll shut off their supply of red pills."

Blip had lifted the canvas to leave but held it there and

frowned at Darla. "Maybe I should go with you?"

"No. You have a much more important job. Talk to the Yardmen. By then, Oberon's army should be here, too. We have to move in before Rud can be injected," he said.

Thoughts and images whizzed through her brain and made her feel almost panicked. She'd have to learn how to focus on grabbing the information she needed. One image at a time.

* * * * *

Oberon found Grant double-checking their weapons. "Come with me," he grunted and stalked toward the Nevermore. He ignored his soldier's shocked expression while he led Grant to a secluded section of the camp.

"Sir? How are you up and walking around?" Grant asked.

Oberon rolled his shoulder and showed Grant the old scar. "Somehow, our little psychic has healed me. She's more powerful than she realizes," he said more to himself than to Grant.

"Holy Benevolent." Grant breathed.

"There's more. I'm afraid we have a traitor in camp," Oberon said.

"What? How do you know that, sir? Surely you're not listening to that mutated dwarf Yardman." Apparently, Branson had been talking.

Oberon's gaze narrowed on Grant while he read his friend's body language. "What's going on, Grant? Do you know who the traitor is?" Oberon recognized his change-the-subject tactic instantly.

Grant shrugged. "Course not."

"But you have your suspicions, don't you?"

A breeze rustled the dry brush around them, and both

men surveyed their surroundings. If anything moved, it'd be dead meat. "Who is it?" Oberon asked.

Grant's head lowered. "What if I'm wrong? It's only a suspicion."

Oberon slanted his head and frowned at Grant. "Don't you trust me to handle this situation fairly? Hell, man, you've known me since boot camp."

Grant chewed on his lip. "It's the new kid. His name is Roy. You know, the one we saved from the wolves last year, but not before he lost one hand. He works so hard in camp. Problem is, he goes missing during the night sometimes. Says it's to use the latrine, but there's something off about him lately." Grant rubbed the ruff of hair on top of his closely shaved head. "I tried to put it down to his injuries making him a little odd in the head, but it's more than that, I'm afraid."

Oberon moved his neck back and forth to ease the stiffness lingering there. "We're about to wage war. We can't afford anyone finding out what our plans are. Can you keep him under wraps without him getting suspicious?"

"Yeah, sure."

"If not, we'll have to detain him. Leave him behind."

"But that'd mean…"

"I know, he'd be wolf bait, or worse, bait for some other animal. Not much we can do about it. We can't afford a leak at this point." The worst part, the kid had already been wolf bait. Leaving him behind would be the worst kind of torture.

"Understood, sir."

"If only we had a cage or something with us. We could detain him and know he'd still be in one piece when we got back." Oberon turned, chewing on his lip and trying to figure out a way to keep the kid alive while they were gone. Since the kid had been through so much, it had probably screwed him up pretty bad.

"Let's get back to camp. The rest of our men should arrive shortly after dawn. If our scouts made it back to the city okay, that is."

Grant exhaled heavily. "It's going to be a long freaking night."

"I know," he said, and stared at the shaft of silver light piercing the thickened clouds and illuminating the Nevermore. He knew from reading about the past that once upon a time the world had experienced the sun and moon without cloud cover. It must have been glorious. It could be again.

An idea struck him. "There's another way to find out if Roy's the traitor. We'll feed him disinformation and let him make his way back to Vestro. If we can send them looking for us in the wrong direction, it'd give us a chance to go after the pill factory."

Grant grinned at Oberon. His unshaven face and wide jaw exuded excitement. "That's why you're the leader. That's a brilliant idea. Okay, so what will we tell him?"

"That we're going to the field where I found Darla and Rud. It's at least a day's march away from us. We'll say that Rud dropped a parchment with information critical to our mission."

"Good," Grant said, beaming. "Very good," he said, looking back at the camp, and tipping his head toward the soldiers. "Looks like Roy's on break, having a coffee at the campfire. Think I'll join my men, have a chat about where we're going first thing in the morning." He winked at Oberon and sauntered off as if he hadn't a care in the world.

"Captain Ford, you have my gratitude and respect. Always," Oberon said under his breath.

From a distance, Oberon watched Roy swallow the news with rapt attention. Not too long after that, the little weasel made for the bushes. Oberon stepped into the tent and surveyed its interior.

"Blip gone?"

She nodded.

"Surely not back to Vestro?"

"I don't think so, but I'm not positive. He feels terrible about not helping Rud escape. He knows his position has been compromised and he shouldn't go back, but he needs to bring the big Yardman in on our plan."

"The little guy is brave."

"He certainly is," she said. "Blip will work with Brawn to herd the Yardmen and get them to help us."

Oberon heard the pain in her voice.

"It's necessary, Darla. We need their help if we hope to win this war."

Her eyes reflected every inch of torture she felt at luring witless giants into a battle they might not win. "I know. But I hate it."

Oberon glanced out at his men.

None of them would stand a chance unless they could persuade the Yardmen to join them.

"We have to make up a smaller tactical team for tonight," he said.

"Good. I think I know where the pill factory is."

Oberon grinned. "I know exactly where it is. He pulled a small map out of his pocket. "Blip left this in my tent yesterday. Of course, once we get into the tunnels, the map won't help. Do you think you can take it from there?"

She nodded, trying to answer while focusing on visual messages forcing themselves into her consciousness.

"If what I'm seeing is right, the factory is heavily guarded by the Mortis themselves. We'll have to make the strike without any of them alerting Vestro. It won't be easy," she said.

"Darla?"

She turned to him. It surprised her when he plunged his hands into her hair, wrapped his fingers around the back of her neck and pulled her closer until his breath warmed her face. She'd always been attracted to his blue eyes, but this close she could see the gold and green flecks in them.

He kissed her long and hard, and she felt a different sort of out-of-body experience. The room spun a little, and her knees felt weak. When she'd let Oberon brand her, they'd lit a fire between them that couldn't be quenched in one lifetime. This wasn't just a kiss, but an awakening. They'd been connected when he tried to save her, and again when he'd branded her, severely burning himself. They were meant to be together, always.

His kiss turned her insides to lava. For the first time in her life, she let herself trust. He pulled her tighter against him until they were so close nothing could ever separate them. She sighed against his lips.

A dark evening in the twenty-first century burst forth in her mind. Two people sitting on a bench, enjoying a glass of wine and watching the ocean. It smelled clean and salty, and the breeze felt so pure. It hadn't really been them, but it had been a message to her. They could bring this life back for everyone.

He let go of her long enough to close the tent flap. Now, they were alone. "I've waited so long for this moment." He pulled her against him again and whispered a delicious suggestion in her ear.

"But we just met a few days ago," she said in a teasing tone.

"I've loved you from the first moment we met."

"When you saved me?" she said softly.

"When I let you down, you mean?" His voice grew husky.

"It seems we've always been bound to each other." She felt his mouth against her neck, and her skin reacted with chills of pleasure. Two fingers slipped under the T-shirt he'd given her and unhooked the strap of her bra and then slid it down her arm. She couldn't wait for his hands to be on her bare flesh.

The T-shirt went quickly, then she pulled her bra off and thrilled at the sound of his breath catching. "You're beautiful," he moaned.

"I don't need compliments, Oberon. I need you." She took his hand and led him to his cot, the bed that an hour ago had held his severely maimed body. Only now, he'd healed. Completely.

And so would she, or she would after he made love to her.

He settled her back on the cot and knelt beside her, helping her yank off her Uvlar pants and then removing his own. She grinned at him. "It's been a long time for you, hasn't it?"

He shook his head. "I've been waiting for you, my love."

"You have not."

He took her mouth again and slid his tongue against hers. Warm and erotic, he slowly explored inside, while his hands explored everywhere else. On fire now. And when she touched him, her desire and her love for him grew with each second.

His mouth slid down her neck, and he suckled one breast and then the other, while she stroked him until she thought he might begin to purr.

"Don't treat me with kid gloves," she said. "I won't break." Her statement had driven him to the brink, and he stopped for a moment, took a few deep breaths and stared deeply into her eyes.

"You're sure?" he asked. His expression told her he wanted this experience to last as much as she did. But they both knew the chances of them both surviving their upcoming battle were slim. Tonight was their only chance, and they didn't have long.

"It's too bad we didn't meet sooner," she said, sliding her tongue along his earlobe and making him shiver.

He grinned. "We did, but you hated me." Oberon kissed her again, like a man possessed, a man who needed to possess in order to save his own soul. And she needed him to save her, too.

They caressed each other until she thought she might dissolve into liquid. And then his mouth moved lower, and she tried not to cry out in ecstasy. "You're making me crazy," she panted as low as she could. No way did she want the soldiers to know what was going on inside the tent.

She'd never made love, ever. And this man, all muscles and tough outer exterior, was as gentle and wonderful a lover as she could have imagined.

"I need you now," she said. "If you continue doing that, I'm going to be unable to hold in the scream of pleasure. The whole camp will know you're doing the down-and- dirty with me in here."

His head lifted, and his eyes sparkled at her. "Far from dirty, more like doing what comes natural—especially for us. Even though it's best not to shout it to the rafters now, I will be telling everyone how I feel. After we've won the battle and you're out of danger. And," he said, grinning, "when you're not stuck in a camp full of men who'll be jealous of what we're doing right now."

She'd already heard some of the soldiers speculating that Oberon had followed the dissident's advice because he had the hots for her. They hadn't sounded impressed.

"You and I are bound to each other, but not because we have to be, because we want to be," he said and kissed her collarbone.

"Make love to me," she said in a gritty voice, her teeth tight together.

"With pleasure," he whispered and covered her with his impressive body and slowly, gently buried himself inside her. "You okay?" he asked.

"Never better. Now move!"

He inhaled, kissed her deeply and began the in-and-out motion that created mind-blasting friction between them. Who knew it would be this erotic, this sensual, this unbelievable? "Oh, oh, I don't know if I can be quiet." She grabbed his buttocks and held on with everything she had inside while his rocking tempo picked up its pace.

Hot, slippery and edged with passion, they moved against each other until the night became theirs alone. Her emotions raw and with unadulterated passion pulsing through her, she tightened rhythmically around him. His breath faltered. He groaned and began moving against her again, harder this time. She bit her lip when the sensation built to another crescendo, and she began meeting his thrusts with her own until her world exploded into a dazzling climax that went on and on.

She could tell by his ragged breathing that he went over the edge of the cliff with her. They fell through the sparkling lights, and floated on fluffy white clouds, then landed softly. Their breathing gradually returned to normal, and he kissed her again.

"I've died and gone to heaven," he said.

She smiled against him and tried to push away their reality. Tomorrow, they might just die. Period. But at least they'd experienced each other before that could happen.

Oberon's watch beeped. He raised his arm. Nine o'clock. "Crap." He jumped up and started yanking on his clothes, then ran a quick hand through his hair and winked at her. "Get dressed. I forgot I called a meeting." He checked his ancient wind-up watch again. "In half an hour, actually. Here." He breathed hard. "I'll go fend everyone off until you're ready."

She smiled. "Too bad, I'm ready for round two."

"Jehova," he said. "Don't do that to me. I have to be able to walk when I get outside." He smiled, and then forced a professional expression onto his face. "We need a few minutes alone again before we go into battle," he said, his expression suddenly very serious.

She grinned hopefully.

"No time for anything that good, my sweet." He quickly remade the bed, military-style, then ran a hand over the blanket to make sure it was taut. He turned and grabbed her hand, brought it to his lips and kissed it. "I'll go distract my officers for a few minutes to give you time to slip out and freshen up. Meet us back here as soon as you're ready, okay?"

Mindless of him staring greedily at her nakedness, she

pulled on her panties and bra, then slipped into her Uvlar. "I could never make a bed that well," she said. "No one will even know I've been here."

"Oh, I'll know," he said with a wide grin. "And I won't forget it for a very long time," he said in a low voice charged with emotion.

"Me either." She yanked up the back of the tent, Blip style, and before she ducked out, said, "See you in a few minutes, Mister Dictator."

"Governor," he said in fake exasperation. Normally, she was able to push every button he had. But those last few buttons were the best yet.

He met Grant crossing the encampment coming toward his tent. "Sir, our plan worked. Roy didn't come back this time."

Oberon sighed. He felt bad for Grant, who really liked the kid. "Good. Hopefully, he made it to Vestro and will deliver our message."

"I imagine he's there right now, spilling his guts. And, I doubt he'll come back, this time."

They returned to the tent and laid their papers out on the table. The rest of his officers arrived shortly after that. The men stood around the table, staring at the map they'd be following tonight, when they weren't following Darla.

He felt her presence before he even saw her. And he smelled that wonderful scent she always seemed to have in her hair.

"Glad you're here," Oberon said, as if he hadn't seen her in hours. His gaze lingered on her for a moment too long, before he shifted to address his soldiers. "Our initial plans have changed, men. Some of you may have heard we're going to an open field on the way back to the city in the morning. That's been scrapped. A small group of us are going into Mortis territory tonight. Hopefully, we'll have the element of surprise."

The place went silent. "If you have questions…" Oberon began. The men started talking at once. Oberon held up a hand for the soldiers to be quiet. "Grant has more information for you. He's going to fill you in on all the details. For example, where we're going. Who the enemy is. Hold on to your hats, men. You're about to come up against the most dangerous foe you've ever seen. If anyone feels he isn't up to this mission tonight, don't be afraid to say so. This isn't a task for a soldier who's unsure." He glanced at Darla. She already had her pistol on her belt. She appeared anything but unsure.

"Follow me, Darla," Oberon said. "I think you need better weaponry before we leave."

Oberon held the tent flap back for Darla to exit before him and turned back to his dark ops team. "After you've been briefed by Captain Ford, gear up and meet Darla and me near the central campfire."

After getting a blade that tucked nicely into her belt and a newer, better pistol, she waited with Oberon for the rest of the men to arrive. Donning her face shield, she paused and let her mind travel out into the Nevermore to find their destination. "There are only two Mortis on guard at the factory right now. They've sent most of the others into the Nevermore tonight, to the field where the creatures attacked Rud and me." She frowned at that. "But why are they going there?"

"I've sent them a little disinformation. They're off on a wild goose chase." He grinned and continued yanking his headgear into place.

"How does she know that?" asked Grant, who'd approached just as she'd given the message.

"Long story, my friend. But believe me when I tell you that you can trust what she says."

Five of them started through the Nevermore, but after a short distance, Darla felt out of body and then dizzy. She paused, then realized she was standing on a steel manhole cover. "We can go down here. Then we can make it most of the way below."

"Good," Oberon said. "Someone help me lift this cover, and let's get our asses out of the Nevermore before something decides we look like tasty morsels."

CHAPTER TWENTY-FOUR

They made it through the tunnels in good time. There were only two partial cave-ins. Easy to get past them. Traveling underground made the trip easier in the dark, but it was a long hike. At this point, no one questioned Darla's directions. They'd been following her because of Oberon's orders, but sometime during their twists and turns in the tunnels, they'd learned to trust her.

"This is it," she said on a shiver. "Mortis territory. Above us."

The team stopped and took a few minutes to mentally prepare themselves.

If her visions were accurate, the Mortis had a community miles from the stronghold, specifically positioned near the pill factory. She didn't blame them for not wanting to be far from their salvation.

It didn't matter any longer that they'd once been human. They'd been turned into mutated killers, and there was no going back for them. Worse, her visions seemed to indicate they'd take over Central City and beyond in the not-too-distant future, if they weren't stopped. If they won the battle, they'd eventually kill Vestro—and the country would be theirs for the taking.

While the soldiers caught their breath, she distanced herself.

Oberon got up from his crouched position near the soldiers and dropped to the tunnel floor beside her. "It's darker in these tunnels," he said, holding up a small lantern that burned animal fat.

She nodded. "Yeah, no electricity here."

Oberon met her gaze. Moisture glistened on his brow, regardless of the cooler temperature down here in the tunnels.

She glanced at the soldiers to make sure they weren't listening. "What if all of this is wrong?"

"Not possible," he whispered back, then pointed to his healed shoulder. "Does this seem like something that could happen to a faithless person? I have faith in you, Darla Rune. I will help you complete this task, no matter how difficult."

"Or deadly?"

His expression turned intensely personal and extremely hot. She'd have given her worldly goods for another kiss. And it was becoming increasingly difficult to concentrate whenever he looked at her like that.

Beyond them, the soldiers started shuffling. They got edgy whenever Oberon left them to talk to her in private. "We'd better go," she said.

He nodded. "Follow my lead out there, okay? I know you're the one with the knowledge, but I have experience in battle. We can win this thing if we work together."

"Agreed," she said. Her shield felt tight against her face. And her heart felt tight from fear. A few days ago, she'd scrounged to live day to day, and now, to live, she had to battle monsters.

Oberon led the way out of the tunnels. They found themselves on the outer edge of the Mortis village. Decayed and fallen buildings surrounded them, and a well-used trail wound its way through the rubble. She glanced at Oberon. Her visions had been accurate. They were on the right track. He nodded to her. Respect shone in his eyes.

Footsteps sounded, coming their way. He indicated a nearby derelict building and gave the hand signal for them to hide.

Her blood turned to ice when she saw the creature stalking past them. This had to be a Mortis. His forehead erupted with spikes over each eyebrow, and his arms were peppered with spurs that could do a lot of damage if he wielded his arms like weapons. And he would.

His expression appeared the most disturbing. His mouth had curled back over an overgrowth of teeth. She'd seen a picture of teeth like that once in an aquatic fish of some sort in one of her mother's well-loved magazines, that showcased the planet as it used to be. And just like the fish, his eyes were dead, too. Emotionless.

As if his built in weaponry wasn't enough, he wore two curved blades on a belt around his waist. He shuffled along, his shoulders curled in toward his chest and his head bowed. She felt his constant agonizing pain. It radiated off him like a living entity. No wonder Mortis had become killing machines. Pain like that probably drove them out of their minds.

While they hid just inside the rotted shell of the building, a building that could theoretically collapse at any moment, her thoughts shifted to Rud. She couldn't bear to think he'd be turned into something like this creature, or what he'd do to her mother if they failed.

Dread settled over her, as did the heat, like a strangling blanket making it hard to breathe, especially through her face shield. The unaware Mortis carried some sort of lantern that gave off better light than she'd ever seen before.

He slogged past them, taking one agonizing step after another. If he was an example of their sentries, this job might be easier than they hoped. On the other hand, Mortis probably didn't expect anyone to be brave enough to come into their village.

"He's gone," Oberon whispered. "Move out."

They moved back onto the path, knowing full well they could run into another Mortis at any time. Pinpricks of fear shuddered through her. "The factory is in that direction. From the outside, it looks like a wrecked building, but it has a red door with a big M scraped into it."

Grant's expression narrowed in disbelief. He shook his head.

"You heard her," Oberon said. "We go this way."

They found the door quickly. In fact, they nearly walked into the line of sight of the Mortis on guard at the door. Only one Mortis. But massive. Sitting on a piece of rubble and snoring very loudly.

"Let me go first," Darla said. "I'll distract him in order to give you the upper hand."

"No way," Oberon grated. "He's a psychopathic killer. He's not going to be distracted by a beautiful woman."

Had he just called her beautiful? Her skin flushed all over. Just when she didn't need to feel any warmer. In fact, she'd have liked nothing better than to peel off the Uvlar suit, but right now she needed every inch of protection it could give her.

Oberon whispered orders to the men. Soldiers named Josh and Fred were sent to flank the Mortis and wait for Oberon's signal to attack. Grant stood next to him. "You and I go full-frontal attack, while Darla stays here."

"I'm not staying here," she said. "Besides, another Mortis might come along. I'm going with you."

He must have seen the validity in her response, because he said, "You'll come, but you're not to be involved in the fight, do you hear me?"

She nodded but gritted her teeth and bit back a comment, because even though she could never be an amazing soldier like him, she'd do whatever she had to do to win this battle. And if that meant doing something risky, so be it.

Meanwhile, the Mortis slept soundly, completely unaware of his enemies sneaking up on him. Darla noted the way the beast's body structure and exaggerated muscles covered his thick bone structure. And those horrible, sharp bones, slicing through his skin. The skin appeared to have healed around some of the bones, but other places had been newly torn, like his bones were still growing. This one's bone spurs were different than those she'd seen on the first Mortis a couple of minutes ago. This creature had horns on his head, like a devil, and his fingernails were razor sharp. He was twice as large as the other Mortis while sitting down. She'd guess he'd be half a foot taller than Oberon, at six-three. No wonder this giant had been left on guard, and no wonder he'd dared to catch a catnap. Who in their right mind would mess with him?

Air seemed to stagnate as they waited for everyone to find their battle stations. When the last soldier waved his okay, Oberon and Grant moved in. She followed them but, as directed, kept several feet back.

She hadn't noticed that Fred had climbed a piece of the broken building façade and had a rope ready to loop around the Mortis' head until she caught Oberon signaling to him. He'd firmly wrapped his end of the rope around a steel column to give himself purchase against the strength of the beast below. All he had to do was loop it over the creature's head. Sounded simple enough but more difficult than it appeared.

Oberon and Grant pulled out dangerous-looking blades of their own. She'd never seen anything quite like them before. But, then, she'd never farmed in the Nevermore and protected herself from beasts like they had.

By mistake, Fred's foot sent a rusted bolt flying off the column to land next to the Mortis, who jerked awake on a growl that reverberated through her bones. His bloody eyes snapped opened and narrowed on Oberon and Grant in front of him.

Before the beast could charge forward, Fred dropped the noose. The Mortis reacted violently, yanking the rope so hard, Fred had to hang on to stop from being pulled off, but somehow the rope held tight wrapped around the column.

Just that second of distraction gave Oberon the chance to swing his ax with every ounce of his energy, but the Mortis jerked sideways so the blade missed hitting his heart. The ax sliced open the giant's shoulder and he barely flinched. Grabbing the noose, the Mortis slashed through it with those long knives at the ends of his fingers.

He was totally free now, and Oberon and Grant found themselves in grave peril. The Mortis dove at them and slashed out and caught Grant's chest. His fingernails sliced through the Uvlar way too easily.

When the Mortis opened his mouth, Darla sensed he was about to shout for backup. Luckily, Grant dove around him while Oberon distracted the brute from the front. Grant grabbed the remaining rope still hanging from the balustrade and swung past the giant, chopping at the back of his neck. He hit his mark, and the Mortis' head fell oddly forward while he dropped to his knees—dead.

"Benevolent Murphy, that was too close," Oberon said, wiping sweat from his brow. "And this one was sleeping. I hate to think what'll happen when we have to fight one who's wide awake and on his guard."

"At least we know now where their weakness lies. The back of their neck," Grant said, bending over and pressing his fingers against his ribs where he'd been slashed. He unzipped his Uvlar and gauged his injuries. "Just a flesh wound," he said on a grin.

* * * * *

"Okay, let's hide this one and get inside." Oberon said.

As the others went inside, he kept lookout. Darla followed last, and he wanted to grab her and hold her close, keep her safe. So what if she'd been the one everyone had waited for for two centuries? She couldn't do it on her own.

"We stay together inside," he said.

She nodded in agreement.

They went down a narrow hall into an open room. It wasn't a huge room, but machinery lined the walls. Machinery. Running all by itself. Little red pills were coming out at the end in clear plastic bubbles.

"How can there be electricity?" Darla asked. "Why haven't the EMP storms taken it out?" She touched the machine. "That bastard. He's been eliminating any hope for electricity for the last twenty-five years. The EMP storms were once a weather phenomenon, but it's now man-made."

"Benevolent fuckers," said Grant. "We should wipe them all out."

"But first we have to stop this. Break these machines so they can't make the pills. We also need to dump the raw material they're being made from."

There were at least fifty paper bags and a few barrels of product in the room. They'd need hours to get rid of this stuff.

"Where do we dump it?" Fred asked.

Oberon peered inside one of the barrels. He grabbed a handful and let the red powder stream through his fingers. "Pour it into the sink over there. We can dissolve it with water."

Fred and Josh rolled the barrels of powder toward the oversized sink. One started pumping the water, while the other one dumped the powder.

"How do we break this machine?" Oberon said, almost to himself. He had no idea what part of it was critical.

Darla had a metal pole in her hand. She'd picked it up from the end of the conveyor belt. She reached out and touched the housing of the machine. She paused, and closed her eyes. "Shove this into the center of that engine, exactly where you see a green rectangle with lots of little wires on it. It'll fry the whole darn thing." She touched another piece of machinery. Then went to the wall and monitored the pipes running across the ceiling. "Water pipes and a sprinkler system," she said.

"A what?" It still baffled him that she understood these strange machines. "How do you know how these things work?"

"That's one thing I've always known," she said, running her hand lovingly across the metal. "I hate to damage the one piece of working mechanical equipment I've ever come across." She pointed at the pipes. "See those little knobs on the ceiling? They're fire extinguishers. When it gets to a certain temperature in here, those little metal bits will rotate and shoot out water."

He glanced around the room. Besides the barrels, bags had been stacked in three corners of the room. He stared at the ceiling again, and then at the slow process of pumping water into the sink. They'd never manage to dump all the bags on time.

He shifted his focus to Darla. "If you can make water fall from the ceiling, it would most likely ruin the dust concoction. Besides, we don't have time to dump it all down the sink."

"Great idea," Grant shouted. "Just tip over the barrels and let the powder spill across the floor, men. Spread the bags out."

Oberon surveyed the room and rubbed the back of his head. Strange that this place had no Mortis guarding the inside, given its importance. Vestro couldn't have pulled everyone to go into the Nevermore? Or had he? Was he that desperate? "Stay on your guard," he shouted.

A second after ramming the pole into the machine, he registered a warning deep inside. He wasn't psychic but his gut instinct had just kicked in.

Seconds later, two Mortis charged into the room and moved in on Fred and Josh.

"Stay back there," he said to Darla, before he and Grant ran to help.

A Mortis had sneaked up on the two privates while they'd been dumping powder. Too late for Fred. His scream had been short lived. Before they could reach him, he'd been snapped backward over a container at a disturbing angle.

Oberon attacked one beast, while Grant took the other. The Mortis began to spin, making his shoulder blades into a devastating weapon. How could he battle a freaking moving blade?

Nevertheless, Oberon swung his ax and felt bone against it before it bounced back. How could this beast's bone be stronger than steel? It seemed the only place they'd been left vulnerable was the back of their necks, but it'd be fucking hard to get close enough to strike at that possible weakness right now.

He took a chance and threw his ax at the Mortis moving in on Grant about ten feet away. It slammed into the Mortis' neck, and the thing went down hard, his shoulder blades cutting into the floorboards and pinning him there. Grant finished him off. Blood spurted out of his neck.

Grant fought another Mortis off Josh. A quick scan let Oberon know Josh had been cut in the leg, and it bled profusely. Oberon had seen those kinds of injuries in the field. Even if he survived, the poor kid wouldn't last long if infection set in.

The Mortis Oberon had been battling, growled at him, and his blood-red eyes narrowed.

"Okay, big guy, you know you're going to die trying, right?" Oberon gritted out, and the Mortis roared in anger and charged him.

Oberon had spotted Darla in his peripheral vision. She'd jumped onto the conveyor belt and was running the length of it. Panicked for her safety, he attacked the Mortis like a crazy man, and managed to keep the beast distracted while she rammed her knife into his neck just as he was about to rip Oberon a new one.

"Thanks. Now get back." His expression begged her to get out of the danger zone now that she'd save his life. He reached down and grabbed the ax he'd thrown minutes before.

Now, he went after another Mortis who'd just entered the room. This one had blue eyes. The others had black pupils and no irises? Maybe a new convert?

Suddenly, Oberon's blood turned to slush in his veins. What if this creature was Rudyard?

He tried to swallow down the lump of fear as he raised the ax over his head. Either way, he didn't have to make the choice of possibly killing his brother, because Grant attacked from the other side and slashed across the back of the creature's neck with his weapon of choice: a heavy-assed sword.

The Mortis dropped like a chunk of mountainside during an avalanche. Oberon's gut twisted, and he prayed this beast had not been his brother. Rud wouldn't have wanted to be like that.

He stared at the Mortis.

As if Grant knew what he was thinking, he said, "Get your ass moving, sir. We don't have time for any regrets."

Just before Oberon turned away, he noticed a faded tattoo on the arm of the Mortis. Not Rud's tattoo. Not Rud's arm. His lungs filled with air, and he released it slowly. He realized he was shaking like a goddamn newborn puppy. He had to get his shit in gear. Get ready for whatever might come. And he had to face the fact that he might not be able to save his baby brother, whom he'd raised since they were mere pups themselves. He tasted bile.

For just a second, the thought of tearing off to the stronghold and getting his brother out took hold of him. But given the strength of these few beasts, he'd never make it, not even with his ax, an old-style Viking ax that came in handy when he wasn't using a gun.

He'd been trained to be better than this. He shouldn't act like a raw recruit. He swallowed down the anger that threatened to make him lose control and pulled himself out of his own self-pity. That's when he realized Darla had climbed up and was holding a lighted match to the metal thing in the ceiling.

"What are you doing?" he shouted, quickly checking the room to make sure no Mortis were near her.

Bodies littered the factory floor. Somehow they had managed to kill them all.

Before she could answer, water began to spray on him—on everything in the room, including the bags of powder. Water started to break down the bags and saturate the irreplaceable powder inside. Just in case the water didn't reach the ones on the bottom, he shouted, "Spread the bags out, and open them." He ran from bag to bag, slamming his ax into each one to spill the contents onto the factory floor. "Open all the bags."

By the time he and Grant finished slashing the bags open, Darla had jumped down and brushed off her gloved hands. He met her near the main doors.

"Fred?" She stared at the soldier's body, now in Grant's arms.

Oberon shook his head. "Dead."

"We have to go. There's probably a silent alarm ringing somewhere else," she said. She kept looking at Fred as if he might stand up and smile at her.

"Sometimes it's like you're speaking a foreign language. Alarms ringing somewhere because you've made this place rain inside?" He shrugged. The world before must've been very complicated before.

According to her expressive features, she bled for the loss of a soldier, one soldier. Imagine how she'd feel when the battle ended and bodies lay strewn across the countryside.

They stacked the bodies into a back room and covered them with a tarp, the longer they went unnoticed, the better.

Slogging through the tunnels took longer with Oberon and Grant carrying Fred and with Josh limping along behind.

No one spoke.

Back in camp, they set Fred's body down near the central fire pit. All eyes were on him. A sullen, dark mood fell over the men. Even the Nevermore sounded quieter than normal while the medic worked on Josh's slashed leg. Fred had been the first, and he wouldn't be the last to die out here this week.

Oberon's jaw tensed. He would have to come up with a helluva battle speech to encourage his men after this. Just glancing at his haphazard crew of soldiers, he understood how they must feel. They'd only just ended one battle against Vestro, and that had taken nearly all of their strength. No matter how tired they were, they needed to win this. It would be all or nothing.

Darla dropped to the ground on her knees beside Fred's body and slipped off her headgear. Her hair spread over her shoulders in waves, and she closed her eyes. "God, grant this man peace and take his soul into heaven where he will feel no pain and where the sun shines and the sky is blue." All the soldiers lowered their heads and closed their eyes. "Lord, we ask that you bless this man and welcome him into your Kingdom," she said. "And give us all strength for what we have to do tomorrow."

Oberon gaped at the soldiers' respectful reaction to her prayer.

Was this a sign of respect for the dead man or did it mean they sensed her importance to their cause? Intuitively?

The sound of horses' hooves pounded in the distance. "The rest of the soldiers are here," Oberon said, and a shout went up among the men.

Very good timing.

CHAPTER TWENTY-FIVE

An hour later, Darla got up and trudged to one of the secondary fires on the outskirts of the camp. She practically collapsed onto the hardpan and blessed the fact that the two soldiers next to the fire got up and left immediately. She wanted to be alone anyway. Her new psychic abilities were hard to control, and she fought off waves of random images that threatened to shut her down. Sometimes they were too dark, too horrifying. She couldn't allow the worst of the images to become full-blown in her head or she'd fall apart. Worse, amidst the terror and chaos, there were images of her and Oberon together. Just brief flashes. But the heat of their coupling strengthened her. Could it possibly be her future? Did that mean they'd survive the battle? Or was it wishful thinking?

She forced herself back to here and now. Hanging on to reality helped ground her.

The flames of the campfire lit the night and created a barrier between herself and Oberon. She watched him helping the rest of his men settle into the camp that had drastically increased in size. She'd been surprised to see so many of them. Who knew Central City's army was so large? There had to be at least a thousand men in the camp now. And they'd need every one of them.

They were a ragged group, thin and rangy, but tough. And they'd need to be. Her heart felt like it pinched in her chest.

But how many Mortis were there? And what ratio of human to Mortis would it take to win the battle? They had to hope getting rid of the pills had made a difference.

She gazed across the camp at the body of the fallen soldier still lying out in respect.

Until this moment she hadn't allowed herself to even think about the consequences of this battle on her mother. She held back a sob that threatened to let loose the floodgates of her emotions. She hadn't seen her mother in years to keep her safe from being branded a dissident. Marilee would have helped Darla in any way possible, but that would have been too dangerous for her. Her mother would never have survived the meager pickings Darla had subsisted upon. But now she might die a horrible death at the hands of Rud, anyway—and all because of Darla.

And Rud, who'd done nothing but try to help her, might soon be turned into one of those horrible beasts. It seemed incomprehensible.

Darla's stomach protested. She pressed her fingers into her sides and leaned forward with her eyes shut.

"Pssst."

The voices of many men talking at once dissolved into the background, and Darla opened her eyes and scanned her surroundings. Had that merely been the fire hissing?

She didn't think so.

"Pssst."

The logs snapped and cracked, and heat warmed her face. She searched the edges of the camp, squinted into the darkness. Everything in the camp had stayed the same as it had been a moment ago. Had she really heard that noise, or had it been another of her weird flashbacks?

"Over here."

She jumped when the dry brush rustled next to her. Blip peered out at her from the brush, his tiny black eyes blinking at her, the light of the fire mirrored in their unfathomable depths.

He seemed even more nervous this time. Maybe because of the sheer numbers of the soldiers in the camp?

She pushed off the ground and quietly went to the edge of the brush. Looking over her shoulder to make sure no one watched, she hunched down. Her hair fell forward, and she shoved it behind her ears and smiled at Blip. "Why are you hiding?"

"You must come with me, Ms. Rune," he said. "I have something very important to show you."

It didn't escape her that Blip might be trying to pull one over on her. But, Moses, if she could go up against full-sized Yardmen, she could follow a miniature Yardman to see what was so important. It felt right, at least. There were no alarm bells or frissons of fear zinging along her nerve endings. Besides, she was desperate to save her mother.

She felt her holster nevertheless. Her weapon remained tucked safely inside.

Blip watched her check for the gun, and she noticed the instant disappointment on his little round face. Her stomach took a hit. For some reason, she didn't want to ever let him down. He'd been through enough in his life. And that came straight from the ether, nothing she knew for a fact, just everything she felt about him.

"Sorry, Blip. It's not you. It's habit. I'm used to looking out for myself. Besides, there might be animals out here," she said, while she continued to follow the little man through the brush. He moved considerably quicker than she'd expected he could. Also, she had to keep a close eye on him, because he tended to disappear completely when the brush was taller than the top of his head.

Fear rippled through her while she listened for rustling in the surrounding brush. Every footstep felt like her last, but she had to follow Blip. She knew it in her bones. Still, no animals attacked. There was no way could they walk through the Nevermore at night without animals finding them. Yet, somehow, the Nevermore remained virtually silent.

"Why aren't we being attacked?" she asked. "Is Maribel somehow keeping the animals away?"

Blip nodded as if it was a fact he'd already known and continued leading her further from safety.

Ten minutes later, and with the last bits of light from the campfires disappearing in the distance, she said, "How far are we going?" Oberon would be ticked that she'd left camp without telling him, but she was the only one invited on this excursion.

"Not much further," Blip said, pointing with his stubby finger. "Just past that hill, there's an old overpass that is still partially standing. Underneath, there's a good hiding place. Blocked off from prying eyes."

"How did it go with Brawn and the Yardmen?" she asked, catching up to the little guy. Even in the darkness she saw the overpass superstructure looming in the distance. There must have been a bonfire underneath it, because light flickered on the underside, illuminating the bottom deck and the road, long collapsed from age. Rebar hung out from the ends like rusty entrails.

Central City's outlying structures were mostly gone except for the old power plant's remnants and the Boneyard. This structure rose into the sky like a giant claw. "I've never seen anything like this before," she said.

"We're getting closer to the old city," Blip answered.

"But that thing is huge. Imagine the world full of wonders like this," she said, her words trailing off. "Why are you taking me here?" And why hadn't he answered her question about the Yardmen? Hopefully they had come. Had they lit the bonfire under the decaying rampart of the massive overpass?

"Just follow me a little further," Blip said. "But be careful, it's steep."

She grinned at that comment. She'd been climbing old technology refuse heaps in the Boneyard for years. This was a tiny hill compared to those.

In the Boneyard, she knew where to step and where not to step in order to keep the pile from collapsing, so she could probably get over this rubble without a problem.

They made it to the bottom of the hill, and now the structure loomed over them like a half-finished work of art. She'd seen these structures in her dreams, fully functioning, beautifully formed overpasses, bridges, skyscrapers. Words most people in this present day wouldn't even fully comprehend. Now, seeing the actual remnants of something from her dreams felt eerie, to say the least.

She heard noises coming from under the bridge and stopped. Nerves skittered along her spine.

"Please, keep moving. We must hurry." Blip stopped and motioned her to follow him.

"Is it safe underneath? It looks like it could collapse completely."

"It's safe enough for now. Please hurry. They won't wait much longer. They have to see that you are really here."

The ground under her feet had leveled off but remained littered with rotting chunks of concrete and rebar. She had to step carefully in the dark here. Blip lit a small pocket lantern and held it aloft as they rounded a huge pockmarked column.

She followed. It felt right.

At first, the bonfire blinded her when she stepped out of the darkness. But, seconds later, her vision cleared, and standing under the bridge were at least two hundred Yardmen. She'd had no idea there were that many Yardmen in existence.

Blip called to the crowd, and all eyes turned to her. A rough shout went up. She froze where she stood. Her knees felt a little like rubber. She tried to swallow but couldn't work up enough spit.

Blip retraced his steps to her, and tugged on her jacket. "Come. You have nothing to fear from them tonight."

The tallest of the Yardmen, a behemoth of a creature, stepped forward. "Thank you for coming," he said in perfect English. Even Blip didn't speak this well. She held her breath and waited a moment before she dared speak.

"I don't understand..." she said. "Why didn't you

come to the camp?"

"Ms. Rune," he said. "I speak for everyone here when I tell you we will consider fighting side by side with you."

She gazed over the many large, round faces with black, expressionless eyes. She'd seen Yardmen so many times in the Boneyard, but other than her attacker, they'd never made actual eye contact before, and now there were two hundred staring at her. She hadn't thought the Yardmen could even talk. She'd only ever heard guttural sounds and grunts from them.

"Darla, this is Brawn. He's Vestro's bodyguard. Or he was Vestro's bodyguard." Blip made a little laughing noise. "I was Vestro's servant, and Brawn used to be his guard. Together we know most of Vestro's frailties. We know where his army is weak, and we know where it is strong."

She wondered if, after all that had happened, the Yardmen could ever fit into society. If they'd even want to. She hoped so."Thank you, Blip and Brawn and everyone, for considering helping us in the battle ahead," she said in a raised voice so they could all hear her.

The strange-looking assortment of Yardmen started shuffling and grunting. Did they understand her?

She eyed Brawn and Blip. "Someone needs to explain a few things to me," she said. "How do they communicate with you?" she asked in a lowered voice. "Do they understand what they're considering volunteering for?"

He nodded and said, "They do. But, they haven't decided yet. They wanted to know you'd be willing to meet them face to face before they took a vote."

Her heart ached for these poor mutated creatures. They

were large and strong, but did they have enough intelligence to fight the Mortis, killers with built-in weaponry and intense psychotic tendencies?

Oberon's team had managed to kill the Mortis earlier tonight only because they had caught them off guard, and even then they lost a man in the process. They wouldn't catch the Mortis off guard again, she'd bet on it.

She sighed. It smelled like decay under this old bridge, as if hundreds of years of the dying planet had gathered in the cracks and crevices of this place.

"We have nearly a thousand soldiers back at the camp," she said. And even they won't be enough. With the Yardmen, maybe we'll have a chance."

Brawn tipped his head in the Yardmen's direction. "I'm sorry, Ms. Rune," he said. "If I can convince the Yardmen, we'll fight with you, not with the soldiers. We will be at your side, protecting you. You alone."

She scanned the many faces and suddenly understood what Brawn meant. These Yardmen were as much her family as anyone else. She'd spent most of her life in the Yards, and they'd lived in careful harmony. If only she'd known then what she knew now about them.

"I understand. Thank you, Brawn. Please tell the Yardmen that if they decide to help, I will be extremely grateful for their support. Maybe with them as our allies against the Mortis, we might have a chance."

Brawn's slit of a mouth mirrored Blip's small mouth. They were smiling.

If the Yardmen decided to follow her, could she lead giants who might not truly understand to certain death? Not to mention, the human soldiers would be slaughtered without their help. She focused on Brawn, then Blip. "If you manage to convince them, time is critical. Oberon is going to begin the attack tomorrow."

Brawn regarded his brethren, and several of them nodded as if in acknowledgment. Had she just witnessed something she'd never considered before? They didn't communicate verbally, but they understood. "I'll explain everything to the Yardmen tonight, Ms. Rune."

"As much as we need you, I don't want the Yardmen to come into this thing without knowing what they're risking," she said, her stomach knotting at the thought of what might happen. "Thank you both for what you're trying to do." She glanced over her shoulder, scanned the darkness between her and the camp she'd left earlier.

She didn't have to be psychic to know that, one way or another, tomorrow would bring death.

But in order for life to begin again, there had to be death. Still, that thought settled heavily in her chest.

"I'll take you back to the camp," Blip said.

"Thank you." She took in the Yardmen and smiled at them, thanking them silently for coming tonight. A chill ran down her back.

* * * * *

Unbeknownst to her, Oberon had followed Darla from the camp. He stayed in the shadows, watching what he feared had been a betrayal by Blip, only to find out they had a better chance with these behemoth Yardmen on their side. Why hadn't they risen up against Vestro before, though? That thought sent a squirmy feeling through him. Something was missing from what Darla had been told. Somehow, Vestro had controlled them for years. What would stop him now?

Blip led her back. They were both quiet, so he had to be extra stealthy in the dry brush. He thought of letting them know he'd followed, but decided he shouldn't do anything to lose Blip's trust, so he stayed hidden.

After Darla entered the camp, she leaned over and said something to Blip. He disappeared into the brush quickly.

Oberon circled around and came across the camp from another side so Darla wouldn't realize he'd been protecting her.

She stood near the fire, staring into the flames as if she'd like to jump in and end it all. In some ways, he understood.

"We have to do this," he said, coming up behind her, and seeing her pained expression. She didn't lift her head. Merely nodded.

"So many lives lost," she said in a low groan.

He frowned. "You're saying that like it's already happened."

Her emerald irises had turned luminescent, and even though she stared directly into his eyes, he knew she didn't really see him. They were lit from beyond, probably looking into their future. And if her expression told him anything, their future was grim.

The light in her eyes faded and she started shivering. He grabbed her by the shoulders, and her body reacted, nearly collapsing against him.

His chest tightened, and he regarded his men. They were the toughest soldiers he knew. It hadn't been that long since they'd fought Vestro's human soldiers in the city. They'd won, but it had been a long and difficult battle. His men were tired, but they had to carry this thing through, and if they could defeat Vestro, they might have a chance for a better life.

He motioned one of his men over. "Yes, sir?"

"Please bring Ms. Rune some water."

She had a container of water within seconds. She took a sip and coughed. "It tastes horrible," she said. "The water from the stream is so much better."

The stream ran alongside the camp. Hell, he couldn't believe he'd ever do something like this, but he dumped the water from the vessel, walked to the edge of the stream and filled it with cold, clear water.

No doubt, some of his men watched him in shock. He went back to Darla, handed her the water, and she drank deeply. "Sweet and refreshing," she said after her last gulp. She'd drunk it all.

He hoped giving Darla water from the stream in front of his soldiers wouldn't make them think he'd gone insane, but if nothing else, he'd learned to trust her.

* * * * *

Rudyard had nearly worked the lock free on his cage when his guard woke up and noticed. The creature let out an ear-piercing shriek and slammed his bony, sharp fingers against the side of the cage and smashing the lock. The door flew open, and the Mortis stepped back, daring Rud to come out. He wanted him to try to escape.

"Uh oh," Rud said out loud. "I'm not stupid enough to try that. You have an unfair advantage."

The Mortis bent his head left, then right. The bones in his neck cracked loudly, and he flicked his long nails back and forth. They sounded like blades slicing together.

Double dirty bastard.

Rud carefully reached out and pulled his cage door shut again. He slumped into the corner and crossed his arms over his chest. Locks were nothing but window dressing with something like a Mortis on guard. He was more trapped now than he'd been before.

Suddenly, he heard something across the barn. Not an animal. A person. It sounded like a woman crying, though men could sob just as quietly. He'd learned that by spending time in the most poverty-stricken parts of the city.

"Mrs. Rune?" he called.

The Mortis charged his cage, and Rud jumped to the center of his metal cell where, hopefully, his guard's nails couldn't slice him.

The sobbing stopped. Maybe the person had hear him. "Is that you?" he called again.

The Mortis growled this time. "No talking," he said through his mouthful of teeth.

It shocked Rud to know he could speak.

"I'm a prisoner," a woman's voice said. "Who are you?"

"I'm Rudyard James," he answered, glaring at the Mortis. He'd risk injury to speak to another human at this point. Desperation made men braver than they'd be normally. "Are you Darla's mother?"

"Yes, I'm Marilee Rune," she said.

So the little guy had been right.

Silence again, then the voice. "Have you seen my daughter? Is she alive?"

The Mortis seemed to be entertained by the talk now, even though he'd tried to make it look otherwise.

Rud would have to be careful not to give any crucial information away. At least, not the little bit of information that he actually knew.

"Alive and well the last time I saw her."

"Oh, thank you, Maribel," she said.

Rud's eyebrows rose. Darla's mother knew about Maribel, so why hadn't Darla? He eyed the Mortis, who hovered over him now, his yellowing eyes staring hard at him.

"I heard two guards talking, though. Something is going to happen in the courtyard tomorrow. I think I'm going to be part of the main event," she said.

Rud knew instantly that it had to be a tactic to draw Darla and Oberon into the stronghold. And they would come.

He looked at the cage he'd been in for nearly two days. He'd only been given a little muddy water since the fresh water he'd received from the tiny Yardman. He hadn't seen him for at least twenty-four hours. What had happened to him? Caught for helping him, maybe. Rud hoped the little man got away.

He tried to swallow but his throat had gone dry. He needed fluids. His legs felt weak. Would he have the strength when it came down to it? He glared at the ugly, bony face of his guard and knew he'd never be strong enough against a beast like him.

"Hang in there, Mrs. Rune," he said. "I have the feeling we're just the bait. Nothing will happen to us until Oberon and Darla come through the gates of this nightmare place." And then he'd be turned into a monster and kill her as part of the main event. Hell, he hoped his brother got to him first.

He heard her voice catch in her throat. "I'd gladly die to save my darling daughter."

"As would I," Rud said under his breath. "And my brother."

CHAPTER TWENTY-SIX

Vestro paced back and forth in his basement sanctuary. It infuriated him that just as he got ready for battle, the Mortis continually balked against his orders. He had to use coercion in the form of their pills as insurance that they'd do what they were ordered to do. But now the factory had been severely damaged. They'd managed to save only a day's worth of product. He'd be in deep trouble if his men didn't get his backup supply from the caves deep inside the mountain before tomorrow. And, that was improbable at best.

If he hadn't needed the Mortis so desperately right now, he'd have called in the Yardmen. Problem was, even though they were afraid of him, they weren't as deadly, or as controllable.

Ironic that his own nephews were his worst enemies. He rubbed two fingers against his thumb in that soothing way that helped to calm him. He'd kept his relationship a secret from them. He'd planned to use it against them at the right time. They'd be shocked when they learned the truth. The pompous asses thought they were better than he was, when in reality they were just the same. Same bloodline and, obviously, the same need to rule the country.

He half growled at that thought, then grinned. Yes. They'd be surprised.

If they lived long enough for him to get the satisfaction of telling them the truth. He went to the video screen and watched Rud in his cage. The dumb sap knew nothing about electricity or technology. The previous governments had secretly kept a small amount of electricity going since the War of Neutrality for their own benefit, but he'd taken the use of electricity to the next level with Rhino's help. For years a pervasive form of Electro Magnetic Pulse storms swept across the land and persisted in the atmosphere, wiping out everything electronic, except the machinery deep under the earth and known only to him. The people barely remembered electricity.

When he'd taken over the city by force, he realized the EMP storms were dying down, and he'd lose his ability to keep the people desperate and in need of him. It had been pure luck that he'd found the EMP machines used in the war and managed to get them working again. They'd been buried deep inside the mountain where he now stockpiled the pills for the Mortis.

He always seemed to be able to get machinery to work. He had a gift. His gift, not Darla Rune's. He'd seen her trying to re-create technology. She knew what to do, but he always made sure her attempts were wiped out by his own pulse technology.

He pushed a button on the wall. A long pause stretched his patience, until finally one of his servants came on the line. "Yes, sir, how may I be of assistance?"

"Where's Blip?"

Another irritating pause. It had been a shock when the Mortis pill installation had been infiltrated last night. Three of his guards were still missing. He suspected they'd stolen a supply of the pills and had taken off deeper into the Nevermore. There'd only ever been one Mortis who'd taken that kind of initiative, so it surprised him when three of them tried it after the example he'd made of the last idiot. Damn it. He didn't have time to look for them right now. He had too many things on his mind at the moment.

Creating the deviants had been his crowning glory and his bane, because keeping the Mortis under control had always been tenuous. And now he had to dip into his hidden stores to keep the rest of his guards going long enough to start up production again. They knew their lives depended on the pills. And they needed to know he could provide them, or he'd never be able to keep control of them.

"Blip's not here, sir."

"Well, where is he?" Vestro glanced at the screen, half expecting to see Blip talking to Rud in the barn again. What was his little creation up to? He should have eradicated him long ago. He should have noticed sooner that Blip had gained too much information while pretending to be his half-wit servant.

Whispering crackled over the remote line. His servants were obviously afraid and didn't know what to tell him. "Never mind," he shouted and clicked the line off. His stomach roiled. Something bothered him, but this close to waging war against his nephews, he couldn't afford to be distracted. At noon tomorrow, Rud and Marilee would be brought to the courtyard.

Darla and Oberon had no choice but to show up—or they would never again see their relatives alive.

* * * * *

Oberon prepared for battle. Right now, in their makeshift war room, they gauged their best locations for attack on the blueprints that Blip had provided.

"There's only one good way in, and that's pretty much through the front door," Captain Ford said.

Oberon shook his head. "No, we can't be that obvious. There's another way. There's got to be."

Darla leaned over the map, scanned the layout on the worn plasticized paper printed before the War of Neutrality. A map with streets and cities. But it also marked mountains and canyons. "Look here," she said. "Vestro's buildings are flanked by mountains. I'm sure he thinks that means he's safe from an attack back there."

"But we can't come in from that side. We don't know the terrain. It's too rough. Too risky," Grant said.

"There might be a way. We have a tiny Yardman who is willing to help us." She rubbed two fingers on the bridge of her nose. "We have to try! Or they'll kill Rud and my mother."

Oberon frowned. She'd spent more time with Rud than she had with him. Had they formed a deeper connection in that time? He couldn't let jealousy sideline him now, so he stared at the map and bit his lip. He wanted to save his brother and Darla's mother as much as she did.

Sounds of footsteps running, soldiers shouting and guns cocking filled the virtual silence of the night as a large shadow loomed in the growing dusk. A huge

Yardman stood in front of the tent as if he belonged there.

Benevolent hell. Oberon glanced down, half expecting to see the miniature Yardman with him.

"Don't shoot," Darla shouted, loudly enough to be heard by the slightly panicked soldiers. After the meeting under the bridge last night she assumed Yardmen didn't come into encampments. But now that one did, the soldiers would probably expect the worst.

"Get back, Ms. Rune," Grant shouted, but Darla rushed forward and took the Yardman's hand in her own.

"Don't shoot him. This is Brawn. He's going to help us beat Vestro."

Brawn nodded his big round head and took in the soldiers around him. Darla squeezed his hand and wondered if he could even feel it, his fingers were so big and calloused. "They're good men," she said to Brawn. "They just need time to get to know you and the others." Don't give up on us, she prayed.

He didn't look convinced. "Blip sent me. He says they're going to torture Rud and your mother tomorrow, Ms. Rune."

"If they lay one hand on Rud or my mother, I'll make them pay with their own blood." She blinked. Had she really just said that?

Regardless of his size, Brawn looked unnerved by the leery humans around him. His head bowed in apparent subservience.

"How is it you speak?" Grant asked, coming out of the tent with Oberon close behind him.

"Vestro created me this way." Brawn's coal-black eyes and slit of a mouth were the very same as any Yardman Oberon had seen before, but he knew from following Darla that this one had always been different.

His demeanor characterized that of a thinking person. His stature might be huge, but the big behemoth had been broken. Broken by Vestro. For the first time, he felt sorry for Yardmen.

"Welcome to the camp," he said. "My name is Oberon."

Brawn bowed his head. "Nice to meet you, sir."

Oberon inhaled and hoped he wasn't about to make a mistake in judgment by welcoming the Yardman into the war room.

"Come inside. Tell us what you know," he said, holding back the fact that they were going to wage war at dusk tomorrow.

Brawn edged uncomfortably between two of Oberon's top men to enter the tent. His head pushed against the canvas ceiling. He gazed at the map and shook his large head. "This map is old. There's a new entrance at the back wall." He pointed. "Right here. The rest of the map is okay. The roads around the structure are accurate."

"Can we get in through that door?" Oberon asked.

"Maybe, if you can get across the mountain top and down into the valley behind the building. It's not as heavily guarded by Mortis back there. But they'll be starting to feel the effects of the lack of medication. They're angry and mean enough now, and they'll be rabid and desperate tomorrow. I'm not sure how to get around that fact."

"We could wait another day," Grant said.

"Not if you want to find Rud and Mrs. Rune alive," Brawn said.

Grant leaned both hands on the table and let his head drop.

"We have to get through the viper's nest of Mortis

however you look at it." Oberon gazed at Brawn. "Will there be other Yardmen?" He tried not to give away the fact that he'd followed Darla last night and listened to what had been said.

"I'm afraid not, sir. I don't think they're coming. You see, they're very afraid of Vestro. He does horrible things to Yardmen who go against his wishes."

If her expression told him anything, her hopes were suddenly dashed.

"But as a group, you are stronger than Vestro. You have strength behind you in numbers," Darla said.

Oberon figured Brawn already knew that.

Brawn stared in Darla's direction. "We have a lot of hope in what you can do to make our future better," he said.

"But we need the Yardmen to succeed," Darla said in a desperate voice.

"We probably do. Without them, fighting an enemy like the Mortis will be a blood bath," Oberon answered. "They're virtually unbeatable unless we can get close enough to their necks, and in doing that, we'll most likely die trying. But we will fight—with, or without the Yardmen—we have to."

"But Yardmen's arms are longer, and they can swing a weapon to strike at their necks."

Oberon nodded. "They can—but only if they want to."

Brawn released a breath that shook his whole chest cavity. "I'm going back. I'll try again to convince them. If I can, I'll meet you here in the morning." He pointed at the map.

"What's there?" Oberon asked.

"It's a meeting of trails on the way to Vestro's stronghold. Yardmen know this route well."

"Thank you, Brawn. I hope to see you there." Brawn turned and left without another word.

Oberon exhaled heavily. "Let's try to get some rest, men. We're heading out at the crack of dawn."

After the others left, Oberon stared at Darla. Her size even smaller and more vulnerable in this light. But she had a determined expression on her face.

"Good night, Oberon," she said.

"Darla, I'd rather spend the rest of the night together," he began.

"Not possible. We need sleep. We probably shouldn't have expended as much energy as we did earlier."

He grinned. "I could expend that kind of energy all night long, my sweet." He stepped closer and ran two fingers under her chin and tipped her face to his. "But you need to be rested tonight, too."

She stepped back and his fingers dropped. "I'll say good night, then." She sounded disappointed. Hell, he was, too.

He reached out for her and kissed her on the mouth in full view of the soldiers. "What are you doing?" she gasped.

"Marking you as mine. I don't want any of those men out there to get any ideas about you. And I want them to know how important you are to me and that they'd better protect you with their last breath. As will I."

He grabbed his kit bag and stepped outside the tent, leaving her inside.

"Where are you going?" she asked.

"I'll sleep nearby. Tonight, you sleep inside. And, don't worry, you can rest easy tonight. This tent is always well guarded."

She smiled at him. "No one has ever done anything

like that for me."

"Oh, my darling, you have no idea what kinds of things I can do for you." He grinned back at her before he threw his bag onto the ground near the campfire and lay down with his head resting against it as if it were a pillow.

She noted the other eyes in the camp watching her, waiting to see what might happen next. She smiled, flipped the canvas down and closed herself inside. She quickly crawled into bed and tried to turn off the thoughts running through her brain.

After closing her eyes, she silently asked Maribel to give her strength for tomorrow. It would be hard to do what she had to do with the thought of her mother's very life on the line. Her instinct would always be to protect her mother first.

The next morning when Darla arose, the soldiers were already preparing. Oberon had suited up in full Uvlar gear, his face shield in place. "Morning," he said. "We'll be going soon." He eyed her up and down. "Were you able to sleep?"

"A little. Probably, as much as you did." She tried to grin but fell short.

The men had been given their orders. Half of them gathered on the west side of camp and the other half on the east. Her half—without Oberon. He'd go west.

Would she ever see him again after today?

At least they'd march together until the halfway point, where they hoped to meet the Yardmen, and at which point, they'd break off. She'd have a chance to say goodbye then, if all went well.

After walking the trail for a couple of hours, Oberon stopped the troops at their designated meeting place. He waited. He double checked the position on the map with Grant. Grant agreed, this was the location. With no sign of the Yardmen, he made his way to Darla.

She couldn't stand the thought of leaving him but they had to do this.

"It's time to split up. Are you ready?" he asked.

She nodded and said in a sad voice, "The Yardmen didn't come."

"I guess we can't blame them," he said, and stepped toward her and fingered her face shield. Should she rip it off to kiss him?

"Looks like we're on our own," he said. " I'm not saying good-bye. I'm saying, watch your rear. Don't do anything stupid and don't be a hero."

She laughed halfheartedly at his last word. "Isn't that what the prophecy expects of me?"

He exhaled. "It doesn't mean you have to be deliberately careless, okay?"

She nodded and felt his fingers lift the edges of her shield. He pulled it back, yanked her close to him and planted his lips on hers. He kissed her like he'd never kissed her before. "Come back to me," he demanded, then searched for Grant who'd taken a couple steps back to give them privacy. "Keep her safe, my friend."

"You know I will," Grant said.

Oberon searched for the Yardmen one more time, then shook his head in disappointment, and gave a hand signal to his troops. She watched as they moved away in another direction. They'd have to travel up the mountain and around to the back of Vestro's stronghold. A circuitous route that might keep their position from the Mortis until they were ready to attack.

Tears burned at the backs of her eyes and she gritted

her teeth together, yanked her face shield back on and said, "I'm ready. Let's get this thing done."

Her stomach felt hollow.

* * * * *

By mid-afternoon, they'd made it to the agreed location on the approach to Vestro's buildings. From here they were to wait for a sign from Oberon, to attack. If all had gone well, by now, Oberon would have penetrated the building and had found Vestro.

Darla's nerves had frayed beyond their limit and tension filled the air. She'd been prostrate in long grass, and keeping a watch over the building below when a shout broke the silence. Her heart lurched, and her mouth went instantly dry. Mortis were attacking from the cover of the half-dwarfed trees on their left.

With no time for fear, she jumped up and joined Grant in a charge toward their enemy. Now, fighting a Mortis with ten times her strength, she ducked when he swung a mace at her. It whizzed past her head and continued in a circle. He swung again, and she dove to the ground and rolled out of its range.

"Get behind me," Grant shouted and pulled out his pistol and shot the beast twice between the eyes. It only slowed him down. His thick protrusion of skull actually protected his brain, capturing the bullets that had only slightly buried into the bone. But it did slow the angry creature long enough for Grant to get behind him and slash his neck with his ax. The beast went down and for just a second, Darla would have sworn she saw relief in the eyes of her attacker.

They were severely outnumbered. She heard soldiers screaming, but her tunnel vision kept her focused on her own survival. She prayed they could stand their ground here, because Oberon needed their help.

When Grant touched her shoulder, she whipped around and nearly stabbed him with her knife. He jumped back just in time. He pointed, and her gaze followed the line of his finger. Yardmen thundered toward them from the east. They were in a long line, and their large feet stirred up the dust, spreading clouds of it into the wind. She couldn't believe it.

"They're going to help us," she said to Grant.

Grant spun away and fought off a Mortis holding a twin-bladed sword.

It took two or three soldiers to fight a single Mortis. She raised her pistol and tried shooting the beast in the forehead. It had worked last time. But this time, the bullets ricocheted off and didn't even slow the creature down. Grant managed to stay out of range of the blades and his ice pick fingers, swords clashed while she worked her way behind him.

She caught this one across the back of the neck, and he fell just before he could pierce Grant through the chest.

Grant's eyes were huge, and his hands were visibly shaking. "I owe you," he said quickly, then spun away to fight off another charging Mortis.

Suddenly, Mortis started dropping at the hands of the quiet and brutally strong Yardmen. They didn't need to slash the beasts across the neck. They crushed them with their pummeling fists and stepped on them. They used their arsenal of weapons built in the yards, too. Their sheer brute strength began to turn the unlikely odds in their favor. It didn't hurt that the Mortis had been weakened by their loss of pills.

When the skirmish ended, she stared at the wasteland

around them. The scents of blood and dirt filled her nostrils. She felt like she might be sick, especially at the sight of too many fallen soldiers. Bodies littered the ground. At least a hundred or more were dead, one tenth of their soldiers. Men with families in Central City. Families that would suffer greatly without their ability to pay for food.

Grant staggered toward her, his energy all but drained. "I didn't think we'd be able to do this," he said. Until then, Darla hadn't realized Grant had thought this battle would be a certain-death sentence. She drank in the sight of her avenging Yardmen. Even though the big men appeared to plod along, their long legs moved quickly through the Nevermore, and they'd proved themselves an awesome foe against the Mortis.

Blip ran to her. He made the face that she now recognized as a smile. "Took some convincing, but we made it."

"And just in time," Darla said, trying to calm her heaving chest.

"Yardmen always wanted to support you, Ms. Rune, but they were also afraid of what Vestro would do to them."

"Here's hoping we can make sure Vestro never torments anyone again." She stared at the faces of the Yardmen. Efficient killers—they'd fooled Vestro, who thought the Mortis were stronger. She scanned the remaining soldiers who were covered with gashes and bruises, while they helped their new comrades move the dead into a line. She'd had the Yardmen all wrong.

"We would have died today if not for all of you," she shouted. "Thank you."

A roar of appreciation went up from the soldiers,

along with guttural sounds from the Yardmen.

They took the time for Grant to say a prayer over the dead. Yardmen stood in silence.

Darla listened but kept her face averted from the bloodied bodies. She didn't need to look. She'd seen it all in a vision back at the camp. The Yardmen had been a surprise, though. Maybe because it had been a last minute decision.

When the prayer ended, The Yardmen, working in unison, stacked the bodies on top of each other, three abreast, then they picked up the biggest boulders in the area and stacked them on top of the men until the bodies literally stood no chance to ever be ravaged by beasts.

Soldiers remustered and stood side by side with the Yardmen, waiting for orders. Blip had climbed onto Brawn's shoulder.

"Are you ready, Darla?" Grant asked her.

"Very."

"Move out." he shouted.

They had a chance to get through this thing. They moved on foot, as silently as possible. But to everyone's surprise, except Darla, not one man could move through the Nevermore as silently as a Yardman.

* * * * *

Oberon slinked quietly into the building. These ancient stone walls had stood the ravages of the War of Neutrality.

So far the halls were quiet and echoed like an empty chamber. Every footstep made a sound, no matter how quiet they tried to be.

"Fuck," he whispered. Sweat beaded inside his Uvlar suit, and he pushed his face shield and helmet onto his back.

"It seems like this hall encircles the building but goes nowhere," a soldier said. "There are no doors."

"Wait. Isn't that a door down there?" Oberon pointed.

"But, sir, metal doors, with no handles? How do we open them?"

They approached the door and stared at it. One of the men put his fingers in the cracks and tried to pry it open, but it wouldn't budge. A green button was embedded in the wall to the left. "What's that for?"

Oberon reached out and touched it. A bell dinged, and the doors opened. "We've found our way in." He pointed at two of the men. "You two go back and tell the sergeant I'm going after Vestro. Leave the back door open. Half can come in this way, and the rest can flank the building."

Corporal Mann was the only soldier still accompanying Oberon. His eyes practically protruded when the doors closed on them. "What now?"

"We go down." Oberon pushed the lowest button. Sublevel four. If he knew Vestro, he'd be cowering in the basement.

The elevator began downward movement.

They gripped their weapons tighter and waited for the doors to open. And when they did, Oberon's breath froze in his chest.

CHAPTER TWENTY-SEVEN

At last, the signal came. A spiral of smoke rose from the mountain. Oberon had made it inside.

Grant went to work sending the message down the line. It spread like a palpable wave of excitement. This was it, their one and only chance to make the world a better place. She glanced at Brawn and Blip who stayed by her side. "I'm taking the Yardmen with me. When the word comes down, we're attacking the courtyard," she said to Grant.

"We'll take soldiers with us, too," he replied.

She figured he'd considered Oberon's orders to look after her when he rounded up the soldiers to go with her. But, honestly, as long as she had the Yardmen at her side, she'd be perfectly safe.

An unlikely lot of Yardmen, soldiers and one skinny girl from the wrong side of the government. What better way to lead soldiers into battle?

They took a wide berth around the main road to the stronghold then began creeping forward toward the front gates.

So far, there was no sign of Vestro. The Mortis in the courtyard were either unaware of the battle that had just taken place on top of the hill, or didn't care. They were preoccupied at making a sort of raised platform in the centre of the courtyard. She nearly called out when she saw her mother, crammed inside a cage, being carried out to the platform. A few minutes later, another cage, holding Rud, was dropped next to her mother's cage. The two cages faced each other.

An extra-large, grotesque Mortis carried out a syringe so big she could see it from her position outside the courtyard gates. That horrified her.

"We can't wait any longer," she said, wondering why Oberon hadn't ordered his men to attack. If someone didn't stop this, it would be too late for both Rud and her mother.

Glancing at Brawn and Blip, she said, "Tell the Yardmen to get ready to attack."

Blip nodded at the same time as Brawn. She touched the small Yardman. "Blip, I don't mean to insult you, but maybe you should stay out here."

His little body stiffened slightly. "I understand why you're saying that, miss, but I'm no more vulnerable than you are." She knew he didn't mean to insult her any more than she did him.

Her gut clenched, though. She liked this little Yardman.

"I can't thank you enough for all you've done, Blip. If we make it out of this…"

"We will," Blip interrupted. "And the Yardmen will protect you, Ms. Rune. It's why they're here."

What could she possibly say to that? She turned. All

eyes were on her now. Apparently, Brawn had given them some kind of hand signal, and they were prepared to go.

She adjusted her face shield, yanked out her new pistol and new, highly honed saber that Oberon had given her. She raised the saber and pointed at the courtyard. *Oberon, I hope to hell you're okay,* she thought, as they began the charge on the courtyard.

The normally quiet Yardmen deliberately stamped their feet on the way down the hill, creating a rumbling noise that practically moved the ground. They added a battle cry, a roaring from deep inside their chests, reverberating sounds that built to a terrifying tempo. Noises like that would surely scare their enemies. Their battle cry bolstered everyone and no doubt shocked the guards on the roof and the Mortis in the courtyard.

They made it to the gates with only one casualty, a Yardman who'd been shot with a compound bow.

She couldn't think about that now. A ferocious battle waged around them. She focused on getting her mother and Rud to safety. Then she'd find Oberon.

* * * * *

Oberon sent his last soldier back when he saw signs that Vestro was on this floor. He also sent an order for the attack to begin.

His solitary goal at the moment—kill that bastard, Vestro. Cut off the head of the beast and maybe he could stop this insanity.

Since the branding, he felt a strong connection to Darla. She was here, too.

He needed to speed up his plan, but he had to keep ducking out of sight when servants scurried in and out of

369

a room at the end of the hall. None of them were happy. More often than not, they appeared to be afraid after they exited the room in question. Yeah, Vestro was inside.

He touched his sidearm and gritted his teeth. Before long the battle would start above ground, and he wanted like the Benevolent to be there for it. He feared for Darla. He wanted to be the one protecting her right now.

He approached the room. A servant spotted him and froze in an alcove nearby. Would he sound the alarm? Oberon eyed the man, whose expression of terror soothed when he saw Oberon only wanted Vestro. He backed away and pointed to the spot where the ex-dictator could be found.

Oberon now stood in the doorway, watching an unwitting Vestro, sitting at a desk while he talked to someone in the opposite corner. Oberon couldn't quite see who. Hell, maybe he was talking to himself?

No. There was another voice. He chanced a peek around the door. In the corner hovered a shadowy feature.

"You ignoramus," the shadow said. "You've ramped up the plans too soon. You're supposed to wait until I can come to the future. Time travel still hasn't made the leap. Don't fuck this up before I get there."

Vestro gurgled out a phlegm-filled laugh. "Too late. The war will start the moment Rud is injected." He raised this watch. "That will be in two minutes."

"I can't believe you're doing this. I gave you everything. The know-how, the information about how to keep people repressed and under your thumb. I want to be the one who creates the new world, you double-dealing bastard."

"Yet, even though you ruined your own future by causing the war that destroyed the planet, you're stuck there." Vestro laughed again. "You deserve it. How many innocents did you kill? Hundreds of millions?"

The voice hissed at him. "It's necessary. We needed to start over. Mankind needed to be refreshed."

"And ruled by you," Vestro said, still not noting Oberon in the doorway.

Oberon couldn't believe what he was hearing. Some man from the past caused the War of Neutrality and all of their suffering so he could transport to the future and create his own world? What kind of sick effing human being would do that?

"Looks like I got the last laugh," Vestro said. "You can't come here. Probably never will be able to, and you've ruined your world. Now, I can re-create this world to my standards. Already have, with your information on genetics. No one can beat my Mortis."

"It wasn't my intention for you to create monsters with that genetic information," the voice shouted. "You were supposed to start creating more humans. A bigger workforce, so I could rebuild."

"Slave labor, you mean," Vestro said. "I've created that and an unbeatable army, too."

"That you barely control. What if they learn how to create their own pills to sustain themselves? What then?"

Vestro paused, and his body stiffened. Oberon stepped back out of view so he could continue hearing this conversation. Obviously, Vestro had been a witting pawn in this whole thing, but it had backfired on the evil fucker from the past.

"It would've been nice if your previous employee, the then-Senator, Maribel Rune, wasn't giving Oberon information about ways to stop you," Vestro said.

The other man laughed, but the anger in his voice bled

through. "They're not stopping me, so much as you, you idiot!"

A servant in the hall spotted Oberon lurking outside the door and dropped the tray he carried. The teapot and cutlery shattered and clinked across the floor. Vestro's attention turned to the doorway. When he caught sight of Oberon, he jumped out of his seat and yanked open a desk drawer, grappling for something inside.

Oberon dove at him, trying to get to him first.

CHAPTER TWENTY-EIGHT

While the rest of the soldiers stormed into the courtyard, Darla slashed and shot her way toward her mother.

She was flanked by Yardmen, though. Massive Yardmen fists and homemade blades were able to stop the Mortis in ways that a saber and gun couldn't.

A Mortis attacked the Yardmen to her left, taking out one of her protectors by cutting his Achilles tendons with the twin blades he wielded. His Mortis eyes were clotted red, and his overgrown teeth obviously bloodied by biting his enemies. She found herself face to face with the heartless killer. Was this the moment she'd expected? Her final moment? Hopefully, he didn't think she'd given up—not until she tried everything in her arsenal to stay alive.

"Die, deviant!" She shot him twice, and he jerked back for a second. The bullets pierced his skin and, like the others, but deflected off his massive bone structure. He growled at her, and his evil eyes narrowed on her. Now she knew what it felt like to be a gnat.

He charged her, and she raised her saber. Even though she had little hope, she'd fight with everything inside her. Just before he lashed out at her, his eyes widened, and he fell forward. Blip hung on to his back with a bloodied knife in his hands. He'd climbed up the beast's back and cut through his brain stem.

She'd definitely misjudged Blip's size. He'd saved her life.

"Thanks, Blip." They didn't have time to say anything else. Two more Mortis came at them. Brawn rushed over and stopped one while Darla and Blip took out the other. Again, she managed to distract the beast while Blip climbed up his back and stopped him cold. They made a good team.

It seemed to take hours before she managed to make it to the platform. Rud and her mother were still inside their cages with the keys dangling on a post near the stairs. She quickly freed her mother then turned to Rud. "Did they inject you?" she asked before she opened his cage.

"No, and thank the Benevolent you're okay Darla," he said. "And Oberon?"

She let him out of the cage. "I'm going for Oberon now. Rud, promise me you'll stay here and protect my mother."

He weighed her request. He finally nodded but obviously wanted to go with her. Something flew past them, a knife that barely missed Darla's head. She pulled them both down. "Please, Rud. Get my mother out of here. I'll make sure Oberon is okay. Besides," she looked into his eyes, "you of all people know it's Oberon and I who have to do this thing."

He made a pained face. "I'm sorry if I made things

worse, Darla. I wanted to help."

"I know. And if you save my mother, I'll be forever in your debt."

"I'll get her out. But promise me you and Oberon will get out of this thing in one piece."

"I'll do my best," she said, and after grabbing her mother and hugging her, she turned and jumped off the raised platform onto the back of a Mortis, Blip-style, and shoved her blade into his brain stem. He dropped to the ground.

She ran for the building. When she reached the doors, she turned long enough to see Rud and her mother making their way up the side of the hill, with two Yardmen flanking them. He'd gotten her out.

Now she needed to find Oberon. She felt it in her bones.

She raced into the building on pure instinct, her psychic radar pressing her forward, in the only direction that seemed plausible. She raced down several corridors until she found a stairway, making her way down several flights without running into a single soldier or Mortis.

When she'd left the battle, the Mortis appeared to be losing.

She exited the stairwell, and her gaze homed in on a room at the end of the hall. This place had more light than anything she'd ever seen. Again, electricity. She started down the hall, noticed employees peeking out from behind partially closed doors. They appeared to be no threat. They were curious and afraid. She imagined they wanted Vestro dead, too. She waved for them to escape. They ran like rats.

Then she heard voices. Vestro and Oberon.

She made her way to a room that had a huge pool of

water in the center and tanks against every wall filled with colorful fish. In the pool in the floor, large gray creatures swirled and thrashed through the water.

Vestro and Oberon were arguing too close to the edge, and she nearly screamed out but didn't want to startle Oberon and put him at a disadvantage.

"This is why I've survived, you idiot," Vestro spat at Oberon. "These are the creatures that will bring about the new world order."

"They're effing fish." Oberon said in a stern voice, trying to break into the madman's obvious delusion.

"They're the fathers of the Mortis. They are becoming rulers of the planet."

"And when they rule, what happens to you?"

Vestro hesitated for just a moment. His stature had become small and painfully thin, as well as stooped and crazy.

This must be the room he used to kill Yardmen, and to terrify the others. Was he going to do that to Oberon? Not if she could help it. She felt panic stir inside her breastbone.

While she watched, Oberon took something out of the pack on his back and set it on the floor. A jade box with inset stones.

Blip entered the room from the other side. He held a stubby finger over his slit of a mouth, signaling for her to keep his secret before he disappeared into a room at the back."You're conspicuously alone in here, Vestro." Oberon's words pulled her attention back to him. "None of your soldiers care to protect you, it seems," he said.

"I think that's where you're wrong, James." Vestro snapped his fingers, and four Mortis came out from behind the tanks. "During a revolution, a leader never goes anywhere without backup." He sneered at Oberon as if he'd been a fool to think otherwise.

Oberon caught sight of Darla and said, "Actually, my backup arrived a few moments ago, too."

Vestro turned his head, and his lids lowered over bloodshot eyes. "One little girl? That's your backup? Excuse me if I piss myself laughing."

Darla grinned. She knew her bodyguards wouldn't be far behind. They'd sworn to protect her, and they had followed her inside. She'd heard them on the stairs when she reached the bottom.

She moved toward Oberon, stood next to him and had to stop herself from reaching out and touching his hand. She didn't give Blip away by looking in his direction.

Vestro kept looking at the casket on the floor, practically drooling.

"What is so interesting about this box?" she asked, touching it with the toe of her boot.

Vestro lurched forward, hands out. "Don't, you'll damage it."

Darla exchanged glances with Oberon. "How can I damage a stone box by merely touching it?"

"Stupid Runes. You and your family are all alike. Meddling in things you shouldn't. If Maribel hadn't hidden this for so many years, I'd have total control now. I'd be the king of New North America, not just leader of Central City."

She cleared her throat and considered his sanity. "Ex-leader," she reminded. "Stone boxes can do amazing things in your delusions."

He cursed under his breath, his thin chest heaving erratically. A slight tick over his left eye told her she'd hit him where it hurt.

The Mortis were moving in, Yardmen behind them, in an ever-tightening circle with her, Vestro and Oberon in the middle. And with Oberon way too close to the edge of the pool. She'd never seen real sharks before, but the way they were swirling around at the top of the tank, she knew they were hungry.

Oberon motioned for her to stay away from the tank. She stepped back a little. She had no desire to be fish food. She'd rather go at the hands of a Mortis. A visceral grunt behind her reminded her that that was still a possibility.

"What does this box do?" Oberon asked. "Maribel asked that I bring it here, that it is very important."

"It's everything," Vestro spat. "But why would she tell you to bring it to me?" He frowned.

"What is it?"

"It's my ticket to the past. Back to before the War of Neutrality. They couldn't figure out time travel back then. I saw the schematics. What they failed to realize is this box takes people back, not forward."

"That doesn't make sense. You created these abominations because you wanted to rule this world, did you not?" Oberon asked.

Vestro glanced at the shuffling Mortis, their pain-filled eyes glaring at him. Darla realized then that he knew he'd gone too far. He feared them.

"No," she said. "Because he can't control them anymore. He needs to escape." Darla practically pulled the information straight from his subconscious.

Oberon laughed at that realization. "But you won't be welcome in the past, either. I heard you speaking to that man who set you up in this sick new world order. You screwed him over, and he's stuck back there. He wants to be the one in control."

Darla felt buzzing in her head. "We're missing the big picture here, Oberon. It's not about him and his control. It's about the fish. This, and the surrounding buildings are a repository. He's keeping them from being put back into the rivers and streams. They are the start of bringing life back to our existence, and he knows it. He wants to keep us from becoming part of a healed planet."

He frowned at her. "How do you know that?"

"Maribel."

Vestro scoffed. "Not possible."

"I'm psychic. We have a connection, and it seems even stronger when I'm near your empty box." She looked at the casket with renewed interest. The reason, all of a sudden, she had a closer connection to Maribel? She realized that Oberon had been secretly carrying the casket in his backpack, and when she'd gotten close to it, she'd gotten stronger messages.

Footsteps thumped down the hall, and Rud burst into the room. "Oberon, you're alive! I feared I'd be too late."

Darla glared at him. "What about my mother?"

"She's safe, don't worry. She's under the protection of that huge Yardman, Brawn." He glanced into the tank. "Damnation, what are those things?"

"Man-eaters," Vestro said. "They're particularly fond of scrawny losers, so watch out."

"Bastard." Rud pushed through the Yardmen and the Mortis, who, for some reason, let him inside the circle.

Darla wondered why Oberon had been so silent. As if he understood her line of thinking, he glanced at her quickly. Then he shifted his attention to the area behind her. She understood and stepped back a couple more steps, almost into the arms of a seven-foot, pitchforked Mortis with oily gray skin and bloody eyes that pierced her with intent.

He didn't attack—yet. She gripped her blade and glanced quickly for Blip. Where had he gone?

One of the Mortis raised an arm when Rud attempted to get to Darla. Before he could slice Rud, Darla spun toward him and gripped her knife, stared him in the eyes and said, "We're not the ones who did this to you. We want to help you."

Vestro snorted. "Don't believe her. She sabotaged the pill factory. She doesn't care whether you live or die. Scratch that. She does care. She wants you to die— painfully."

The four Mortis in the room began shuffling a little more than before. Angry sounds emitted from their bony throats.

* * * * *

Oberon bent down, grabbed the box and held it over the water. "Tell them to back off, or this goes into the tank."

"No. Don't do it." Vestro pulled a triangular golden icon from a chain around his neck and began fiddling with tiny knobs on the sides. The casket began to hum, and a purplish light leaked out of it.

"What have you done? It's getting hot." Oberon quickly set it down near his feet, where he could kick it into the water if he had to.

Glancing at Darla to make sure she was safe, Oberon shifted his attention to Vestro's beasts. The Mortis were looking more uncomfortable by the moment. The groans coming from them, and their inability to stand still, made it obvious their connective tissues were failing.

"My Mortis are in need of their fix, it seems. They'll rip you to shreds for taking it from them, I imagine." Vestro laughed maniacally.

Oberon glanced at the biggest Mortis in the room. His skin, a black-blue color, accentuated his protruding and darkened bones that had oxidized with age. He'd obviously been this way for a long time.

"Are we winning the battle?" Vestro pointed up, meaning the courtyard.

The Mortis shook his head in the negative.

Vestro exhaled. "Damn it. Kill them now. I'm tired of being fucked sideways by these assholes. Kill the girl first and throw the rest to the sharks."

Before the Mortis could move a muscle, three Yardmen were on top of them. They started punching the Mortis. Their roars were ear-shattering.

"Get back," Oberon shouted when Vestro made a grab for the box and managed to snag it away. The box was too hot to handle, and Vestro screamed and dropped it again. He gaped at his hands, still steaming from the heat.

Fighting continued until they were all involved. She fought off one of the Mortis, who'd gotten past her two bodyguards who were partially paralyzed in fear, no doubt by the shark tank. They would only fight a distance away.

"I'm going to kill you, Vestro. You've made my life a misery from day one," Oberon growled, moving in on him.

Vestro laughed. "Funny, that's the same thing your father used to say to me when I got him in trouble."

Oberon punched Vestro in the gut. He puffed out a loud breath and hunched forward. "What are you talking about?" Oberon asked. "You didn't know my father."

Vestro heaved a couple of times, trying to catch his breath. "Really, well, I should hope I'd know my own brother."

Oberon had been just about to sucker punch him when his fist froze. He stared at the meanest, worst man on the planet. Could it be true?

"I don't have an uncle. Nice try, though."

Suddenly, an ethereal woman's voice came out of the box. "He is your uncle, Oberon."

"He can't be."

"Blood or not, you must defeat him, and wipe the Mortis out completely. They can't survive. Not even one of them."

"Oh, that'll be a simple task," Oberon ground out, more to himself than the disembodied voice.

"You've already wiped out most of their pill supply. The rest is hidden, and hopefully, they'll never find it before it's too late for them. Poor creatures."

Vestro tried to slink out of the room.

"Stop him," Oberon shouted to one of the Yardmen who'd been fighting a Mortis with all his strength. Blades clanked and swished as they swiped through the air at each other. The Yardman's arms and torso were slashed and bloody, but he still managed to hold off the Mortis long enough to yank the illustrious dictator back, sliding him across the floor toward the tank.

Vestro bristled with anger when he climbed to his feet again. "You big oaf. I made you. Who do you think you are?"

Anger magnified, and the Yardman screamed out. Vestro froze for a minute. The Yardman slashed the Mortis so hard his head nearly came off.

"Oh boy," Rud shouted. "It appears Vestro has no allies left. He's put himself in a very bad spot."

Another voice came out of the box, a man this time. "Kill them, Vestro. Don't let them win. We can still take over the future."

"Hey, that's the voice of the person who gave me the combination to the vault," Rud shouted.

"I knew it couldn't have been Maribel," Oberon grunted, then grabbed for Darla, and the two of them dashed to the corner of the room, away from the fighting Mortis and Yardmen. Their massive bodies could easily have crushed a human being, and they wouldn't even have known they'd done it.

"Wait,' he said, once he made sure Darla was out of harm's way. "Where's Rud?"

"He's still over there." She pointed at the spot where two Mortis were moving against him.

"Stay here," he ordered, then glanced at her quickly. "Promise me!"

"I will," she said.

He took off across the room, diving over a dead Mortis, and landing on his feet behind his brother's attackers.

"Nice to see you, brother," Rud shouted. "Can you please kill one of these things, while I handle the other one?"

"Happily," Oberon said, and readied himself while one of the Mortis, the biggest of them, the oldest of them, turned on him and snarled.

"You die tonight, James," came out through mangled teeth.

"You first," Oberon said, and dove at the beast with his blades slashing the air.

When he got a shoulder spike in his upper arm it burned and hurt like being branded, and he could feel the heat of his blood running down his arm. "Now you've made me angry," he shouted. He turned and jumped on top of the dead Mortis behind him. The gigantic Mortis laughed deep and loud, practically vibrating every bone in Oberon's body. His mistake. While he laughed, Oberon jumped into the air and slammed his blade down into the beast's neck before he'd registered what had just happened. He shouted and then gurgled and fell to the ground. Their major weakness seemed to be their deluded sense of invulnerability.

"A little more help, if you're not busy," Rud shouted.

Oberon had to grin at that. He raced to Rud's side, and the two of them beat another Mortis down by cutting him behind the knees. From there, Oberon managed to get behind him and drive his blade into the monster's brain stem.

"No wonder your soldiers respect you, brother. I had no idea how mean you are."

Oberon grinned at him. "I take that as a compliment."

"He's getting the casket," Darla screamed from across the room.

Vestro cowered over the vibrating box, his handheld control glowing the same color purple as the box. "It's working," he shrieked. He seemed to have forgotten he wasn't alone. "I'm going to travel back to the past. I'm going to make you all sorry for what you've done to me this day." Spittle flew out of his mouth, and his eyes were crazed. Skin hung from his burned hands.

Oberon frowned and glanced at Darla. Maribel wouldn't have sent him the box if she thought it worked as a time machine. He had no idea about the purple light, but he didn't think he wanted to experience it the way Vestro seemed to be. He was too close. His own flesh had started to glow.

"Yes, yes," Vestro shouted. "Send me the scientific information you promised me. The portal is open to bring me back to you. Since it's only one way, you owe me that much."

"Darla made her way to Oberon and Rud. The fight had ended down here. Two Yardmen were injured but okay. She ripped off her face shield and used it to cover a wound on one of them. The Yardman nodded his head in reverence while she helped him. She wrapped her hand around one of his large fingers. "Thank you for helping us. We are in your debt," she said.

Rud leaned in to Oberon. "By the way, brother, when this thing is over, remind me to tell you we've got a much bigger family than we knew."

"What?" Oberon said with irritation. "What are you talking about?"

Before Rud could answer, a man's voice came out of the box again, and everyone turned to watch Vestro, so close to the shark tank, and so wrapped up with the box. "You idiot. Don't do anything to damage the box, or I'll never make it to the future. We still haven't quite figured out time travel, but we're close."

"Maybe I don't want you here," Vestro sniveled.

"Goddamn you, you've done enough damage. I want people to be subdued, not dead. I need an army of followers. You're turning them away from us. If this keeps up, the James' family will win, and I can't have that. That bitch Maribel is giving me enough trouble in this time."

"I am a James, too, Rhino, or have you forgotten?"

"No, I haven't forgotten. But you're the black sheep, the fragile X member of the James family. The rest are bleeding hearts, who spend all their time trying to save humanity. Gives me a pain in the ass just thinking about it."

"Where is Maribel? Have you killed her yet?"

"Have you killed Oberon and Darla yet?" He sounded very angry.

"I am going to very soon." Vestro started laughing. His whole body was glowing now. "Very soon."

"What is he talking about?" Rud asked his brother.

"I don't know."

"You've lost your power, Vestro. Don't tell your deluded friend from the past otherwise," Darla said.

Vestro's attention shifted to her. One finger pointed at her. "You think you're so smart. You think you know everything, don't you? Well, you don't know this."

"I don't think I like the sound of that," Oberon said under his breath. "Darla, I think you should tell the Yardmen to get out of here, and we should leave, too."

"Wait," Rud said. "What about him and the box?" He pointed at Vestro.

Oberon put a hand on his brother's shoulder. "Do you see how his body is lighting up?"

"Yeah?"

"That same purple light seems to be sparking along the edges of the water."

"Okay?" Rud sounded unsure as to where Oberon was going with his suggestion.

"I have the feeling this whole place is going to be alive with whatever that stuff is. And I have the feeling it's not going to be healthy to be here when it happens."

"Wait," Darla said. "What about Blip? Has anyone

seen him?"

"No, where did he go?" Oberon asked, casting a worried glance at the shark tank.

Blip shot around the corner of one of the fish tanks. He had paperwork in his small hands. He could barely lift it. Darla reached down and took some of it. "Blip, what is this stuff?"

"It's important information you're going to need to carry out your quest. It's information that Vestro stole from Oberon's father. He's kept it hidden. With these papers, we might be able to change things."

Oberon reached down and patted Blip's shoulder. "You're a good soldier, Blip. Glad you're on our side."

"What about the box?" Blip asked, looking almost shocked when he saw Vestro through the purple, sparking haze.

"It's history, and we're the future," Darla said.

The vibrations were building, and the glass tanks were starting to rattle. The box had started jumping on the floor, getting dangerously close to the tank. Vestro, cackling like a crazy man, leaned toward the water to try to stop the box from falling in. When his hands touched it he screamed and jerked uncontrollably. The last one out of the room, Oberon cast one quick glance back just as Vestro fell into the pool. He barely had time to scream before being ripped apart by the hungry sharks.

Oberon cringed. Death by sharks might be a little more humane than whatever the box was going to do to him.

He grabbed Darla's hand.

"We'd better hurry," she said. "I think this whole place is going to blow."

"Lead us out of here, my love," he said to her. They

ran for the elevator. The old rusted plaque on the wall said it would hold twenty-one people. Thankfully, it held three people and two and a half Yardmen. They were crammed in very tightly, but when the doors opened on the top floor, they heard the rumbling start from deep below the ground.

"Run!" Oberon shouted.

They made it to the courtyard with the building writhing and rumbling as if the demons from hell itself were about to burst forth.

"Retreat," he shouted, running alongside with the Yardmen, his brother and the woman he loved beyond all measure.

They made it to the mountainside. Yardmen, soldiers, and even a few Mortis scrambled into the brush, getting as far away from the building as possible. Blip rode on Brawn's shoulder.

"Where's my mother?" Darla asked, grabbing Rud by the sleeve of his Uvlar suit when they were able to stop running.

"I'm here, darling," Marilee shouted. She approached with a Yardman on each side of her. She rushed forward, hands out, and when her arms wrapped around Darla, their smiles could have lit their world a thousand times over.

Oberon's stomach curdled. As good as their reunion must be right now, he'd personally caused them many years of despair. How could he ever forgive himself? And the rest of their people had suffered at the hands of his own uncle. He shook his head. The James family had a lot to make up for.

Grant approached. "Some of the Mortis are getting away, sir."

Oberon shook his head. He'd seen them retreating through the brush and toward the mountain. He sighed. "We'll never catch them in that scrub," he said. "Their leader is dead. Their source of pills is gone. Maybe this'll be the last we see of them."

Grant met Oberon's gaze. He could read Oberon well. Neither of them really believed they'd seen the last of the Mortis. But they had no choice. They'd won this battle, at the very least.

The building rumbled deep underground again, and a series of explosions sent debris skyward. The ground rocked, and some of the men lost their footing.

Oberon moved to Darla's side and slid a hand under her elbow before Rud could get to her. Rud eyed his brother's protective hand on Darla and measured Darla's reaction.

His brother's mouth went thin, but Oberon knew the moment Rud realized Darla belonged to him. Disappointment flitted across his face, but then faded away.

Oberon leaned down toward her ear. "We should go, at least back to camp before heading back to the city." He also took Marilee Rune's elbow. "Are you okay, Mrs. Rune?"

Dirty and disheveled, she said. "I'll survive. Now that I have my daughter back."

"Mom, there's a stream at camp, cool and clear. You can take a bath there."

Her mother didn't even question the sanity of that comment. "Lovely. I can't wait."

Rud stepped up and joined them. The four of them, with Grant close behind and two very special Yardmen, led the troops back to their encampment.

* * * * *

Later that night, Darla settled her mother down to sleep. They'd bathed. They'd eaten. And now she searched for Blip and Brawn. The Yardmen were in the vicinity, but they wouldn't stay in the human camp. She needed to thank them, but at the same time, she wondered what their world would be like in the future and how the poor gargantuan Yardmen would ever fit in. Would people ever accept them? Oberon's soldiers had accepted fighting with them. They owed their lives to the Yardmen. Maybe that meant there was hope that the rest of society would accept them, too—given time.

She'd barely stepped a toe out of camp when Oberon appeared next to her. "Going somewhere, my love?"

"I have to thank the Yardmen," she said.

"The Nevermore is still dangerous. You can't just go out there alone."

"What was I thinking? Will you come with me?"

"Try to stop me." He grinned down at her. Wrapping her in the warmth of the adoration shining in his eyes as they stepped into the brush.

How'd she ever get this lucky? She thought of the dreams of her running into his arms. They'd never really been in the past, but maybe they could re-create a future that would be just as good.

"Are you upset that we lost the Neo-Verolli Casket?" Oberon asked her as they made their way through the Nevermore.

"No. I think it served its purpose. Besides, there's nothing for us in the past, even if that box worked as a time machine. Everything is in our future." She paused and listened for a moment. As if whispering in her ear, Maribel had just given her the best message of all. Darla grinned and touched her stomach. "We want to make the world a better place for our child, after all."

Oberon froze. He grabbed her shoulders and kissed her until she could barely breathe. "Oh my, darling. You have given me the world."

###

MESSAGE FROM THE AUTHOR

Thank you for investing that most precious of commodities—your time—in my book! If you enjoyed GIFT OF PROPHESY, I would be thrilled if you could help us buzz it. You can do this by:

Recommending it. Help other readers find this book by recommending it to friends, readers' groups and discussion boards.

Reviewing it. Please share with other readers what you liked about this book by reviewing it wherever you purchased it, or at readers' sites such as Goodreads.

Again, thank you for choosing to read my book!

If you don't want to miss my next release, you can sign up for Lina's newsletter here:

Lina@LinaGardiner.com

A bonus to signing up? Pop-up Giveaways which are open only to newsletter subscribers.

OTHER BOOKS BY LINA GARDINER

Jess Vandermire Vampire Hunter Series
Grave Illusions (Book 1)
Beyond the Grave (Book 2)
Grave New Day (Book 3)
Grave Expectations (Book 4) — coming in December
2014

The Black Moon Series
Black Moon Awakening (Book 1)

What She Doesn't Know (Romantic Suspense)

ABOUT THE AUTHOR

Lina Gardiner lives in New Brunswick, Canada. She is a Daphne DuMaurier and Prism Award winner in Dark Fantasy and has garnered a fabulous Kirkus review for Romantic Suspense. Her previous publications include romantic suspense and paranormal romance novels targeted to the adult market. She loves to hear from readers! Learn more about them on her website.

Connect with the Author:
Email: Lina@LinaGardiner.com
Website: www.LinaGardiner.com
Blog: http://www.LinaGardiner.blogspot.ca
Twitter: https://twitter.com/LinaGardiner